TILL
HUMAN
VOICES
WAKE US

Till Human Voices Wake Us

REBECCA ROQUE

BLACK STONE
PUBLISHING

Printed in the United States of America

Young Adult Fiction / Thrillers & Suspense

Blackstone Publishing
31 Mistletoe Rd.
Ashland, OR 97520

www.BlackstonePublishing.com

for Ben,
for the indigo nights of summer and the enigma of fireflies
who despite everything
refuse to dim their glow
for DOS and demonslaying and crunchy mac & cheese
for Tiger & Mallory, and all of the other fae we probably
shouldn't have named for stolen treasure
(sorry you got busted)
for interstate odysseys in truck beds under the darkest of moons,
and for the audacity to truly choose my own adventure

PART ONE

We have lingered in chambers of the sea
By sea-girls wreathed with sea-weed of red and brown
Till human voices wake us, and we drown.

T. S. Eliot

Chapter

1

When the rain comes, it starts with a sigh. The leaves at the top of my tree whisper secrets to be carried away by the wind, heavy with promises of its own. I turn my face to the sky. I think about how mine might be the first skin this rain touches today, and I smile.

My rain.

My storm.

I want to pretend the shiver humming through my body is electricity, that I am a lightning rod in the gathering storm, but it is both more and less than that. I'm shivering with fear, the kind that lives in the dark hollow spaces in your bones but sometimes leaves its burrow to take your whole body for a ride.

I'm familiar with this fear. I've invited it out to play, after all. I called it out when I lifted one foot off the ground, and then the other, and climbed this tree as high as I could go, until the branches grew too slender to support me. Even now its skeletal arms sway in the storm's breath, warning me that I might have gone too far this time.

As the storm gathers strength, so does the force of my

heartbeat. I am dizzy with the press of it behind my eyes, in the back of my throat. The silent sky tilts.

The fear murmurs, *You will fall.*

The fear promises, *You will break.*

The fear is strong. For as long as I can remember, heights have terrified me; I have a distinct memory of Dad swooping me up onto his broad shoulders, and the meltdown that followed, screams giving way to hiccups and then sleep and then, inevitably, the nightmares.

The fear is strong. It has always *been* strong.

But I am stronger.

I am in this tree because *I* choose to be. Because the fear would keep me grounded. I am in this tree because it is exactly the opposite of where the fear wants me to be.

But I still think I might throw up.

———

"You have a leaf in your hair, fairy girl." Alice leans over and plucks it free. She examines the orange stain creeping across its green veins, autumn bleeding summer away in the palm of her hand. Then she drops the leaf onto my lap and I slip it out the window, watching it drift to the ground as we pull away from my house.

Alice's tight black curls are swept up in an asymmetrical cascade, accenting her high cheekbones and soft brown eyes. There are shadows beneath those eyes this morning though, and I suspect I might not be the only one facing down some ghosts lately.

"Late night?"

"Yeah." She doesn't need to elaborate. Alice has had her eye on valedictorian since kindergarten, but for her parents, that journey began at conception. She's had exactly one boyfriend in her seventeen years, and after the way that ended, I'm pretty sure the Bookers have rescinded dating privileges for the next decade.

"Let's caffeinate our woes away, then. My treat."

She eyes the dash clock. "Think we have time?"

"Homeroom is negotiable. Coffee is not."

Finally, a smile. "Fair."

———

The drive-through line isn't outrageous for once, and I order my usual venti Americano with a splash of cream. Alice orders a caramel macchiato, decaf. I stare at the alien who is wearing the body of my friend as she drives up to the window.

"Decaf?"

She takes one look at me and laughs. "Jesus, Cia, your face! You look like I just farted in church."

"I repeat: *decaf?*"

"I have a test in Mandarin second period." Alice passes the barista my debit card. "I'm already nervous. I don't want to be a twitchy wreck."

"Heresy," I mutter. "Both the blasphemy against caffeine and the implication that you are capable of anything less than acing a test."

She keeps her eyes fixed on the drive-through window. "I'm only human, Cia. I'm as capable of fucking up as anyone else."

Now I *know* she's a pod person. My Alice swears about as often as a politician tells the truth. I open my mouth but the barista returns with our drinks, and we're half a block away before I have a chance to respond. "Al, are you okay?"

She waits until the next light, draws a deep breath. Lets it out in a curl-fluttering gust. "Yeah. I just didn't get much sleep. Sorry for being a bitch."

"My best bitch," I remind her.

She smiles. "Always."

"You know you can talk to me."

"I know."

But she doesn't say anything, and I don't push again. "Want to skip first period and take a nap?"

She glances at me, aghast, and my Alice is back. "Have you lost your mind?"

I shrug. "Grumpy babies get naps, maybe grumpy Alices could use one too."

She sips her frothy mess of a drink before turning into the parking lot of Summerset High. "I'll be alright." She cuts the engine, but hesitates before opening her door. "Lunch in the quad?"

"It's a date."

But now things feel off again. We always have lunch in the quad. It's our midday therapy session, keeping us sane in the bizarre social experiment that is high school. The fact that she even asked gives away a need for reassurance that is very un-Alice.

We succumb to the gravitational pull of responsibility and make our way toward the school. As the doors swing shut and the raindrops dry on my arms, unspent electricity still dances through my body, prickling and buzzing in currents just beneath my skin—or maybe it's just the quadruple shot of espresso.

———

"Are you going to eat that?"

I hand Alice the chocolate pudding cup. "Not since I was twelve. But don't tell Papa that."

She peels it open and spoons a glob of goop into her mouth. "Your dads are so cute. My mom decided her morning momming duties were over the second I figured out how to nuke a Pop-Tart. Does he still do that thing with the notes?"

"Oh yeah." I pull out the folded paper from my lunch bag, smiling before I've even opened it. "'In a world full of Cheerios, be a Froot Loop.'"

Alice laughs. I fold the note back into the bag. Papa had packed extra snacks this morning, and my initial confusion turned to gratitude when I realized why—at least one of us had remembered my CPR class after school today. While my track shoes collected dust at the bottom of my closet, I'd upgraded my wardrobe with a junior EMT jacket this year. To say Dad wasn't thrilled about my choice would be like saying Zeus wasn't thrilled about Prometheus stealing fire from Olympus. He doesn't like anything that might conceivably put me within the same zip code as danger. Thankfully it's illegal to tie your seventeen-year-old daughter to a rock while giant birds eat her liver.

The storm this morning proved to be all bluster, a promise unfulfilled, charcoal clouds burned away and now only ashes on the horizon. The tree we're sitting under fractures the light into a mosaic on our skin, but the shadow that crosses Alice's face has nothing to do with the sun.

"Cia," she says. "I have to tell you something, but you have to promise not to be mad."

Somebody shrieks and I look across the quad. The jocks own the middle of the courtyard, mostly seniors like us, but with the grace and strength (and social skills) of apex predators claiming their space at the default center of attention. Cheyenne's cry dissolves into giggles as Darius holds her up for a few overhead presses before swinging her back down to her feet with elegance and complete indifference to the fact that he just flashed the whole senior class her panties.

A couple of the jocks catch my eye, and we exchange subtle

nods—I'd had a place at that table once, when I obliterated the state record for the 1500 meter run my sophomore year. I don't run track anymore, but I still own my place at the top of the leaderboard. Not that I care, but it keeps me out of the prey category when the jocks start looking down the food chain for entertainment.

One gaze lingers longer than the others: Judah Hayes, fellow ex-track geek. My retirement had been served up by an ACL tear and the joy of spending summer break in physical therapy. Judah stopped running two months ago, when his twin brother went missing and Judah stopped doing *everything* besides looking for Noah. There is something heavy and helpless in my chest as I watch him watching us. It must be a little like waking up one morning and finding the mirror empty. Or like your shadow is gone, no matter where you stand in the sunlight. Judah has only been back in school for a couple of weeks, and the sovereigns of Summerset High closed ranks protectively around him the second he walked through the double doors. Whether that was from genuine empathy, I couldn't say. Maybe it was just a carnivorous desire to be closer to the bleeding meat, the way some people get when they catch a whiff of tragedy.

From where I sit, I can see that Judah's wavy brown hair probably hasn't had anything more hygienic than his fingers through it in the past week, and his lean runner's frame is harder than it used to be. More sharp angles. He's a tree without leaves and out of season. There is no mistaking the look on his face: he doesn't want to be here. But equally clear by the intensity of his stare: for some reason, he *really* wants to know what we're talking about.

Come to think of it, *I* really want to know what we're talking about. I lob my wadded-up lunch bag into the trash and brush crumbs off my jeans. "What's up?"

"Okay." Alice exhales as if I've just given her permission to breathe. "I've been looking into the fire."

I go still. "Why?" I don't need to ask which fire. She means *my* fire. The Fire with a capital F.

"I don't think it was an accident."

"Why are you thinking about it at all?"

"Cia." She takes my hands. Her brown fingers are smooth against the patchwork of scars stitched into my skin. "I know you don't want to hear this. But there's so much more to the story."

I wore compression gloves for all of kindergarten and half of first grade, keeping my grafted skin pliable and marking me as different even among the glue-eating, booger-picking crowd. My hands are hypersensitive in places, even now, twelve years later. The nerve endings haven't forgotten. I feel Alice's touch all the way into the bone.

I feel her words even deeper. "It isn't a *story*."

"I know. I didn't mean it like that. But I don't . . ." She draws a deep breath. "I don't think it was an accident like they said."

The sandwich I'd eaten turns to lead in my stomach. I take my hands back. "An accident? An accident is when a bunch of random bullshit crashes together. What happened back then was no accident. My bio dad was a sick, crazy person who thought God wanted him to cook bonedust, and our house blew up because he wasn't very good at it, and my mom died, and my sisters died, and that's it. There's no *story* there, Alice. Not one that hasn't been told a hundred times before."

"I know." Her voice is a whisper of an apology, but not the kind of apology that means she's going to stop. "But who was buying the drugs, Cia? We've both watched enough Netflix documentaries to know that there are no lone wolves in that world. He had to have been connected. Who was financing him?"

Alice has wanted to be the next Nellie Bly since she joined journalism club freshman year. I think her first word must have been *Why?* But she's never turned that laser-focus on me. It's why I sat at her table in kindergarten—she was the only one who thought my jumbo 64-count box of Crayolas was more interesting than my shiny gloves and robot leg.

"Look. I should have asked you before I started digging, but cross my heart and hope to die, I was looking at something else entirely." Her eyes are all aching sincerity. I wonder what mine are.

"Noah."

Her fingers curl in the empty space where mine had been. "Noah."

"He broke up with *you*, Alice. You don't owe him anything." It comes out sharper than intended—as if I don't know all about wounds that refuse to heal.

Hurt flickers across her face. "I know that."

"Does Judah know what you're doing?"

She doesn't look at him. "Listen to me, Cia. Noah isn't the only kid who went missing this year in Summerset, not by far. I found eleven more just in public records. But the Hayes family was the only one that got any publicity at all."

"What does Noah have to do with my fire?"

"Nothing. Not . . . directly." She blows a curl off her face in frustration. "Except bad things happen to kids here, and no one gives a shit."

Alice has always been fanatical about ethics in journalism. And everywhere else, for that matter. I know that, and the words come out anyway. "So is this your big in for Emerson? Trading on your friends' personal tragedies for your admission portfolio?"

She flinches. But she doesn't back down. "I'm telling you because it's the right thing to do, Cia. I'm not asking permission." She leans closer, speaks quieter. "There are a lot of unanswered questions about the night of your fire, questions that never got asked in the first place. Why is that? If your—" she pauses. "If

John Bennett was the Walter White of Summerset, why didn't they find any paraphernalia in the rubble? Why were all of the doors locked from the outside? And why—"

The wetness on my cheek surprises us both, I think.

"You deserve the truth more than anyone," Alice says quietly. "Cia . . . Do *you* remember why the doors were locked?"

Hush now. Everything is going to be alright.

The voice of a mother I don't remember breathes smoke into my ear, my lungs, and there isn't enough oxygen in the quad for both of us—me and this memory I didn't ask for.

I haven't answered Alice's question. Whatever she sees in my face must tell her I'm not going to.

"Did you know there were over three hundred house fires in Summerset that year? That's almost double the national average for a town our size. But almost none of them made the papers. Doesn't that seem strange to you? Even yours barely got a mention, and three kids di—" She stops, but it's way too late to unsay it.

Three kids died. I was supposed to be number four. "Why are you doing this?"

"Because kids disappear and nobody in this town misses a beat. Because kids *die* and nobody asks the right questions. Or *any* questions. Because something is really wrong with Summerset, Cia, and I think your family was involved."

Those who hope in the Lord will renew their strength. They will soar on wings like eagles.

"Just hear me out."

Close your eyes, sweetheart. It's time to fly.

I am ash, weightless and gray. I float up and away from her.

"Don't walk away, Cia. Please."

I'm not walking. The wind has taken me, and I don't know where I'm going.

Away.

"You're not the only one with secrets, you know!"

I do know. But the wind is carrying me away, away from my best friend, away from the quad, down a hallway to a class I won't pay attention to, because for the first time in more than ten years, my leg hurts. The leg I haven't had since I was five, and the fire took it and everything else away.

———

Pause.

Play.

That was yesterday. My phone says 0742.

> **alice.books113** 15:36
>
> ▌ we have to talk.

> **alice.books113** 15:55
>
> ▌ i know you're mad. this is important.

> **alice.books113** 16:18
>
> ▌ whatever you think you know, don't trust it. trust me.

> **alice.books113** 16:19
>
> ▌ i wouldn't hurt you.

Between then and now, Alice reached out to me seventeen times—four calls and thirteen Snapchat messages.

> **alice.books113** 16:21
>
> ▌ will you just hear me out?

alice.books113 17:05

come on, cia. we're better than this.

alice.books113 19:06

i can't do this alone. i need you.

Between then and now, Alice drowned in the quarry.

Chapter

2

I sleep through all of it.

As the jogger crouches at the edge of the quarry, hoping the yellow sundress he could barely see floating in the water two hundred feet down doesn't have a girl in it—

As the sheriff's deputy and ambulance pull up to the east rim, lights and sirens off because the one thing they know for sure is that they are too late—

As the divers attach ropes or straps or a thousand yellow helium balloons to my best friend to lift her out of that icy water, the sun comes up and my dad doesn't wake me up for school, and so I sleep.

When I race into the kitchen, frantic about missing first bell and AP World History, Dad and Papa are sitting at the kitchen table.

"Why didn't anyone wake—"

I only see that they are holding hands when their hands fall apart as they stand. Dad's dark eyes are inscrutable as always, but Papa's are hazel and soft.

My first thought is, *Cancer.*

"Is it back?" I ask, stopping short.

Dad looks confused.

Papa doesn't. When you have scars like we do, you don't ever get to forget what made them. "Come sit, sweetheart."

I don't want to. I don't want whatever is coming to catch me on my ass. "What's wrong?"

"Silencia." I've always loved the way Dad says my name. My bio father had clear ideas about the qualities he wanted in his daughters, chaining us to his doctrines with our very names: Prudence, Grace, Faith. Silence. But from Dad's lips it became something musical, something beautiful. As the only child to survive our father, I honor my sisters by keeping my name but giving it wings. It was Papa who'd thought to give me the choice, when I was six and the adoption was finalized, but it was Dad who'd made it an easy one. "It's Alice, mija."

I hold on to the kitchen counter. It's not that I don't trust my prosthetic to hold me up; it's the other leg, the one that's all bone and flesh—the human parts of me aren't nearly as trustworthy. "What about Alice?" My own voice feels like sand in my throat. I hadn't left her on read out of spite. After she'd blindsided me in the quad, I'd needed time for the hurricane of sensory echoes and visceral emotion to downgrade at least a category or two—time she'd been in too much of a rush to give me.

But why? Whatever secrets might be buried in the cinders of my fire have kept for twelve years. What difference did another few hours make?

"Sit down with us," Papa suggests again.

"What *about* Alice?" I repeat.

Dad crosses the kitchen. He is built like a Cuban Dwayne Johnson, an unstoppable force to my immovable object, but his gravelly voice is gentler than I've ever heard it. "Alice died last night."

White noise roars in my ears.

I can't breathe. The sound that comes out of me is too small to be words, but they hear me, and I'm in their arms before I can turn to ash again. I'm wrapped in their warmth, in the puzzle-piece fit of my head beneath Papa's chin and Dad's arms around us both, and I think Papa cries before I do but when he does I know this is real. I don't know anything yet about the jogger or the divers or Brouardel's five stages of drowning—I will, that's all coming—but for now I just know that nothing is going to be the same.

————

Papa taps gently on my door. I'm lucky if Dad gives me a warning knock before blowing in whenever he wants, but Papa is a social worker at Summerset Juvenile Corrections and tells Dad all the time that kids in my *developmental stage* need privacy to develop independence and identity.

"Come in." I put my phone and all of its accusations facedown on my nightstand.

i need you.

I've been imagining Alice as they pulled her out of the water, lavender and full and soft, like a mermaid who wished to be a human so that she could dance with her love on shore, whose wish was granted while she was still too deep, still down in the depths where the sun is only a myth whispered among anglerfish, and the strong beautiful tail that was perfect for weaving between the currents split into legs that were not, and so she tried to swallow the sea to get to him. Only he turned out to be a tired EMT named Jack, and when he brought her to shore the magic that gave her breath under the sea was long, long gone.

Pancakes, my Australian Shepherd mix, squeezes in before Papa can get through the doorway. She collects her due—ear scratches and a nose smooch—before finding a square of sun-warmed carpet to flop down in.

Papa has brought me orange juice, coffee and Elvis toast—peanut butter and bananas on wheat, my childhood favorite. I think of Alice in the quarry, belly full of water and algae and maybe minnows. I leave the toast and sip the coffee.

My room feels normal-size until Papa's in it. Then it somehow feels too small for human inhabitants, especially six-foot lanksters like Papa who fold in triplicate to sit on the edge of my bed.

"How are you holding up?"

"I don't know yet." It's the truth. Nothing makes sense.

"The Bookers called. They wanted to make sure you were OK."

That *really* doesn't make sense. My brain misfires a few times before words assemble themselves into a sentence. "Alice's parents called to check on *me*?"

"You're like a second daughter to them, sweetheart." He hesitates. "And sometimes, when these kinds of things happen . . ."

"These kinds of things?"

I wonder if Alice's eyes were like fishbowls when they pulled her out. Opportunistic sea creatures staring out at the world of landwalkers for a few brief moments until the water started draining out of her and they drowned too, sea-lungs tearing like tissue paper against the invading oxygen.

Papa's talking but it's like watching Netflix on crappy wi-fi—there's a few seconds of lag before the audio catches up. "Suicide?"

He nods. "The police will want to talk to you. Your school is going to offer counseling, and hold a memorial. They will probably ask if you want to be involved." He puts one of his big hands on mine, squeezes. "We'll run interference for you as much as you need. Everybody grieves differently. You just tell us, sweetie."

Grieving? Is that what I'm supposed to be doing? "How do they know . . ."

"There was a letter."

Dad's a firefighter, friends with half the police force in Summerset. They probably called him before the coroner, because good news travels fast but bad news is wildfire in a small town. I suddenly wish he hadn't gone to work. Papa is Elvis toast and coffee, intuition and warmth. Dad is facts and action.

Right now, I need facts.

"What did the letter say?"

Papa sighs. "I can't tell you that, monkey. There's an investigation—"

This betrayal lances through me, hot and sickening. "You can't tell me?"

"The police want to keep certain things private, Cia. The Bookers do too. They have every right to it."

"Then why do you get to know?"

He doesn't answer the question, just gives me that infuriatingly gentle look of eternal patience he's perfected over twelve years. "I know you want answers, sweetheart. I would too. Give it time, but realize that the answers that come may not be the ones you want. They may not be enough, or they may not make sense. Nobody can know what Alice was thinking or feeling last night, and it may not be our place to understand."

I could have known. If I'd answered the damn phone.

"You said last night. Do they know when she . . . went in?"

Her last message had been sent at 7:06 p.m. I'd still been at school, counting the clicks of a dummy heart beneath my palms as I tried to get the cadence right.

i can't do this alone. i need you.

"Not yet. The water gets so cold in that quarry, especially after the sun sets, it would have slowed down . . ."

He doesn't say decomposition. Or rigor mortis. Or whatever other clinically horrible thing happened to my best friend while I . . .

Clear your airway, Lucero!

Breathe.

Breathe.

My shiny new CPR certification card is in the front of my wallet. I think about giving it back. I think about setting it on fire.

Deeper. Push hard. Push fast.

Be ready to feel ribs breaking under your hands. Don't be afraid. This is life, in the palms of your hands, and you can't be afraid.

Had I been breathing life into the shell of a mannequin the very moment Alice's bubbled out of her lungs into that cold, dark quarry water?

Papa can't tell me, or won't. There will be a postmortem, and the grown-ups will know then, and somehow I'm going to make one of them tell me because *I need to know.*

Papa tells me he's taken the day off and he's here if I need him. He leaves me alone, Pancakes following reluctantly.

I snatch my phone back up the second he closes the door, save Alice's last messages before they disappear forever into the Snapchat ether.

i don't know who else to call

Answer: anyone but me.

Breathe.

Breathe.

Chapter

3

The only warning I get is a shadow passing behind my curtains before—

Bang!

I unlock the window and slide it open.

Will Mason spills into my room like the world's least graceful burglar, tripping over my backpack and nearly sending us both to the floor.

"Cia." Spiky lashes around his bright blue eyes; he's been crying. "They're saying Alice is dead."

Hearing it from my dads had been hard enough. Hearing it from someone who hurts with it as deeply as I do undoes me. I start to shake, the parts of me held together like splintered glass one breath away from disintegration. "I know."

He wraps me up, and I can feel the warmth of his skin through his long-sleeved black shirt. He smells like yesterday's Old Spice and fabric softener. I close my aching eyes and let his warmth fill the fractured spaces in me.

He holds me for what feels like forever. My mind comes up

for air a few times but mostly I just float in his embrace. Will goes back even further with Alice than I do—their mothers were in the same new moms playgroup while mine was barricaded in our home, keeping newborn me secret and safe from the evils of vaccines and social security numbers.

When he finally lets me go, I sit back on my bed and gather my tangle of wavy brown hair into a loose knot over one shoulder. Yesterday's mascara smears across the back of my hand as I swipe the wet from my eyes.

Will drops into the chair. His jeans look like they went through the washing machine with a feral cat. His trademark gray beanie is pulled down low, but not enough to keep tufts of brown hair from escaping, and I resist the urge to tuck them back in the way Alice always does.

Did.

"What do you know?" He leans forward, elbows on bony knees.

whatever you think you know, don't trust it.

What do I think I know? My best friend is dead. What else is there?

It hurts to swallow past the boulder in my throat. "They called Dad this morning. She was . . . They found her in the quarry. They're saying she drowned." The word almost falls apart before I can say it.

"How? We've been swimming in that quarry since sixth grade."

How? There's only one way *to* drown. You open your mouth and water goes in instead of air. And it keeps going in and your alveoli exchange carbon dioxide for quarry water until your veins run green-blue and you become a mermaid forever and ever.

"She left a note, Will."

It takes a second. Then anger pulls his face into angles I hardly recognize. "No. Screw that! She wouldn't off herself. Not Alice. Who told you that?"

"Papa said—"

He slams his fist onto my desk, and I wince as a framed photo of Pancakes falls over. "He's a fucking liar!"

"Will."

"What? Do you think she did it? Come *on*, Cia. She was your best friend."

I don't say anything. He wants something to fight. I do, too. But not him.

Will rubs his face, breathes out through his fingers, and rights the photo, fidgeting with it for a few extra seconds before meeting my eyes again. "I just . . . It doesn't make any sense. What did this note say?"

I take a shuddering breath. This rage/regret two-step has become a too-common dance with Will lately. He has his reasons, and right now I need him so much more than I need an apology. "I don't know. Papa knows but he won't tell me. They seem to think it was pretty . . . unambiguous."

"Well, they didn't know her. Not like us."

My stomach twists. "No. But even we didn't know *everything* about her."

Will's brow creases. "What the hell does that mean?"

I trust Will. We've been the two hydrogens to Alice's oxygen for almost as long as I can remember. When Papa was going through treatment and basically radioactive from the chemo/radiation carpet bomb the doctors dropped on his lungs, the Masons became my surrogate family. Will is my brother, my best friend. The only one I have left now.

I *really* don't want to tell him about the fight. I'm not sure I'm ready for Will-level honesty about that part. But I brace myself for it anyway. "We had a fight at lunch. She sent a few messages but I . . . I didn't talk to her after that."

Will's eyes flash up to me. "What did you fight about?"

"She's been looking into the fire." I add softly, "*My* fire. She said there was more to the story than people knew. She seemed to think there was some kind of cover-up."

He looks as confused as I'd felt. As I still felt. "Why was she investigating your fire?"

"She said she wasn't. Or at least, that she hadn't meant to. That she'd started out looking for Noah."

"That asshole again." Will's never been a fan of Noah Hayes, even before Noah's orbit collided with ours when he became Alice's first serious boyfriend last year. His resentment crystallized when Noah dumped her out of nowhere, breaking her heart into a zillion pieces that took us weeks to reassemble. That was where I jumped on the Noah-sucks train. Before that, he'd seemed nice enough, if a beat out of step with the rest of us—the kind of guy who would probably become art school gentry if he managed to survive high school. He'd been suspended for spray painting a Pablo Neruda poem on the school doors for Alice last Valentine's day, subsequently commissioned to paint a mural of the school mascot on the gym wall, and re-suspended when instead of a cartoony pirate, he had covered the wall with a Banksy-style condemnation of the student athletic industry.

I get why she'd been into him. I really do. What I don't get is following the snake into its den after it's already bitten you once. What I don't get is why she'd gone there alone.

"She never stopped missing him, Will. Even when she said she was over it, and went out those couple times with that tennis guy, I think it was just to make us stop asking her about it." I hug my pillow. I hadn't known how much she was still hurting over Noah. She'd seemed . . . okay. Not great, but not *not* okay.

Hadn't she?

My vision is swimmy all of a sudden. "How did we miss this, Will? How was she hurting this bad and we didn't know?"

He's beside me on the bed and hugging me again before my eyes spill over. "Stop, Cia. We didn't miss anything."

But there's something in his voice, something in the space between his words. I've known him too long. When I pull back, he drops his gaze first, which tells me everything. "Will?"

"Shit," he mutters.

I stare at him. "Did you know she was looking for Noah?"

"Everyone's looking for Noah, Cia. It's a small town."

"*Nobody's* looking for Noah! That was her whole point." I try to shove him off the bed, but he doesn't budge. "I can't believe you knew about this."

"There's no *this*, Cia! She wasn't getting anywhere. I thought she'd dropped it. I had no idea she'd started looking into your fire." He finally meets my eyes again. "I swear. I would never have kept that from you. I would have told her not to, either. But, Cia . . ." He hesitates. "I don't think loving someone means that you owe them all of your secrets."

"That doesn't sound shady at *all*, Will."

"You know what I mean!"

"I really don't!"

"Just because there are *things* we didn't know about Alice doesn't mean we didn't know *her*. Alice was our best friend, and I'm not buying their story. She didn't do this."

Now I'm angry, like *really* angry, because I want to find comfort in denial too but my brain won't let me. The unanswered messages on my phone won't let me. I grab my phone off the nightstand. It hits him on the chest and bounces on the bed.

"She *did* do this, Will. She reached out to me and I wasn't there and she . . ." My throat closes off whatever else I was going to say, and the tears burn fresh trails down my already salt-raw cheeks.

Will unlocks my phone, and I watch him open Snapchat.

It takes him all of sixty seconds to read Alice's messages. I don't need to look at the phone—I've memorized all of them.

I know exactly when he reads the last one, because his expression goes to a dark place. "Jesus."

I don't say anything.

"This looks bad."

"Thanks," I say icily, and reach for the phone.

He pulls it away. "No. I mean, you don't look great. But Alice—it makes her sound really desperate."

"You think? Give it back."

"The cops can't see this."

That is *not* what I was expecting. "Excuse me?"

"They can't see this, Cia! Not yet. This is all they'll need to close the investigation entirely. If there even is one."

The thought of my dads realizing I'd hung Alice out to dry when she needed me most makes me want to crawl under the bed. But . . . "Will—"

He jerks the phone out of my reach. "Cia! How can you seriously think she did this?"

"If she didn't, who did?" A sob breaks the sentence in half. "Tell me! I'd love to know how this is anyone's fault but mine!"

"Maybe someone who wanted whatever she was digging up to stay buried." He stands up. "I can't believe how easy it is for you of all people to just write her off!"

I flinch. "How can you say that to me?"

Will is supposed to be my brother, my safe place. He showed his colors during my first official throw-down brawl. I was eight and growing faster than my prosthetist could keep up with, and my leg came out of its socket during kickball. I picked the prosthetic up and whacked the first kid that laughed with it. I didn't see the brat's big brother coming up behind me until I heard him—well, more accurately, heard the ball *thwack* into the side of his head. Will actually got into pretty big trouble for that one.

Will is my best friend. Still and always.

But he doesn't back down. "Alice should have called me instead of you. I would never have turned my back on her."

Rage.

Regret.

He doesn't get a monopoly on either. I reach out again. "Give. Me. My. *Phone*."

He turns and hurls it against the wall.

Plastic shrapnel flies everywhere. I recoil, hands out to protect my face.

Will looks almost as shocked as I am at what he'd just done, but his expression quickly goes grim and flat. "There," he says. "Problem solved."

The door bangs open. Papa slows his momentum a few steps into my room, but Pancakes barrels in and puts her body between Will and me. Her tail wags the whole time, because she adores Will, but she makes no attempt to go to him.

I understand her ambivalence.

Papa takes in the open window, my broken phone and Will's hunched shoulders, his clenched fists, before I can even say a word.

"Will," Papa says, calm. "You know our front door opens as well as our windows."

Will doesn't look at either of us. "Window. Whatever gets me out of here the fastest."

He's as good as his word.

"Are you okay?" Papa brushes the hair out of my face. "What was that about? I don't think I've ever heard you and Will fight."

Every inch of me is trembling. "He heard about Alice."

Papa picks up the pieces of my phone, frowns. "So he broke your phone?"

I hold out my hands. "How bad is it?"

"Terminal, by the looks of things." He hands over the remains. "Cia. The Masons will always be family for the way they stepped up when I was on chemo. Will's going through a lot with his mom, and now this. You know Will gets a lot of leeway from us. But I'm your dad, not his. And that can't happen again."

I start to speak but he raises a hand. "Let me finish. We didn't raise you to be a princess we have to protect. We raised a strong, smart, capable young woman who takes shit from no one. So you tell me: how are we handling this?"

I can't help smiling, even though my eyes are still wet. Papa swears about as often as Mr. Rogers. "He'll pay to get it fixed, for one."

Papa raises his eyebrows.

"After he apologizes . . . to us both," I add, watching his expression, "he'll finally learn how to use the front door. No more window."

"No more window," Papa says firmly. "And he's going to talk to his parents about what happened, or I will."

I nod.

"I'm sorry, monkey. It's been a hell of a day for you, and it's not going to get any easier."

Bananas were the first solid food little Silencia could handle when the doctors took the feeding tube out. Once I traded my track shoes in for rock climbing kicks, any chance of escaping the nickname went kaput. I stop trying to cram my battery back into the shell of the abused phone. "What do you mean?"

"The police called," he said. "They'll be here in an hour."

Chapter

4

I am in a parent sandwich. Dad sits to my left, having left work early, Papa to my right. Dad's leaning forward with his elbows on the table, owning the middle ground between us and the two detectives across the dining room table.

My stomach lets everybody know that I shouldn't have turned my nose up at Papa's Elvis toast, but Will's parting shot had left my belly in knots. He'd acted like a complete ass, but he hadn't been totally wrong. I *had* turned my back on Alice last night, justifiably or not. I owe it to her not to turn away now.

The younger detective chuckles. He looks like he should be modeling board shorts for Hurley, not grilling teenage girls about their dead best friends. He'd introduced himself as Dan, but his badge says DET. TIMMERMAN. "Must be lunch time."

Nobody else smiles. The other cop has not invited us to call him anything except Detective Rojas. His patchy black mustache is slightly off center, and when he talks I find myself watching it ride his upper lip like a caterpillar. "I'm sure everybody agrees that lunch can wait a little while longer, given the situation," says Rojas.

Twenty-four hours ago, Alice was a beautiful, smart, fiercely stubborn seventeen year old girl—a big sister, the journalism club president and the student voted most likely to expose a politician in a sex scandal. Now she's a *situation*.

I take a deep breath. Papa squeezes my knee. We've already run through the interview hors d'oeuvres: my name (Silencia Lucero, née Silence Bennett), age (17), grade (senior), how long I've known Alice (twelve years, since the Department of Children's Services placed me with Dad and Papa and I got to go to actual school for the first time).

"So she drowned?" I ask, preempting whatever Rojas had been about to say, and the caterpillar goes flat. "I mean . . . it's for sure? She didn't die some other way?"

"The postmortem is still pending," Timmerman says. "But it looks that way."

"We make no assumptions in this stage of an investigation." Rojas frowns at his partner. "Is there a reason to think she died some other way?"

I don't like how careful he is to use my exact words in his questions. Despite the mustard smear where his shirt is pulled tight across his belly, I get the impression Rojas is very good at his job. That should reassure me—Alice deserves the best.

Still, I don't like him. I don't like Timmerman either, for that matter. He's too pretty. "Nothing. Except that she wouldn't . . . the Alice I know wouldn't have done this."

Neither one of them bothers stating the obvious.

I took a shower after Will left, but I skipped the blow-dryer and makeup. The detectives could deal with my wet, messy bun and tear-burned face. Instead, I spent half an hour reading everything I could find online about drowning.

About how long it takes. About how it feels. About what exactly happens to your body when you go from girl to *situation*.

I need to know. I wish I didn't.

"We've been swimming in that quarry since we were little,"
I say, echoing Will, and it sounds softer and sadder than I mean
it to.

Timmerman nods. "Then you know how cold the water
gets at night. I grew up here too. It doesn't take long for your
muscles to cramp up in that kind of cold. Once you cramp up
it gets really hard to keep your head above water."

I do know. I've been learning all about it from Professor Google. Nineteenth century forensic pathologist Dr. Paul
Brouardel established five distinct stages of drowning, as illus-
trated by some of the cruelest animal testing I've ever heard of
in his drowning lab. You know you're in a whole different era
of medical ethics when you have a *drowning lab*.

Rojas flips the pages of his notebook noisily. "Would you
say Alice was depressed?"

"I didn't, did I?"

Dad gives me a look. Papa hides a smile behind a cough
that doesn't fool anyone.

Timmerman shows me an orthodontist's wet dream. "Was
Alice seeing anyone?"

"No. Nobody serious since Noah."

Rojas: "That's Noah Hayes."

"Yes."

Rojas: "Tell me about Noah and Alice."

"Why? He's been gone for months. He didn't have anything
to do with this."

"Indulge me," Rojas says, not buying the ignorance act for
a second.

I hate this line of questioning, and I'm sure it shows on

my face. If Will is right, and they are only looking to confirm what they've already concluded about what pushed Alice into the water last night, this is not going to convince them to look deeper. But . . . she *had* been chasing Noah. And now she's gone. Maybe getting them to look in his direction isn't a complete waste of time.

Papa puts his arm around the back of my chair, and I take a deep breath. "Noah had a crush on Alice since freshman year. We all had the same art class, and he used her for his figure study. Not like, naked," I say quickly, as if it matters to the four men staring at me. "They had a professional model and everything. But while Alice and the rest of the class were drawing the model, Noah was drawing Alice. Alice is a really terrible artist, so hers looked like the marshmallow monster from *Ghostbusters*, but his was beautiful. I mean really beautiful." This part hurts more than I expected.

"So Noah was a bit of a rule-breaker," Rojas observes. "Did Alice generally go for that sort?"

"No," I say, annoyed at how far off the mark he is. "He just . . . thought outside the lines. Alice is very serious about her grades. She reads college prep books like some girls read *Cosmo*. Noah wasn't like that. He got okay grades but I think school was just something to do for him. Like, to pass the time. And he found all the high school soap opera drama stuff funny. He didn't ever talk about college, but he did this thing with a local group of . . . they called themselves renegade artists. They did pop-up galleries in empty spaces, overnight street art where people would see it in the morning, making social or political statements, that kind of stuff. They were always talking about how careful they had to be so they didn't get busted. I don't know if he ever got arrested."

"We do," Rojas says.

I pull the sleeves of my hoodie over my hands so Dad and Papa can't see my fingers knotting together. "He used to say that he and Alice were going to change the world. He was going to make people see the truth, and she was going to make people listen." I shrug. "Then he broke it off, and a month later he was gone."

"Wow," Timmerman says mildly. "Just like that."

"Just like that," I mutter.

"That'll make your head spin."

I shrug again.

"What did it do to Alice?"

I meet Rojas's eyes. They're bloodshot and steady. "What did the note say?" I ask.

"The family has asked that we keep that information need-to-know at this time."

"Okay, well, I need to know."

Dad says, "Silencia. We all want to know *why*. It's their job to figure it out. Don't make it harder."

My right knee bounces hard under the table.

I don't want to be here.

I don't want to be here.

I don't want to be here.

"What did it *do* to her? It destroyed her! What do you think? She didn't see it coming and it broke her heart, and Will and I helped her put it back together, and it sucked for a while and then she was okay. Not great but *okay*. She didn't kill herself over Noah freaking Hayes."

Rojas pulls a piece of paper out of a manila folder, slides it across the table. It's a photocopy.

A photocopy of a typed note.

Chapter

5

Dad swipes the letter up before I can read it. "Franco. Yo no creo que sea bueno para mi hija ver eso." As Battalion Chief of the Summerset Fire Department, Dad knows just about everyone on the police force. I don't get the impression he and Rojas are particularly friendly, but there's a kind of respect between them. It doesn't apply to Timmerman, though; Dad pretty much ignores the younger cop entirely.

Growing up in Dad's house, I know just enough Spanish to know when I'm in trouble—my understanding is half vocabulary, half flavor of the delivery. If my radar is properly calibrated, Rojas isn't in trouble, but he's close. He looks from me to Dad, nods slowly. "I think she needs to."

Dad sighs, hands me the paper. My triphammering heartbeat goes strangely quiet.

Alice's note is deeply creased from several uneven folds. It is only three lines long.

Think of her still the same way, I say;

She is not dead,

She is just away

I stare at the spaces between the letters, willing there to be more. When nothing magically materializes, I drop it on the table. "What is this trite bullshit?"

Papa, Captain of the Manners Police, lets that slide. "I think," he says carefully, "it means she didn't want you to think differently about her. To be disappointed in her, or to doubt how much she loved you."

Dad hands the paper back to Rojas. When he opens the folder, I see another photocopy. "What's that?"

Rojas hands it over. "This was in a Ziploc bag in her pocket, along with the note."

It's a picture of Alice and Noah.

They're standing in front of a dilapidated building with half the stucco smashed off the exterior. The word FOREVER loops across the exposed bricks, thin rivers of spray paint running down from the Rs. Noah's face is in profile, smiling, eyes fixed on Alice, one arm around her waist pulling her in close, and the other hanging loose at his side, the dot-matrix evidence of aerosol paint marking him from fingertips to elbow. She's off balance, on one foot and mid-laugh, nose crinkled up with one hand coming up to cover her mouth but too slow, the camera caught her anyway and I have never wished for anything as much as I wish I were in on the joke, because maybe then I'd understand, maybe then this would make sense.

I don't notice the tears until Papa gets up from the table and comes back with a Kleenex.

Rojas takes the photo back. "When did you last speak to Alice?"

"Yesterday. At lunch." Not a lie. Not the entire truth, either.
"And?"

I unravel the Kleenex into tiny, soft fibers. "She was working on her capstone project for journalism club. She seemed
excited about it."

Timmerman: "Do you know what the project was?"

Dad looks at me when I don't speak right away.

I hate giving them this. It feels like I'm betraying Alice. I
don't want to give them one more ounce of evidence to support
the decision they've already made, that Alice killed herself over
Noah. I want them to keep looking, keep digging, because Will
is right: our Alice is not that girl. She is so much more than just
one narcissistic boy's broken ex-girlfriend, which is what I'm
afraid is all the detectives see when they look at her.

"She was looking for Noah." It comes out quiet, angry.
"She said there were other missing kids, kids whose families
never reported them missing, or whose reports never went anywhere. She thought there was a story there. We had a—a fight,
I guess. I told her to let it go. To let him go. That wasn't what
she wanted to hear."

Rojas makes a note in his pad. "So you didn't talk to Alice
at all after lunch?"

"No." It hits me then: the police don't have her phone. If
they did, they would know about the calls and text messages.
But if they don't have it, where is it?

"Do you know where she went after school?"

"Yesterday was Wednesday, so she would have gone to
debate club. After that I don't know."

"She didn't show up for debate club," Rojas observes. "Or
any of her afternoon classes, actually. It seems she left school
right after lunch. Right after the two of you fought about
Noah Hayes."

Alice ditched an entire afternoon of classes? The same Alice who lost her mind if we were five minutes late to homeroom?

Rojas reads the surprise on my face and makes another note, then looks back up at me. "Did you go straight home after school?"

"I had junior EMT class. We got out around 7:30."

Rojas nods but doesn't write anything down. He already knows all of this, I'm sure of it. He's not asking because he doesn't know the answers. He's asking to see how I react. "And did you go straight home after that?"

Dad: "She said she didn't talk to Alice after lunch. Asked and answered. Move on."

Rojas is unruffled. "You looked surprised when I said Alice left school early. You didn't know?" He doesn't wait for my answer. "You two were best friends, weren't you?"

It is as much accusation as implication. I force myself to meet his eyes. "Just because you love someone doesn't mean they owe you all of their secrets." Will's words taste like sawdust, but he wasn't wrong about that, either.

Papa stands up abruptly. "Excuse me." I hear the bathroom door close behind him.

Dad shifts his gaze from the closed door to Rojas. "Silencia was home with us all evening. It was not her job to know where Alice was, or what she was thinking."

"No doubt you have a point there, sir," Timmerman says. "Nobody's saying that your daughter had anything to do with Miss Booker's death. We just want to make sure we understand the whole picture."

My right knee is still going. It could power our whole neighborhood at this rate. Hook me up to the power grid. The idea that the cops could think I had anything to do with Alice's death had never even occurred to me, but clearly it had to Dad. Does that say more about him or me?

Rojas, out of left field: "What do you know about the disappearance of Noah Hayes?"

"Silencia had nothing to do with that boy running away," Dad says. "I don't see that this is relevant."

"How long had he been using bonedust?" Rojas asks me, and my leg freezes. My everything freezes. "Did he and Alice ever use together?"

Now Dad stands up. "Sabe algo, esta conversación acaba de terminar."

Rojas sits back in his chair but makes no move to get up.

Smoked, snorted, or shot, bonedust is cheaper and easier to get your hands on than anything else our small town can brew up or import. It flows through Summerset like the collateral blood supply of a diseased heart. Our art, our music, our violence—all of it laced with dust until it's impossible to separate one from the other. I can't remember the last party I went to that didn't serve up dust alongside whatever cheap keg somebody's uncle had been bribed to supply.

Yet for all the local news outlets running special reports calling it the epidemic of this generation, for every emergency bill allowing over the counter sales of nasal sprays loaded with reversal agents because Summerset Memorial Hospital needed bunk beds to keep up with the ODs and business owners got tired of finding corpses in their shop doorways, for all the public hand-wringing and pearl-clutching that goes on over bonedust, nothing changes. Except maybe they're a little quicker to clean the streets in the mornings.

My teeth grind together so hard my jaw hurts. "Alice *hated* what bonedust has done to this town! She would never have touched the stuff. If Noah was messing with dust when they were together he sure as hell was good at hiding it, because she didn't know anything about it." I may be the world's worst best friend, but at least this I know for damn sure.

The doorbell interrupts whatever Rojas might have been about to say, and I'm out of my chair like a jack-in-the-box wound way too tight for way too long. "I'll get it."

Pancakes races me to the door. Pure enthusiasm goes a long way toward making up for what arthritis and cataracts have taken away, but it still hurts my heart to see her limp.

The man at the door smiles warmly. He's head and shoulders taller than me, and built like he lifts cars off old ladies for fun.

"Uncle Sean," I try to say, only I end up mumbling it into his shoulder because he's already got me in a rib cage-splintering hug.

"How's my best girl?" he asks. He's not my biological uncle—nothing about my family has to do with biology. What ties us together is way more important than genetic coincidence. Sean and Dad go way back, though; Sean started in the police academy the same year Dad got into the fire academy.

"She probably needs to breathe if you actually want an answer to that question, Dad," Remy Walsh says, stepping inside once Uncle Sean stops linebackering the doorway. If Detective Timmerman is Hurley, Remy is Ralph Lauren; his gray suit jacket is open over a light blue button-down, collar perky but parted over a white T-shirt. He wears his sandy hair in the same neat side-parted style he has since Little League, but today a few strands have escaped their posts.

"Been better," I say when my lungs reinflate.

Uncle Sean's stubbly face softens. "No doubt. I'm so sorry about Alice."

I nod. "Dad's in the dining room with the detectives."

Remy's arms replace his father's, less beefy but no less welcome or familiar. He doesn't say anything stupid like *How are you holding up?* and I'm grateful for it.

"I don't believe it," he says into my hair, quiet. "Not like, *I can't believe this happened.* But like I just don't *believe* she's dead. I mean, I know the police aren't lying, but . . ."

Remy's only two years older than us, but he started college at sixteen, pre-med. He used to hang with Alice, Will and me, by virtue of our dads being BFFs and dragging us to the same endless parade of social functions, and Will and Alice coming along for solidarity and free grub. Since he started college our lives haven't overlapped nearly as much as they used to, but that doesn't make him any less one of us.

"I know." And I do. My brain says *This is real,* but my heart can't begin to accept the enormity of what that means. Of being the girl who used to be half of an Alice-and-Cia whole, and is now just half. Of people's eyes scraping over me like tongues in search of wounds, like they do to Judah Hayes.

Voices murmur from the dining room, and Remy pulls back just enough to give me a questioning eyebrow.

"The cops are here," I tell him. "Pretending like they give a shit about Alice, but really just looking for reasons to write her off."

Remy frowns. "What kind of questions are they asking?"

"About Noah, mostly."

His eyes darken. "That kid really hurt her."

"He did. But she was getting better. She was moving on." I don't like the neutrality of his expression. "She *was*, Remy."

He doesn't disagree. Instead, he loops his arm around my shoulders and lends me the courage to walk back into the room with my own personal interrogation panel.

Everyone is standing when we enter the dining room, but their faces look like the pain scale spectrum on hospital whiteboards: Dad's expression is unreadable, Timmerman looks vaguely embarrassed, and Rojas looks like he ate a bad grape.

"Sir." Timmerman nods at Sean, his back boot-camp straight.

"Deputy Chief Walsh," Rojas says sourly. "I wasn't aware you were personally overseeing this case?" He makes the statement a question.

Sean ignores them both for the moment and walks around to give my dad one of those one-arm man hugs. "Sorry about all of this, Javier."

Dad nods. "It's all right. The detectives were just leaving. I believe we've answered all of their questions for now."

"Actually—"

Sean cuts Rojas off. "Thank you for your diligent efforts on this case, Frank. And Detective Thompson, is it?"

"Timmerman, sir."

"Sure. Your attention to detail in this tragedy is appreciated. If you have any further questions for Miss Lucero, you can come to me directly."

I take great satisfaction in watching Rojas's face go from hypertension-pink to angry plum, but he otherwise manages to keep his shit together. "With respect, sir, that isn't exactly protocol."

"Respect acknowledged, Detective, but you will do it anyway." Sean smiles pleasantly. This ruthlessness is a side of him I've never seen, and I'm fascinated. "Battalion Chief Lucero and his family deserve a little more compassion than simply following protocol to the letter in light of this terrible tragedy. Your lieutenant agrees, of course. I'll expect a report on your progress at 0600 tomorrow." He winks. "I'll even bring the go juice. The shit that passes for coffee at your station is a federal crime."

The detectives leave just as Papa emerges from the bathroom. He gets another man-hug from Sean.

"Good to see you, Liam," he says. "I wish the circumstances were happier."

"Don't we all." Papa looks at me, and suddenly I have to be somewhere else. My body isn't big enough to hold this kind of sorrow for this long. It burns hot and dark and fills me with smoke, and I look at the faces of the men around me and I can barely breathe.

"I have to go."

"Go where?" Dad asks, and their faces all take different but similar shapes. Confusion. Concern.

"Climbing. I need to clear my head. Can I take the car?"

Dad and Papa exchange a look, communicating something via Parent Telepathy that ends with Papa scooping his keys out of the bowl and tossing them to me, and then I'm out the door.

Outside, the sun is warm and the breeze stirs the leaves that have started to drift free from the trees and it's actually a pretty perfect day in every way except that Alice is dead and I have no one to blame except a missing boy who looked at her with stars in his eyes until he didn't anymore and now no one can ever look at her again.

Chapter

6

My muscles scream in protest as I reach for the next hold. The one I want is just out of reach, so I strain further, and my arm trembles with the effort.

My right foot slips off its narrow perch.

Brouardel's first stage of drowning: surprise. The animal gasps for air once, twice. Feels only cold water rushing in.

The weight of my entire body wrenches through my right arm. I kick out my left leg toward the closest foothold, slide off, kick out again.

Muscle to tendon to bone to ligament, every part of my right shoulder is on fire.

Stage two: the animal fights violently to reach the surface.

I am not going to fall.

I am *not* going to fall.

My left foot finds solid purchase, but my prosthetic relies on dynamic movement for push—I have no isolated active ankle flexion to propel me those last few centimeters to the hold I need. I have to get the other foothold back.

I risk a glance down. The ground looks impossibly far away, but there's my foothold, and I edge my right foot into the narrow crevice.

Stage three: the animal calms. The animal swallows the water.

I push up with everything I've got. My Achilles tendon vibrates.

My fingertips slide into the crimp.

I get my rhythm back. I climb. I step and reach, step and reach.

Until there are no more footholds.

I stare at the sheer wall, the next handhold so far out of reach I could laugh.

I'm going to fall.

Stage four: the animal loses consciousness. Pupils dilate.

"Move, Cia!" Rob shouts from a hundred miles below me. He works here at the rock gym, but he's not on the clock now. He was practicing some bouldering when I coerced him into belaying for me. "Trust yourself!"

My left hand is cramped into a claw, my flexor muscles abused past their limit. I think it could be stuck like that now, fused with the crimp hold, keeping me safe.

I do not want safe.

Safety is static, and static is the enemy of progress.

I plant my shoe against the sheer surface. I trust my foot. I trust my leg.

I trust my body.

I push my hips off the wall.

I lift my other foot. Plant it.

Push.

Reach.

Stage five: terminal gasps, involuntary and likely far too late.

Fall.

Chapter

7

My muscles hum with the promise of future ache, but that's what I was after. The gnawing beneath my skin is gone, the suffocating smoke forced out through my pores. My body feels like doll parts, strangely-jointed and held together with taut rubber bands.

It's barely one o'clock. Besides Rob and me there'd been only three other people inside, so it's odd that someone has parked next to me in the large parking lot, kind of like taking the seat right next to a stranger in an otherwise empty movie theater.

Even odder, there's someone leaning against my car.

Judah Hayes straightens as I approach but doesn't step away from my car. His jeans are frayed over his Converses, which look like he's been hiking somewhere muddy. I can't help but notice the way his black T-shirt stretches across his shoulders, the glint of a fragile silver chain disappearing into it, or the fact that he seems to have gained an inch or two over the summer. He's always been taller than me but now I'm eye level with his chin. Noah never had more than a sprinkle of stubble along his jaw, but Judah looks like he probably has to shave every day; there are shadows under his skin that make him look older. More dangerous.

I can see my reflection in his sunglasses. "What are you doing here?"

"I heard about Alice." He uncrosses his arms . . . and doesn't say anything else.

That's fine. If I get any more sympathy today, I might choke on it. I walk past him, unlock the car and toss my bag into the back seat. "Okay."

"Alice was a great girl. She deserved better than what my brother did to her."

Would you say Alice was depressed?

Nobody can know what Alice was thinking . . .

Alice was a great girl.

"You all talk about her in the past tense so easily," I say, without really meaning to say anything. "It hasn't even been a day, and already, Alice *was*. Alice isn't anymore. How is that so easy for everybody?"

"Asks the girl who's hanging out at the gym hours after finding out her best friend is dead."

I slam the door. "Fuck you, Judah." I can't believe he went there. Then I remind myself he's carrying the weight of his own tragedy, and it buys him exactly one ounce of patience. "What do you want from me?"

He takes his time. I'm suddenly supremely aware of the sweat between my breasts and in the groove of my spine, my tank top clinging to my skin.

Whatever. He's seen me sweatier. We were track nerds together for two years.

"The police never looked for Noah," he says. "Not really. We turn eighteen in two months, and he'd . . . had some problems this summer. I guess they figured good riddance."

The bitterness in his voice cuts through my defenses. "He's still a minor."

"A minor with two arrests for possession and three for criminal trespassing. He had a court date coming up and was facing jail time. When he bounced, they probably just figured they'd save the taxpayer dollars and let the problem take care of itself."

Alice hadn't mentioned any of that. "Possession of what?"

"Anything he could get his hands on. My brother is an addict." Mirrored lenses or not, there's no hiding the pain when he says the word.

Oh, Alice.

Rojas had hinted as much, but Alice had never spoken a word about anything more serious than pot. Why hadn't she told me? Had Will known?

"I'm sorry, Judah. I didn't know."

"Why would you? My brother is all about *the experience.* Opening his mind, letting the universe in." The sarcasm is strong in this one. "This year he got into that bonedust shit, though, and when he broke it off with Alice . . . Things changed after that. *He* changed."

I hug myself, let my keys jingle. "What your family is going through sucks, Judah. I can't imagine what it's like."

He doesn't take the hint, remains in front of the driver's side door. "The cops wrote my brother off, but Alice didn't. She was looking for him."

"I know."

He cocks his head.

"She told me. Yesterday," I say.

"Is that what you were fighting about?"

I remember him staring at us across the quad. Alice, holding my hands and pleading with me to hear her out. Guilt forms a blade of ice in my gut, and I turn it against him before it can cut me. "It's not really any of your business."

"My brother is my business," he snaps. "What do you know, Cia?"

He halves the distance between us with a deliberate step. The vehemence in his voice startles me, and I stand my ground even though I really, really want to back away.

Daddy didn't raise no princess.

"She trusted you," he says. "What did she tell you? And who did *you* tell?"

My adrenaline is already up from the rock wall. The waves of intensity coming off of Judah kick my pulse back into high gear. "She told me she was looking for him. That's it."

"Bullshit, Cia. She was onto something, and the day after she confides in *you*, she's dead. Tell me that's a fucking coincidence!"

"Step *off*, Judah!" I hiss, keys poking out between my fingers in case I need to throw a punch. "You don't want to do this."

He smiles then, cracking the mask. I see fury there, but also pain. It comes alive in me, recognizing itself.

"I will do whatever it takes," Judah says, "to find my brother." He opens the door, holds it out in a mock-gentlemanly gesture.

I get in, beyond ready to put him in the rearview mirror. When I try to pull the door closed, he holds tight. Leans in, and the stray thought flashes through my head that an onlooker might think he was leaning in for a kiss goodbye.

"Whatever it takes, Cia," he says softly.

Not a kiss. A threat.

He shuts the door gently, taps the roof of the car. Doesn't move as I gun the gas, just becomes smaller and smaller in the mirror until he could be anyone, and then, as I pull out of the lot, no one at all.

Chapter

8

The water below me is still, keeping its secrets.

Across the quarry, yellow tape stretches between the dirt patch that serves as an unofficial parking lot on the cliff's edge. The lone police car parked there hasn't moved for ten minutes. I'm pretty sure it's occupied by some poor rookie assigned to make sure Alice's idea isn't contagious.

I'd genuinely planned to go home when I pulled out of that parking lot, but I can't say I was surprised at the sound of my tires chewing up loose rock instead of smooth concrete. The usual road to the quarry was cordoned off with cones and wood barricades, so I'd taken the back way, which isn't really a road at all and requires walking about half a mile through the woods when the trees get too close together to squeeze a car through.

The surrounding forest exhales, stirring the loose strands of hair that are no longer sweat-glued to my skin.

I don't know what I expected to see.

The sides of the quarry are gray streaked with rust, tiered like a stairwell for giants. The water looks Gatorade-blue due to the way the high content of rock dust digests and spits back the sunlight.

I don't know what I expected to feel.

I know that what I do feel is *pissed*.

When I wrote a report on the quarry for seventh grade science, I felt a connection to the place immediately. I learned about how it had helped Summerset grow from a village to a town to a city with its jobs and exports and easy access to building materials, and how it had been abandoned, the way Americans abandon everything we view as old and used up, left to fill with groundwater and reclaimed by the forest and teenagers looking for a place to smoke and drink and swim and get laid . . . and now, apparently, to die.

I am pissed at the quarry. It was our refuge, our oasis. When grown-ups warned of the dangers of the quarry, they said things like *toxic runoff, industrial waste, steep drop-offs.* They never said anything about despair grabbing you by the throat and pulling you in.

I am pissed at the miners who started digging Alice's grave in 1840, when they laid the first explosives in the earth and blasted out the gypsum that used to live here but is now wrapped around millions of humans as plaster walls to keep us warm and dry, molded by doctors into casts to heal us when we're broken.

I am pissed at Judah.

What did she tell you? And who did you tell?

Alice didn't tell me *anything*. In fact, it seems like I've learned more about Alice in the hours that she's been dead than I have in the last three months of being her best friend.

"Damn it, Alice," I whisper.

A clatter from the edge of the forest makes me jump. I wipe my cheeks with the back of my hand and drop my shades back down over my eyes.

"I knew you'd come here," Will says. I turn back to the water, leave my eye-armor in place.

"I had no right to talk to you that way, Cia." He sits beside me in the dirt, our feet dangling over the edge. Tugs his beanie down half over his eyes, the way he likes it, as if the world makes more sense when viewed in slivers instead of the whole.

"No, you didn't."

He puts his hand on mine. His scruffy fingerless glove scratches my skin, his warm fingers curl between mine and he puts our hands together on his knee. "If I was another guy who'd treated you that way, I'd punch me in the throat."

I don't pull my hand away.

"I'm a real piece of shit sometimes." He doesn't look at me. "I can't remember what it's like to not be angry all the time. What really sucks is that this is me doing the best I can. And it's not good enough. I know it's not."

My heart hurts too much for this. What he did isn't okay, not by any stretch, but I need my best friend right now, and he needs me.

I squeeze his fingers.

He sniffs. When he speaks again, his voice is splintered in a way it wasn't before. "I miss her so much, Cia."

I rest my head on his shoulder. "I do too."

A few minutes pass. The cop car doesn't move. The sun dries the tears we're both pretending not to cry for some reason. We compare our interviews with the police, finding few differences except that I'd seen the note and he hadn't.

When I recite the poem from memory, Will scowls. "That's some trite bullshit if I ever heard it." He pauses. "What if . . ."

I know exactly where he's going, because my mind had seized hopefully on the most literal spin as well.

She is not dead, she is just away.

She is not dead.

"The Bookers identified her," I remind him softly, and we both fall silent again. He whips a rock across the quarry, and it reminds me of something else. "Judah Hayes ambushed me outside the rock gym."

Will takes a second to follow me around that switchback. "What did he want?"

"I don't know how, but he knew she'd been looking into Noah's disappearance. He wanted to know what Alice had told me."

"What *did* Alice tell you?"

"Literally just that. And that my fire hadn't ever really been investigated." I hug one knee to my chest. "Not that I gave her time to tell me much else. But Judah seemed to think she'd found something."

"Something like?"

"I don't know. He saw us arguing in the quad yesterday. He thought she told me some big secret about Noah. He basically accused me of selling her out, because we had that fight and then she . . . then she was dead."

"So he doesn't buy this Ophelia shit either. I guess we know which twin got the brains." Will turns his eyes on me. "That leaves you, Cia. What do you believe?"

That's a great question, one I don't have an answer ready for. "Does it matter? I obviously didn't know her as well as I thought I did."

"It matters." He pulls at a thread on his glove. "I have to tell you something."

My heartbeat stutters before finding its rhythm again. More secrets. "Spit it out, Mason."

The thread on his glove is long, and suddenly half the thumb seam is coming undone. I put my hand over his to stop him from unraveling the whole damn thing at the same time he blurts out, "Alice was pregnant."

I freeze.

"The police don't know yet," he says, "but they will."

I can't hear this.

My legs twitch with the sudden urge to run, heat streaking through my muscles in a *need* to run I haven't felt since the last time I stood at the starting line watching the starter's finger curl around the trigger.

But where would I go?

Is there a place where Alice isn't lavender-cold, blue lips and mirror-glazed eyes, baby mer-child in her belly now forever lost to dreams and could-have-beens? Is there a place where best friends don't keep the kind of secrets that eat you away like cotton candy left in the rain?

If there is, it's miles away from here.

I stay.

"How do you know?" I whisper.

He looks embarrassed. "She said I could borrow her notes from English Lit that day I skipped last week. She was in the bathroom and I didn't want to forget, so I went through her backpack. I found an ultrasound photo."

"How . . . ?"

He knows what I'm asking. "They told her she was about fourteen weeks along. So . . . right before Noah broke up with her." He takes out a lighter, scorches the thread to a blackened nub. "She made me swear I wouldn't say anything. Her parents didn't even know yet. She wanted to tell you herself."

"But you've known for a *week*. She didn't say a word to me."

"I don't think she was ready for anyone to know. Not even us. I think she still hoped Noah would come back. That when he found out about the baby, things would be all right again."

That doesn't sound like the pragmatic Alice I knew. But then, I'd get into a windowless van with strangers promising candy before I'd trust my judgment about anything Alice-related right now. "I can't believe she didn't tell me."

Will turns to face me. "But don't you see? That's why this doesn't make any sense. Alice *loved* kids. Remember when Teddy was born? You'd have thought her parents got her a pony instead of a little brother. She would never have done this, Cia. Never."

The breeze grows teeth, drags them across the back of my neck until the hair raises on my arms. "What are you saying, Will?"

"What if she did find Noah?"

"I don't—"

"What if she found Noah," Will asks me, "but Noah didn't want that baby?"

He might as well have pushed me off the edge. I feel like I'm free falling. "He would never hurt her."

"He did hurt her."

"Not like that." I want to be certain. I want to trust what I thought I knew.

But Will doesn't hesitate. "Well, *someone* killed Alice. And right now, they think they got away with it."

Chapter

9

My hands are trembling as I throw the car into reverse and kick up a thick dust cloud.

Fact: Alice was pregnant.

Fact: Alice was looking for Noah.

Fact: Alice was looking into my fire.

Fact: Alice is dead.

Will's arms around me had felt heavy and safe before I left him at the quarry's edge, but that feeling slips further away with every mile on the odometer.

Alice hadn't done this to herself. The baby proved it. It might look otherwise to the cops, who just see a desperate, lonely girl chasing her ex off a cliff, but Alice wasn't either of those things.

I feel sick as my thoughts take shape in the silence.

Alice was.

Now I'm doing it too, making her past tense.

Fact: Alice did not kill herself.

What if Judah's right? Alice *had* found something. She'd

been trying to tell me about it yesterday. What if it had been Noah, and he hadn't wanted to be found? What if he'd seen Alice's pregnancy as a threat, and they'd fought?

My knuckles whiten on the steering wheel. I want to believe what I said about Noah. But if it wasn't him, who was it? Who else had a secret worth killing for?

Fact: Alice's murderer is out there somewhere.

If whatever got Alice killed isn't about Noah . . . then it's about my fire.

It's about me.

Fact: I am in way over my head.

———

The porch swing *skrees* softly as we go back and forth, back and forth. Papa lit a few citronella candles before disappearing inside, smears of orange in the pale blue blanket that's fallen over the world, that dusky limbo between sunset and full dark.

Remy is relaxed beside me, long legs outstretched, ankles bare between the cuffs of his brown pants and loafers. The tails of a white shirt have liberated themselves from his waistband and hang loose under his gray sweater vest. Cricketsong and the shushing of leaves are the only sounds, but our silence is comfortable, comforting even. Remy's well acquainted with the futility of words in the face of loss—Papa won his battle with cancer two years after Remy's mom lost hers.

"When you weren't home, I went to see the Bookers," he says eventually. "They're pretty devastated, but they're hanging in there. The little guy seemed to be taking it the hardest."

"Teddy."

He nods. Teddy's five and worships his big sister. By the time Teddy entered the picture Remy was exiting stage left, trading our lazy summers at the quarry and scary movie nights under blanket forts for private tutoring sessions and college prep intensives.

No one's said anything about Alice being pregnant. Is it even possible that Will and I are still the only ones who know?

"I know it sounds stupid," Remy says, "but I still can't believe she's gone."

Back

and forth.

Pancakes's tail thumps against the porch.

"Did you know I was her first kiss?" he asks suddenly.

My jaw drops. "No way! Carter Whitman, sixth grade, T-rex exhibit at the museum. She'd had a crush on him for months."

"I know," he said mildly. "That's why she didn't want to be a bad kisser."

"So you were the dry run?" I can't help laughing.

He looks offended. "As an older man, I was happy to share my wisdom with the next generation." Then he frowns, all teasing gone from his expression. "What happened, Cia? I didn't know this Noah kid as well as you guys did. Dad says he was into drugs? Bonedust?"

I shrug. "I knew he smoked pot. I didn't know about the rest, but apparently you could fill the quarry with all the things I didn't know about Alice's life."

"Hey." He grabs my hand. His eyes are the color of the moss that grows on the trees around the quarry, but the fading daylight turns them ash-gray. "This is not on you, Silencia Lucero. Not one ounce of it. Do you hear me?"

I swallow hard past the sudden rock in my throat. "I hear you."

Will and I agreed to keep what we knew between us for now, until we have more information. Until we have something stronger than *Alice wouldn't kill her baby*. But this is Remy. He loved her too.

"She didn't do it, Remy."

A lock of beach-sand hair falls across his forehead as he tilts his head. "What do you mean?"

"I mean she didn't kill herself." He opens his mouth but I pick up steam, talking over whatever he was about to say. "I know everyone thinks she was devastated over Noah. And maybe she was. But Alice wasn't the kind of person to let sadness break her. She turned it into action. She was looking for him, Remy, and she was asking a lot of questions. Maybe she found an answer someone didn't want getting out."

I've left out the baby. For now, that tragedy is just for Will and me to bear.

I have his attention anyway. "What kind of questions?"

He hasn't taken his hand back, and heat is slowly blooming between my skin and his.

"Missing kids, for one. She said that there were a lot more kids missing than the official reports showed, at least eleven this year alone, and that Noah's family was the only one that got any media coverage at all."

He looks thoughtful. "That doesn't seem that unusual, to be honest. Especially if they were teenagers. A lot of times they don't even take a report if the kid is seventeen."

I hadn't known that, but I press on. "She was looking into more than just that, Remy. I don't know everything, but I will."

There's blond fuzz on his jaw I've never noticed before, nearly obscuring the scar from the time he took one of my soccer cleats to the chin. He looks older than nineteen. "How?"

"Will and I are going to get her laptop. It's either at home or at school. That seems like the best place to start."

"Was that Will's idea?"

I hate that the answer is, *mostly yes.* I hate that I let what I didn't know about Alice count for more than what I did know, because the person I knew was a bright, passionate girl who never for all the boys in the world would have given up that fire. "We both know it's true, Remy. Alice just isn't—*wasn't*— the girl they're trying to make her out to be."

"Have you told the police about this stuff, Cia?"

"No. Detective Rojas just wants to close this case, and we want to blow it wide open. I don't think he wants to hear anything I have to say."

"I want to hear everything you have to say." He looks down at our hands, seems to notice suddenly that they're still pretzeled together, and blushes. Both of our hands creep back into our respective laps. "I mean, I want to help you, Cia. My dad, too, if you let him."

"No," I say, too sharp. "I mean, not yet. Thanks, Remy. I mean it. And I'll take you up on it when the time comes. We just don't have anything to show yet."

Is that the truth?

Or is there something else?

I know that I want Will and me to be the ones to find Alice's secrets. To decide which ones stay buried and which see the light of day. We who loved her should make those choices, not strangers with badges and bylines.

Why am I trying to protect her, still, now?

Because she deserved so much better than she got, from any of us.

"Hey." He lifts my chin, thumbs away the tear that snuck past my barbed-wire defenses. "What just happened?"

"She called me, Remy."

My tear glitters on his fingertip. He doesn't rub it away. "When?"

"Right before she died. She called and texted me, seventeen times. I didn't answer . . . I ignored every single one, and then someone killed her—"

"We don't know that—"

"I fucking know it, Remy!"

"Okay." He blows out a breath. "Okay. Why didn't you answer?"

"We'd had a fight and I just needed some time off from her. She could be so intense when she got her teeth into something, and normally I'm game for the chase, but this time it was . . . It was me, Remy."

"What do you mean?"

"She wasn't just looking into missing kids. She was looking into fires. *My* fire. She thought there was something fucked-up about it."

"There *was* something fucked-up about it. John Bennett decided to cook bonedust in his basement, and blew up his house with his wife and four daughters in it. It doesn't get much worse than that."

"Alice thought it did."

"What did she find?"

"Something about the way the doors were locked, and how the investigation was conducted. I don't know yet."

Remy's lips tighten. "Listen, Cia. I know you want answers. I do too. But your *dad* was first on scene. He's the one that found you in the grass—"

"I *know* that, Remy, Jesus—"

"—so if you have any questions about that night, he should be the first person you talk to. Don't go around him on this, kid. You'll break his heart."

"Don't call me kid." He has a point, and guilt makes me surly. Twelve years ago, Dad had still been riding a rig at Summerset

Station 4, coming up on five years out of the academy. He'd been playing video games at the station when the call came in.

Ten minutes later he was on his knees in scorched grass, breathing through the smoke-parched lips of some stranger's little girl while the rest of his crew went face to face with a fire that, in the glimpses that only come to me in nightmares, had serrated claws and a yawning hole of a mouth like Abaddon himself crawling up out of hell.

Too late. All of them, too late. My sisters were dead, Grace and Faith and Prudence, none of us existing on paper before the fire and the three of them existing only on paper after, on paper and etched into small smooth stone blocks at the cemetery to be remembered by a town that had never known them, by a sister that can only piece together enough memory for a single recurring nightmare—

Hush now.

No.

I don't

won't

remember this.

Everything is going to be all right.

"Cia."

I look up.

Firelight reflects in his eyes, and I flinch.

There's no fire.

The sun is gone, and the porch lights have come on, and Remy is looking at me with way too much sympathy stamped all over his face.

I get up abruptly. The swing bumps the backs of my knees. "Will you help me?"

He stands up, too. "With whatever you need," he says.

His cheek is Velcro on my lips. "I hoped you'd say that."

Chapter

10

"¡Mierda!"

The seat belt bites into my collarbone as Dad stomps on the brakes. Inches from the bumper, a thin woman in a sundress slowly looks up at us. Her pupils are blown out holes in a sea of blue.

"Don't stare."

"I'm not," I say, staring. The woman moves around to my side of the car, but Dad hits the accelerator the moment she's out of the way.

"Wow, Dad."

"She is high, Cia. She had no business talking to you."

She is also someone's daughter. Sister. Someone's *something*.

My Dad is a good man. He's spent his life in service of this town. But even he had looked right through her.

Is that what's happened to Noah? Missing not because he's not here, somewhere—but because no one bothers to *see* him?

Alice would have seen him.

Had she?

"Dad, have they said anything else about . . . about Alice's . . ."

I can't say *body*. He doesn't need me to. "Like what, mija?"

I hold my coffee with both hands, mostly so he can't see them trembling. "Would they be able to tell if she'd been pushed?"

He takes until the next red light to respond, and then he looks at me. "Is there someone you think may have pushed her?"

"That's a non-answer."

"So is that," he observes.

I watch the light flip to green. "No. There's no one. I just can't believe she jumped." I can't mention the Noah theory, not without breaking my promise to Will to keep Alice's secret. "Your turn."

Dad sighs. "Not necessarily."

"Not . . . necessarily?"

"Not likely. Pero, Cia . . . she *did* jump. Eso lo sabes, ¿sí?"

I can't give him the answer he wants, so I don't say anything at all.

Not likely, he'd said. Probably even less likely if she'd been caught by surprise. If she'd been with someone she trusted, and it had happened too fast to fight back.

I wedge my cup into the holder. My churning stomach doesn't need any more caffeine.

When we pull up to the drop-off zone at school, Dad squeezes my hand. He's wearing his Class A's today, the jacket pressed stiff, buttons shiny. He'd said something about a meeting downtown, which is Dad-code for anything involving politicians. He rubs his neck under the collar; he just shaved this morning but I can already see a sprinkling of black under his skin where his beard refuses to accept defeat. Impulsively, I reach over and give him a hug.

Surprised, he hugs me back. These arms have been safety

almost as far back as I can remember, and I need them around me now, before I face this shitshow of a day. "Do you need one more day at home, mija?"

I open the door. "Miles away from okay. But sitting in my room another day isn't going to bring me any closer."

He nods. You don't fight fires for the better part of two decades without staring death in the face a few times, and feeling its chill as it passes you by to take the man beside you. He gets it, sort of.

I step out, sling my backpack over my shoulder. It feels light, and I realize I have no idea what's in it. Are my books at home? In my locker? What day is it even?

When I woke up this morning I made it halfway to the bathroom before I remembered, the truth stabbing me in the sternum like a surgeon's scalpel. I thought for a split second I was having a heart attack, until I realized that it was just Alice, carving out space. That's where she lives now, in a torn-out hollow just beneath my heart.

I hip-check the door closed. "Have a good day at work, Dad."

"Sea lo que sea lo vamos a superar, todo va a estar bien."

"I know. Love you."

"Loved you first." He pulls the hybrid away from the curb, leaving behind a minimal-carbon-footprint ghost of warmth.

———

I wait outside until just after the homeroom bell. Everybody knows Alice was my best friend. Since I missed school yesterday, the sharks are going to be *ravenous* today, stirred to a frenzy by rumor and the scent of blood in the water.

By the time I enter the building the usual hallway mob scene has mostly trickled away, and I make it to my locker with an impressive zero incidents of eye contact. I stuff thirty pounds of World History and Pre-Calc into my backpack, then stare at Alice's locker, five down from mine.

I have it open in five seconds, her combo as familiar to me as my own. Alice's locker is a mini-IKEA of everything-in-its-place-ness, with actual extra shelves placed inside to facilitate extra obsessive-compulsive orderliness.

Or it used to be.

Now it stands empty.

I take a step back. I close and reopen it before I realize the ludicrousness of what I'm doing, as if Alice's stuff just happened to disappear into a pocket alternate universe for a moment, but would blink back to my reality if I just tried again.

Still empty.

Small fingers touch my shoulder and I nearly jump out of my skin.

Ms. "Call Me Gwen" Fletcher is a couple of inches shorter than me, but her Medusa-mane of curly brown hair makes up the difference. She's not the kind of Medusa that you look at and turn to stone, though. She's the kind that looks at you with big eyes the color and invitingness of fondue chocolate and before you know it you're vomiting up your feelings all over the place and she's handing you a box of Kleenex.

Not today, Medusa.

"I'm sorry if I startled you," the counselor says. She's maybe in her early thirties, pretty in an absent-minded way. I bet she spends more on lint rollers to get the cat hair off her hippie skirts than she does on makeup.

"It's okay." I readjust the leaden weight of my backpack before it completes its slow grind off my shoulder. Down the hall, a still form amidst the weaving bodies catches my attention.

Judah is watching us. Watching *me*, specifically. His dark eyes hold mine without flinching; he isn't embarrassed to be caught.

And I have nothing to hide, no matter what he thinks. So let him watch. I blow him a kiss and turn away.

Ms. Fletcher looks over my shoulder. "I didn't know you and Judah Hayes were . . ."

"Oh, we're not. We're *definitely* not." I gesture to the empty locker. "Do you know what happened to Alice's things? Did her parents come by?" I can't imagine clearing out their dead daughter's locker was high on their list of priorities yesterday, but maybe the school had done it for them.

Ms. Fletcher shakes her head. "No, the Bookers haven't been here."

"Did the police—?"

"The police were here first thing yesterday morning," she says. "It was already empty."

"Someone took her things?"

Google image search "compassionate patience for the mentally slow," and you'll see Ms. Fletcher's face. "Alice did, Silencia."

I look back at the locker. Yup, still empty.

"We think she cleared it out Wednesday afternoon," she says. "She wasn't planning on coming back."

"You don't know that." I slam the locker shut.

She looks puzzled.

The late bell saves me from whatever had been about to come out of my mouth. "I have to get to homeroom," I say instead.

"You don't, actually. I'll sign you in." She nods down the hall toward the guidance counselor offices. "Coffee or hot chocolate?"

———

I go hot chocolate, because I am jittery enough without more chemical assistance today, and because Call Me Gwen has some dark chocolate salted caramel concoction that she says must be tasted to be believed.

Her office is comfortable, with a couple of afghans slung over the chairs and a small library of books on how to make a living caring about other people's problems. She's nixed the overhead fluorescent light somehow, which is actually kind of impressive since I know they're on a timer, not a switch, so Ms. Fletcher must have climbed up on one of these afghan-covered swivel chairs and disabled it herself. A floor lamp behind her gives the room a soft yellow glow, and a few loops of what look like wooden beads hang from one of its arms.

"What are those?"

She looks over her shoulder, lifts one off and gently hands it to me. "It's called a *mala*. They're Buddhist prayer beads. Each strand has a hundred and eight beads."

It feels warm in my hands, the beads heavier than I expected. "It's pretty."

"The mala has been used for thousands of years as a meditation tool. As you touch each bead, you repeat a mantra, or just take a deep, healing breath. The intention is deeper connection with the universe. Stillness of mind."

I nod, rolling one of the smooth beads between my fingers. I like how it feels.

When I hand it back, Ms. Fletcher shakes her head. "Keep it," she says. "I have a feeling you could use some connection and stillness of mind these days."

I wrap it around my wrist. "You're not wrong." Having a social worker for a dad has some advantages; when she gives me silence to fill, I recognize the tactic and keep my mouth shut, fiddle with the beads she probably already regrets giving me.

Thing is, if Alice really had killed herself, I probably would talk to Ms. Fletcher about it. She's a nice lady, and she's been one of Will's biggest advocates since the accident. She's got more to offer than beads and exotic beverages, but I don't think her repertoire includes solving murders.

Ms. Fletcher: "I'm not going to tell you how bright and kind Alice was, or how much this school will feel her loss. Other people will, to the point that you'll probably be sick of hearing it. The truth is you feel her loss deeper than anyone here will, and you know who she was better than anyone here does."

I look up, surprised by the next-level honesty from an adult in authority.

"Everyone is going to be asking why. The police, her parents, your peers. You're going to hear a lot of rumors, things young people make up to fill the empty spaces because suicide is scary and most of us don't know how else to make sense of how it makes us feel." She swirls her coffee. "How are you making sense of it?"

"I went to the quarry," I say. *Damn it, mouth!*

She nods, as if the most logical thing to do when your friend dies is go scope out the scene. "What was that like?"

"It's the same." I shrug. "But different. We've been playing there since we were kids. It was our safe place, and now it's Alice's grave."

"But not really," she says gently. "She isn't there anymore."

She's right. Alice is nowhere, and everywhere. She's a dull ache beneath my heart and a rumor whispered in the halls. She's in the pollution-rainbowed waves of the quarry and a metal drawer at the medical examiner's office.

Ms. Fletcher has said something that I missed. "Sorry, what?"

"If Alice was here right now, what would you say to her?"

"I wouldn't say anything." I look away. "I'd just listen."

Ms. Fletcher slides the Kleenex across her desk.

———

I make it to AP World History in time for the Christians to pooh-pooh all over the Romans' wine-fueled orgies. Maryam Hadad gives me a sympathetic smile from behind her librarian glasses, the Bergdorf Goodman clones in the back tap their Jimmy Choos and whisper, and the teacher, Mr. Chen, pauses to nod at me as I drop my late pass onto his desk before continuing his lecture.

I actually really like World History, but Mr. Chen might as well be speaking Latin today. I slip my phone out of my backpack. Papa helped me resurrect my last phone from the grave of forgotten technology last night, while the one Will broke is on life support at Verizon's repair facility.

My messages and photos had transferred over in a matter of minutes, superimposed over what seem now like artifacts from another era. Another lifetime. I kept my old wallpaper: a group selfie of Alice, Will, and me squeezed into a metal bench shellacked in decades of cotton candy and vomit goo, riding the Ferris wheel at the state fair. The city lights are a rainbow blur behind us. Will's smile is still genuine, Alice's heart was still whole, and I still believed neither of them would ever lie to me.

We all look so young.

I have a couple texts waiting for me from Remy. Will too—guess I'm not the only one risking Summerset's zero tolerance cell phone policy this morning.

SexyBeast 07:51

> you here?

SexyBeast 08:23

> maryam said she saw you go into call me gwens office.
> bet im next. you doing ok?

I'd forgotten that Will had gotten into my phone and changed his name not long after that picture was taken. Those had been the pre-Snap days, since my dads had stood their ground on sixteen being the age at which I magically became mature enough for untraceable communication.

me 08:55

Alice's locker is empty.

SexyBeast 08:56

empty empty?

me 08:56

empty empty. they think she did it on her way out.

SexyBeast 08:57

it wasn't empty weds afternoon when i put her english lit notes back

But by the next morning it had been cleaned out completely.

I realize with a jolt that this is it—the first objective hole in the story the cops are trying to sell. Alice couldn't have emptied her locker if she'd left after lunch.

I turn my attention to Remy.

remy w 08:04

I meant what I said last night, just so you know.

me 08:57

which part?

remy w 08:58

> All of it. Did you talk to your dad?

me 08:58

> only to ask if he heard anything else about alice

remy w 08:58

> Any news?

me 08:59

> no. her locker is empty. the school says she cleared it
> out, Will says she didn't.

remy w 08:59

> What do you say?

I don't hesitate long.

me 08:59

> I believe Will. if Alice was killed because she
> discovered something, then whoever did it would
> want to cover his tracks.

I take some notes for appearances' sake, but they have nothing to do with the decline of the Roman empire.

MISSING: CELL PHONE. ?LAPTOP?

Mr. Chen turns around to write something on the smart-board.

ALICE'S LOCKER   WHO HAD ACCESS?

And more importantly, what were they looking for?

remy w 09:01
> So what's next?

me 09:02
> I need to know what she knew.

remy w 09:02
> How are you going to do that?

Now that is a damn good question.

When the bell rings, I hustle out of Mr. Chen's room before the mouths paired with any of those hungering eyes can attack, but the hallway is far from sanctuary. I keep my head down as the whispers swarm me like a thousand stinging flies, my grief like honey, and the most painful words are the ones that stick.

"—total duster like her boyfriend, he probably got her into it—"

"—she was like a straight A student, I heard her mom was a Nazi about grades, that's probably why—"

"—hooked up with her after her boyfriend peaced out, he said she was like super obsessed with death—"

"—selling it online, I shit you not, my friend said he saw her on a cam site—"

"—killed Noah Hayes for cheating on her and the guilt—"

"—find out she was a lesbian—"

"—sex tape—"

"—pregnant—"

My head snaps up.

"Who said that?"

Everyone is staring at me. Most—but not all—have the decency to shut their lying faces when I make eye contact.

"*Who said that?*"

A poloed boy with pressed khaki pants and a watch that probably cost more than Alice's car smirks.

Rage bubbles up in me, sorrow distilled to its purest form, and before I know it, I have closed the distance between us, because too much is fucked up today, and somebody has to pay for something, and it might as well be him.

Chapter

11

A soft arm loops through mine.

"Walk with me," Maryam murmurs. The thick lenses of her glasses give her owl eyes in her round face.

I look back at J. Crew.

"Whatever he said, it probably isn't the stupidest thing you're going to hear today," Maryam says quietly. "Come on."

The thing is, if he's the one that said it—it wasn't stupid at all. And I need to know how he knows.

He probably doesn't know anything, my internal voice of sanity says reasonably. *He's just shooting in the dark like everyone else.*

But what if he isn't?

I let Maryam lead me past the pack of hyenas out to the quad. I go straight to our tree, mine and Alice's, and sit. Maryam offers me water, maybe literally trying to douse the fire she sees burning behind my eyes.

I accept the paper cup and take a sip. "Thanks, Maryam."

"No prob." She doesn't say any more, or ask me any

questions, and in doing neither moves way up my list of favorite people. Maryam is smart, but subtle about it. With Alice gone, she's got valedictorian in the hole if she doesn't drive her grades off a cliff.

Off a cliff? Really?

Second bell rings, and Maryam shifts anxiously. Late to class is definitely not her MO. any more than it was Alice's.

"Go ahead. I'm okay."

She goes. The last stragglers dribble out of the quad and I watch the halls clear through the tinted glass.

I blow out a deep breath and lean against the tree. Like the rest of Summerset, its leaves are contemplating autumn, tinged with red and gold. Soon they'll fall, crunched into dust by careless feet. The tree will stretch skeletal arms toward a gray sky that has no answers. The quarry will freeze and keep its secrets just as well.

I unlock my relic of a phone. I hadn't wiped the phone when I'd replaced it—there's still that cheesy wallpaper, a photo gallery full of ancient history, and all of the apps I hadn't been able to live without.

I tap the Kik icon. Will had us all download it two years ago, with the reasoning that it was a way to send messages that our parents couldn't track via the phone bill since my dads wouldn't let me use Snapchat yet. We went back to regular texting when we all realized A) our parents were way too busy to pay attention to our text logs, and B) our texts were not exactly the juiciest of classified material. For a while it had felt like something secret and exciting, though.

Thank God my password is still saved, because that was during my regrettable boy band phase and typing out the phrase I suspect fifteen-year-old me chose for a password would cost more dignity than I have to spare today.

It's all still there.

Every message, every selfie, every secret.

I open my conversation with Alice. Her screen name was Elizabeth Cochran— the actual name of legendary investigative journalist Nellie Bly. Mine was somewhat less ambitious.

Most of her pictures that summer were of Teddy. He was two or three and a complete ham.

One exchange in particular catches my attention.

> **silencia_luc**
> i think noah hays likes you.

> **silencia_luc**
> hes pretty cute.

elizabeth_MF_cochran
i guess so, if you notice that stuff. i'm too busy for boys. maybe in college.

> **silencia_luc**
> lol. you'll be too busy winning the pulitzer by then. these are supposed to be our wild years. have you ever even been grounded?

elizabeth_MF_cochran
i'll add it to my list of things to do before school starts. but only if you get grounded too.

silencia_luc

duh. best bitches don't let each
other suffer alone.

elizabeth_MF_cochran

damn straight.

silencia_luc

what are you going to do, get a
B+ on a paper?

elizabeth_MF_cochran

let's not be hasty.

My eyes blur with tears.

"Fuck, I miss you," I whisper to the screen.

I spend most of Pre-Calc traveling back in time, until my heart can't take any more. I close the conversation, knowing I'll be back.

Then I reopen it.

still my best bitch, I type, and hit send.

An *S* appears next to the message. Sent.

My thumb hovers, but before I can close the app, the *S* turns into a *D*.

Delivered.

What?

Alice's phone.

Somewhere, it is still on. And for some reason, it is running a chat app that we kept secret from everyone but the three of us. A chat app we all deleted over a year ago.

Except one of us didn't.

I stare at the *D*, willing it to vomit up GPS coordinates. It doesn't oblige. It doesn't turn into an *R*, either, so the message hasn't been opened and read.

I don't realize my hands are shaking until I type again. *Alice?*

She doesn't answer.

Of course she doesn't answer.

Third bell rings.

Does Will know Alice still used Kik? Who was she talking to?

The phone maintains its serene neutrality. I stuff it in my pocket and stand up before I am stampeded. I've barely crossed the quad when I hear shouting, and my heart stutters into a dubstep remix of its original beat.

I know that voice.

I run into the hall just in time to see Will throw the first punch.

If Kyle Kaufman could catch a football as well as he catches that punch, the Summerset Pirates wouldn't be 0 for 3 this season. Kyle's head snaps to the side, Will's fist connecting with the angle where Kyle's jaw meets his ear, and Kyle reels backward, but only for a moment.

Then a whole lot of things happen all at once.

Darius McMillan jumps on Will from behind. Will staggers under the weight of our Big Mac-loving quarterback, but doesn't go down. Darius wraps one beefy arm around Will's neck, and Kyle seizes the opportunity to punch Will square in the stomach.

I don't even think. One second I'm in the doorway to the quad, the next I'm standing between Will and Kyle, staring into Kyle's red face and wild eyes—and the second after that I'm on the floor, because Kyle is way too pissed to pull punches no matter who gets in the way.

"Kyle, man, hold up," Darius is saying, I think. My ears are ringing as I jump back up to my feet.

"Touch her again and I'll fucking kill you!" Will shouts, landing a kick to Darius's shin, but Darius is fairly used to abuse. All that's missing is a chorus line of cheerleaders in nanoskirts cheering him on.

I'm not stupid. Going head-to-head with a roided-out wide receiver is not a hobby I plan to run with, but the truth is I can take it. Will can't. As hot as he's been running lately, I don't believe at all that he will know—or care—when to stop. This will end with him in handcuffs or the hospital if I don't slow it down long enough for someone to call security.

By some miracle of my lizard brain reflexes I duck Kyle's next swing.

"Get the hell out of the way, Lucero," he spits. "He's had this coming since his mom killed A-Ray."

"That has nothing to do with him," I snap back.

"The fuck it doesn't!" Kyle steps so far into my bubble I can smell the breakfast burrito on his hot breath.

"You're a smart girl, Cia, but you got this one wrong," Darius says, grunting as Will lands an elbow to his eight-pack. "Step aside and let him take his medicine like a big boy."

"Back off," I say to Kyle's chin. He's got eight inches and sixty pounds on me, and uses all of it to hulk over me. Caveman intimidation tactics 101. "Your parents can't afford this lawsuit, Kaufman. Not with Daddy K.'s expensive side piece *and* the alimony he's going to be paying your mom when she finds out."

I've never been part of the jock crowd, but when I ran track I was definitely jock-adjacent, and gossip trickles down pretty much unfiltered from country club to locker room in a town like Summerset. I have no idea if it's true but Kyle's reaction is exactly what I was after: blind fury, diverted mid-course from Will to me.

He drives me into a bank of lockers like a steer impaling

its prey against a wall. The back of my skull slams hard into the metal.

Fireworks bloom at the edges of my vision, purple and red and oil-spill shimmer, and I think, *Pretty*, and then I'm rag-dolling it to the floor. I grab Kyle's ankle as the tile gets closer and closer . . .

At least I'll have company down here, I think as two hundred pounds of testosterone-laced Grade A grass-fed American beef hits the floor.

"What the hell is going on here?" Some Grown-Up bellows, not a moment too soon.

I look up and notice with some pride and way more concern that Will has given Darius a bloody nose, which he only could have done by slamming the back of his skull into the QB's face.

Some Grown-Up turns out to be Coach Andersen, followed quickly by Vice Principal Holland and Call Me Gwen.

The crowd scatters like grease fleeing from a drop of Palmolive.

Show's over, don't forget to tip your bartenders, I tell them silently, and the first drop of blood trickles down my neck.

———

"I'm going to choke Kaufman to death with his own jockstrap." Will is still shaking with anger. "Or maybe Darius's. Whichever one has more HPV on it."

"Gross, Will. And no more death threats when Holland comes back. You know they're mandatory reporters of that stuff."

"Whatever."

"Not whatever." I sigh. My head is already starting to ache. "What did he say?"

"He's an asshole."

"Nobody's debating that. What did he *say*?"

"That I killed Alice just like my mom killed Aaron." Hurt flashes behind his eyes, quickly slips away behind the shadows that have taken up permanent residence there. "That everybody close to me pays for it, and I should kill myself too."

"Oh, Will." Now *I* want to choke Kyle with his grody strap. "Nobody thinks you killed Alice."

His expression says otherwise. "I don't want to talk about it anymore."

"Will—"

"I mean it, Cia. Let it go." He touches my neck. "I can't believe he hit you. Are you okay?"

"I'm fine." I pull my hair forward over my shoulder. If VP Holland sees blood it'll be Go Straight to the Nurse's Office, Do Not Pass Go. That would change the phone call my dads get from "Your well-intentioned but robustly stupid daughter was in a fight," to, "Your well-intentioned but robustly stupid daughter was in a fight and is now in the nurse's office," which in all likelihood would lead to Papa leaving work to come check on me, thus ratcheting up the drama of this whole situation exponentially.

We're in luck. Coach Andersen has silver-tongued Holland into chalking the whole thing up to misplaced grief, a possibly-inevitable teenage response to the shock and fear of losing one of our peers and being confronted with our own mortality, and Darius and Kyle should definitely still be allowed to play Friday night because kids need a physical outlet for their emotions and also, a return to normal routine will help everyone move on.

Not to mention, Summerset High really needs that W.

———

Ms. Fletcher keeps Will back while I am sent on my way with another late pass.

I step into the empty hall and realize I have no idea where I'm going.

I don't even know what time it is.

I wander vaguely for a few steps before someone calls my name and I turn around.

Santi's red-heeled boots click on the waxed tile. Wavy black hair cascades down one side of her head, the other shaved smooth, unadorned except for a feathery earring that looks like it could be used to catch exotic fish.

"Silencia, you are a mess," she says. Santi has been a theater geek since she learned to talk, so her particular elocution is less affectation and more job hazard. She hooks her slim arm through mine and for the second time this morning I am being led somewhere by someone who knows better than I do where I should be going.

I must look particularly lost today.

———

The warren of rooms behind the stage of Summerset High's auditorium are the sole domain of our theater club, and in the land of drama Santi reigns supreme. She leads me through a set of double doors, then one I thought was a closet, down a flight of stairs I'm pretty sure is a fire escape of some sort, and through a third door that is, honest to God, completely hidden behind a black velvet curtain.

"This can't be up to code," I mutter as Santi sashays me through an abattoir of gowned, pierced, and bewigged mannequin carcasses, most missing some essential limb, and into a dressing room.

"Honey, we make our own code down here," Santi says, closing the door behind me.

Lengths of multicolored fabric are draped over every available surface, the walls strung with pearls, cantina lights, and masks of every shape and material: glitter, feathers, leather, flower petals all adorning the empty-eyed visages of demons, deer, butterflies, cats, and something that looks like a bird skull.

"Welcome," Santi says with a flourish, "to my court." She drops elegantly into a director's chair before a large oval-shaped mirror and lights a joint, offers it to me. I pass, but the small room quickly fills with the slightly sweet scent of smoke.

"Sit," she says. "As a visiting noble, you are hereby granted sanctuary within these humble walls."

Floor aside, the only other option is an overstuffed pink ottoman beside Santi. I sit. She brushes my hair back, shakes her head with a *tsk*, and nestles the joint into a slender black cigarette holder a la Audrey Hepburn.

"Kyle Kaufman is a complete cretin," Santi says.

I smile. "I don't think I've heard anyone our age say *cretin* before."

"And?" Santi plants the cigarette holder in the soil of a potted orchid and dabs what looks like—what I hope is—peroxide onto a lacy handkerchief and pats at my neck.

"And it's a good word for Kyle Kaufman."

Cretin Kaufman got my ear pretty good when he rang my bell with his first punch. The bleeding is from behind my ear, where two of my earrings sliced away a fair ribbon of flesh. Santi's attention draws some fresh blood flow, but not too much, and the Hello Kitty band-aid she presses on my skin makes it all better. Or close enough.

"Thanks, Santi." I pick at dried blood in my hair.

She gestures. "Take off your sweater."

I swear under my breath. I hadn't noticed the line of blood running from beneath the sleeve down to my wrist, but Santi misses nothing. I peel it off along with the thin layer of scab that's formed over the split skin of my elbow.

"This isn't going to be the end of it, you know."

My head throbs. "I know. They blame Will for Aaron Raymond."

"Of course they do."

I'm immediately defensive, even though I know Santi is an ally. "It wasn't Will's fault. It probably wasn't even completely his mom's fault. Aaron was totally hammered, out of his mind."

"That's the story."

"That's the truth."

"And when in history," Santi asks, "have men in power cared about the truth?"

Chapter
12

Santi has a point, of course. The good people of Summerset didn't care about the truth when Will's mom was arrested for vehicular manslaughter, and they don't seem to care now that Alice is dead. The easy headlines have already been printed. Why complicate things?

The cantina lights make everything hazy, soft. The pot smoke might help too. Santi's handkerchief is more red than white now, and my mind slips back in time to another creeping bloodstain, another microburst of violence.

———

It was two summers and a lifetime ago. The party was going to be legendary. A twofer—we were celebrating the end of sophomore year at Kyle Kaufman's house. Not really my scene, but as the girl that proved everybody wrong and grabbed that state record for Summerset, I was on the VIP list. I hadn't told them yet that race had been my grand finale, that I wasn't taking track again next year. They'd figure it out when they saw the fall roster.

Will came with a girl he wandered away from ten minutes into the party. Alice and I had gone together, though when the Hayes twins arrived, she wandered off with her boo for some art history lessons on various pieces in the Kaufman collection, and possibly some less PG activities.

Cheyenne Stokes handed out her infamous Red Solo Cup Specials. The drink tasted like pineapple and nail polish remover, and gave me a tingly all-over buzz that I didn't hate. I did refill it with cranberry juice at the earliest opportunity though, and sipped on that for most of the rest of the night. I wanted to at least vaguely remember the party, and preferably not swap spit with anybody I'd regret.

At some point Will found one of Mr. Kaufman's old acoustic guitars and began strumming outside next to the fire pit, where he could give gnarly side-eye to the guy with his arm around me every time that arm went somewhere he didn't approve of. The guy, Finn, was a cute chess team captain/baseball player hybrid just unlikely enough to be interesting, but not so interesting that talking was the only thing I wanted to do with him. Somebody brought laced brownies and the entire cheerleading squad was feeling *really* good, euphoric from both the pot and the only carbs they'd eaten all year.

Santi had three lacrosse players down to their underwear and a single sock among the lot of them in a cutthroat game of strip poker. The rules seemed nebulous but somehow always favored Santi, who had magnanimously doffed her beret more out of pity, I suspected, than because she had actually lost a hand.

Aaron Raymond did a line of dust off of Cheyenne's cleavage and invited his best friends Darius and Kyle to do the same. More than once. Cheyenne giggled and jiggled. The boys roared like mountain lions scenting prey, showed rows of white teeth like chum-drunk sharks.

Finn's kisses were promises I was willing to believe for the moment.

Will played some Clapton, some Dylan. There were shots, something blue and glittery. Finn called a toast to me, pointing out to the cringes of many and the cheers of a few that I had brought home Summerset's only gold in any sport all year. The football crowd scowled, emptied their Solo cups, refilled them. The night got darker. The fire burned lower.

Cheyenne made out with Alex Franklin in the hot tub. Alex thought this was the coolest thing since Doritos tacos, but Cheyenne's boyfriend Aaron had a different opinion, and made it known in the language he and the rest of the Summerset KGB disguised as football players spoke most fluently: brutality.

He smashed Alex's face with his fist enough times to turn the bubbling hot tub water pink. Alex's friends dragged him out and stuffed him into the back seat of somebody's dad's Lexus. Aaron's rage wasn't spent, though. He shattered his beer bottle on the patio, declared the party to be fucking bullshit, and went for his Audi. Half the football team tried to stop him, but they all scattered when Aaron floored it in reverse down the driveway, tires spraying gravel like shrapnel.

We'd piled into Alice's car not long after that, Will and Noah and Alice and me. When I woke up the next morning, it was to a dull headache and a newfound conviction to put any future invitations from Kyle Kaufman directly into the shredder.

When Will woke up, it was to his dad and stepmom sitting on his bed and trying to find the best way to tell him that his mother had been in a horrific wrong-way accident, and that if she survived her injuries she would be going to prison for murder. The charge had been upgraded from manslaughter as soon as her toxicology panel came back positive for bonedust.

Not just any murder, either—the body they'd dragged out of the mangled remains of an Audi RS3 had belonged to Aaron Raymond, who'd been far too high himself to see her coming, even on that long stretch of straight highway. He should have had plenty of time to brake, to recognize the danger and get himself out of her way. But the only skid marks had come from her tires, not his.

Turns out, there is no best way to tell your kid any of that. Also turns out, the whole town looks at you a little different when your mom takes out a star high school football player. Especially when said football player is the son of elites, and said mom just finished her fourth stint in rehab two days before.

It was an accident. A tragic, stupid accident.

That was the story, anyway.

———

Santi says, "I'm sorry about what happened."

I know she doesn't mean the fight. I also know that Santi glides between worlds with the charisma and savvy of a politician who has a little bit of dirt on everybody; the jocks go to Santi for the kind of favors that turn a party into a Party, the stoners go to Santi when they want to track down some obscure strain of pot that's supposed to make you be able to taste music, and the cheerleaders go to Santi when they've exhausted their moms' supplies of Xanax and diet pills.

I *also* know that the bonedust that turned Aaron Raymond into the Hulk at Kyle's party didn't get there without Santi's help. Will knows it, too. But Santi doesn't name her sources—ever. Not even for a childhood friend on a kamikaze mission to find out who turned his mother into a loaded gun.

Will's mom had been three months clean and full of promises the morning of Kyle's party. I'd seen Will choose to believe those promises, despite everything that had come before. And I'd seen him crack down to the core of himself when, once again, they'd been broken. I'd seen him glue himself back together with the promise of vengeance on whatever operation is pumping bonedust through our town like a poison pulse, and I'd seen his friendship with Santi turn to hatred when she refused to give him names.

Santi isn't exactly a dealer . . . more of an illicit concierge. She's the spider queen at the middle of the web, at the heart of the interconnectedness of everything. Nearly everybody at Summerset High needs something from Santi at some point, and Santi takes her payment in secrets or favors owed. It keeps her safe in a world that frequently tries to destroy the unknown rather than understand it, and I respect that, even if it seems like a precarious way to survive.

It also makes her the one person in this building who might be able to help me.

"Did you know Alice was looking for Noah?"

Santi's pause while quilting together enough bandaids to cover my elbow is so slight, I almost miss it. Almost. "I did."

"Did she come to you?"

"She did."

". . . and?"

She takes a drag of the joint, tilts her head back and exhales. "*And*, people come to me because they know I'm not going to go all Edward Snowden the second someone asks nicely."

"Alice is dead, Santi. Don't you think you can stop protecting her secrets now?"

Santi's black-rimmed eyes hold mine. "On the contrary. I think they are more dangerous than ever."

My hands go cold. "What do you mean by that?"

"People are dead, Silencia. Maybe you should let Alice, and her secrets, rest in peace. For everybody's sake."

"Santi—"

She stands up abruptly. "Places to go, people to see, darling. Stay as long as you like. There's more grass in the ceramic cat if you change your mind."

The door closes gently behind Santi, leaving me alone with her stash and my own unanswered questions.

I've never seen Santi scared before, but the look in her eyes just before she left . . . Will and I aren't the only ones who know Alice's death wasn't an accident.

Santi knows something. I'd put money on it. Something that scares the hell out of her.

Something that means Alice's death isn't the end, unless we let it be.

Let it be?

I'll take Yeah, That's Not Gonna Happen for $500, Alex.

Silence might be my name, but it's never been my style.

Chapter
13

TWO YEARS AGO

elizabeth_MF_cochran:
> cia! I know what we're doing for Halloween.

will_inthelongblackcoat:
> it's only April

silencia_luc:
> we don't need that kind of negativity around here, will.
> al, please continue

elizabeth_MF_cochran:
> Freddie and Truus Oversteegen.

will_inthelongblackcoat:
> gesundheit

silencia_luc:

do I google or do you just want to tell me?

elizabeth_MF_cochran:

they were sisters who joined the Dutch resistance when they were 14 and 16 to fight nazis. nobody suspected them because they looked so young and innocent, but they lured their targets from bars and murdered them in the woods. think Black Widow meets Lolita.

will_inthelongblackcoat:

gotta go, but don't worry, I'm definitely going to think about that tonight

silencia_luc:

you had me at resistance. what do we wear? blood-spattered aprons, clogs, revolvers tucked into our bonnets?

elizabeth_MF_cochran:

that's a good start.

silencia_luc:

do you think we'd have been that badass back then?

silencia_luc:

i mean, it's easy to identify with the heroes, but the truth is the vast majority of people were silent, & let the world be shaped around them by whoever turned out to be the strongest . . . and people haven't changed that much.

elizabeth_MF_cochran:

> I think most people want to do what's right. sometimes
> it just takes the right spark to light the fire.

silencia_luc:

> what would our spark be?

elizabeth_MF_cochran:

> we don't need one.

elizabeth_MF_cochran:

> we are the fire.

Chapter

14

I am flying through a sea of stars, purplewhite and brilliant, holes torn out of the thickest black velvet curtain. I am flying, and there is no fear here, there is no sorrow and no grief, and the stars are humming with eldritch fire.

I fly too close.

In this dream, I always fly too close.

I've been here before. I've made this mistake before.

I will make it again.

I reach out with both hands, longing to be filled with star-light, for my blood to turn opalescent, for my eyes to shine lavender and aching, to see what lies on the other side of that midnight curtain.

I reach . . .

The star explodes in my hands.

I have never known such pain.

I have always known this pain.

———

I wake up gasping, the breath nightmare-scorched out of my lungs. I am soaked in sweat. The skin of my hands sparks with starfire, the nerve endings strung with sand-shards of broken glass, and my leg . . .

My leg aches.

I start to tremble, and it isn't just the chill of the air on my damp skin. This dream has haunted me for as long as I can remember, but I haven't had phantom pain like this in years.

For just this moment, the parts of me that I don't have— Alice, my leg—hurt worse than the parts left behind.

The pillow muffles my sobs so that Pancakes doesn't even stir.

I don't fall back to sleep for a long, long time.

———

The Booker house looks like a photo with the saturation slider pulled all the way to the left. All of the color has been leeched out of our faces, our clothes—everyone is wearing some shade of black or gray, the pink rims of Mrs. Booker's eyes a shock of color in the otherwise monochrome portrait of grief that is Alice's memorial Saturday afternoon.

My dads are in the sitting room with the Masons, Alice's dad, some extended Booker family members I've never heard of . . . and Detective Rojas. He's cleaned up at least, no condiment stains that I can see, but the sight of him sitting next to Mr. Booker sparks a blaze of resentment.

He doesn't belong here. He didn't know Alice. He didn't *love* her. His narrative of the broken girl pining after the lost boy is so grossly reductive, I want to throw him and his stupid notebook in the quarry.

The medical examiner hasn't released her yet, which I hope

means that someone with the credentials to make their opinion matter more than mine has questions. It for sure means that the Bookers can't plan a funeral. It also means my brilliant, beautiful, uncompromising best friend is lying in a meat cabinet.

I wonder if they will take her baby from her. If they will put it back in her belly, or in her arms, or at all.

The clatter of glass saves me from my spiraling imagination. Will and I are in the kitchen, ostensibly trying to help Mrs. Booker find room for a never-ending onslaught of Tupperware from guests but realistically just getting in her way. Will looks like a throwback from another century in pressed pants and suspenders, shirt sleeves rolled up to his elbows. He has even taken off his signature beanie and combed his hair. Alice would have loved it.

"Is this the stew Liam made for the block party last fall?" Mrs. Booker asks me.

"I think so."

"That was really good," she says softly. She considers the geometric arrangement in front of her, then pulls out a foil-wrapped baking tin and drops it straight into the garbage, sliding Papa's stew into its spot. "Mrs. Ferguson's lemon tarts," she explains. "She always brings them to bake sales. Alice was the only one that could stand them."

"She actually hated them too," Will says, and I give him a look that hopefully reads *Maybe we don't correct the grieving mother about her dead daughter.* He just shrugs: message received and ignored. "She spat one out in a planter when Mrs. Ferguson wasn't looking. She didn't want to hurt her feelings."

Mrs. Booker's smile is creased with pain but genuine. "That poor tree."

Will winks at me, and I guess maybe he's right. Mrs. Booker is wounded, not broken. I shouldn't underestimate her—she did raise Alice, after all.

A girl I recognize from Alice's journalism club hesitates in the doorway before being nudged forward by her mother. Apologies are murmured, hugs are exchanged, and I stare hard at the girl. I can't remember her name.

Do you know something?

Did Alice trust you more than she trusted me?

Will squeezes my hand. "Time to go," he whispers.

We take the escape Mrs. Booker's distraction offers, but instead of heading back into the living room, we duck into the hallway. The lights are off back here; this part of the Booker house is not intended for public consumption today, but what we need to do can't wait any longer.

Alice's room is upstairs. I try and fail to force my eyes straight ahead. Photos in simple, sophisticated frames are staggered up the wall, a timeline of the Booker children milestones. Infant Alice held in her parents' bare hands, curled up like a little bug. Teddy crawling through a cloud of toilet paper he'd unrolled from the spool. Alice's first day of school, first lost tooth. Teddy sleeping on our back porch, using Pancakes for a pillow. Alice and me building sandcastles. Alice, Will, and me at the eighth-grade dance, Will with the cocky raised eyebrow he'd been practicing all year. Alice with her Girl Scout Gold Award, surrounded by boxes of the donations she'd solicited from the community for a domestic violence shelter.

There's a blank spot where another photo used to hang. The fastidious observer might notice the barest of rectangular outlines on the wall, but I don't have to look that closely because I know what's missing. It was a photo of Alice and Noah, taken at Homecoming last year.

Alice had looked so, so beautiful that night.

And after that, nothing but blank spots that Teddy will have to fill with his own memories and moments, because Alice's are over.

I touch the wall at the place where Alice's story stops. Will continues a few steps ahead of me before realizing I'm not following.

"Cia," he says.

It hurts.

God, it hurts.

He sees it in my face, comes back down a step or two and holds out his hand. "I know," he says quietly.

I let him lead me the rest of the way upstairs.

Alice's door is locked. Frustration heats my skin. Of course, the Bookers wouldn't leave her room open for randos to wander into.

"Damn it," I whisper. It isn't going to take our parents long to notice we've slipped away. We don't have time for this.

"You're not asposed to say that," comes a little voice from somewhere in the vicinity of my hip.

"Oh, Teddy." I kneel and wrap my arms around Alice's little brother. He's a skinny kid, his weight against my body slight, and his Tootsie Roll Pop immediately sticks in my hair.

"Mama locked the door." He seems baffled, as if the mechanisms of adult logic make no sense to him. Will goes in for his hug and frees my hair from the lollipop. "But what if Alice comes home and can't get in? Then she'll have to sleep in my bed, and where am I going to sleep?"

"That's not something you need to worry about, kid," Will says, the delivery much gentler than the words.

"Will!" I hiss.

But Teddy just nods somberly. "I know. But what if she does? Won't she be mad?"

"Not at you, little bear," I tell him.

He smiles mischievously. "I know! Know why?"

"Because she loves you very much."

"Duh. And because of *this*." Teddy scampers off into his parents' room.

I whirl on Will. "Seriously?"

"What? It's the truth." He is defensive, not understanding my anger. "Should I have lied to him?"

Teddy returns, triumphant. His sticky fist opens to reveal a silver key on a loop of blue yarn.

"Good man," Will says, and they high-five.

Teddy gives me the key. "Will you leave it unlocked?" he asks me. "Just in case?"

I don't know which of us is more tragic: him, believing hard enough in *just in case* to hold grief at bay, or me, wishing desperately that I were young enough to believe it too.

"Go on downstairs, buddy," I say. "Your mom's probably wondering where you are."

He nods, takes the stairs down with the grace of a baby hippo.

I slide the key in. The knob turns easily in my hand.

———

It's clear someone has been through Alice's things, or more likely several someones. Her room isn't trashed or anything, but everything is just slightly *off.* Her bed is made too neatly, corners tucked in in a way that Alice would have found claustrophobic. Her corkboard, covered in photos, scraps of paper, fortune cookie strips, ticket stubs, random detritus of the life of a teenage girl—it has a few gaps, things missing that I'm so used to seeing I don't even register what they were, only their absence, and I wonder what the police found compelling enough to take. Anger simmers through me at the thought of sour-faced Detective Rojas going through her things.

Most conspicuously absent is her laptop, its charger coiled on the floor beside her desk. My stomach sinks.

I drop onto the bed as Will shuts the door silently behind us. "The police must have taken it. Of course they would."

Will sits beside me. "I'm surprised they did, actually. Given how *sure* the cops are that she killed herself, this is starting to look suspiciously like an actual investigation."

I flop onto my back. "Maybe on their part. Not so much on ours." I drag one of Alice's pillows over my face and scream my frustration and disappointment into it, leaving it there until Will removes it.

The air is cool on my hot face. "She deserves better than this, Will," I say, staring at the ceiling. "She deserves better than *us*. She deserves a real investigation."

"Hey." He reaches across the bedspread, puts his hand on my fist. "Don't count us out yet, Watson. We're just getting started."

"Watson?"

"Sure."

"That makes you . . . Sherlock?"

"It's hard being both the beauty and the brains of this operation," he says, tapping his head. "But you always get there eventually."

But where are we starting from? And with what?

The ceiling gets blurry and I shut my eyes. I know we don't have much time, but everything just feels so heavy. We *needed* that laptop.

The bed lifts slightly as Will stands.

"Can I tell you something?" The question is so quiet, I almost miss it.

I don't move. "God, Will. Please. No more secrets."

"It's not a secret. It's . . ."

Silence stretches long enough that I open my eyes. He's

standing next to her corkboard, holding a photo of him and Alice dressed like pilgrims in a school play. He holds it up with an unsteady grin. "Kindergarten. By sixth grade she was staging walkouts until the school district stopped celebrating Columbus Day."

I remember. And I get the feeling whatever he wants to tell me doesn't really have anything to do with the criminally white-washed American history curriculum.

He returns to my side, tracing a corner of the photo with one finger. "She would have been something. I mean really *something*. If she'd had the chance."

"I know," I whisper.

A few more beats pass. Then: "I told her I'd be the father."

My eyes spring open. "You what?"

He doesn't look at me. "Not the real father. Obviously. But I told her we could . . . we could tell everyone the baby was mine. We could raise it together."

Five minutes ago I'd thought it was impossible for my heart to shatter any more completely than it already had. I was wrong. It turns out there is always a new way to hurt. "Oh, Will."

"I told her we didn't have to . . . *be* together. Not like that. Not if she didn't want to."

Not if she *didn't want to.*

That last part says everything.

It was his rapid pivot on Noah, from friendly acquaintance to sworn enemy, that had first hinted to me that Will's feelings towards Alice had changed. I'd seen it way back then, and then I'd let myself forget because it seemed like he had let it go. He'd seemed happy that she was happy. When Noah blew that up, Will was there for her the same way I was, nothing more . . . I'd thought.

How had I missed it?

I sit up. His eyes are bright and wet. I don't say anything—this isn't a hole that words can fill. I take his hand. He squeezes mine hard enough to crack knuckles. I don't pull away.

My chest aches with the weight of what I know and the helplessness of what I don't. With her laptop we would have had all of her saved logins and passwords, all of her history—assuming she hadn't purged it—and bookmarks, the cookies to track where she'd been and when. Her email. Her music. Her messages.

Her messages . . .

"Shit. Will, I forgot to tell you!"

He looks up from the photo. "Forgot to tell me what?"

I slide my phone out of my pocket. "This is my old phone, from before I upgraded last year."

Will grimaces. "I haven't forgotten. I'm going to pay your dad to get the other one fixed—"

"That's not it, Will. Remember how we all used that chat app a couple years ago?"

"So we could keep our messages secret?" He snorts. "Yeah, I vaguely recall a time in my life when I felt that righteous a level of self-importance."

"Have you used it lately?"

"No. My phone kept running out of space so I deleted it."

"So did Alice. But you two were the only people I talked to on there, so I totally forgot about it when you guys stopped using it."

"So?"

"So," I say, opening up the app, "*look.*"

It doesn't register right away. I watch Will read and re-read the last few lines.

still my best bitch.

He blinks. "You sent that Thursday?"

"Yeah."

"And . . . it says delivered."

"*Yeah.*" I squeeze his knee.

"Ouch!"

"Sorry. But you know what that means, right?"

He rubs his leg. "No?"

"If it was just floating in the ether, it would say S for sent. It only registers a message as delivered when the other account has actually received it. Which requires the other account be logged in, and active." I shake the phone at him. "You know what, you've been demoted. You're definitely Watson. What it means is that her phone is still *on*."

"And if it's still on . . . it definitely isn't sitting at the bottom of the quarry."

"It definitely is not."

"And . . . she reinstalled Kik." He frowns. "Maybe nostalgia. Or maybe there was someone new she wanted to exchange untraceable messages with. Someone she was keeping secret from all of us."

"That's what I'm thinking. And it's a stretch, but I don't think whoever killed her has her phone. Why would they leave it on? The cops can trace that stuff, ping cell towers or whatever. I think it's still out there somewhere."

"Send another one," he says, new urgency in his voice. "See if it's still on."

My thumb hovers over the screen. I am suddenly self-conscious, and I sneak a glance at Will as I type. His expression is intense, focused.

we know you didn't do it.

Will makes eye contact, nods. I hit send.

Seconds tick by, meld into a full minute. The *S* remains unchanged.

"Okay," I say at last. "The battery must have finally died."

"Or someone turned it off."

"Or that," I admit. "But it's something."

Will nods again, but his expression mirrors my own disappointment as he stands up. "We should get back downstairs before we get busted."

I put the pillow back in its place, and a memory jostles loose. "Just a minute." I jump up and grab a small notebook from Alice's desk.

I don't hesitate before I write: *Whoever did this to you is going to pay.*

"Cia?" Will asks from the doorway.

I tear the page free and roll it up tightly. "Did Alice ever tell you about the magic bedpost?"

He laughs a little. "She definitely didn't."

"It started in first or second grade. We were having a sleepover and we knocked the knob off the bedpost . . . here." I pull the knob off easily; it's just a ball of wood with a peg to keep it from rolling off the post. "There's a hollow space in there where we used to put secret messages."

"Kind of a recurring theme with you guys."

"Kik was *your* idea," I remind him. "And this wasn't for messages, so much as . . . wishes, I guess. We wrote things we wanted to come true. Like, 'Mom will take me to see Harry Potter.' I think that was Alice's first wish."

He's looking at me thoughtfully. "What was second-grade Cia's first wish?"

"Who knows?"

"Come on. It can't be that embarrassing."

"Oh, it can." I tuck my wadded-up note into the cavity.

Only it doesn't slide all the way in.

I pull it out, peer inside.

"Will," I whisper.

"What is it?"

I turn around and show him: in the palm of my hand is a flash drive.

Chapter

15

"Holy shit," Will murmurs. "You are literally the only person in the world who could have found that."

I know. More importantly, Alice knew.

I stare at the tiny rectangle. She had hidden it there for *me* to find.

She had been counting on me to pick up where she left off, if something happened.

The ghost of hope begins to wrap its ephemeral limbs around my heart.

We aren't wrong.

It was one thing to believe that Alice hadn't killed herself. That she had loved us, her baby, her life way too much to write such a pointless ending. I hadn't wanted to admit it, but that belief wasn't absolute. Can belief ever be? Isn't that what keeps it from being simply knowledge, not faith—its imperfection, its room for doubt?

There's no more room for doubt.

Alice had been *afraid*. She saw something coming on the

horizon and she prepared for it as best she could. But why hadn't she gone to the police?

Only one answer makes sense. Alice didn't trust the police to protect her.

That means we can't, either.

I slip the flash drive into my wallet and shove it deep into my purse. Detective Rojas can keep the damn laptop. Alice has given me what I need. "This wasn't her only hiding spot," I tell Will, and head for the door.

———

I ask Mr. Booker for Alice's car keys so I can get back a sweater I'd loaned her. He doesn't ask any questions, just hands the keys over. He looks blank, slightly confused, his audio track just a second off.

Broken.

Alice's car in the driveway is still covered in a layer of quarry dust. I get in the driver's seat, Will climbs in the passenger side, and once the doors close, we just sit for a few long moments, cocooned in heavy quiet and the faintest hint of strawberries.

I reach under the seat. I have to feel around for a minute before I find what I'm looking for: a hole torn in the upholstery, so far back and to the side that I practically dislocate my shoulder rooting around for it.

Alice used to keep a small change purse full of condoms in there. The Bookers are smart, progressive people, but when it came to their little girl, they'd been a little medieval. Mrs. Booker's version of "the talk" had been so clinical we'd had to Google half the words she'd used, and they'd given Noah the side-eye whenever he even held Alice's hand.

The condom stash is gone, but in its place is something *way* more useful to me at this juncture of my life.

"No fucking way," Will says.

I hold up Alice's dead phone. "This," I say, "is why I am obviously Sherlock."

Will inclines his head. "I concede."

"Okay." I pull the plastic rectangle out of my wallet. "Divide and conquer. Phone or flash drive?"

He reluctantly closes my fingers around the flash drive. "Neither. I have an iPhone, you guys both have Androids. And I'm grounded for what most reasonable people would consider prudent and justified self-defense."

"Breaking Darius's nose?"

"Yup."

"Grounded from what?"

"Just about everything that makes life worth living. You. Playstation. Netflix. My computer."

"That's some serious lockdown."

"I've drafted a letter to the Human Rights Council," he mutters.

"Would it help if I talked to them?"

"Probably not, since you got busted too, buddy." He looks at the phone in my hand. "Be careful with that, though. The cops are probably looking for it."

"I know. I'll give it to them," I say. "Eventually."

———

Will leaves first, his parents flanking him with extra static cling. I wave from the end of the driveway. He breathes on the window and writes "HELP ME" in the fog as their car pulls away.

"Nice dress."

I spin around.

Judah Hayes is standing beside the mailbox.

"Thanks. I was wondering when everyone would stop talking about my dead best friend and notice how cute I look." My sarcasm is scathing. "What are you doing here?"

"Paying my respects. Alice was a friend." His suit fits his lanky frame as if it'd been sewn around his body. It looks vaguely familiar, and I think it might be the same one he wore to Homecoming last year. At least his hair finally looks like it's had a passing encounter with a brush.

The breeze stirs the hem of my black dress around my knees. Summer's gone, its memory kept by some late-blooming shrubs dividing the yards, but it's too cool out to be outside without a jacket, and my arms prickle with goosebumps beneath my lacy sleeves.

I glance back at the house. It doesn't seem like anyone else has noticed him yet. He and Noah are not identical, but it's easy enough to see one in the other's face—the Bookers are not going to welcome his presence. "Tell me about that friendship," I say, moving between him and the door to lean against the Jetta. "When exactly did you and Alice become so close?"

"After Noah disappeared."

"Why?"

"You know why. We were looking for him."

"She was looking for more than Noah. And I think you know that." I'm gripping her phone in my hand, and his eyes wander to it.

"Why do you have Alice's phone?" he asks me slowly.

Damn it. I can't even pretend it isn't hers. We'd spent a lazy afternoon this summer bedazzling our phone cases, mine in a black and teal spiral, hers in Emerson purple and white.

The prickling of my skin isn't just about the cold

anymore—there is a darkness in Judah's eyes that shines like lava rock. He sees my secrets but cannot name them, and that makes him furious. "More importantly, Cia, *how* do you have Alice's phone?"

I jam it into my purse and cross my arms. "How do you know it's hers?"

"Give me a break. We spent plenty of time together before she and Noah broke up. I can tell you about her wallpaper and her ringtone too, if you want."

"Sounds like you spent plenty of time together after, too."

He doesn't argue. "The cops are looking for that phone."

"I know. They're not asking the right questions."

"And that's yours to decide?"

"Yeah, Judah, it is," I snap. "She was *my* best friend. She trusted *me* with—" I shut my mouth.

"With what?" When I don't answer, he steps away from the mailbox. Toward me. "Cia, what do you think is on that phone?"

My pulse ramps up. "I don't know! It's dead. I haven't gotten into it yet."

"I don't believe you." He's so close, the temperature of the air between us rises a few degrees.

I raise my chin, meet the darkness in his gaze with the fire in my own. "That's your problem, not mine. You should go, Judah. I don't think the Bookers want to see you."

Hurt ripples underneath the anger. I shouldn't feel bad, but I do. I don't want to care about Judah's feelings right now. I can't afford to, not if I'm going to do right by Alice. "I cared about Alice," he says.

"Did you? Or did you care about what she could do for you?"

"What's that supposed to mean?"

"I don't think you gave a shit about Alice. I think the only thing you care about is your brother, not the girl whose heart he broke and definitely not any of the rest of us. I think you saw Alice as a way to get answers, and you didn't care if it kept her from moving on. You didn't care if it put her in danger. I think you used her, and you never once stopped to think about what it might cost her!"

Is that really what I think? I wonder. But the words are already out.

Fury rolls off him in waves I can feel on my skin. "Then you should probably give me that phone," he says, gritting his teeth. "If you're right about me, who knows what I might do?"

I know exactly one thing for certain in this moment: I am *not* giving up Alice's phone. "Or what you've already done?" I ask him.

He doesn't flinch. "Give me the phone." This close, I can finally see the intricate etching of the tiny silver pendant he's always wearing: two robed saints, side by side, the letters around them too small to read.

"What are you going to do, Judah?"

His chest rises and falls, but instead of lashing out he goes stone-still.

He's not like my dad, whose anger ignites like a flash fire, sears everything close to it, and then winks out as fast as it came. Judah is a slow, controlled burn. He's not going to be baited, but neither is he going to be easily put off.

It hasn't occurred to me until just this moment to be, maybe, a little bit scared.

"I already told you. Whatever it takes."

"Hey!"

We both look over my shoulder.

Remy takes the steps down from the Bookers' porch two at a time. "Get away from her."

Judah leans in. His lips, close to my ear, brush my hair when he says, quietly, "Your stick."

A memory, triggered by the warmth of his breath on my neck:

Running practice relays just before what would be my last competition, the changeover box looms ahead, Judah's feet pounding the track behind me. Lips salt-stung with sweat, but pushing harder to see if he could keep up, a challenge sung in sneaker percussion and rhythmic breathing.

"Your stick," he says in the space between breaths.

A blind hand-off of the baton, a brush of fingers on wrist, the slightest dyssynchrony. A tangle of limbs on the rubberized track, Judah on his elbows over me, baton forgotten for the longest two seconds I'd ever known. Eyes that live between brown and green meeting mine with a different kind of challenge.

Judah steps back.

Remy stands beside me, looks at Judah and then me. Judah is taller but Remy *claims* the space like he always has, in that effortless way that made unnecessary any discussion about things like who would be team captain or whose idea for how to spend summer break days was best. I used to find it annoying when we were little, and I still do, kind of, but in this moment it's also a little welcome because for some reason I am out of my depth with this dark-eyed boy.

"What's going on here?" Remy asks, his voice slightly deeper than I've ever heard it, and I recognize the thinnest layer of threat there.

"Judah was just leaving," I say. Alice's phone is burning a

hole in my purse. I stare at the boy in question, daring him to say otherwise. *If you out me for having this phone, we both lose,* I tell him silently. *Go.*

He gives an almost imperceptible nod that I'm certain Remy doesn't notice, but which says more than any parting shot could—acknowledging the lie implicit between us, and my willingness to let Remy have my back but not to tell him everything I know. My cheeks burn with anger, but Judah isn't its target this time. I don't know what is.

I am sick to death of secrets.

"See you soon," Judah says pleasantly.

"What was that about?" Remy asks me once Judah is out of earshot.

Your stick.

He was telling me that the next play is mine. But in relay, just because someone else has the baton, that does not mean you are not also running. Anticipating. Planning your own move.

Whatever it takes.

I can almost hear Alice's phone ringing in my purse, a twenty-first century telltale heart. I don't want to lie to Remy. He might technically be an adult now, but he was one of us. *Is* one of us. I wait until Judah's car rounds the corner and disappears from sight.

"Is your dad still here?"

Remy glances at the house, then back at me. "No. He got a call, had to leave. You and Will were in the kitchen with Mrs. Booker, I think."

I am still angry, angry at Judah's satisfaction in our shared lie of omission, angry at a world that has warped my childhood friends into a noir ensemble of liars, killers, and victims. If I am going to find Alice's killer, I too have to become a liar. But I don't have to like it.

And *I* get to choose who I trust. Not Judah.

I pull Alice's phone from my purse.

Remy's eyes widen. "Is that hers?"

I nod. "It's dead. I'm going to charge it at home."

"Cia, you can't keep it. The detectives—"

"Can wait another few days. Please, Remy. I just need some time. I'll turn it in soon." I already half-regret my impulsive decision to show him the phone. It hadn't been a conscious decision to let Remy in as much as it had been to spite Judah and that knowing little nod.

But then I remember Remy on my back porch, swinging with me in the glow of candles and fireflies. *Whatever you need.* He hadn't hesitated, then or now, to back me up.

I can see the gears turning. "That was Noah's brother, wasn't it?"

"Yeah. Judah."

"Biblical. Religious family?"

"Their mom is." Noah's only religion had been Alice, as far as I know. Until he lost faith.

"What did he want from you?"

"He and Alice were working together to find Noah. He wants the phone."

"Did he threaten you?"

"Not . . . exactly."

Remy's jaw tenses. "Do you think he had something to do with what happened to Alice?"

"I . . ." I don't honestly know how to answer his question. I only have Judah's version of events to support my current operating premise, and that might be a big mistake.

What if they weren't working together at all? Judah had confirmed what the cops said about Noah taking a nosedive into bonedust prior to his disappearance. A teenage boy doesn't sustain that kind of hobby on a minimum-wage job, and he hadn't even had one of those as far as I know. Noah chose a path of some seriously shady shit when he walked away from my best friend—the kind of shit that makes everything it touches stink.

Despite their differences, Noah and Judah are *twins*. Growing up, one was never in the nurse's office without the other somehow knowing and magically appearing there within moments, whether it was a cold or a skinned knee to blame. Could Judah really be as in the dark as the rest of us about where his brother had gone when he'd left Alice alone at a table set for two?

It doesn't seem likely.

"Judah's acting really strange," I admit to Remy. "He's definitely hiding something." I think of all the times we hung out after track meets, never just the two of us of course, the whole team, back when Judah's smile still reached his eyes and he ran not because he was haunted, but purely for the pleasure of it. I think of sweaty socks tossed across the locker room, endless hours beating the track flatter with the pounding of our shoes, and the stolen champagne he smuggled in when I brought home that gold. It tasted like carbonated spit and victory. "But I don't think he's a killer."

"Are you sure about that, Cia? Really sure?" Remy's expression is grave. "Because if you're right about Alice, then chances are the killer is someone you both knew. You need to be very careful with who you trust."

"I don't trust him," I say quickly. "I just don't know that I'm ready to believe he's a murderer. Not yet."

"If Alice didn't kill herself, Cia, you're putting yourself in danger as long as you have this phone." He touches my hand, the one holding the phone. "Let me take it. I'll get everything I can off of it for you, and make sure it ends up somewhere my dad will find it without ever knowing where it came from."

I'm tempted. Real tempted. I'd have whatever information

is on that phone and so would the cops. I've no real desire to play martyr, or to keep looking over my shoulder.

But . . .

I tuck the phone back in my purse. "Thanks, Remy. But I need to see what's on it for myself first." Alice was *my* best girlfriend. It's like the porn stash rule guys have—I feel a duty to protect Alice's memory as best I can, which includes but isn't limited to deleting any sexy photos she might have sent to Noah over the year they dated.

"I understand." He sighs. "Just promise me you'll be careful."

"Of course. Besides, I'm tougher than I look. Bionic leg, remember."

Remy doesn't smile back.

I don't have time to worry about what might be lurking in the shadows, though. I've got a phone to break into . . . and a flash drive full of secrets meant for my eyes only.

Chapter

16

Turns out, Alice's flash drive is a tiny plastic Fort Knox.

PASSWORD REQUIRED, the pop-up tells me helpfully for the hundredth time. It gives no clue as to how many characters it wants, no *forgot password?* link to bypass this part for a few generic questions about her mother's maiden name and the color of her car—nothing but an empty box. No glimpse into what kinds of files are hiding behind its castle walls, either.

"Damn it, Alice." I drop my head onto my desk, give my eyes a brief respite from the computer screen. It's been over an hour since we got home from the memorial, and I've run through every possible combination of birthdays, nicknames, band names, favorite characters, and inside jokes I can think of. She'd left it for *me*, after all. Only me. So it wouldn't make any sense for her to have locked it up behind a password I could never figure out, but so far all I've figured out is a hundred things it isn't.

Hiding it in a place no other human being would think to

look wasn't enough, apparently. To be fair, her next-level paranoia turned out to be more than justified.

My phone rattles on the desk, left on vibrate since the memorial. I drag my head back up to see what it wants.

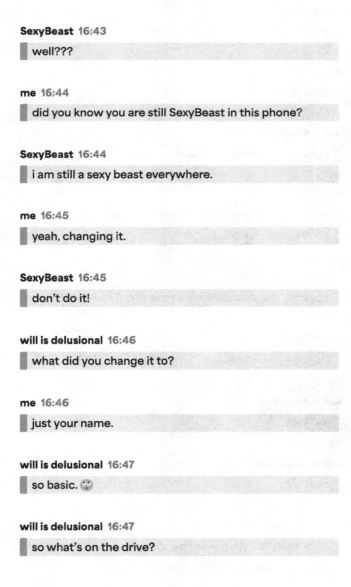

SexyBeast 16:43

well???

me 16:44

did you know you are still SexyBeast in this phone?

SexyBeast 16:44

i am still a sexy beast everywhere.

me 16:45

yeah, changing it.

SexyBeast 16:45

don't do it!

will is delusional 16:46

what did you change it to?

me 16:46

just your name.

will is delusional 16:47

so basic. 🙄

will is delusional 16:47

so what's on the drive?

me 16:47

> it's locked down tighter than meghan markle's playboy pics. i can't crack the password. any suggestions?

will is delusional 16:48

> meghan markle took pics for playboy?!

me 16:49

> priorities?

will is delusional 16:50

> right. um . . . teddy's birthday?

me 16:50

> tried all the obvious stuff. birthdays, names, combinations thereof

will is delusional 16:51

> i got nothing. sounds like it's time to call invisigoth

me 16:51

> . . .

will is delusional 16:52

> X-Files?

will is delusional 16:52

> no?

will is delusional 16:53

> think buffy season one willow, not gay yet, tons of black eyeshadow and inexplicable hacking prowess

me 16:53

do you know any hackers, will?

will is delusional 16:54

i know where you can hire one on the dark web

I blink. You'd think nothing Will said would surprise me now, and yet . . .

me 16:54

filing that away as a maybe.

will is delusional 16:54

i did use to build gundams with a guy who's president of the computer club now

me 16:54

i have no idea what that means

will is delusional 16:54

giant robots

me 16:55

of course. if you think he can help us get into this thing maybe it's time to rekindle your incredibly nerdy bond

will is delusional 16:55

gundams are huge in japan, judgy mcjudgerson

me 16:55

so is buying used underwear from vending machines, that doesn't make it cool

will is delusional 16:55

i should so apply to college in japan

will is delusional 16:56

how about the phone?

me 16:56

charging. didn't have enough power to boot up. might
now. checking.

I flop onto my bed, grab Alice's phone. The screen flashes
with the image of a battery and a lightning bolt, but the juice
in the bottom of the battery is green now, not red. Enough, at
least, to power on.

The phone chirps at me and shows me nine gray dots. This,
at least, I know. I swipe my thumb over the screen, unlocking
it with a heart pattern.

Eureka.

I smile grimly. Time to get to work.

———

I am lost in Alice's world for at least an hour before Papa knocks
on the door. I jam her phone under my pillow as the door opens
a crack.

"Hey, sweetheart. Dinner in twenty minutes, okay?"

"Okay." I realize I must look weird, lying on my bed still in
the dress I'd worn to Alice's memorial, with no phone or book
or anything, as if I'd just been staring off into space before he
poked his head in. "I fell asleep for a minute," I explain lamely.

His face is full of concern. "Are you feeling all right?"

"Just tired. Today was . . . not easy." I can tell he's about to come in and give me a hug, maybe feel my forehead. I sit up and say quickly, "I should probably change out of this dress."

He nods and closes the door.

I dive back in.

I'd gone to her call log first. For some reason I needed to see it from her side, the string of outgoing calls with my name on them like an accusation.

Alice hadn't called anyone else the night she died. Not Will, not Judah, not the cops. Just me. Regret breaks over me in relentless waves, filling my eyes with useless water and burning in the back of my throat. I wish so hard that I could undo what I'd done. No vengeance will ever be as satisfying as simply having my friend back.

But vengeance is all I have left. And I don't even have that, yet.

The call log shows two inbound calls that night from *Blocked ID*. Unlike the calls to me, these were answered. One lasted a couple of minutes, 2:32. The other, received just before 9:00 p.m., had been a much shorter conversation: 0:47.

Alice had multiple voicemails. Five from her parents, with escalating notes of panic when she didn't come home that night. After the first one, I skip through the rest. I am filled too full with grief and guilt to hold their voices in my memory forever as well as hers.

There's also a voicemail from Judah.

"*Hey, Alice. I waited for you after school in our spot, did you leave early? I saw you talking to Cia. Guessing she didn't take it too well. Call me.*"

They had a spot?

He'd sent a smattering of messages on Snap that afternoon and evening, too—messages she hadn't opened, or else I wouldn't be able to see them now. I save them quickly before they can go poof.

judah.runs.good 15:17

> you coming?

judah.runs.good 15:31

> I guess something came up? Let me know everything's
> OK when you see this.

judah.runs.good 17:52

> Alice?

judah.runs.good 19:06

> you're starting to scare me.

judah.runs.good 21:58

> I'm not going to sleep until you tell me you're OK.

He called several more times but didn't leave any more messages.

Maybe he really did care about her.

He cared enough to pick up the phone, which is more than you did, my asshole brain whispers.

But also:

They had a *spot*?

Or maybe this was just his clever cover.

I can't rule out Judah as a suspect. But I can understand why he can't rule me out, either.

I open her browser. I have dozens of tabs open at any given moment but Alice had only three: Summerset High's online portal, a half-completed application for a spring internship at the Summerset Free Press, and . . .

My stomach sinks. The last tab is an article about foods to avoid during pregnancy.

Alice had wanted to protect her baby.

It had been one thing to hear about it from Will. This is a gut punch I should have been ready for, but am very much not.

Would the baby have had Alice's springy curls? Noah's deep dimples?

I close my eyes against this torrent of pain, let it crash and break. I can't even begin to grieve Alice's baby, too. Not yet.

I close the last tab. That's one land mine I'm not stepping on again.

I am going to need days, not minutes, to dig through Alice's Snapchat. I skim the surface of her feed for now, noting conversations with Maryam Hadad, several other journalist club kids, Judah, and of course Will and me. Most of her chats are empty, their contents erased on viewing. Alice hadn't been a hoarder. She'd saved very few texts or Snaps—except when it came to Noah.

He had sent his final messages to Alice nearly three months ago. Of course she'd saved them.

wayward.son1117 June 13 - 23:02

> none of this was ever your fault. i let this poison in.
> maybe i am the poison. maybe it's always been me.

wayward.son1117 June 13 - 23:03

> what we had was a beautiful dream. but i am awake
> now. you have to wake up, too.

wayward.son1117 June 13 - 23:04

> stop looking for me.

wayward.son1117 June 13 - 23:04

> i don't want you here.

She had not saved her side of any of their conversations, so I'll never know what she said back. My imagination more than fills in the blanks. What I can see are the messages she'd sent in the past thirty days, both marked Delivered but neither opened, running out the hourglass sand before it would be as if they'd never existed.

alice.books113 September 2 - 09:21

> there is nothing too broken to be fixed. nothing. not us, not you. never you.

alice.books113 September 7 - 09:21

> you don't need to protect me. I will NEVER stop looking.

She'd thought he was protecting her? From what?

I remember vividly how lost and unanchored I'd felt when I texted Alice the day after they told me she was gone. It's no stretch to imagine what Alice had been feeling when she'd messaged Noah long after the conversation had become a soliloquy.

That reminds me—why had Kik been running to receive my message in the first place? Before Wednesday I hadn't even thought of it in so long, especially with Snap to give us all the privacy we wanted. It's not until I open Kik on Alice's phone that the bomb drops, and all the air goes out of the room.

"Holy shit," I whisper into the void.

Will and I had thought Kik was our secret, just the three of us, and one that we'd outgrown a long time ago.

But Alice hadn't. And she'd invited two more people to the party.

———

Dinner is—surprise—Papa's famous stew. Usually it's one of my favorites, but tonight the tender beef crumbles in my mouth like dust, the savory broth tastes like quarry water, and I ask to be excused early. My dads exchange a look but for once let me go without an interrogation. Pancakes trails after me and claims her spot between my bed and the door with a *whuff.*

I listen for footsteps in the hall. Only the soft murmur of their voices carries from the dining room, but that can change in seconds. I close the door silently and slide Alice's phone out of my underwear drawer, my heart already pounding.

The first stranger appeared in Alice's Kik messages three weeks ago.

Serpico
I don't like this.

elizabeth_MF_cochran
It's all right. This is safer than email.

Serpico
None of this is safe. You're being careful?

elizabeth_MF_cochran
Of course. Don't worry about me. You said you had more to show me?

Serpico
Not like this. We should meet. I'd rather give it to you in person and be done with it.

> **Serpico**
> Are you still there?

> **elizabeth_MF_cochran**
> No meeting. That would risk exposing us both. Send it to the same PO box as last time.

> **Serpico**
> It'll be in the mail tomorrow.

I'm struck by two things. Alice playing the part of the calm, cool professional, reassuring her source—and the fact that Alice is *playing a part*. Whoever Serpico thinks she is, it definitely isn't a high school journalism club student.

Three days later:

> **elizabeth_MF_cochran**
> Got your package. I have questions.

> **Serpico**
> No more questions. You have all the information you need to find the answers you want. I'm done.

> **Serpico**
> Don't let me down.

> **Serpico**
> And be careful.

> **elizabeth_MF_cochran**
> If you change your mind, you know how to reach me.

The last message is marked with an *S*. Sent two weeks ago but never delivered, and the account shows as deactivated when I try to call up their profile. Serpico wasn't kidding about being done.

The hair on my arms rises as I open the next conversation, dated two days before Alice died.

Wolf_theChemist
I hear you've been looking for me.

Wolf_theChemist
Stop.

elizabeth_MF_cochran
I know what you're doing.

Wolf_theChemist
You know nothing.

elizabeth_MF_cochran
Then why are you talking to me?

Wolf_theChemist
My Netflix is down.

elizabeth_MF_cochran
Funny.

elizabeth_MF_cochran
You know who's not laughing?
All those missing kids.

Wolf_theChemist
Not my fault they're not in
on the joke.

elizabeth_MF_cochran

I think it is, actually. Where is
Noah Hayes?

Wolf_theChemist

Who cares? The cops don't.

elizabeth_MF_cochran

Tell me, or I'll give them something
they will care about.

Wolf_theChemist

You are in so far over your head
you don't even know you're
drowning.

I can hardly breathe.

elizabeth_MF_cochran

Takes a big man to make threats
behind a screen.

Wolf_theChemist

Merely an observation. Netflix is
back up, is there anything else?

elizabeth_MF_cochran

Brush me off at your own risk.

Wolf_theChemist

I don't talk to dead girls.

elizabeth_MF_cochran

[attached file]

I open the image. It takes a moment for me to realize what I'm looking at: a death certificate. I don't recognize the name, Reginald Goodwyn. Age: 19. Cause of death: respiratory failure due to poisoning.

Alice sent two more photos.

Rohit Shah. Cause of death: asphyxiation due to acute smoke inhalation. Age: 18.

Serena Clay, a month shy of 18. Cause of death: respiratory failure due to poisoning.

Poisoning?

Google informs me that poisoning is often code for drug overdose when the doctor writing the death certificate gives a damn about the family reading it.

elizabeth_MF_cochran

Let's play a game. What do
Reggie, Rohit, and Serena have
in common? I bet you know . . .

I wish to hell I knew.

Wolf_theChemist

Besides being irrelevant nobodies?
Scratch that—DEAD irrelevant
nobodies. RIP, losers.

elizabeth_MF_cochran

Last chance.

Wolf_theChemist
You're not very much fun.

elizabeth_MF_cochran
Noah Hayes.

Wolf_theChemist
Alice Booker.

Ice jolts through me at seeing her name. How had he uncovered her real identity so fast?

Maybe it hadn't been that fast. He had, after all, heard that
she had been looking for him.

The realization that this had been going on for so long
without me—and that I had completely shut Alice down when
she'd finally tried to bring me in—seeps into my bones, Ophelia's stones, making me heavy with hurt.

Wolf_theChemist
Hello?

Wolf_theChemist
Don't play coy, Alice.

Wolf_theChemist
You're so sweet with little Teddy,
Alice. He could almost be your
own.

Wolf_theChemist
Do you think you'll ever have
children, Alice?

elizabeth_MF_cochran

Stay away from my family.

Wolf_theChemist

My game, Alice. My rules.

Wolf_theChemist

Talk soon darling.

Chapter

17

I should give this to the cops. They would have to listen now
that I have proof.

Proof of what?

Someone was threatening Alice.

*What threat, exactly? Pointing out that Teddy is cute? Threat-
ening to talk to her soon?*

Okay, so hardly a smoking gun. I can hear Detective Rojas
in my head now, jabbing me with probing questions I don't have
answers for or worse, dismissing me altogether. Again.

It boils down to: what did Alice have that someone would
kill for?

I stare at the flash drive sticking out of my computer, serving
no more purpose than to keep dust out of my USB port until I
can figure out the damn password. *That* is what Alice had, I'm
sure of it. That drive has to be what Serpico sent to Alice, the
information it contains enough to unsettle Wolf_theChemist
into taking her seriously. But until I can crack it, all I have are
the names of three dead kids I've never heard of.

And Noah.

Why had she said his name right after theirs?

My heart is lead-heavy with the implication, one I'm still not ready to accept. Maybe she'd just been fishing, baiting the Chemist into filling in the blanks. I don't believe that Alice could have known for certain that Noah was dead and not given his family all the answers she had. Or that she could have known and kept it from Will and me. We would have seen that kind of faultline in her, that kind of break.

I know we would have.

I get the idea to compare her browser history to Serpico's first contact. If I can figure out where she found him, maybe *I* can find him. But three weeks might as well be three years in teenage girl internet use, and after the foods to avoid during pregnancy bomb, my emotional bandwidth is thin as spiderwebs. I scratch down the names of a few websites to check out later, mostly local and community news pages with a couple missing persons/cold case sites mixed in, and put Alice's phone back on the charger.

I text Will a brief update—it'll be easier to show him the phone at school tomorrow and let him meet Serpico and the Chemist for himself. A chill crawls down my spine with the hundred filament legs of a centipede. Alice died because of whatever is on that drive, and now I have it.

But Will and I are the only ones that know about the drive.

I keep telling myself that, over and over, but secrets aren't the solace they used to be, and sleep doesn't come easy.

———

My dads aren't quite back to the level of trust required to let me ride my bike to school, especially after that sad excuse for a fight with Kyle and Darius. I might be grouchier about it but judging from the longer-than-usual line of cars in the dropoff lane, they're not the only parents in Summerset feeling extra helicoptery right now.

Will is waiting for me in the quad with a venti Americano and a hug.

"You're everything I want and need in this life," I say lovingly.

"You're talking to the coffee," Will observes.

"Obviously." I pull Alice's phone from my pocket, unlock it and hand it to him, watching his face as he begins to read.

"Holy shit. You're a teenage Abby Sciuto, if you swapped the Doc Martens for Pumas and updated the wardrobe from the shameful back closet of 90s kindergoth to . . ." Will eyes my outfit: cuffed jeans Papa calls holey-er than the Pope, white tank top, cropped oversize sweater. ". . . uh, regular girl clothes."

"Thanks?"

He turns his attention back to Alice's phone. "How did this Chemist guy find her?"

"I'm not sure if he found her or she found him. She was definitely looking." I sip the coffee. Perfection. "But how did she even know where to look? How did she find *any* of this?"

Will looks up at me, a strange expression on his face. "Um. That might have been partially my fault."

"If you don't tell me exactly what you mean in the next ten *milliseconds* I swear to God, Will, this coffee is going up your—"

"I showed her how to access the dark web."

I take a deep breath. Apparently Will's idea of *no more secrets* is miles away from my own. "You what?"

"It's nothing you can't Google," he protests lamely.

"What were *you* doing on the dark web?" I backpedal. "What even *is* the dark web?"

"It's the Upside Down of the internet. No IP addresses, no

cookies, no rules. You need a special browser to even access it. Some of it is mirrored from the regular internet, but a lot of the content is there because it can't exist anywhere else. All the dark, illegal shit you'd expect, but also like . . . oppressed people under totalitarian regimes trying to organize revolutions. All the major news organizations have darknet sites for anonymous submissions to protect their sources. It's entirely self-regulating. Like I said last night, you can find whoever you need to get you whatever you want."

Wheels spinning, I stare hard at Will. "That answers one of my questions. And the other?"

"You know what I was doing there." The words are equal part resignation and resolve.

"I really don't," I tell him. But then I do. "Wait. Your mom?"

"She still won't name her dealer. One year into a fifteen year sentence, and she still won't say a word to defend herself. She's that scared, Cia."

"Will . . ."

He squeezes Alice's phone so hard I half expect it to crack in his grip. "Don't. She was *clean*. She meant to stay that way. I know she made her own choices, but dammit, Cia, whoever gave her that dust took all of them away from her except one."

His pain is palpable and contagious. "And if you find her dealer?"

"When," he says grimly. "Not if. *When* I find them, I'll be a good citizen and give the cops a chance to prove they give a damn about actually helping people and not just breaking up families to meet quotas."

I don't ask what happens if the police let him down. I don't want him to think about it any more than he already has. "Have you asked Santi?"

"Santi," he repeats darkly. "Santi looks out for Santi. She

doesn't give a shit about me, my mom, or anyone else as long as she gets hers."

I blink. We've known Santi since elementary school, and while we've always been more friend-adjacent than friends, I hadn't expected this level of venom from Will. "That's harsh."

"Yeah, well." I watch Will force his fingers to relax. My own tension is slower to dissipate. "Anyway. I just showed her the basics, which browser to download, et cetera. Whatever she got up to from there, she never mentioned it again."

"Not to us, anyway." But maybe to Judah? I move around the table to sit next to Will. "The bell's going to ring any minute. Here . . . read this one."

"Yes, boss lady. Reading."

I watch over his shoulder as he scrolls through the other message thread. "Serpico . . . why do I know that name?"

"Al Pacino, 1973," Will says absently. "It got him his first Golden Globe, even though he got cheated out of the Oscar."

"It was a movie?" I translate.

"It wasn't a porno."

I punch his shoulder.

"Ouch! Just kidding. They don't give Oscars for porn. Unless you count the AVNs, which I personally find to have much more merit—" Will ducks another swing. "Okay! Relax, Rowdy Ronda. Serpico was a cop—a real cop—who went undercover to expose corruption in the NYPD, took a bullet to the face for his efforts."

"Grim choice for a pseudonym."

"Kind of, yeah. I mean things ended pretty well for the real Serpico. He won a bunch of awards and retired in Switzerland. And got to hang out with Al Pacino."

The first bell rings. Will hands the phone back and stands up from the table as the quad begins to empty.

"We have to get into that drive," I tell him.

"Alternatively, we could find Serpico. Do you really think he didn't keep backup copies of whatever information he gave Alice?"

"I kind of don't. It sounds like he really wanted to be out of it."

Will shrugs. "Might be easier to find him than to crack that drive. We don't even know if Alice set the password or Serpico did."

The hope that began to bloom the moment we found the flash drive starts to wilt, but I won't let it. It is a strange kind of flower, fed by anger instead of sunlight, sorrow instead of water. "Then I guess we'd better hope your boy Gundam comes through with his hacking skills."

———

I wade through my classes like a shipwreck survivor looking for shore. I try to pay attention, I honestly do—Alice would be pissed if I start failing classes in her name—but my notebooks are full of potential password combinations and the names of three dead kids I've never met instead of polynomials and papal states. Kyle Kaufman whacks Alex Franklin in the face with a soccer ball in phys ed, which no one who knows Kyle believes is an accident.

Mr. Melendez teaches our phys ed class and is also an assistant coach for the Pirates. He sends Alex to the nurse's office and gives Kyle a bro-y smirk. "Slow it down a little, Kaufman. Not everybody's in your league."

I physiologically can't help the fact that my eyes roll so hard I can see the back of my skull. High school is a four-year cage fight. The question isn't who will win—that's been decided years ago, by genetics and parental income brackets—but how broken you will be when you crawl out the other side.

I can't wait to graduate.

———

I ask to leave gym class early when I can't even pretend to focus anymore. Mr. Melendez says no. He's of the suck-it-up-snowflake breed, and grieving my best friend apparently doesn't buy me any grace. Thankfully, his buttons are easy to push.

"Fine. Do *you* have a tampon I can use, then?" I cross my arms. "Preferably the super-max kind. This place is about to look like a scene from *Dexter*."

Mr. Melendez's cheeks turn the color of bologna and he waves me away without another word.

Easy.

I should have at least ten minutes to change out of my gym clothes before Melendez cuts the rest of the pack loose. The locker room should be empty.

It isn't.

I can't see over the banks of lockers that stand like rows of metal soldiers at attention, but I hear the rustling of paper and the faint clank of metal.

I'm not alone.

I don't call out. Instead, I ease the door just short of closed and walk toward the sounds, my chest thumping and my sneakers silent on the concrete floor.

Until the weight of the door I'd just walked through pulls it shut with a heavy *click*.

All at once a locker slams, four or five or six rows ahead of me, and footsteps pound the concrete. I break into a sprint, on the theory that anyone running away is guilty of something, but I come to a dead stop when I realize the locker hanging open is my own.

"No," I whisper.

The door to the hallway bangs open, slams shut again behind the thief, but all I can think about is Alice's phone.

My civilian clothes are draped where they were probably thrown, over the bench that divides my row from the next. The floor in front of my locker is covered with the innards of my purse: lip gloss and body spray and gum wrappers and old lunch notes from Papa and whatever else was lurking in the bottom of my vintage Kate Spade, which, speaking of, lies under the bench about five feet away.

My mind stops rambling. The percussion in my chest turns into a wrecking ball of fury in my stomach.

I'm too late. Alice's phone is gone.

And it's not the only thing missing.

———

"That son of a bitch." Will slams his fist down on the lunch table, making milk cartons dance and the kids at the other end of the table stare. "He's trying to cover his tracks, but it's too late. We already know what he did."

"What who did?" I'm not tracking, until I follow Will's glare across the cafeteria to where Cheyenne appears to be crying about something. Probably the injustice of the three-day suspension Darius had bought himself, not because he'd started the fight (from my perspective, that honor went to Will) but because it was his third one this semester and it's only September. As usual, at least half a dozen girls sit around her, wolves circling a wounded cub. It's unclear whether they are guarding her or waiting to tear her apart. In that crowd, either outcome is equally likely.

Judah sits a little ways apart but still within the protective periphery of the jock squad. He might as well be in another solar system for all the attention he's giving them, barely nodding when someone jostles him for a reply. I can't see what he's fixated on since he's sitting with his back to us, but given our last couple of encounters, I doubt it's anything you'd find on a syllabus.

"You think it was Judah?"

"You don't? He knew you had the phone. He *threatened* you, Cia. And now it's gone."

"Sort of." I absently play with the scrap of paper holding Papa's words of wisdom for the day:

CUPCAKES ARE MUFFINS THAT BELIEVED IN MIRACLES.

Will takes it, reads it, shakes his head and hands it back. "It's *sort of* gone?"

I shake my head. "He sort of threatened me. He actually kind of suggested I give it to the police first. That doesn't seem like something a killer would do."

Will rolls his eyes, exasperated. "He knew you weren't going to give it to the cops. He was just trying to throw you off."

"Maybe." I'm just not sure. I wish I was, one way or the other. I kind of envy Will's snap judgment, but I've seen too many sides of Judah Hayes to easily fit him into any one category. "Maybe the person who stole Alice's phone isn't the same person who killed her. If he is the one who broke into my locker, maybe Judah really is trying to find out who killed her, too, and that's why he went after the phone."

Will looks dubious. "I think you're making this too complicated."

"Whoever broke into my locker took more than just the phone, Will."

"What else did he take?"

I hesitate. "My bra." Lacy and lower-cut than my dads needed to know about, it was one of my favorites and now it's in the hands of at best a creepo thief, and at worst, a murderer with an agenda I've placed myself at the top of.

He blinks. "You were running around gym class without a bra? Is that a girl thing?"

I cut him off before I completely lose him to his imagination. "No, and can you be less of a teenage boy for two seconds? I had a sports bra on. Nobody wants to be walking around the rest of the day in a sweaty underwire."

His eyes come back into focus. "Wait. So—"

"Yeah. I think he—whoever he is—wants to scare me. To make it personal."

Rage darkens his face, a total eclipse of everything rational, and Will rockets to his feet.

The fact that I am between Will and the jock squad buys me an advantage of only a second or two, most of which I lose trying to untangle my legs from beneath the table after he shoves it away from him.

"Will!" I shout, but even I can't break through the noise this time. His eyes are fixed on Judah, who still hasn't looked up even though most of the rest of the cafeteria is gawking by now.

I follow him step for step across the line of tables, trying to make him look at me. Will is having none of it, and when he rounds the end of the table, I am forced to jog backwards to keep myself between him and the target of that blind fury, who has finally noticed the Mack truck barreling toward him.

Judah rises.

We're less than twenty feet away.

"Damn it, Will, stop!" I shout.

"Get out of my way, Cia." He looks over my head. "You're fucking dead, Hayes!"

I waste time I can't spare glancing over my shoulder. Judah looks confused, but then his shoulders square up, his hands go loose, and he looks resigned.

Resigned to violence.

That glance costs me. I trip over someone's backpack and land flat on my butt, the impact sending lightning bolts up my tailbone. Will pauses, looks down at me, but I can't find my friend behind the curtain of rage that has fallen across his eyes. He steps over my legs and keeps going.

Half the football team and a few basketball players close ranks around Judah, smelling blood in the water and wanting their piece.

I don't know what kind of magical radar she has, or how she teleported from her office on the other side of the school, but Ms. Fletcher appears in front of Will so fast he nearly steps on her.

I can't hear what she says, but he loses momentum when he elects not to steamroll over the petite guidance counselor, and that second is all it takes for the cafeteria aides and a security officer to close in.

They've hustled him out of the cafeteria by the time I get to my feet, and by the time anyone thinks to turn those hungry eyes on me, I'm gone too.

Chapter

18

I hardly register the rest of the school day even as I'm moving through it. Dad's working late so I take the bus, and I retreat to my bedroom the moment I've cleared a Papa-approved portion of my dinner plate. Will remains incommunicado, even on Snapchat, which I'd downloaded to my old phone this afternoon. I wonder if his phone has been added to the list of lost privileges after today's cafeteria blow-up. That makes me think of Judah, who had caught my gaze for a few long beats as the adults scrambled to get Will out of the cafeteria. I'd been the one to look away this time, fleeing the scene in true accomplice style to avoid interrogation round two. In those seconds, though, his confusion had truly looked genuine.

I've glimpsed the darkness in Judah, but skulking around doesn't seem like his style. I can absolutely see him taking Alice's phone if presented with the opportunity. In his shoes, I wouldn't hesitate. The rest, though? Stealing my bra, trashing my stuff? That just doesn't feel like the Judah I've known since middle school. But if the past few days have taught me anything, it's that I don't know the people around me nearly as well as I'd once thought.

Alice's phone . . . I'm so angry I could scream. I'd had so little time with it. I hadn't gotten to her emails at all, and I'd barely scratched the surface of her Snaps and browser history. The idea that whoever had stolen the phone might not even be able to unlock it gives me small comfort. If they'd stolen it to cover their tracks, it doesn't matter if they were locked out, only that I don't have it anymore.

Her browser history . . . The notepad on my desk is open to the page where I'd scribbled the names of the sites Alice had been using when she'd established contact with Serpico. I wake up my laptop. I may not have her phone anymore, but that doesn't mean I have *nothing.*

I start by searching Alice's favorite usernames, tracing her footsteps through the murky anonymity of the internet mirror-world back to the time when I'm guessing she met Serpico—about a month ago, with a few weeks of wiggle room. Finding her is easy: her usernames are predictable iterations of Elizabeth Jane Cochran and Nellie Bly. The hard part is readying myself for what I might find. For when Noah's story intersects inexplicably with mine, the boy Summerset forgot and the children Summerset never knew.

I've never gone down that road. To what was probably my parents' deep relief, I hardly remember the hurting that brought the healing that brought the scars I wear today, and that has always seemed like a fair deal. I've always felt whole enough, suspected those jagged pieces would only cut.

I've never gone down that road, but I will follow where Alice leads me. Even there.

Two frustrating hours later, all I have is a headache and eye sockets that feel like they're coated in Velcro, prickly and sore.

The Summerset Free Press: dead end. Only one article even mentions Noah, posted a week after he had stopped coming home. "Article" is a generous term, as the page features last year's yearbook photo, two clumps of generic sentences that barely qualified as paragraphs, and a link to the Summerset Police Department's website. The comments section is disabled, empty.

Crimewatchers.net: claims to be "in pursuit of the missing, unidentified and justice," but appears to mostly be public domain news regurgitation and speculation. Under the username ej_cochran, Alice posted Noah's photo and information here six weeks ago, got loads of sympathy and zero help. Dead end.

Websleuths.com: a forum for true crime aficionados who aren't content to be simple pain spectators, but actually try to solve crimes via the internet hivemind. bly_dont_lie shared Noah's information on their MISSING discussion board two months ago, received a few helpful suggestions for national databases where she could submit his vital statistics. Those seem more useful for finding a body than a boy, and I can't tell if Alice followed up or not. She goes radio silent on the MISSING board after a week.

But two weeks ago, after Serpico's info dump, she had gone back. Not to MISSING, but bly_dont_lie is all over the CRIMES boards. Favorite discussion topics: interpreting coroner reports, how police departments handle missing persons, post-mortem tox screens, autopsy protocol and procedure, and our little town of Summerset. Most of her posts were seeking information, not sharing, and she definitely preferred to keep her conversations off the board as the majority of her responses were along the lines of "PM'd you" which gets me exactly nowhere. I try every password combination I can think of to get into her private messages until I'm locked out, and the password reset option is useless without being able to get into her email.

I exercise what could fairly be called superhuman restraint and manage not to throw my laptop out the window.

I've saved Reddit for last, because, well, it's Reddit. Generally not 4chan level shitposting, it's still shark-infested waters for the vulnerable, and Alice had been that, even if she'd refused to admit it. I sigh, rub my eyes, and start small.

I sit up straight almost immediately.

/r/SummersetLocal: Six weeks ago eliza_jane_c shared the Summerset Free Press article and some of her own photos of Noah, captioned with a rant about the indifference of Summerset authorities. A chorus of supportive ACAB-style posts followed, but two responses in particular stop my inexorable slouch to the floor.

> **buttOns_for_eyes** July 24 - 03:10
>
> same thing happened to my friend Reggie. they gave 0 fks when he disappeared and then they said he was dead but none of us got to see the body. shady af!! hope your guy's story ends better
>
> > **aggressivesneeze603** July 25 - 01:41
> >
> > he's not the first and won't be the last, **eliza_jane_c.** beware the badge. this town is and has always been their hunting ground.

I know Reggie. At least, I'd read his death certificate on Alice's phone.

Alice had responded right away but buttOns_for_eyes never posted again, according to their Reddit profile. aggressivesneeze603 is a different story.

eliza_jane_c July 25 - 08:26
can you tell me more?

> **aggressivesneeze603** July 27 - 10:41
> sorry. I like being on this side of the ground.

> **eliza_jane_c** July 27 - 10:50
> tell me where to look then. PM if you want.

> **aggressivesneeze603** July 30 - 02:52
> no PMs. try infomarket.

> **eliza_jane_c** July 30 - 07:12
> I don't understand.

> **aggressivesneeze603** July 30 - 02:52
> down the rabbit hole, little girl.

Alice said nothing else, and neither had aggressivesneeze603.

I stare at the screen, willing it to decrypt that last exchange for me. Searching "infomarket" yields nothing relevant, with the exception of a Moldovan news site I dig through for way too long before realizing it's nothing more sinister than an eastern European Yahoo.

eliza_jane_c July 30 - 07:12
I don't understand.

"You and me both," I mutter. As if the condescending "little girl" isn't enough, "down the rabbit hole" is such an overused trope I want to reach through the internet and slap the person who'd typed it.

Reach through the internet.

The cogs of my brain whir, slip, spin, and finally catch.

It's the Upside Down of the internet. No IP addresses, no cookies, no rules.

Crap. Alice is going to make me follow her to the dark web.

I send Will a Snap of my progress bar as I download the Tor browser, which according to Google is the key to the dark kingdom. *following breadcrumbs*, I caption the photo. *gonna make me do this alone?*

Nothing. Either he's asleep, or they really did take his phone. Double crap.

I can't name the reason for the sudden apprehension that settles over me, other than the fact that I am following a ghost to a place I've only heard about in stories, every one of which involved people with very good reasons to do very bad things to keep their secrets.

You can find whoever you need to get you whatever you want.

Had Will told Alice the same thing?

Professor Google taught me that the dark web is not indexed the way the regular web is, not searchable. You have to know the exact address of what you are looking for, and odds are it's a nonsense jumble of characters that defies memorization and changes frequently, so if you luck into it once, you may not find it in the same place you left it.

But Prof. G also taught me that when sites *want* to be found, they can list themselves on the Hidden Wiki. I extrapolate that an infomarket, like any other market, benefits from a large number of shoppers. I hope that means it wants to be found, but the gods of the dark web are fickle.

I find Infomarket much quicker than I'd expected. A thrill zings through me, but fizzles a moment later when I realize that Infomarket purges posts every seventy-two hours. Alice has been gone longer than that—any evidence of what she'd been looking for here, or what she might have found, is long gone.

I look anyway. There's no option to search by username. Infomarket takes simplicity to an annoying level, providing only two paths: I HAVE INFORMATION ABOUT . . . and I AM LOOKING FOR . . . , both bold red hyperlinks on a gray background. It does give the option to zoom in on a map to a particular geographic area. I click the first link and zoom in to Summerset. Several flags pop up, offering tips on everything from the dirty secrets of local politicos to where to buy the best painkillers to who's offering no-questions-asked, cash-paying gig work. Every tip comes with a price tag, payable by crypto.

No mention of missing kids or bonedust. No Serpico.

No Chemist, either.

I click the second link, consider making my own post to see if I can draw Serpico out. What would I even say?

I am looking for . . . Noah Hayes.

I am looking for . . . a tipster called Serpico.

I am looking for . . . the reason my best friend is dead.

The cursor blinks in and out of existence, waiting.

I am looking for . . . payback.

I close Tor.

This is how Serpico found Alice, I'm sure of it. Or how she found him. But he's as much of a ghost as she is, at least to me. Who the hell is he? Why would he go to Alice with his secrets and not the police?

Because in doing so, he put Alice between himself and someone who would clearly kill to keep those secrets. Did he know what he was doing?

Did Serpico know he was risking Alice's life as well as his own when he sent her that flash drive?

Of course he knew.

In Will's telling of it, the real Serpico was a hero, risking everything to expose deadly corruption. But our Serpico seems like a coward to me, kicking the hornets' nest and leaving a teenage girl to face the swarm.

Not that I can claim to be much better.

19:06 [alice.books113]: i can't do this alone. i need you.

I close the laptop and sprawl across my bed, dropping an arm off the edge of the bed to scratch Pancakes. Her tail thumps the floor cheerfully.

Alice had needed me and I hadn't been there. Now I need her. I need her like thunder needs a storm, needs its ferocity to give it force and direction. I need Alice to talk to me, and she won't. She never will again.

Regret carves out a hollow in my throat that threatens to fill with enough tears to drown me, an ocean with no horizon. I am Brouardel's dog, holding fast somewhere between clinging to hope that my lips will taste the air again and giving in to the underwater, to the places where light doesn't follow.

I choose hope. Tell myself it's no choice at all, really.

But my lips still taste like saltwater.

I run my fingers over the beads of the mala and come up with a mantra of my own: *I will get this bastard.*

Next up: Instagram. Alice and I made our accounts at the same time and I've seen every one of her posts, but since not noticing what's right under my nose seems to be one of my talents, I go back through anyway.

This is what I find: unlike many—maybe even most—people, Alice didn't do a social media purge of all traces of Noah when they broke up. In fact, as far as I can tell, she didn't delete anything.

That probably hadn't been a good sign, but it was one we'd all missed because Alice had smiled and said she was OK and we'd all let her down by letting it rest there.

I'm a hundred percent positive the cops didn't miss it. One

more nail in the "Alice offed herself because she couldn't handle living without Noah" coffin.

But did they miss this?

I roll off my stomach and sit up. The picture had been posted in February, long before Noah became the shadow of hurt that never left my best friend's eyes. She'd used a black and white filter—she always liked the simplicity of monochrome photos, which leave only the space between light and shadow to tell the whole story.

I already know the story behind this one. Noah had taken that picture he'd drawn of Alice way back in freshman year and blown it up into a huge, splattered-pixel mural on a wall in a housing development on the outskirts of town that had stalled years ago, and now the only money being invested in it was to pay a security guard twelve bucks an hour to drive around in a golf cart and make sure kids like Noah weren't painting pictures of their girlfriends on the plaster walls of houses that had failed to become homes.

It was Valentine's Day and he'd taken her there for a picnic. They'd talked about the future, their dreams. They'd kissed and his hands had been stained with paint and it got on her dress and she never wore it again but she didn't get rid of it either.

In the photo, Noah is slightly blurry and his painted hands are out of the frame because he was laughing and trying to get out of it too, but the mural is in perfect focus and I remember how much I've chosen to forget about Noah, like what an amazing artist he is and how all he'd ever wanted to do was draw and love Alice and how I wish more than anything I knew when and why that changed, because when that changed so did everything else, for all of us.

The picture is seven months old, but a month ago, Alice left a comment. It doesn't take much imagination to see her as she

must have been, curled up in bed, holding on to the pain because sometimes pain hurts less than the emptiness that follows.

I'm not giving up on you, she wrote. *Not ever.*

The last comment had been posted less than twenty-four hours
later from queen_0f_d1am0ndz: *he's moved on bitch y don't u?*

queen_0f_d1am0ndz's account is private, the tiny profile
photo showing me nothing but pouty red lips.

I hate her immediately.

And I have to know who she is.

———

The next morning, I follow Santi out of World History and
into the girls' bathroom like the weirdo stalker I'm more than
willing to be if it gets me answers. When I lock the door behind
me, Santi spins around.

I raise my hands. "It's just me."

She turns back to the mirror. "What does *just me* need today
that warrants a private audience?"

"I need to know who this is." I hold up my phone, queen_0f_
d1am0ndz's Instagram profile filling my screen.

Santi takes one look and turns away with a grimace. "Girl,
you don't want anything to do with that one. The only diamonds
she knows anything about are the kind you stick down a pipe and
smoke." She leans closer to her reflection, adds another layer of
dark berry stain to her lips. "Besides. There's only room for one
queen in Summerset, and she ain't it." She pouts and kisses the air.

I've come to the right person, at least. Santi knows everyone in this town. "Who is she?"

"Nobody you want to know, darling. Trust me."

"Maybe not, but she knows something about Noah, which
means she might know something about Alice."

She offers me something in a mint tin that is either an Altoid or half a Xanax. I don't want either. "Santi. I'm serious."

She pops the Xanax/mint and puts the tin away. "So am I." But then she sighs, long-lashed eyes meeting mine in the mirror. "You aren't going to let this go?"

"No."

Somewhere in a galaxy far far away, second bell rings. I don't move.

Santi sighs. "Her name is Jenna Reglin. She was a year ahead of us."

"Never heard of her."

"She wasn't exactly setting track records," she says drily. "That girl never met a chemical she wouldn't snort, shoot, or smoke."

he's moved on bitch

Is Jenna Reglin really what Noah moved on to?

My chest aches for Alice. She wouldn't have let that comment go without asking questions. Did those questions lead her to Jenna?

Santi writes down an address. "If she isn't there she isn't far. That neighborhood is one big petri dish."

"Thank you."

"Don't thank me." She passes the scrap of paper to me as if handling a used Kleenex. "I feel sorry for what happened to Alice, but if I were really doing you any favors, I'd have sent you packing the moment you walked in here."

There's nothing more to say. I turn to leave, but Santi calls me back.

"Don't go after dark," she says. "And don't even think about going alone."

———

I am half-obedient, which my dads would agree is about on par with my average. It's full daylight when I walk out of school after second period, but I haven't said a word to anyone about where I'm going. I feel a twinge of guilt about not telling Will, but between picking a fight with Kyle last week and going after Judah yesterday, he's too much of a loose cannon to bring to a situation that might require a little more finesse. He's got his phone back but he hadn't been in the quad this morning, so I haven't seen him since yesterday's blowout.

I'm halfway across the parking lot when I hear my name. I walk faster, recognizing the voice.

"Cia!" Judah calls again. "Slow down!"

"Hard pass." I glance over my shoulder to see the fire exit doors close behind him, the same stairwell I just snuck out of. "Why are you following me?"

He sprints up to walk beside me. "Getting into fights and now playing hooky. I figured something interesting was happening."

"It isn't. And I wouldn't invite you if it was." My annoyance rises. "What do you *want*, Judah?"

"I wanted to say thank you." He pauses, I don't, and he jogs to catch up with me again. "Can you stop for a minute?"

"Thank you for what? For kindly leaving Alice's phone in a place where you could find it? You are *so* welcome." I'm still not sure I believe he's the one who broke into my locker, but I lob the bomb anyway. Unless he's an exceptional liar, his reaction will tell me everything I need to know.

Puzzlement pulls his brows down low. "What are you talking about?"

His confusion seems kosher. And yet, petty larceny would probably be small potatoes to Mr. Whatever It Takes. "Nice try." I turn away but he touches my arm—touches, doesn't grab, this time.

"Cia, wait. Please."

I stop and face him. "What?"

He hesitates. "I heard your locker got broken into. Is that what they were after? Alice's phone?" It almost seems as if he'd been about to say something else, but changed his mind.

"Sure looks that way, since that's what they took."

"Damn it!"

Judah looks so genuinely pissed that my doubts about his complicity creep up again. The wind shifts, tossing my hair over my shoulder and carrying the scent of him to me. He is the woods and sweet smoke and stolen whiskey around a secret fire when the darkness is waiting all around. I want to trust him. I know I'd better not.

And I know from the way he watches me that he knows better than to trust me, too.

Secrets. Lately it feels like we're all choking on them.

But I don't give mine up and he doesn't either.

"Will thinks you did it," I tell him.

"The locker? Or . . ."

I shrug. "Either. Both."

"Of course he does." He exhales heavily. "I knew there had to be a reason he came charging across the lunch room yesterday." His eyes find mine. "That's what I wanted to thank you for, by the way. Slowing him down before there was any carnage. That was either very brave or very stupid of you."

"My dads would say that where I'm concerned, those two things usually go together."

"Still. You could have gotten hurt."

"Will is my friend." I add, "I didn't do it for you."

"Oh, I got that part." He smiles. It's a good smile, a little crooked. You don't spend hundreds of hours grinding out laps alongside someone without learning when a smile is real and when it's a mask, hiding a side stitch or shin splints or the guilt of a trashed locker. This one? Real.

Shit. I don't want to like the way he smiles. I look away.

Judah follows my gaze to the city bus stop. "Where are you going?"

"Away," I say. He's making this too complicated. "Good talk." I head off again.

He manages to keep up. "It occurs to me," he says, only slightly out of breath, "that I might have gone about this the wrong way."

I check my phone. The next bus should be here in less than five minutes, assuming it's on time.

"Look. *Cia.*"

I stop again.

"Look at me."

He has a dimple on the opposite cheek from Noah. Now that's weird.

"I know you didn't do anything to Alice."

"I wish I could say the same."

"You know I wouldn't hurt her," he says quietly. "The only reason you're scared of me is because I gave you reason to be. Because I threatened you. That was a mistake."

I hug myself. The breeze is sharp and my sweater is worn thin from too many tumble-drys. "I'm not scared of you."

His raised eyebrow tells me exactly how convincing that wasn't.

"Three days ago you were convinced enough that I had something to do with what happened to Alice that you almost made a scene outside the Booker house. Now you're sorry? What changed your mind?"

"Don't misunderstand me, Cia. I still think you know more than you're telling. But I suspect that's because you don't know who you can trust, and not because you're the one that shouldn't be trusted." He shrugs, the intensity in his eyes giving the lie to the nonchalant gesture. "You didn't break into your own locker, after all. Ergo, you're probably not the bad guy."

"Did you?"

"Break into your locker? No. I was in Spanish class. I might have tried to, though, if I'd known her phone was in there." All traces of apology are gone. "I wasn't exaggerating when I said I'll do whatever it takes to find my brother, Cia. You don't want to be in between me and finding Noah. I thought you were, before. But now I think I might've been wrong. Now I think maybe you're the best chance at finding Noah I've ever had."

Neither of us speaks for a few beats, each weighing the other. Or at least that's what I'm doing.

Can I trust you?

The only reason we have to trust each other is the people we lost, and how much we loved them. Is that enough?

I hand him my phone. He squints, the bright sunlight giving the screen a radiant sheen.

"Who is she?" he asks.

"She left a comment on Alice's Insta a month ago implying that Noah was with her. Her name is Jenna, and she's about to have an unexpected guest." I eye him, deciding. "Or two."

He jingles his keyring. "I'll drive."

Chapter
19

Jenna Reglin's neighborhood reminds me of a row of plaster dominoes waiting to tumble over. One house looks like it started to burn down but ran out of motivation. Through broken, charred boards, I see color and movement: someone still calls that house home. A tricycle sits overturned in the dirt yard, weeds sprouting between the spokes of its wheels.

Judah parks across the street and down a few houses from the address Santi had given me. We step out onto cracked concrete, seemed like the face of an old man who has seen too much to ever be surprised again. I can feel eyes on us, but only shifting curtains and shivering blinds greet me when I glance up and down the street.

Judah hands me his keys as we cross the road. "If things go south," he says, "I want you to get out of here and call for help."

I frown. "You must have me mistaken for the kind of girl who gets out when things go south."

"I'm serious, Cia. These people don't fuck around."

I tuck his keys into my purse, step past him and ring the

doorbell. "Then it's a good thing I let you come with me, isn't it?"

The doorbell doesn't work, of course, and even gives me a spiteful little zing as the circuit shorts. I curse and press my fingertip to my lips. Judah bangs on the door. I am hyper aware of his physical presence behind me. It excites my skin, a static charge before the storm.

I don't know Judah like I once thought I did, when we'd pushed ourselves past our limits every day as teammates. I have no idea what his limits are anymore. He's a lot angrier than he used to be, but so am I. Our alliance feels brittle, tenuous. What if Will's horrible suspicion was true, and Noah did kill Alice?

At the end of the day our paths are temporarily parallel. They are not the same. But even cloaked in everything I don't know about him and his motives, I'm glad Judah is here with me now.

Metal grinds across wood and the door opens all of six inches. "What do you want?" The voice is husky, rough with sleep or smoke.

"Are you Jenna?" I ask.

A watery blue eye scrapes over my body. "Who the hell wants to know?"

Judah tags in. "Hey. My name is Judah. I think you knew my brother."

The eye widens as she takes him in. "Holy shit. Holy *shit*!" The door starts to slam shut. I wedge my foot in the narrow space, the foot that science made, that doesn't feel pain even when Jenna throws her weight against the door. "Go away!"

We don't need any more attention than we've already got. Judah leans into the door, muscling it open without much effort, and once we've slid inside and shut the door behind us I see that Jenna Reglin can't weigh more than a hundred and ten pounds.

Low-watt bulbs filter through red bead curtains and smoke-stained lampshades, casting Jenna's home in a blood orange glow that almost camouflages the creeping mold stains on the drywall. I smell weed and patchouli and . . . baby powder.

Oh, hell.

The toddler sitting on the floor looks up at us with startled baby deer eyes, searching her mother's face for cues. Cry? Scream? Go back to watching cartoon kitchen utensils singing about teamwork? She's chubby, old enough to sit on her own and reach for things she shouldn't have, and much better fed than her mom, though a day or two overdue for a bath.

It occurs to me they might not even have running water.

"Please don't hurt my baby," Jenna whimpers.

I freeze, unused to playing the role of threat to babies, but Judah doesn't miss a beat. "We're not here for that," he says, and I don't have time to figure out what exactly he means by *that* before he continues. "We're here about Noah."

"Watch your show, baby. Mama will be right back." Jenna kisses the top of her daughter's head and we follow her to the dining room, set in the rear of the house beside a kitchen too small for anything more adventurous than opening a can of Chef Boyardee. Heaps of papers and half-opened mail cover the surface of a small round table, where Jenna gestures for us to sit.

Movement catches my peripheral vision and tugs my gaze away from the scorched glass pipe resting inside an empty baby food jar. What I had taken for a shadow along the floorboards of the kitchen is actually crawling with more legs than I want to imagine.

"No, thanks," I say.

Jenna collapses into one of the chairs, folding into herself at sharp angles. She never stops moving; her hands tremble as she lights a smoke, and one leg kicks while the other foot taps.

It's almost impossible to believe she's only a year older than us, barely out of high school, and this far away from hope. What had happened to this girl? For all of the mold stains and hostility, it's still obvious that she's trying. And that she loves her daughter with the ferocity of someone who has only one beacon left in the whole world to steer by.

he's moved on bitch

My walls slam back up.

"He's gone, your brother," Jenna says. "Been gone a few weeks now."

"But he was here."

"You knew that before you came bustin' down my door."

Judah glances back at the child on the floor, who is still more interested in us than the cartoon. She smiles shyly and covers her eyes.

"You're confusing her. She thinks you're him. Probably wondering why you haven't picked her up yet." Jenna barks out a laugh. "But don't get any ideas, Noah's Brother, she isn't his. She's nobody's but mine and it's gonna stay that way."

Judah looks relieved. All I feel is more sadness—this kid's safety net is more hole than weave. And, piling on top of that depressing thought, realization that Judah's relief is misplaced. He has no idea that Noah is, in fact, a father.

Or would have been.

Alice aches in her spot beneath my heart, and I have to force my lungs to take in air. It tastes like cigarettes.

Judah takes the other chair at the table. "When was Noah here?"

Jenna shrugs. "Summer."

"July? August?"

"Sure."

He keeps his voice level, but I can see the tension flickering through his muscles. "When did he leave?"

"Couple weeks ago."

"Be more specific."

"Be less of a dick," she sneers.

My turn. "Jenna," I say. "If you don't want to talk to us, it's okay. We can go. But Noah is still a minor, and next time it'll be the cops knocking on your door. Maybe knocking on a few doors. And I don't think your neighbors will appreciate you drawing that kind of attention."

She mutters something around her smoke that rhymes with *itch* and flashes me a look of hate. It's amazing how quickly her eyes shift from predator to prey and back again. They go soft and wet, sliding back to Judah. Jenna is a chameleon, constantly assessing what she needs to be at any given moment. I recognize the hallmark of trauma when I see it. "He was a good kid, your brother. Didn't belong here, but then I guess none of us do until we realize we don't belong anywhere else anymore."

She sifts through the papers on the table, unconcerned about the small landslide she causes off the opposite end. "He drew this. That's my Margaret." She hands Judah a piece of construction paper and nods at the baby.

I was expecting something more along the lines of Summer or Stormy or Heaven and it must show on my face because Jenna says, "It was my grandmother's name. She's the last one who gave a damn about me 'til the cancer got her."

I follow her gaze to see Margaret stuffing something into her mouth. I hope it doesn't have legs.

Judah passes me the drawing without a word. It's definitely a Noah Hayes original, Crayola and dollar-store construction paper instead of acrylic and canvas, but he captured a laughing Margaret as vividly as any camera. If we'd had any doubt before, it just went up in a cloud of cigarette smoke and cheap incense.

"I want that back," Jenna says sharply. I hand it to her, and she's careful not to bend the paper as she places it back on the table.

Noah had *lived* here, in a strange little family with this fanged chameleon girl and her sweet, grubby daughter, and he had left Alice to do it.

I can't wrap my head around it. All I know for sure is that impending fatherhood as a motive for murder is off the table. Even Will has to see that now.

Judah picks up one of the envelopes that slid to the floor. "What's this?"

Jenna squints at it. "Check stub. Take it, take all of 'em. Not like we were gonna file joint taxes or anything anyway." She snorts at her own joke, but it seems forced. The sadness that settled over her when she found Noah's drawing seems to have taken root.

Judah hands me several unopened envelopes. They're addressed to Noah, with the return address that of one Rearden Health Alliance.

I feel suddenly queasy in a way that has nothing to do with insects and mystery stains, and everything to do with something being where it very much shouldn't be.

I've seen that company's name before. I've never been more certain of anything.

But where?

Judah's voice forces me to refocus. "Noah was working?"

"It was, like, a research thing."

"What kind of research?" I ask, earning myself another scowl from Jenna.

"Girl, he treated us good and helped with the bills, do you think I was about to ask what he did for that money?" She shakes her head. "Maybe where you all live, guys like that grow on trees or some shit. Not here."

Judah goes at it one last time. "So you know absolutely nothing about what kind of work he was doing?"

"I know he wasn't *doing* the research. He *was* the research. It was some kind of study thing. All's I know is they did check-ups and stuff, made sure he was healthy. They even helped with the surgery when he got sick."

The storm-static swirls across my skin, Judah's tension spilling over. "When he got sick? What kind of surgery?"

"It was just, like, his gallbladder or something. It wasn't even a real surgery. Just a couple little cuts here—" Jenna gestures vaguely at her abdomen. "—and some antibiotics. And some *real* good pain meds." She starts to grin, remembers, sinks back into sullen resistance.

How is it that Noah was reported missing almost three months ago but has continued to walk around Summerset as if he were invisible? I want to doubt Jenna, but then I think about how my dad had looked right through the woman in the street the other day, a traffic obstacle instead of a person. He could have driven right past Noah himself and not seen him. But what kind of clinic treats minors, *experiments* on minors, without parental consent?

Rearden Health Alliance. It sticks in my memory like gum in my hair, as I cram the envelopes into my purse. I'll figure it out later, when we're out of hostile territory.

I pick up where Judah left off. "When did he leave, Jenna? Where did he go?"

"Hell if I know. Everybody leaves." She aims for bitter and gets close, but something in the way her voice cracks tells me this one really hurt.

Does it hurt because she really cares about Noah?

Maybe.

"What aren't you telling us?" I ask softly.

She sniffs, wipes her nose with the back of one thin hand. "I'm telling you the same thing I told that bitch who came by two weeks ago—Noah's *gone* and he ain't coming back!"

Judah grabs for my arm but I'm too fast—I slap the cigarette out of her mouth before she can even flinch. She stares up at me, only slightly more surprised than I am, as a trickle of blood stains her cracked lips.

"Her name," I say, "was Alice." Anger roils through me like molten lava rock, black and heavy.

The curtains pull shut behind Jenna's eyes. "Get the fuck out of my house," she whispers hoarsely. "Get out get out get *out!*"

Margaret watches our every move, neurons synapsing and forming conclusions about how the world works that I wish to hell were wrong, and the cigarette smolders in the matted carpet. Nobody moves.

Jenna shoves her chair back and stands. "What do you mean, her name *was* Alice?"

That's so far from what I expected to come out of her mouth that it takes me a second to find words again.

Judah speaks quietly. "She died last week."

"She was killed," I say. "Pretty soon after she talked to you."

Jenna's translucent skin goes even paler. "I didn't tell her nothing she didn't already know." She hugs herself. "Besides, she got what she wanted, didn't she? They're together now."

The anger turns to ice in my veins.

They're together now.

This time it's Judah that nearly loses his shit. "What did you say?"

"I said, get out of my house."

"What the fuck did you just say?" he demands. The storm-static rolls over me, thunder poised to fulfill its promise.

Margaret starts to cry. Jenna does, too.

"You want to know the truth? You really want to know? Fine! He's dead, okay? Is that what you wanted to hear? He's *dead*. Just like everyone else who ever gave a shit about me."

My breath is vacuum-yanked from my body. Judah reels, sucker punched. My hand is on his shoulder with no memory of putting it there, both of us leaning into that connection as Jenna's words sink in.

Noah . . . dead?

And Jenna had known, but let Alice keep looking for him anyway. Had let Alice keep asking questions until someone—not Noah—put her in the quarry to shut her up.

———

Jenna goes on talking. "We'd just got the food stamps card and Mags and I went shopping to make us a special dinner because it was our one-month anniversary as a family and when we came home he was dead. I know a fucking OD when I see one, and I wasn't about to call no cops and have children's services take Mags away so we took care of it and he should never have been here anyway but at least he's in a pretty place now. I tried to do right by him, so don't you judge us." Tears pour down her face and she shoves past us, picks up Margaret and bounces the kid on one hip. "Don't you *dare* fucking judge us."

A muscle beneath Judah's eye tics. "I'm going to ask you one more time," he says, slow and gentle in the way that smothering someone in their sleep is gentle. "Where. Is. My. Brother?"

"If I tell you, will you go?"

Judah says nothing, so I nod.

She tells us.

———

As we walk back to the car, Jenna stands in the doorway of her house, Margaret's sticky baby fingers tangled in her hair.

"I loved him too, you know!" she shouts across the street, then slams the door for punctuation.

I flinch at the sound, every muscle in my body strung tight. My thoughts are fractured and racing. I don't want to have enough room for this sorrow. I want to be full of Alice and only her, protected from this new hurt, but somehow that isn't the way pain works and the world is tear-blurred in front of me. I see Noah's laughing face, soft and out of focus. I see Noah's painted hands. I see the word FOREVER on a broken wall. I see Noah's eyes when Alice came down the stairs in her Homecoming dress.

I see Noah's broken brother, holding it together with stillness and silence like a storm holding its breath.

Judah's stare is fixed in a place I'm not sure I want to go, but I can't let him stay there alone.

I don't speak as I start his car. When I turn the wrong way, further away from town and home, he doesn't say a word either.

Chapter
20

Jenna wasn't lying when she called the place pretty. Technically it's the wrong side of the river, not far enough downstream from the plastic factory for the water not to have a rainbow sheen, and the cattails along the banks are blossoming with fast food wrappers and beer cans and plastic bags—the river's natural filtration system, plucking out the debris so the suburbanites further south can enjoy it without being forced to think about the massive socioeconomic chasm in between. But two ancient willow trees trail their leafy fingers through the water, and wildflowers explode from a blanket of vivid green grass, their riotous color camouflaging the debris. The air here smells like damp earth and lavender.

Sssh, the willows whisper in a breeze too gentle for me to feel. Asking us to keep their secrets? I only asked Judah once if he wanted to call the police. *Not yet* was all he had said, and I don't push it. All we have to show them is proof of exactly what they had already concluded: that Noah had walked away from his old life voluntarily. Besides, if I could have had a few minutes with Alice to say goodbye—if the first hands to touch her cold skin could have been mine instead of a stranger's—there isn't much I wouldn't give for that.

The flora here is ravenously efficient, every shade of green pushing and tangling together, but it's clear the earth here has been disturbed, and recently. It looks more like the hungry digging of paws than the careful excavation of shovels, and I swallow hard, not allowing myself to think about what we might find.

Judah walks around the gnarled trunks, and when he comes back to me he doesn't need to ask. We go to our knees in the tumbled earth and begin scooping it away with our bare hands. It doesn't take long.

My fingers graze something firm yet yielding, white and round. Dull horror rolls through me as I register it as the toe box of a Chuck Taylor shoe.

A Chuck Taylor shoe too solid not to have a foot in it. I brush the dirt away, tracing the tiny Sharpie heart Alice had drawn there with my thumb.

"Judah," I whisper, but he doesn't respond. I scoop more dirt away.

Black sock.

Pale blue skin.

"Judah!"

"Cia." Dandelion snow floats on that sneaky breeze, swirling around Judah when he turns to me, and something shining and fragile dangles from his fingers.

"He's here," Judah says, and his voice is stripped bare. "Noah's here."

I move closer, take his hands in mine to steady them because he's shaking now, a solitary earthquake with a magnitude I can't begin to imagine. The pendant in his hands is twin to the one that's hung from his neck for as long as I've known him: two robed figures, side by side, saints of something or other. Saints who fell asleep on the job.

I don't ask if he's sure. I don't tell him it's time to call the police. I don't say anything at all.

Sssh, the trees say, and for once in my life I listen.

"I can't breathe," Judah gasps, doubling over, curling his fingers deep in the soft soil like roots with Noah's necklace still tangled between them. "I can't breathe."

I drop to the ground and wrap my arms around him. One of his hands comes up and grips my wrist hard enough to grind bone, hard enough maybe to anchor him, and neither of us lets go.

———

"How sweet," a voice drawls from behind us, I don't know how much time later. Probably only minutes, but possibly eons.

Judah whips around, on his feet in an instant and tugging me half behind him before releasing my hand.

There are four of them, the tallest clearly in charge. He looks like he'd shaved everything above the neck with a dull straight razor. A guy with beard stubble and a black beanie pulled low over twitchy eyes stands to Baldy's left. To his right, another guy with acne scars and a sprawling neck tattoo swings a baseball bat loosely at his side. The fourth wouldn't have looked out of place at Alice's debate club, generically handsome in a Teen Vogue kind of way except for the giant hunting knife on his belt.

Fear strings me tight. High school hallway brawls are all about ego, any harm done being incidental to the actual end goal of social status. I have never had to defend myself from someone whose endgame was harm itself. Until now. The hunger in their eyes tells me they like to take their time with their meals, these predators. Only one person had known where we were going to be—these four are almost certainly a love letter from Jenna, sealed with a bloody kiss.

"You fucked up," Baldy says, shaking his head in faux sympathy. "This ain't got nothing to do with you. But now you gone and seen things you shouldn't."

"We were just leaving," I say, not knowing if it's the truth. If there's a chance in hell of prying Judah away from his brother now that we've finally found him.

Baldy smiles. "Nah, that ship has sailed, bitch."

"Don't talk to her that way," Judah says, voice gravel-scratched by grief to a low growl. "In fact, don't talk to her at all. Talk to me."

"You're not nearly as pretty," Baldy says. "But I guess that don't matter. Ain't neither of you gonna be very pretty when we done here."

"What do you want?" I ask, because they didn't just come here for blood. Not that that wouldn't be reason enough for them, but it's too convenient, the timing too perfect.

The twitchy guy smirks. "Don't worry, sis, you about to find out."

Judah simultaneously tenses and relaxes, his spine going rigid while his arms hang loose by his sides, and I feel more than hear him take in a slow, deep breath. The chain tightens around his knuckles as his fingers curl. I know what he's doing, can feel the danger vibrating off him in the prickling of the fine hairs on my arms, but they don't see it, or don't recognize it because their violence is such a simple thing while his . . . has layers. Judah's darkness hides until it's time to come out and play. I've seen its shadow a few times in the past few days but he never let it slip further than that, because until today he hadn't been sure—hadn't known if I was friend or foe, if the secrets I was keeping were stained with guilt or fear.

He has no such doubts about the four people advancing on us.

"I wouldn't," he says softly.

If they hear, they only laugh.

I step to the side, away from Judah, and blast the first one to come within range—Teen Vogue—with a triple-street-legal-strength pepper spray facial, courtesy of Uncle Sean. His scream drowns out the pleas of the willows for quiet, and then it's *on*.

Judah doesn't wait any longer for them to come to us—he runs at Baldy and Twitchy, catching them off guard, and lands a punch to Twitchy's ear that sends him staggering.

I can't spectate for long. Teen Vogue is down on his knees, clawing at his inflamed eyes, but the guy with the bat shoves him aside and comes at me. I take a step back and aim the spray again, but three feet of Louisville Slugger slams into my wrist before I get more than a spritz out in his direction. Fire lances up my arm as the small canister flies from my fingers into the tangled weeds a few feet away.

I only got Slugger with enough pepper spray to make him call me names Dad really wouldn't approve of and he barrels toward me again, even more pissed off than before. I drop to my knees in the grass, searching for the canister in a snarl of green. I'm not fast enough, coming up with a Taco Bell wrapper and what I really hope is a deflated child's balloon before the bat cracks against my back.

I can't help the cry that explodes from my lungs as the air is smashed out of them. I feel my purse torn away from my body, the strap briefly catching and ripping at my hair before its weight on my shoulder is abruptly gone. I roll to the side as the bat comes down again.

This time it lands with a dull *thunk*, and Slugger frowns as the impact vibrates up his arms.

"The fuck?" he mutters.

The source of his confusion—my metal and carbon fiber leg—lashes out and catches him mid-shin. As he topples down I spare a glance at Judah, who has left Twitchy in a groaning heap while Baldy chews dirt, one elbow twisted behind him, Judah's arm crooked around his throat. Baldy's spine bends like a bowstring as he arches up, fighting for air. Judah yanks brutally on the arm he's got trapped, and the bowstring snaps, goes limp.

Slugger and I get to our feet at about the same time. He swings the bat again and I leap back, but if I go much further I'm going to be swimming, not walking. Teen Vogue is on all fours not far from me, frantically splashing river water into the raw craters of his eyes.

There's nowhere else to go.

"Hey, asshole!"

Slugger hesitates.

Judah drops Baldy's face back into the dirt, darkened to mud by their mingled blood, and stands up. He isn't unscathed, not by far—streaks of red and brown paint the left side of his face and his damp shirt clings to his skin, riding up one side of his abdomen.

"Your turn," he says, and I'm pretty sure Slugger and I see the blood in his teeth at the same time.

"Fuck this," Slugger says, and throws the bat at Judah before taking off. He swoops up my purse, and I start after him but Judah grabs my arm.

"Let it go, Cia!" The thread of fear in his voice isn't for him, and I know it, but I've lost so damn much already and watching this one last thing disappear—

"Let it go," he repeats, quieter. "You still have my keys?"

I pull them out of my pocket. Now he is the one to steady

my shaking hands as he holds them with one of his own and takes the keys from me with the other. "We have to go. Now."

Slugger's home run swing has messed with the fit of my prosthetic, and the squelchy mud and the lightning bolts still shooting up and down my legs conspire to throw me entirely off balance. Judah sees my limp and closes the distance between us, winding one arm around me.

"I'm fine," I mutter, but I slide my arm around his waist because the only other place to put it is pinned between us like a weird T-rex arm, and I can feel the curve of his obliques beneath my fingers.

"You're something," he says, and I'm not sure if that's a compliment or not, but then we're at the car and the engine is roaring and the tires make a squealy chewing sound and we're leaving Baldy and Twitchy and the pretty one weeping acid tears far, far behind.

———

"Where did you learn to channel Bruce Lee like that?"

Judah almost smiles, just enough to send a fresh trickle of blood creeping down his split lower lip. "More Hélio Gracie than Bruce Lee. Mom put Noah and me in martial arts classes when we were four or five. Noah lost interest around seventh grade."

I can tell the adrenaline is still searing through him the way it is through me, like we're both holding the same live wire. His brother's name lingers, the reason we are bleeding and the reason at least one of us can start to heal, but there is too much noise in our bloodstreams to face that yet. "Here I thought you were just a track geek."

"I only started track for the cardio conditioning. I didn't plan on taking it that seriously." He glances at me sideways as

I sift through the makeshift medical kit I've assembled on his dashboard from whatever I could scrounge at CVS. "Until a certain girl started running circles around me and I had to fight for my honor."

"Stop talking," I murmur, hoping the dim lighting of the car's interior hides the pink creeping across my cheeks as I place my fingers on his bloodied lip. It's warm, soft, and his eyes catch mine, or are caught there—I'm not sure who's hunting whom. Heat floods my skin, tingling down deep.

Focus.

I try, I really do. I gently bring the edges of the shallow cut together. Is this what falling in love is supposed to feel like? Pulling one another's wounds closed, blurring the edges between what's broken in whom? Because between the adrenaline and whatever *this* is, every inch of my body is sparking.

"This is going to burn a little," I warn him. He shrugs, and I brush liquid bandage over the snaky red line. His nose wrinkles as the stuff touches the open wound, but he is a good patient and doesn't move. I give it a few seconds to dry and apply another coat.

"That tastes terrible," he observes when I remove my fingers.

"Don't eat it then." I press a two-by-two gauze pad over his left eyebrow. The skin there had split as if it had just been waiting for the excuse, leaving him with red dirt-crusted warpaint.

"Pro athlete *and* sage wisdom," he says. "Is there any talent you don't have?"

"I can't give you the stitches you need for this." I get most of the dried blood off his skin with a saline-soaked gauze square, but the split in his brow has already started to trickle again. "Unless you want me to run back in for some dental floss and a sewing needle, you should probably go to an urgent care."

He winces. "Not gluable?"

"I can try. It'll probably reopen the second you raise your eyebrows, and even if it heals, it'll leave a serious scar."

"Don't girls like guys with scars?"

"Some girls." I hold the wound together as best I can with two fingers while I try to paint it closed with the liquid bandage. "Who don't mind their merchandise a little damaged," I add.

I rest my hand on the side of his face as I work, and his eyes don't leave my face the entire time. He waits until I am done and recap the small bottle before taking my hands in his. The hypersensitive skin effervesces awake beneath the warmth of his palms.

"Isn't everybody a little damaged?" he asks. A thin rope of angry pink stripes his knuckles where Noah's chain had dug into his skin, the chain still wrapped around his hand like a rosary. "We don't have to be defined by our damage. What matters is what we do with it. Scarred skin is tougher than skin that's never been tested, right? Broken bones heal stronger? You know that better than anyone."

The air in the car is hot, buzzy, and there isn't enough of it.

Judah gently turns my right wrist over. "Does it hurt?"

Nothing hurts. Everything hurts. I wonder why I've never noticed that his hazel eyes are struck with flecks of gold, tiger eyes, and it takes me a second to realize he means the growing violet stain where bat had met bone.

"It's not broken," I manage.

"Not broken isn't the same as not hurting." His voice is quiet. "We *both* know that."

I look down at our hands, back up to those vibrant eyes, the intensity behind them stirring up all kinds of trouble deep in me.

"Listen." He touches my bruise, whisperlight. "I need to apologize for how I acted towards you . . . before."

"No, you don't. We were on the same hunt, we just didn't

know it yet. Alice deserves that ferocity." My stomach twists. "So does Noah. God, Judah. I'm so sorry."

If ever there was a word more pathetically inadequate than *sorry* for the meaning it's meant to carry, I'd like to hear it.

His eyelashes cast shadows across his cheekbones as he closes his eyes, takes his time reopening them. They aren't dry when he does. "It's strange. Noah left almost three months ago, but I've been missing him much longer than that, and I . . ." Judah leans back against the headrest. "It's hard to explain, but I feel like we'd already been saying the world's longest goodbye. He's felt far away for a long time, even before he left. Finding him . . ." His voice fails him, and it takes a moment to come back. "Finding him now just means I've really lost him. Forever."

I can't imagine what it feels like to lose a twin. Once, when I had been Silence and not Cia, I had lost three sisters. But I had been too small, my memories of them too ephemeral, to feel that hurt as deeply as Judah is feeling this. "You wear the same necklace."

He lets go of one of my hands, fingers finding it beneath the stained cotton of his shirt. "Our grandfather gave them to us when we were born. Twin brothers Cosmas and Damian. In Brazil, where he grew up, they were believed to be protectors of children."

I don't respond right away, reluctant to break the spell that pain has wrought, to let others into the world that has formed between us, but I braid my fingers into his and he tightens his grip.

"We need to call the cops," I say at last.

"I already did. When you were inside."

I blink, through apprehension replaces my surprise almost immediately. "What did you tell them?"

"As little as necessary to get them out there." He sees my expression. "Don't worry. I left you out of it. I don't know what

Jenna's going to say, but I told them I was alone when I found him. I'll probably steal your found-Jenna-on-Instagram story though. Is that okay?"

"Very okay. I've hit my interrogation quota for the month."

"I thought you might have." He lets go of my hand and starts the car. "I should take you home."

I grimace. "How about to the border instead? *Everything* was in that purse. Dad's going to kill me when he finds out I lost my house keys and my ID. He'll have a locksmith over changing all the locks within the hour." I glance at the freshly-cracked screen of my phone. "At least that was in my pocket."

"I'm sorry about your purse." He looks thoughtful. "Those men followed us there because Jenna sent them, or someone watching the house did. Whatever my brother was mixed up in, someone didn't want him found. Do you think they took your purse to make it look like a simple mugging?"

"No. I mean, maybe that was part of it, but I think they wanted my purse because of what was in it. Or what they thought might be in it." I am pissed about losing Noah's mail. Those check stubs were the only clue we had about how he'd been spending his time since he'd gone AWOL, and the only chance *I* had at figuring out how any of this is tied to Alice.

But if Twitchy and crew had thought they were getting any more than that, they'd been sorely mistaken. I shift my arm slightly against my shirt, and there it is—a slender, firm rectangle pushing against the fabric of my bra.

After the locker break-in, I am not taking *any* chances with losing this damn flash drive. Even though it's as useful as a calcified stick of gum without the password.

Judah watches me, waiting. He doesn't know what it is, but he can tell there's more.

The ghost of his touch sparks over my skin still.

I remember how easy it seemed for him to slip into violence, like a comfortable suit well-tailored to his body.

I make a decision.

———

Somehow it's barely one o'clock, and neither of my parents are home when we pull up to my house.

Judah clearly doesn't like the fact that the bad guys have my address any more than my dads are going to, though he's trying not to be all toxic masc about it. I can't say Dad will give me the same respect. "Can I walk you in?"

"There's an alarm," I tell him.

He doesn't budge.

"Suit yourself." He follows me around back to Papa's garden, a cobblestone path that winds through a jungle of wildflowers.

"This is beautiful," Judah says, hushed.

I retrieve the spare key from beneath the hat of one of a dozen garden gnomes. "Dad planted it when Papa was going through treatment for lung cancer. Papa was basically radioactive. We weren't allowed to touch him, or even be close to him. I was too little to understand, so they sent me to stay with Will and his family during treatments. But I think it was pretty hard for Papa." I point. "That's their bedroom window. Dad wanted to give him something beautiful to look at, something that would be even more beautiful when he woke up every morning. He started with peonies—he said they symbolize healing. Then the bellflowers, for love."

"Your dad could teach Nicholas Sparks a thing or two about romance," Judah says, a smile playing at his lips.

"That's the funny thing." I shake my head. "He really couldn't. Dad's about as sentimental as the guy who shot Bambi's mom. But for Papa . . ." I try to see through Judah's eyes, to see the garden for the first time, and the depth of my parents' love for each other pulls at my heart. "For Papa, he could."

I hurry up the steps and let us in before he can see the sudden sheen over my eyes. When I think about how close we came to losing Papa, I ache with the kind of fear that only comes with true and absolute powerlessness.

Fuck cancer.

Pancakes greets us at the back door, tail swishing happily. I punch my code in to reset the alarm. "Happy?" I gesture to the panel. "Nobody's been in that shouldn't be."

"Happy is a strong word." But the alarm seems to have set Judah somewhat at ease. I walk with him back out to the garden. Pancakes winds between our legs as we descend the porch steps, then finds a patch of midday sun and flops onto her side.

"Thank you," Judah says, pausing at the gate. "For trusting me. For helping me find my brother."

I only nod, because he's touching my face, and his fingers are warm and the air is heavy-sweet with the last late blooms of honeysuckle.

"You're a strange girl," he tells me, and I like the way he says it, as if normal might be the worst thing and having explored my scars with his fingers and his questions he has lost his taste for normal altogether. "Most people run from what scares them. You . . . You get mad. You run at it full-bore."

"Yes," I say, because what else is there?

He laughs, eyes tracing my face as if seeing something unexpected there, not the girl he'd coexisted beside since grade school but something new. Something intriguing and possibly, from the apprehension edging his gaze, dangerous.

Judah's fingers find the bruised part of my jaw from Kyle K's right hook and it occurs to me that in one way or another he has found every part of me that hurts today and yet pain is the opposite of what is roaring through my body right now, and as his eyes burn into mine I know that I don't want him to stop and unless I'm still concussed from Kyle K's Hulk fist, he doesn't want to stop either.

His lips meet mine with surprising gentleness, but his mouth is hot, my blood is champagne bubbles, and his hand slides down to my jaw, my neck, and my breath is stolen away and with it, just for this broken-glass shard of time here in Papa's garden, with it goes my grief and my rage and my fear and everything, everything that isn't him.

Chapter
21

In the end I lie, which is not really my forte, but it'll cause my parents much less stress to think I had a space cadet moment and left my purse on the city bus after skipping school than to know I'd gotten mugged while digging up a body. The skipping is no secret, unfortunately, and my phone rings less than ten minutes after Judah leaves. Thankfully Papa is first on the school's call list, and he lets me off easy when I tell him I needed some breathing room from all the gossip about Alice. Dad will be a different story, one there's no point worrying about now.

I do need breathing room, but I also need an ice pack and some Advil. I gather both and retreat to my room, no longer bothering to hide my limp now that my only audience is half-blind and lost interest as soon as she realized the pills in my hand weren't treats. On close inspection I find a sweeping dent down the side of my prosthetic, but no structural damage. No capris for me until I figure out how to explain that one. I wrap my throbbing wrist in one Ace bandage and wrap the ice around it with another. I should be grateful that the bat hadn't hit any lower down my arm, or I'd be wearing a cast for the next six weeks.

But I am feeling many things in this moment, curled up on my bed in the only position that doesn't send stabbing spasms down my back, and gratitude is not one of them. Sorrow—check.

Noah's painted hands.

Noah's dimpled smile.

Claw marks in soft earth. Noah's muddy Chucks. The smell of dandelion and copper, the blood of brothers mixing in the dirt.

What would it be like to see a face so like your own in a coffin?

Fear—check.

They have my purse, ergo they have my driver's license . . . ergo they have my address. I don't even know who *they* are, and they know where I sleep. The temptation to call Uncle Sean and come clean is real and strong. He has always been a superhero to me, a bastion of strength and safety standing beside my Dad to keep Summerset safe. And yet . . . *beware the badge*, aggressivesneeze603 had warned Alice. *this town is and always has been their hunting ground.*

Paranoia? Or prophecy?

Alice was one of the most by-the-book people I've ever met, and she hadn't gone to the cops. I don't know why yet, but I'm choosing to trust her. She's never let me down before.

She never will.

Anger—check.

No, scratch that.

Fury.

Alice was right. Bad things do happen to kids here. Maybe we never fought back because we weren't aware that we are at war. *I* know, because Alice told me. I didn't listen at first, and I still don't know the face of our enemy, but I'm about to bury two of my friends. That's all the information I need to know which side I stand on.

On the list of things I don't know: why they put Noah in the ground at all. If it truly had been an overdose, why not just dump him at a hospital? Maybe that made sense in Jenna-logic, but it doesn't fly with me. You only hide a body when that body holds secrets you need to keep hidden. Serpico had turned Alice on to the idea that not only were there others like Noah, those kids dancing so far out on addiction's edge that a few were bound to fall, but that something more malevolent than gravity was to blame. How close had she gotten to the truth before they'd pushed her, too?

Close enough to see what I still can't: the thread that binds Noah's story to mine. Fire and ash, bonedust and shallow graves. John Bennett had cooked dust, Noah and the others chased it off a cliff. But that can't be all there is to it, because I know all that already. Whatever Alice had been trying to prepare me for—it's something new. Something worse.

Baldy and his sidekicks hadn't only meant to scare us off. The more I think about it, the more I believe that grabbing my purse had been at the top of their agenda. They wanted back what I'd taken. They'd gotten it, but Judah and me finding Noah before they caught up to us clearly hadn't been part of the plan.

We've lost every round so far: Noah, Alice, Alice's phone, Noah's mail. But we're still in this fight. I'd gotten more out of Alice's phone than even I had realized at first. And Judah and I had both seen the name on the corner of those envelopes.

The crack in my phone screen catches my fingertip with every swipe, promising to make me bleed sooner or later. I am trying to figure out where I have heard of Rearden Health Alliance, but Google is being about as useful as nipples on the Batsuit. This was always Alice's thing, finding things that didn't want to be found, and it's total amateur hour where I'm concerned.

I know you don't want to hear this. But there's so much more to the story.

I wish to hell I'd listened to that story when she'd been around to tell it.

Public records inform me that Rearden Health Alliance is a Nonprofit Corporation, designated Charitable, registered to a P. O. box right here in Summerset, established the year before I was born and in good standing since. Also listed is a board of directors chaired by one Arnold Miller, MD, with several other directors beneath him, most with a string of letters of their own trailing after their names. None of the names ring any bells but I write them down anyway. I chase my own tail around the state corporation commission website trying to find more information for half an hour before switching gears and following the money instead. According to their public IRS forms, Rearden Health Alliance claimed just over $12 million in assets as of their last disclosed filing two years ago, most of that in the form of "contributions and grants."

And with that my Lisbeth Salander moment has run its course. I have *zero* idea where to go from here.

I rub my eyes. My brain hurts and I'm no closer to figuring out what the hell Noah was doing for Rearden . . . or what Rearden was doing *to* Noah.

My phone chirps, the pile of neglected messages politely demanding attention. I open Snapchat. Santi hopes I'm not doing anything stupid, which I definitely was at the time she'd sent the message. Maryam has an extra copy of her notes from the English Lit class I missed today and hopes I'm feeling better.

I have messages waiting for me in two other chat threads: judah.runs.good and h4n_sh0t_f1rst. I start to open Judah's first, then feel guilty. I've been besties with Will my entire life. I only kissed Judah this afternoon, and he's already getting first dibs on my attention? That is definitely some kind of Bechdel test fail. Will it is.

> **h4n_sh0t_f1rst** 11:18
> lunch?

> **h4n_sh0t_f1rst** 11:23
> are you even here?

> **h4n_sh0t_f1rst** 11:28
> are you OK?

> **h4n_sh0t_f1rst** 12:48
> you're scaring me. please tell me you just took a mental health day and didn't fall on your head at the rock gym.

> **h4n_sh0t_f1rst** 14:56
> if I don't hear from you in ten minutes I'm coming over.

> **cia_luc0204** 14:58
> relax, I'm fine. sorry for not texting back.

> **h4n_sh0t_f1rst** 14:59
> jesus horatio christ, C, don't do that to me. why did you skip today?

I hesitate. But not for long.

> **cia_luc0204** 15:01
> call me. I'll explain.

———

Five minutes into the video chat I'd hoped would be a phone call since it's much easier to play it cool when my face doesn't give me away, Will has finally calmed down. Kind of.

"I can't believe you trust that jackal," he mutters. The black-and-blue checkered wall behind him tells me he's still at school, probably in a stairwell.

I push down a surge of annoyance. "His brother is dead, Will." I'm stretched out on my stomach, phone propped against the headboard, because if he sees me in the fetal position he'll know how much I'm really hurting, and if he knows that he'll somehow turn it into a reason to be even more pissed at Judah. "And he saved me from getting my ass well and truly kicked. I think he's more than proven himself."

"Or he orchestrated the whole thing. When did you become so naïve?"

I have no poker face, so I know my irritation shows. "Honestly, Will? Between you and Judah, one of you is the reason I have bruises and the other one is the reason I don't have more. Do you want to guess who's who or should I just tell you?"

He looks away, shame stamped across his face.

"Will—"

"No. You're right." He's silent for a moment. "I'm sorry I've been off the chain this past week," he says at last. "You deserve a better best friend than that. I have to stop thinking I'm the only one that pays for my stupidity."

"That would be nice," I say, but gently, without heat. "I'm down fifty percent of my best friends these days, so you have a lot of slack to pick up."

His smile is sad and fleeting. "Okay. So Noah was playing house with this Jenna chick and working for a company called Rearden?"

"Yeah. I know I've seen the name before, but I can't figure

out where and it's driving me crazy. Did you ever ask Gundam guy about the flash drive?"

"He's out of town all week." Will sounds as frustrated as I feel. "His sister is getting married in Germany. Really inconsiderate timing."

"No joke."

"So do you think Noah really overdosed?"

"It's possible. But so are a hundred other things. We didn't see . . ." I swallow, and Will's eyes soften. "We didn't see the whole body, but I could tell animals had been there. I'm not sure what they'll find in an autopsy. They have to do one, right? Mysterious circumstances and all that?"

"I think so. But you guys getting jumped right after talking to Mom of the Year definitely makes my Spidey-sense tingle. If it was really an accidental overdose, what are they trying to hide?"

"You ask good questions, Mason. This is why I keep you around." Last bell rings, extra loud through my phone's tinny speaker. I open Judah's message while waiting for the end of the day announcements to wrap up. It occurs to me that I haven't talked to Remy since Alice's memorial, but I'm not in the mood for another lecture—Will filled that quota already—so I put that on hold for now. He's a dual major in two hard sciences; he has enough on his hands. Remy is going to save lives someday, he doesn't need me derailing that until I have something more than bruises and bad news. And the truth is . . . he isn't what I need right now, either.

Or who I need.

judah.runs.good 14:50

| hey. no word from the cops yet. distract me?

judah.runs.good 14:51

| let's talk about your password problem.

I'd made the decision to trust him with everything I know. The messages on Alice's phone—Serpico, the Chemist. The impenetrable flash drive and its mysterious contents.

Well. Almost everything. I hadn't told him I had it on me when we went looking for Noah. Even Will doesn't know that I've carried it against my skin every moment since Alice's phone had been stolen. And I hadn't told him about Alice's other secret, the baby that had only ever breathed water.

The list of people who I know a hundred percent, a *thousand* percent, did not kill Alice is still very, very short. The only name on it is mine.

Even if Judah does kiss like it's his first language. Like my lips are a flavor he is afraid he might forget, and must commit every detail of to memory.

I force my attention back to the square of my screen currently filled with Will's anxious face. "Don't you have to catch the bus?"

"I rode my bike. Are you really okay?" Worry makes him sound younger, vulnerable.

"Really really okay." I smile at him to prove it. "Today sucked for a lot of reasons, but I think it was worth it, Will. I think we're getting somewhere."

"Fine, But no more adventures without me. We're a team, Cia. You and me, not you and Judah. Our Alice, our responsibility."

"Don't forget Noah."

"I wish I could," he says darkly, and then sighs. "Fine. That wasn't fair. But neither was leaving me out of this thing with Jenna. Don't do it again, Cia. Please."

"I won't." I glance again at Judah's unanswered message. "Listen, I have to go. Judah thinks he might be able to help me get into Alice's flash drive. I'll catch up with you later."

"You better." He ends the call.

cia_luc0204 15:25
name your price.

judah.runs.good 15:26
two more kisses

Heat creeps up my neck. And lower.

cia_luc0204 15:26
one.

judah.runs.good 15:27
one, and you tell me what's on the drive after I solve the password mystery for you.

cia_luc0204 15:27
pretty confident in yourself, huh?

judah.runs.good 15:27
not letting you down has suddenly moved rather high up my list of priorities.

I can't help the smile that pulls at my lips.

judah.runs.good 15:28
do we have a deal?

cia_luc0204 15:28
you have a deal.

cia_luc0204 15:29

> what am I going to find on there, anyway? do you have
> any idea?

judah.runs.good 15:29

> some. I know there are others like Noah, a lot of them.
> kids with records, kids with addictions & mental health
> issues. kids you wouldn't think anyone would miss.

judah.runs.good 15:30

> she wouldn't tell me who her source was, but some
> guy she met online tipped her off and sent that flash
> drive to a po box she rented. we used to meet in the
> journo club room after school. we looked through
> some of it together, but not all. she was weirdly
> protective of it.

If she'd decided to let Judah in, why not let him in all the way? What had she been protecting?

It hits me then. Me. It had to be me. She'd seen the Bennett name on one of those files and decided to go down that path alone until she could bring me in herself. That's the only reason I can think of that she would have shut him out—because as much as she trusted Noah's twin, her first loyalty had been to me.

whatever you think you know, don't trust it. trust me.

How could I have ever doubted her?

judah.runs.good 15:33

> cia?

cia_luc0204 15:33

> sorry. but she gave you the password?

judah.runs.good 15:34

> yeah. i don't know what the password was when she
> first got the drive, but she changed it right away

judah.runs.good 15:34

> she never let that thing out of her sight, so I never
> used it, and she was adamant about not writing the
> password down. it's been a few weeks but i'm pretty
> sure i remember it

I grab my laptop and drag it onto my bed. My pulse thrums in my ears as I slip the flash drive from my bra into the c omputer.

cia_luc0204 15:34

> OK. go.

judah.runs.good 15:35

> try weiweiblackwell

cia_luc0204 15:35

> now you're just stringing letters together. did you type
> that with your forehead?

judah.runs.good 15:36

> blackwell was the asylum where nellie bly went
> undercover in the 1800s. blackwell was where all
> the secrets were kept.

INCORRECT. PASSWORD?

I exhale the breath I've been holding.

cia_luc0204 15:36

try again.

judah.runs.good 15:37

damn. i know that's part of it try . . .

judah.runs.good 15:37

weiwei1887blackwell

INCORRECT. PASSWORD?

cia_luc0204 15:38

I'm starting to think you don't actually want to kiss me
again

judah.runs.good 15:38

you couldn't be more wrong, lady.

cia_luc0204 15:38

more wrong than your last two guesses?

judah.runs.good 15:39

ouch

cia_luc0204 15:39

weiwei?

judah.runs.good 15:40

noah was a huge fan of ai weiwei. heard of him?

cia_luc0204 15:41

negative, ghost rider

judah.runs.good 15:41

> he's a chinese protest artist, puts things front and
> center that powerful people prefer to keep hidden.

cia_luc0204 15:42

> i see. that's pretty on the nose.

judah.runs.good 15:42

> alice didn't have much use for subtlety. neither did my
> brother.

Understatement.

I can't stop seeing the Sharpie heart on Noah's shoe. I hope the police took Judah's call seriously.

I hope they are gentle with their shovels.

judah.runs.good 15:44

> weiwei<3blackwell

cia_luc0204 15:44

> cute

judah.runs.good 15:44

> try it.

The password box disappears, and a window with a short directory opens.

"Holy shit," I whisper.

judah.runs.good 15:45

> well?

cia_luc0204 15:45

> I can't believe you guessed that.

judah.runs.good 15:45

> part guess, part genius.

judah 15:46

> mostly genius tbh

The realization is sudden and obvious. Alice *wanted* us to work together. She hid the flash drive in a place where only I would find it, with a password that only Judah knew. She'd been fully aware that she was in danger, and we'd been her contingency plan. She knew I couldn't do this by myself, and neither could he. She'd been arranging this chessboard long before I'd known there was any game to play.

me 15:47

> so what was alice's blackwell? what secrets did she
> think were worth risking her life for?

And possibly mine?

No immediate response—I picture Judah hesitating, and anger trickles in through the cracks. What does he know that he still isn't telling me?

judah 15:48

> just take a look at whatever's on there and call me
> when you're done.

I turn my attention to the laptop.

Chapter
22

Alice had been a very busy girl.

The drive is organized into four subdirectories: DC/PME, FIRE, MEDIA, and MISSING. Most of the files are PDFs, scanned copies of records going back fifteen years.

I start with MISSING, because that's where Alice's journey started, too . . . and because I'm not ready for FIRE yet. I will be—I'll have to be. But there's no harm in stepping into the shallow end of the pool first.

There are almost four *hundred* files in here.

Four hundred kids that never came home.

That's more than the entire student body of my school.

I take a deep breath and open one near the top, AGUIL-ERA.T.16.pdf.

The letterhead reads SUMMERSET POLICE DEPT: Runaway Juvenile/Missing Person Report. Toby Aguilera, 5'8", 165 lbs, brown/brown, Hispanic/Latino, was reported missing by his mother nine years ago.

In the too-short section provided for a narrative, his mom

reported that he'd run off after a fight about him dropping out of school. She'd called the cops five days later, because that was the longest he'd ever stayed gone.

Five *days*.

I came home twenty minutes past my 9 p.m. school night curfew once after a track team pizza party went late and Dad had already called two of the other parents to make sure I was safe and sober. I know I'm lucky. I got dealt a shit hand at first, but after the fire, I guess life got tired of kicking me around. I have two parents who love the crap out of me and a home in which I have never, ever doubted my safety. Those two things alone are much more than most of these kids ever had.

Shauna Zhao, missing at seventeen, has a story similar to Toby's. So does Thomas Anderson, sixteen, and Juan Apreza, fifteen.

These aren't the kind of kids who go missing from the library, softball practice, or the ice cream parlor. These kids don't simply not come home from school after academic triathlon club, or volunteering at the nursing home.

These are kids that had been written off before the ink dried on the reports I have in front of me. Thomas had actually been gone for *three months* before his dad filed a report, and that was only at the insistence of school truancy officers when he didn't come back to school in the fall.

I read through a few more files before I come across a name I recognize, though I don't immediately remember why. Serena Clay, sixteen when she'd gone missing three years ago. Her grandparents had told the police she might have run away to be with her mom, who'd just been released from prison.

It's not until I've trudged through a few of the files in the DC/PME folder—which turns out to stand for "death certificate/post-mortem examination"—that I find Serena again amidst a sea of "Unidentified/Unknown Decedent's," and re-member where I've seen her name.

According to her file, Serena Clay died last year, just before she would have turned eighteen. Cause of death: respiratory failure due to poisoning. Manner of death: accidental. Female: not pregnant. Autopsy: not completed. Certifying coroner: T. Sato, MD, CMDI.

This—this exact file—is one of the death certificates Alice had sent to Wolf_theChemist.

I quickly find both missing person reports and death cer-tificates for the other two Alice had sent: Rohit Shah, 18, asphyxiation due to smoke inhalation six years ago, reported missing by his brother, and Reginald "Reggie" Goodwyn, re-spiratory failure due to poisoning last winter, reported missing by his mother two years ago.

I spend the next hour reading. The foundation of this city has some massive fucking cracks, if all of these kids fell through them and *nobody seemed to notice*.

The names of fifty-two dead kids are burned into my reti-nas, while the greater number of "Unknown's" are burned into my soul. My eyes ache along with my heart as I look back at the notes I've written.

Most of the missing kids are now missing adults—the oldest report goes back fifteen years. Only a handful—such as HAYES.N.17—are still legally juveniles. I wonder if that mat-ters. How many of these kids got anything resembling a search party, and how many got the locks changed behind them?

Most of the death certificates and autopsy reports match up with a missing person report, and all of their stories ended here in Summerset.

Summerset kids dying Summerset deaths, my brain whispers bitterly.

Those that cite an actual cause of death are in the minority—many of them weren't found until weeks or months after they died, the river or the earth having taken its due in the form of most of their soft tissue, leaving only bones and dogged tendons to keep the secrets of their last moments. Lots of *presumed accidentals*. Those that do have a COD tell stories of overdose, smoke inhalation, and two from cerebral hemorrhage. Of note: none of the fire-related deaths are dated more recently than five years ago. Most are way older.

Also of note: nearly all of the death certificates from the last five years are signed by T. Sato. The other signatures are either illegible or one-offs.

The fires stopped when Sato came to town?

At least on paper.

Okay. So what in the hell does it mean?

If Alice's records are up to date, there are still a hell of a lot of missing kids in Summerset, and rather a lot of dead ones. Enough to keep one small-town coroner *very* busy.

MEDIA has a handful of scanned newspaper articles, mostly about the Hayes family in the days following Noah's disappearance, a few pieces about other kids, other struggling families. It's an uncharitable thought, but looking into their grayscale faces, I don't see grief as much as I see numbness. Fatigue. I see life's steel-shod bootprint in the eyes of parents grieving the loss of their kids, parents who also think that maybe, just maybe, things will be the smallest bit easier now.

I climb down to the floor and spend a few quality minutes snuggling a drowsy Pancakes, replenishing my soul, before I open the last folder.

FIRE.

I've never actually seen a Fire Investigation Report, not even my own, even though my dad has been a firefighter for my whole life. Some judgmental types might call that repression, but I've always called it living in the present. Some of the reports in the file are so old they were still filling them out by hand at the time, but reports from the last five years are all electronic, neatly typed and way more legible than their ancestors.

My eyes go right to my file. It's one of the oldest.

I recognize my dad's handwriting immediately.

The first two pages are fill-in-the-blank style forms. With checkboxes and skinny lines covered in my dad's blocky print, they provide the skeleton of a tragedy that the subsequent ten typewriter-stamped pages flesh out with more detail than I ever wanted to know.

Our names had been written in later, in someone else's handwriting. There were no records for us—Father had felt we were *his* property, not the government's. We had all been born in that house, and if our mother had had any kind of midwife or doula to help her, I don't remember them. We did not have doctors, schools, trips to the grocery store. Our entire world had existed between the walls of John Bennett's house. Nobody had known my sisters' names until I could speak well enough again to tell them.

WITNESS 1: JOHN BENNETT, 42. DECEASED.

WITNESS 2: RACHEL BENNETT, 31. DECEASED.

WITNESS 3: ~~CHILD BENNETT~~. DECEASED. GRACE BENNETT, 7

WITNESS 4: ~~CHILD BENNETT~~. DECEASED. FAITH BENNETT, 3

WITNESS 5: ~~CHILD BENNETT~~. DECEASED. PRUDENCE BENNETT, <1

WITNESS 6: ~~CHILD BENNETT~~. SURVIVED. SILENCE BENNETT, 5

OTHER: FETAL REMAINS x2 BEHIND STRUCTURE

My fingers graze the screen, touching their names, wondering if there had been any marker for the graves behind our house. If the two children our mother had miscarried had been given names like ours.

Grace.

Faith.

Prudence.

Silence.

All things my father valued.

All things that kept his family in line, his children well-behaved.

So well-behaved that they didn't even open a window to escape when the house was on fire.

The memory cuts through my focus like a hot knife through butter.

Never touch the windows, Mother says to Grace. I am small and the house is so big. Mother is tall, and so beautiful. *The air outside is not safe to breathe. It will make you sick. Father built this house to protect us. You don't want to be sick, do you?*

I remember feeling loved and safe. Maybe I only remember feeling safe because I had been told how much there was to fear.

I should remember more. I was five when the house burned down—I wasn't a baby. I should remember more than the whispers of a dead mother.

But I don't. And I don't know if I want to.

I click to the next page.

Our property had been a little over three acres, with a two-story house as well as two standalone buildings, a workshop and a garage. The file contains floor plans for all of them.

Floor plans marked with circled X's where the bodies of my family had been found. One X for my father (W1), out in his workshop, where the explosion had started the fire that had spilled over to the main house on the breath of a dragon. One

X for my mother (W2), outside the door of another room with three more X's (W3, W4, W5)—our bedroom.

The three X's are nearly on top of one another. My heart paints the picture before my brain can tell it not to: Grace, the eldest, holds baby Prudence in one arm and little Faith in the other, pressed up against the window the floor plan tells me is there, but which led to a world that the Bennett children had been taught to fear more than the smoke creeping in from under the door.

I touch the lone X outside, between the house and the garage.

W6.

That's me.

Lying in the grass, skin and hair still smoking, breath turned to ash in scorched lungs, that was me.

Those who hope in the Lord will renew their strength. They will soar on wings like eagles.

The first photo looks like something from the set of a movie about hell itself. I don't—can't—look at the rest. Not yet. Maybe not ever.

Alice hadn't been lying about the locks.

Cia . . . Do you *remember why the doors were locked?*

Do I want to?

The report confirms it. My sisters hadn't been huddled up in their bedroom because they'd been small children frozen by fear. They had burned to death in that room because *there was nowhere else to go.*

And my mother, found outside their door, nearly beaten off its hinges by her fists, had not had the key. That, they found in the workshop, on a heavy ring with a dozen other keys.

Why hadn't I been in the bedroom too, locked in for the night with my sisters?

What had I done to be kept apart from them?

I move to the section titled **ELIMINATION OF CAUSES.**

6.1 Natural Fire Cause: Discounted, see below.

6.2 Main Gas Supply: Discounted, no gas supply to Building #2.

6.3 Portable Gas Appliance: Discounted, no portable gas appliances within building . . .

I scan further down the list.

6.9 Refracted Sunlight: Discounted, fire incident occurred at 2010 hrs, sun already set.

6.10 Deliberate Act: Discounted, all indications lead the Fire Investigator(s) to believe the resultant fire was not as the result of a deliberate act.

PROBABLE CAUSE

Chemical Reaction.

The report launches into a chemical analysis that makes my eyes cross, so I skip to the next important part: the end.

The forms and the following typed pages are signed by one Javier Lucero, FF-EMTP, with several other firefighters signing off below.

Alice was right.

I have a *lot* of questions.

I close my file and move on to the next. And the next.

And that's when I see it.

What Alice saw—why she didn't come to me right away. Why she wanted to make *absolutely sure*.

But really, it's pretty clear.

Well, something's clear. I'm just not sure yet what it means.

The year of my fire, and for a couple of years after, Alice compiled hundreds of records of house fires, all within Summerset county limits. She organized them into two folders, about a quarter going into one labeled JL and the rest into OTHER. Both folders house a mix of reports, ranging from minor accidents with minimal property damage to catastrophic or fatal infernos.

It takes me about ten minutes to cross reference the death certificates and make my list, acid crawling up my throat all the while. When I'm finished, I go back to the JL folder. Every single one of the hundred and six fire reports here lists my dad, Javier Lucero, as the lead investigator.

And his isn't the only name I recognize. According to my list, every single person with *smoke inhalation* listed as cause of death had been in one of those houses.

PART TWO

In Mexico, when we want to speak deep secrets, we drink pulgue together. It is a drink made from the cactus plant, and when you take the bottle from your mouth, it leaves a string behind, between the mouth and the bottle, like a spider's web.

It shows that the truth sticks inside.

Alejandro Jodorowsky

Chapter
23

When the knock on my door comes, I'm not surprised. I've been waiting for it. I'd heard the garage door rolling up even as I'd been making my own folder, copying into one place all the records related to the kids who'd been found dead after fires Dad had investigated.

Most of the houses in question had been either under construction or vacant, the kids presumed to be squatters. It looks like the paperwork had taken longer than any actual investigation, but I want to be fair. I want to hear what Dad has to say before I talk to Will or Judah.

"Come in."

I'm in the only chair, so Dad sits on the edge of the bed. "What's going on, Cia? I know the last week has been incredibly difficult, but skipping school? *Fighting?*" Behind the concern in his dark eyes, the stern set of his mouth, I think I see something more . . . something like fear. Or am I imagining things? "Things can't go on like this, Silencia. Talk to me."

"I had the dream again," I blurt out. It's the last thing I meant to say.

His expression softens. "The flying dream."

I slide down in my chair a little. "Yeah."

"It's been a while, hasn't it?"

At least a year since I last flew. Almost three years since I'd last awoken screaming, dragging them from their bed in the dead of night and refusing to go back to sleep until exhaustion took the choice away from me.

"Yeah." This isn't at all where I intended this conversation to go, but now that we're here, I can't stop. "I want to know about the fire, Dad. I want to know what happened to me. I think . . . I think I *need* to know."

He doesn't say anything, and I force my eyes up to his. He looks . . . haunted.

"We don't know for sure what happened to you. By the time we got there you were outside, and the fire had taken most of the house. Based on your injuries, our best guess was that you jumped. None of the others made it out."

Never touch the windows. The air outside is not safe to breathe.

I remember wooden slats nailed over windows, wide enough apart to let sunlight through but not a child. Would I have been strong enough? Brave enough?

It just doesn't ring true, somehow.

"The doors were locked from the outside. My sisters didn't get out because they *couldn't.*"

"How do you know that?" he asks sharply.

The report I hand him is still warm, hot off the press—I'd printed it quickly after I'd heard the garage open. I watch him scan the first page, the recognition instant, and skim the rest, pausing only a moment at his signature on the last page.

When he's done, he doesn't give it back. "How did you get this, mija?"

"It's public record, Dad." It's true but not the truth, not the answer he's looking for, and we both know it. "I have a right to know."

He sighs. "Of course you do. Nobody is trying to keep anything from you, Silencia. We just want to protect you. Papa disagreed, of course, but I figured maybe there was a reason you didn't remember. The dreams were bad enough without the rest."

My stomach flips. "Well, now I'm asking you for the rest."

Dad gazes over my head at the photos I have pinned to my corkboard—Alice, Santi, and me dolled up for a seventh-grade dance; Remy, Alice, Will, Aaron Raymond, and me at a neighborhood Halloween festival ten years ago; an aged and dog-eared shot of Papa and Dad kissing on their wedding day the year before they'd become a family of three. He stares for so long I think he might not speak at all, and then he does. "The fire started in the workshop. Based on the residue we found out there and the spread of the fire, Mr. Bennett was cooking with some really dangerous chemicals, and had been for a long time."

I notice he doesn't say *your father*. I'm glad. But as Alice had pointed out, there's nothing in the record about any drug paraphernalia found on premises. I don't interrupt.

"You girls were all exposed to it, probably for years. You were all so small," he says absently, and I watch as he goes somewhere else for a second, then pulls himself back. "I didn't believe the doctors at first when they said you were five years old. I thought you couldn't be more than three or four, but they said it was your teeth that told the real story, since you weren't on paper anywhere. There were no records of any of you."

"We were his," I murmur. "Only his. I remember that."

When Dad doesn't continue right away, I prompt him. "Why wasn't I with my sisters?"

"We don't know exactly what—"

"But you can guess."

He holds my gaze. "Silencia. Looking backward does not help you to move forward."

"It's my story, Dad. Not yours to keep from me."

He looks ready to argue more, but something shifts, and he lets it go. "When we found you, there was a chain wrapped around your leg, attached to a piece of metal we later identified as part of the radiator from the kitchen."

Understanding flickers, the wet tongue of horror sliding over my neck, but I wait. I have to hear him say it.

"You were chained up in the kitchen," he says softly. "Punishment for whatever a five-year-old being kept like an animal could have done to upset her crazy keeper. When the fire started it spread into the kitchen first. You tried to get away, but you couldn't get the chain off your leg, and the fire was growing . . . We figured that's how your hands got so burned. The radiator blew and you had burns from the steam as well as the fire."

I let it roll over me. I pretend he's talking about someone else, some other little girl's horrific tragedy, even though the scars are and always will be mine. "How did I get out?"

"Your mother," he says. "It looked like she pried the radiator apart with a poker. Just enough to get you free, even though she didn't have the key to the lock on the chain. She didn't have any of the keys. She was as trapped as you were. She brought you upstairs, away from the fire—probably to try to get your sisters out. But the fire was too quick, and I think . . ." He rubs his face. "I think she did the only thing she could think of to save you."

Red and peeling fingers clawing at the boarded-up window, curls of blackened skin hanging like wood shavings from my mother's slender hands. The sound of splintering wood as she wedges the length of the iron poker beneath and heaves with all her strength.

Soft lips on my forehead, whispering against the terror.

Hush now. Everything is going to be alright. Those who hope in the Lord will renew their strength. They will soar on wings like eagles.

Close your eyes, sweetheart.

It's time to fly.

I fall.

Dad is there, then and now.

Too late then, almost.

Just in time now.

———

I don't know where the tears come from, or who they're for, but they don't want to stop. A mother with a face of starlight and smoke, who loved me enough to throw me out a window but not enough to challenge her madman husband or her suffocating faith and give her children a chance at a normal life? My sisters, ash outlines on the floor of a bedroom in which not a single charred toy or doll was found?

Myself?

Dad's shirt is damp when I finally leave the comfortable space he's made for me between his shoulder and his beefy chest.

"¿Estás bien, mija?"

I nod, shifting away from him. Putting distance between us because I'm afraid if I can still feel the warmth of him, still smell his foresty Dad smell, I'll chicken out and the questions still festering in my heart will remain unasked.

"Yeah." I wipe my eyes, careful to use my left hand so as not to call attention to the Ace wrap on my other wrist. Ms.

Fletcher's *mala* rattles gently, the prayer beads I've worn every day since she gave them to me. I could use some serenity right now, but it's a futile thought, because here I sit in my glass house of secrets, about to throw one hell of a stone.

"It was a horrible thing that happened, Silencia. One of the worst I've ever seen. For you to even survive, to be ours and to thrive as you have, is a miracle. Nothing less."

I try to smile for him, but the truth is so much worse than I'd imagined, and my face has no filter. I choose my words carefully. "Dad, there's something else I want to ask you about."

"What is it?"

"Amy Cheung."

Crack, goes the glass, but it doesn't shatter as his expression slips from concerned to neutral. "Who?"

"Jordan Conway," I say. "Rohit Shah."

Crack.

Crack.

"Should I know these people?"

"They're all kids that went missing. Kids that later died in fires you investigated."

Dad's face tightens. "I've been with the fire department for almost twenty years, Silencia. I've investigated a lot of fires. People got caught in too many of them. What are you getting at?"

"There are more. Mauricio Benitez. Adeline Wong. Teresa Schmidt."

Dad is shaking his head. "What are you asking me, Silencia?"

"Kids go missing in Summerset more than they do other places. And things burn down in Summerset more than they do other places—a lot more. But nobody talks about it. And some of those kids, kind of a lot of them, showed up dead in fires you investigated. What did you find out in those investigations, Dad? What happened to them?"

Dad's eyes narrow. "They were probably drug addicts, Silencia. You probably don't remember a time before bonedust hit the streets, but I do, and this town turned inside out overnight. We were finding bodies in the streets, in school bathrooms, in movie theaters. The places they were living weren't safe to begin with, and they were either cooking drugs or falling asleep while smoking them or wiring things together to steal electricity or any of a dozen other stupid, sad mistakes that they never lived to learn from."

"Then why did the fires drop off five years ago? Because as a member of the graduating class of Summerset High, Dad, I can damn well attest to the fact that kids in this town did not miraculously start making better life decisions. But maybe the adults started telling better lies."

My voice is harsh, too loud, a blade cutting through the tenderness that had held us together only moments ago. The words pulse in the air between us, and when Dad finally speaks again, he leaves them hanging there, unanswered. "¿Por qué esta escena, de donde salió todo esto?"

"Alice," I tell him. "She was looking into the missing kids. She was looking for Noah, but once she saw the pattern she started digging deeper. I think she found something, and she got killed for it."

"Alice was sick, mija. She got depressed after Noah disappeared and she wasn't thinking clearly. You're not going to get caught up in her mistakes, Silencia. I'm not going to let that happen."

A small but persistent alarm is going off in the back of my head. "Alice was thinking perfectly clearly, Dad, and so am I. There is something wrong in Summerset—"

Dad raises a hand. "¡Basta ya! He escuchado suficiente. We've let this go on too far. We've given you the space Liam thought you needed to grieve, but I see now that was wrong. I'm not going to make the same mistake the Bookers did."

I flinch. "That's not fair. The Bookers didn't do anything wrong."

"They gave Alice far too much freedom when what she needed was boundaries. To know she was loved and safe. Instead she invented conspiracies and chased after ghosts. I'm not going to let that happen to you. You're *alive*. What happened was terrible, but you still have to go to school. You still have a future. Alice would want that for you, not for you to follow her off that cliff."

You don't know what Alice would want, I almost say, but bite my lip just in time.

Alice wanted me to find that drive.

Alice wanted me to finish what she'd started.

Dad stands up. "You're grounded, Silencia. Effective immediately. No car. Straight home after school unless approved by me or Papa in advance. Do you understand?"

I'm still blinking at him in shock when he holds out his hand. "License."

"What?"

"I said no car. We will take you to school and pick you up."

"How? You both have work."

"I'll leave early," he says. "Or Papa will."

"Dad—"

"Your *license*, Silencia. Now."

Heat flooding my veins, I glare at him. "It was in my purse, *Dad*. It's gone."

"Fine."

"You don't have to do this, Dad."

He turns back at the door. "I think I do. You need to understand that we are not going to lose you, Silencia, and we are not going to let you lose yourself. What happened to Alice is awful, and we all wish she were still with us. But she isn't, and you are, and that means you have to keep moving forward." Silhouetted in the doorway, he is a faceless outline. "That means you have to start letting go."

"Never," I whisper to the empty space he leaves behind, and my glass house finally collapses around me.

I gave him a chance to tell me the truth. I gave him *every* chance.

Dad is lying to me.

I feel like I'm going to be sick, and a moment later, I am. The bathroom tile is freezing, or I am hot, or both. My thoughts tangle up in each other, all teeth and anxiety and fear.

I wasn't certain before, but I am now: whatever this is, my dad is involved.

I'd been willing to be convinced of some kind of unlikely coincidence—*desperate* to be convinced. But he'd barely even tried. Instead he'd iced me out and put me on lockdown. That looks a lot more like a guilty conscience than a clear one.

The man who had literally breathed me back to life, who'd given me his name when my own was too heavy for a child to carry—he's hiding something from me.

I reach for my phone.

Judah's number goes straight to voicemail. I hang up without leaving a message, but my phone blips a moment later.

judah_runs_good 18:43

cops are here. they found him. call you later.

My chest sinks, pain layered on pain pushing my ribs in until my heart protests. There is no Mr. Hayes, hasn't been since he beat feet when the twins were almost thirteen. Judah is all

their mother has. She needs him now way more than I do . . .
even though I ache at the thought of his arms around me in the
garden, his lips and the smell of him laced with honeysuckle
and sunshine.

cia_luc0204 18:44
I need your help.

h4n_sh0t_f1rst 18:44
anything.

Chapter
24

Will shows up half an hour later via door instead of window, so my dads can't be too grumpy.

"She's grounded, Will," I hear Dad say as he escorts Will to my bedroom. "Ten minutes, door stays open."

"Yes, Mr. Lucero," Will says, and I roll my eyes so hard I think they might go back into my head. "I just wanted to bring her the Pre-Calc homework that's due tomorrow, because the teacher said there's going to be a pop quiz."

"That kind of takes the pop out of pop quiz, doesn't it?"

Will laughs dutifully. I sit up as he comes in, shift my crutch so he can sit down. I don't want my parents to see the dent before I've come up with a workable explanation, and my leg is throbbing anyway, so I've left the prosthetic off all evening.

"Ten minutes," Dad repeats before heading back to the living room.

"Yes, Mr. Lucero," I mimic Will.

He makes a face. "Hey, one of us has to stay on his good side."

"You're not even in my Pre-Calc class."

He drops his backpack on the floor. "Then you probably don't have a pop quiz, either," he says.

"That's the best news I've heard all day." I give him a hug. I'm glad he's here. As I pull away he sees my wrist; the Ace wrap has ridden up to show the spreading bruise.

"Christ. Are you sure you're okay?"

I nod. "My back is pretty sore, too, but nothing serious. Judah's the one who's going to have battle scars, since he wouldn't go to urgent care."

At the mention of Judah's name, Will's face sours. "He should have kept you safe."

Irritation spikes through me on so many levels, but before I can retort, Will holds out both hands in submission. "I know, I know. Never mind. Sorry. Moving on. So your dad stonewalled you?"

"Worse. He didn't just deny that he was involved, Will. That would have been easier. He completely shut me down, and now this house is my personal Alcatraz." My shoulders slump. "I didn't want to believe it. Even when I saw his name on all those documents . . . Like he said, he's been a firefighter for almost twenty years. That's a *lot* of fires, and of course people died in some of them. I wanted to be convinced, Will. I wanted him to have an explanation that made just the smallest bit of sense—I would have bought it. But he didn't even try." I hug myself. "I've never seen him look so cold, Will. Never."

"He's hiding something," Will agrees. "So . . . let's find out what it is."

Before I can ask, he lifts his hip and slides something out of his back pocket onto my bed.

I gasp. "How do you have my dad's cell phone?"

Will shrugs. "He left it sitting on the kitchen counter." His voice is a low whisper. "And if he's watching the clock—which, knowing your dad, he is—we have exactly eight minutes left before I get the boot. So I hope your password cracking skills have improved since the Great Flash Drive Caper."

I grab the phone. It only takes me four guesses to figure it out: it's the date my adoption was finalized. Sorrow sparks and gutters—I don't have time for that yet.

I open his email first. His inbox is about as boring as it gets, all work and mortgage and one exchange that leads me to believe he's thinking about taking Papa on a cruise for their upcoming anniversary. His messages aren't any more interesting—I only peek at his exchanges with Papa long enough to conclude there is no big bad conspiracy there, only differing opinions about parenting and what kind of protein to use for Taco Tuesday.

Then the phone vibrates in my hands.

New message from ID BLOCKED. Open?

Hell yes, I open.

⚠ BLOCKED 19:31

> You said this was under control. Obviously, you grossly overstated your ability. If you don't take care of this, I will. And I promise, neither you nor your inquisitive daughter will like that.

Will looks over my shoulder. "Whoa," he breathes. The phone rumbles again.

⚠ BLOCKED 19:31

> Never forget, Javier: what was given can be taken away.

"What does that mean?"

I shake my head, still stunned. Proof: I am holding it in my hands. Someone is threatening my dad. They have something on him and they're using it to keep him in line—using *me* to keep him in line. But what's the rest?

I feel sick again. Will puts his arm around me. "Hey," he says, forcing my attention away from the phone. "Look. All we know is that your dad is trying to protect you. Let's not jump to any conclusions further than that, okay?"

"That's not all we know," I whisper. "Will, he's in this. All these missing kids, these fires—*he's* what ties them together. He covered something up."

"Maybe," he says. "But he's not the only thing. What about the doctor that signed off on all those death certificates but didn't bother to do a single autopsy? And the fact that we'll never know how most of the others died, because someone made sure they weren't found until all the evidence rotted or burned away? This isn't just about whatever your dad may or may not have done more than five years ago."

"Why are you defending him?"

"Because I don't want you to get tunnel vision." He glances down the hall. "Time's almost up, Cia. I have to get this bad boy back on the kitchen counter before your dad comes to haul me out of here. You should probably delete those messages."

I frown, but he's right. Obviously my dad has spoken with this person before and deleted all previous communications. There is no way to mark the messages unread—he will know they've been seen. I hurriedly delete them before I can change my mind and hand the phone back to Will.

He disappears for a minute, and I hear the hall bathroom sink running before he comes back, hands empty. "Done and done," he says. "But listen. There's something else."

I am so in my own misery that it takes me a beat to realize he's waiting for a response. "What?"

"I looked up the names of some of those kids you mentioned. The ones who died."

"And?"

"Noah was friends with at least one of them."

I look up from the phone. "Who?"

"Reggie Goodwyn. He was part of the whole Warhol-wannabe underground art scene Noah was into. He's in a couple of Noah's older pictures on Instagram."

"Show me."

Will plays with his phone for a second. "Here."

The picture is from last October—only a few weeks before what Reggie's death certificate danced around labeling a fatal overdose. He'd lived off the radar for over a year after he'd gone missing. I wonder if, like Noah, he'd wrapped a new family around himself to keep the dark at bay.

Reggie Goodwyn is gorgeous—*was* gorgeous. With dreads down to his waist and a smile that looks like an ad for cosmetic dentistry, he's a little on the thin side in the photo, but he looks happy. The sleeves of his flannel are rolled halfway up his arms, but I squint and think maybe that bruise-smudged shadow in the hollow of his elbow could be the footprint of a needle.

Another satisfied bonedust customer?

I wonder if gorgeous Reggie was the one to introduce Noah to dust. I wonder if there even had been a *one*, or if Noah's brand of nonconformity and rebellion-via-creation had left him chasing inspiration down deeper and deeper burrows until he just couldn't claw his way back up again . . . or if Reggie's death had driven him there. I'd never heard Noah mention Reggie, but then I'd never really heard Noah talk about anyone except Alice, or Judah every now and then.

Is it possible my dad isn't lying? That Reggie, Serena, and the rest of them just took hard paths that met hard ends, case closed? It's possible.

But in the few minutes between the time the garage had opened and Dad knocking on my door, I'd run the same numbers Alice had. I'd stacked Summerset's tragedies against a dozen other towns our size, and we won by a landslide. Or lost, depending on your perspective. Either we live in the unluckiest town on the planet, or we're right.

Dad's heavy footfalls in the hall signal the end of this session of the Summerset Conspiracy Club.

Will squeezes my hand and stands up. "I'll see you tomorrow," he says. "See if you can make it through an entire day this time."

I grimace. "I don't think I have much choice."

From just beyond the doorway, Dad says, "She'll be there. Let's go." Further down the hall I faintly hear him offer Will a ride home, but Will's jailors are more lenient than mine and he's got his bike to cover the handful of blocks between our houses.

Dad's always been the less polished parent, but he's never used his anger to intimidate me before. He's never made me feel small.

Never forget, Javier: what was given can be taken away.

What had been given? Money?

It's always money. But here in the quiet isolation of my room, a tiny voice whispers something even darker.

Me?

No.

My dads are the superheroes of my story. Period. They are everything a broken little girl needed them to be. This can't poison that, too.

I curl into myself. The Advil is wearing off and I am five

feet five inches of pain, which is somehow negligible compared to the beating my heart just took. For a brief, fierce moment, I let myself imagine a world where everything could go back to the way it was. Where Dad scoops me up like he had when I was little and tells me whatever lies I need to hear. I believe him. And I feel safe again.

Chapter
25

The vibration of my phone against my hip wakes me up, which seems impossible because that requires falling asleep, and yet it appears I've done both. Groggy, I drag it out from underneath me. It's just after ten, and Judah's calling.

"Hey," I say, quiet. Dad didn't exactly give me comprehensive parameters for this whole grounded thing, but I'm guessing late night talks with non-Will boys might be off my short list of privileges right now. I grab my crutch and use it to nudge the door closed.

"Hey." He sounds weary, all the energy wrung from his voice. "Did I wake you?"

"I'm glad you did. How are you? How's your mom?"

"Finally asleep." Pause. "In Noah's room."

"Oh."

"Between the Johnnie Walker and the Xanax, I had to carry her up there. But at least she'll get some sleep."

I haven't seen Judah's mom since the track championship sophomore year, but I remember a petite, soft-spoken woman with smile lines almost as deep as her worry lines. I know first-hand what a warm and safe place Judah's arms can be, and I am glad she has him. I think of her burrowing into her other son's space, wrapping sheets that still hold the memory of his skin and his dreams tight around herself.

"She insisted on seeing the . . . on seeing him. We haven't been home long."

I wonder if the medical examiner took Noah to the same place as Alice. If this is how Alice's last wish was granted, like the most awful fairy tale where they are blue instead of the genie, forever cold and wishless. "Did you see him?"

"Yes."

"Judah." His name is soft on my lips. I don't ask if he's okay, because he isn't. There is no universe in which you can see a corpse with a face so like your own that you know the mirror will never truly be only yours anymore, and be okay.

I listen to the sound of him breathing for a minute. The lack of words isn't awkward for some reason, doesn't actually feel like a lack at all. Just grief recognizing itself.

"Jenna wasn't lying about him getting sick, Cia. He had scars on his stomach."

"What do you think it means?"

I can almost hear him shaking his head. "I don't know. Maybe nothing. Maybe something." A clink, the muffled sound of scotch being downed much faster than its makers intended. "God damn it, Noah," he whispers.

My eyes blur with sudden sorrow. This is too heavy. Too much. It's not fair that he's alone tonight, left to stand vigil for Noah all by himself. I wish I was there with him, wish I could wrap myself around him the way his mom has cocooned herself in Noah's memory.

"Anyone who tries to tell me that any of this is part of

God's plan," Judah says at last, "is getting punched in the fuck-ing face."

"I call seconds."

"It's yours."

I almost smile.

"Okay." he says, and his breathing shifts; it sounds as if he's walking up stairs. Heading to his own bedroom? "Distract me again. You've been through the drive. Tell me what you know."

I tell him. I tell him all of it, including Dad's nuclear reac-tion to my questions and what I'd found in his phone afterward. When I am finished, Judah adds another piece to the puzzle that neither Will nor I had noticed: of the very, very few kids who'd warranted full autopsies—none performed on Dr. Sato's watch—nearly all of them had bonedust in their system.

Judah hadn't noticed it either, actually. But Alice had, and she'd pointed it out to him. Only Alice had noticed words like diacetylmorphine and phenethylamine and methylone recurring in the dense cluster of lab results that may as well have been Sanskrit to me. Only Alice recognized their signif-icance in the chemical formulation of the designer drug that had ignited the Summerset party scene like a match dropped into kerosene.

Aaron Raymond had had a faceful of dust before he went American Psycho on Alex Franklin, setting into motion the domino fall that put him in the ground. Its promises aren't worth the dirt we threw on his coffin.

"The fires. Your dad. That's what Alice wouldn't show me."

"I think she was trying to protect me." It hurts to say out loud. "That's what she wanted to talk about when you saw us arguing in the quad. I don't think she meant to keep it from you, but I think she felt like I should know about it first."

"I get that." Judah considers this. "Then you know

everything I know, now. Something is wrong with this town. Kids go missing and it's like they were never here to begin with. They die in fires that statistically should not have happened. But nobody says anything because these aren't kids anybody misses." Anger gilds the pain behind his words. "Not anybody that matters, anyway."

"Easy prey," I say. "Half of the missing persons reports were only filed because Child Protective Services or truancy courts got involved."

"People paid to care."

"Or at least to file paperwork that makes it look that way."

"So young to be so jaded, Lucero."

"You and I both know the system chews up kids like me every day. I got lucky. Most kids don't."

"I think you earned every bit of luck you've ever had, and then some."

My chest warms.

"You're right, though. When you have nobody asking questions, you have perfect victims. And so many of them become victims. We bury more kids than a town twice our size . . . and those are just the ones we find. You saw how many missing persons reports there are. How many street kids do you think have no paper trail?"

If the number of "Unidentified Decedents" in Alice's records was any indicator, the answer is *a lot*.

The answer is too many.

"Listen," he says, as if I'd ever stopped. His voice is softer but still tense; he must be exhausted. "When Alice died the day after she told me she was going to bring you in, it seemed obvious that something had gone sideways there. I didn't know if I could trust you. But Alice never doubted you, and I shouldn't have either."

"You were being loyal to Alice. I'll never be angry at you for that." Part of me still wants more than anything to crawl back into Dad's arms, to say that I'm sorry, and to let him convince me that my worst fears are wrong. "Maybe nobody in this town is what they pretend to be."

"Maybe not," he agrees. "Be careful around your dad, Cia, okay? We don't know who's threatening him, or how far he'll go to protect his secrets."

"My dad would never hurt me," I say automatically.

"What about Alice?" Judah asks. "What about me? If he thought he was protecting you, can you say for absolute certainty he wouldn't hurt someone else, to try to scare you away from this?"

Never, I want to say. *Not in a hundred million years. My dad plants peonies for the man he loves and saves little orphan girls from burning houses.* But now, for the first time, I have reason to doubt that last part. Because the sick thing stretching tentacles out through my gut is whispering, *What if it wasn't a coincidence he was there that night?*

What if he had something to do with my fire?

I say nothing to defend him. I say nothing to accuse him.

"Just . . . be careful. We know almost everything Alice knew, and they killed her for it."

"We've learned so much and I still feel like we don't know anything, Judah. Where do we go with all of this?"

"We dig into these Rearden people, find out what they were doing with my brother. If they were involved with any of the other missing or dead kids. We look at who filed each of their missing persons reports, and we find *them*, and figure out if those kids had anything in common besides bonedust. And if that's all there is, then we dig into that. Where did they get it? Who did they do it with? What did they do to get it?" He sighs. "It's not the clearest roadmap, but it's the one we've got."

"We're still missing something important." I drag my fingers through my hair, wince as they catch on a tangle. "Serpico."

"Alice's source."

"He used her, Judah. He hid behind Alice and let her face this alone. Whoever he is, he's in this, and he has something to lose. I would bet anything that he knows exactly who killed Alice."

"But he's a ghost."

"He's a ghost," I echo, frustrated.

Judah hesitates. "I might have a lead on that."

"Tell me."

"There's nothing to tell yet. I'll tell you if it comes to anything, but it's probably another dead end."

I frown, and then realize how lucky I am that neither of my dads has come in to say goodnight given the late hour. "I better go before my dads remember they forgot to ground me from my phone."

"Alright. Hey, be careful at school tomorrow. I won't be there to have your back, so try not to start any fights, okay?"

"Yeah, yeah."

"And Cia . . ."

I wait.

"Noah would have liked this," he says quietly. "Us, I mean. Whatever this is."

My skin hums again. I like how the word *us* sounds on his lips. "Good," I tell him. "Because I think I like it too."

———

Papa pokes his head in just before I click my light off to let me know he'll be taking me to school in the morning. There's softness in his eyes that tells me he doesn't fully agree with Dad's executive order but will support him in the name of parental solidarity, which I think is kind of like Ephialtes betraying the valiant Spartans but don't tell him so because he'd probably give me a history lesson that won't paint me quite so favorably.

I lay in bed for what feels like hours, but sleep doesn't come back. Dad's words percolate in my mind, ricocheting off the fragments of older memories, all of them sharp, all of them cutting into me.

You have to start letting go.

"I will never let you go," I whisper to the pale blue moonlight spilling over my ceiling, to the ghost-girl who lives somewhere beneath my heart now, to Alice, who will never graduate or break a huge story or get married or kiss the powdersoft forehead of the child she and Noah made. I will carry her with me for all of those moments because I'm all she has left.

And I will get the bastard that killed her.

My thumb slides over the cracked glass of my phone screen without thought, guided by a need I cannot name. Guided by Alice herself, maybe.

> **silencia_luc**
> You fucked up.

My words fly through time and space toward their target, instant and irrevocable.

No going back now.

> **silencia_luc**
> Are you there?

silencia_luc

Of course you are. You have
nothing better to do than hide
behind a screen and make
threats. Here's one you might
like: You fucked up when you
killed my friend. We're coming
for you.

The response comes swift.

Wolf_theChemist

Self-righteousness looks cute
on you.

silencia_luc

An orange jumpsuit is going to look
cute on you.

Wolf_theChemist

I bet this looks cute on you, too.
[image loading . . .]

It's my bra, stolen from my gym locker, draped across a
white pillow.

Wolf_theChemist

You pretend to be so good, but this
tells a different story. It still has your
scent, you know. If I close my eyes I
can see you in it.

Wolf_theChemist

> Smell you in it.

Rage sears through me, black and deep, a kind of fury I have never felt before. Knowing he's using this violation to try to shake me doesn't make my skin crawl any less.

Wolf_theChemist

> If you really want to play, we can play. But you won't like my rules.

Wolf_theChemist

> Cat got your tongue?

Wolf_theChemist

> Oh, you don't have a cat.
> That's right.

Wolf_theChemist

> Just a deaf old dog who wouldn't even hear me coming.

Chapter
26

I drag myself around the house the next morning with the zest of a zombie. My lack of sleep is carved into half-moons beneath my eyes. Dad's gone by the time I'm out of the shower but he's left me a cup of coffee the way I like it, one cream no sugar.

I'm sipping my coffee and staring outside when Pancakes comes in through the dog door, the old plastic flap slapping the trim and nearly making me spill hot coffee all over myself. The threat from last night rebounds front and center into my thoughts.

But he won't come near this house in broad daylight, and Pancakes stays in at night, I try to convince myself.

My block is part of an older neighborhood, and trees grow thick here, their roots and limbs entwined with bushes and flowering shrubs to create what's always been kind of a dreamy feeling of dancing shadows. When I was little, I used to try to find all the hidden burrows under the shrubs, the places where the trees hollowed out a space just big enough to cradle my body during hide and seek on warm summer evenings, the fireflies silently promising not to give me away.

But the shadows don't feel dreamy now. They feel menacing. And the secrets being kept have been paid for in the blood of the same children who used to laugh and play here, fearless and fragile—so much more than we ever thought.

Dad thinks I need to let go, but I should have held on tighter. I should never have let Alice slip away these past few months.

Santi's words from the other day toy with my memory, echoing Dad's sentiment.

People are dead, Silencia. Maybe you should let Alice, and her secrets, rest in peace. For everybody's sake.

I frown. Something isn't quite right.

I put the coffee down, look out at the empty place where Alice's car should be sitting as she waves frantically at me to hurry, because if we aren't fifteen minutes early we're late in Alice Standard Time.

People are dead, Silencia.

People.

Plural.

But at the time, I'd only known about Alice. Noah had still been only missing.

Except Santi knew better.

I pour the rest of my coffee down the drain. My heart doesn't need any more fuel—it's already slam-dancing against my ribs.

What else does Santi know?

———

My homeroom teacher doesn't hesitate to write me a pass to go to the guidance office when I ask two minutes after the bell rings. I disappear the moment he ticks my name off the attendance list.

I look back at the Snap of my bruised wrist I'd sent Santi this morning, more to get her attention than her pity.

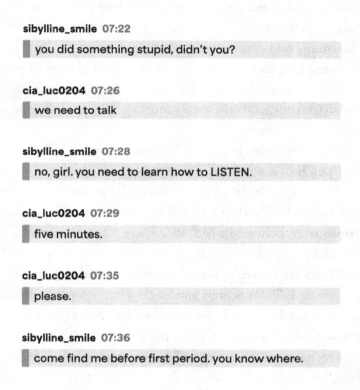

sibylline_smile 07:22
you did something stupid, didn't you?

cia_luc0204 07:26
we need to talk

sibylline_smile 07:28
no, girl. you need to learn how to LISTEN.

cia_luc0204 07:29
five minutes.

cia_luc0204 07:35
please.

sibylline_smile 07:36
come find me before first period. you know where.

King Minos's labyrinth has nothing on the maze behind the auditorium, and Santi has not left me a trail of thread to follow. After five or six wrong turns I think I am on the right path when the air shifts, subtly, to moth-eaten satin and candlesmoke, the light amberwax.

A shattering crash breaks the spell, and before I have time to think, I break into a run.

I push aside the velvet curtain to Santi's lair.

At first glance the room looks empty. Several of the

low-hanging cantina lights have gone dark. An ephemeral curlicue writhes up from a cone of incense and the only sound is my own uneven breathing.

Then the darkness drips.

The lights have not gone out. They are covered in something thick and dark, and suddenly I have tunnel vision, the edges round and swimmy.

Everything in here is wrong. Broken glass glitters all over the floor, the patchwork rugs diamond-struck, and a thick crack runs diagonally across the vanity mirror.

"Santi?" I whisper.

The room holds its breath. Waiting for me.

I step inside, and finally, I see it.

Smeared across the paisley wallpaper, huge slashes of paint spell out: **MY GAME**. Over and between the bulbs hanging forlorn from bent nails: **MY RULES**. I take an involuntary step back, my breath catching somewhere between lungs and lips. Then my tunnel vision zeroes in on something, a heeled boot on its side, innocuous amidst the chaos of strewn fabric and loose pearls and hollow-eyed masks, except for the fact that this particular boot has a leg coming out of it.

I race around the vanity and drop to my knees beside Santi's still form, facedown on the floor in a sea of shrapnel from the overturned side table.

She's breathing, but too shallow and too fast, and her hair is matted to the back of her head, and the sticky puddle I'm kneeling in is too warm to be paint, too vital to be on the outside. A smear of not-paint ends a few feet away: Santi must have crawled over here before losing consciousness.

My game. My rules.

He'd warned me. I hadn't listened.

This is my fault.

I grab a fistful of shimmery chiffon and use it to support Santi's head as I carefully, so carefully, roll her onto her left side, the recovery position, to protect her airway—basic first aid concepts jabbing through the veil of panic that's rapidly descending over me. Junior EMT class doesn't cover finding one of the few friends you have left with her head cracked like an eggshell. What the hell do I do now?

What if whoever did this is still close?

I'm not leaving Santi.

I repurpose a scarf of gauzy white linen, holding it to the back of her head. The broken flesh shifts under the thin fabric between it and my hand, and my stomach somersaults.

What if they're coming back?

I shake off the thought and reach for my phone, holding pressure on Santi's wound as best I can while the dark stain of her blood creeps through the linen.

I give the 911 operator all the information I have, which is not enough, then put the phone on speaker before setting it on the floor. Glancing around, I grab the only weapon I can find—a shard of mirror glass the size and shape of a slice of pizza from under the vanity.

The fingers of Santi's left hand uncurl, bloodied petals unfolding to reveal a scrap of paper in her palm. I only glance at it long enough to realize what it is before I shove it into my pocket and refocus my attention on keeping my friend safe.

I hold my weapon in sweat-slick fingers, fix my gaze on the velvet curtain, and wait for whoever finds us first.

Chapter

27

After an eternity of soft silence, of waiting, of fear so thick it could choke you, time suddenly jumps into high gear. The first person through the doorway is a school security officer, French braid and serious eyes and calm voice and belt full of weapons ready to be deployed if calm turns out to be the wrong approach. Then it's all flashlights and loud directives and firm hands on my arms, and my mirror-knife dropping to the floor to be ground back into sand by a paramedic's boot, and the adults are in control and the fear eases its grip on my throat and I can breathe.

I'm standing outside behind a fire exit surrounded by the principal, two uniformed cops, the security officer, Ms. Fletcher, an EMT, and a couple of other people whose function isn't immediately clear. The abrupt brightness of daylight turns the edges of everything to shimmery lava, my pupils constricting painfully.

The EMT wraps the shallow cut on my palm from the mirror-knife in gauze and doesn't look twice at the myriad other scars tracing up my forearm. From what I can tell, the cops want to take me to the station to give a full statement and Ms. Fletcher and the principal want to wait for one of my parents to arrive.

"Is she under arrest?" Ms. Fletcher wants to know.

"Of course not," one of the cops replies, annoyed.

She crosses her arms. "Then it can wait until she has a parent present."

"She's a minor," Principal Holland reminds everybody who might have forgotten since Ms. Fletcher informed them of that fact two minutes ago. "It's really best if she stays here until her parents arrive."

"Really a pain in my ass," the other cop mutters.

"I don't have anything to hide," says the girl hiding the card from Santi's hand in her pocket and a flash drive full of secrets in her bra. "I'll go. Tell my dads to meet me there."

Principal Holland frowns, and Ms. Fletcher touches my arm. "You don't have to go anywhere. You have every right—"

"If it helps them figure out who attacked Santi, I want to do it." Lie. I do want to figure out who attacked her, but nothing I have to say is going to help the cops. I am positive the police had my enterprising friend on their radar long before today, and not in the role of victim. I want to know what they know. I also want very much to not be *here* anymore, and downtown is as good a place as any. Dad can't be mad at me for missing school to help the police solve a crime.

Ms. Fletcher looks down at her mala wrapped around my wrist. "You're a very strong person, Silencia. It's okay to ask for help sometimes. Why don't I come with you?"

The cops and I all speak up at the same time to shut down that idea, and so it is that less than half an hour later I'm sitting on a plastic chair with a molded butt imprint that seems designed to mimic the discomfort of a wedgie while a Violent Crimes detective named Yates takes my statement. It is a remarkably effective and subtle interrogation tactic, especially when your witness is trying hard to be stoic through the strenuous objections of a bruised spine.

I like Yates. She reminds me that even though the law says I can voluntarily speak to the police as a witness even without my parents present, I have every right to wait for them if I want, and I again say no thanks. She looks relieved. I think we both know that once Dad gets here, this whole process is going to get even less fun for everybody involved.

Yates listens to my story, asks relevant questions. I weave together enough half-truths to hopefully form a convincing picture. Yates is smart, but I'm being so cooperative I don't think she knows whether to trust her BS meter or not. The story: I went down to talk to Santi about Noah being found at last because I knew they'd been friends (half true—Santi had already known Noah was dead, and in hindsight she'd been pretty upset about it). I didn't see or hear anyone else (true). I don't know who would want to hurt her (more or less true). I'm not aware of anyone at school making any more dumb or hateful comments than usual toward those that don't fit into their approved categories of how people should look and love and be (true).

Yates gets up to grab something from the printer, across the busy room. The furniture in here looks like someone's first go at Tetris, all L-shaped desks and modular tables at odds with one another.

Two desks away I see a familiar, though far from friendly, face. Detective Rojas is on the phone, his round face in profile as he speaks heatedly to someone on the other end. His spidey-sense must tingle because he glances over at me.

I look around but Yates hasn't returned yet, so I take the opportunity to go chat with Rojas. I'm feeling strangely buoyant, almost manic. Maybe this is what happens when your brain can't process any more trauma—it stops trying to keep you safe with fear, and just emboldens you for whatever stupid thing you were going to do next anyway.

"What are you doing here?" he asks, not bothering with a goodbye to whoever he'd been talking to before disconnecting the call.

"A friend of mine got attacked at school. I found her."

I can see him struggling. He knows I'm hiding something, suspected as much before I actually was. The thing is I think he might actually be a good cop, simply because he's so unpleasant and tactless, and I think the real bad guys might try a little harder to defy the stereotype. If I'm right, I want to know if he's still buying the suicide story or if he might actually help me find Alice's killer.

"I'm sorry about your friend," he says gruffly. "As you can see, I'm very busy here."

"Busy finding out who killed Alice Booker?"

His black eyes search my face. This guy is *intense.* "Is there something I should know, Miss Lucero?"

So much.

But I can't give it to him. Not yet. There are miles of uncertainty between *thinking* he might be a good guy and *knowing* he can be trusted. "Just that Alice didn't kill herself. But you know that already, because I've been telling you since day one."

"Anything else?" He gives nothing away. "Perhaps pertaining to the discovery of the body of Noah Hayes less than twenty-four hours ago?"

"That does seem suspicious. I'm glad you're looking into it," I say.

Irritation darkens his already flushed skin, but before he can answer, his partner sidles up and plops a hip on the cluttered surface of Rojas's desk.

"If it isn't the accomplished daughter of our esteemed Battalion Chief," Timmerman observes, sounding pleased. A day's worth of stubble contours a square jaw, and his blue eyes are clear. He looks like he should go back in time a few decades and film a surfing movie with Kate Hudson.

By the look on his face Rojas agrees with me. "Get your bony ass off my desk."

"Relax, Frank. Your triglycerides are showing."

I can't help it; I snort, and Timmerman smiles at me. "Oh, hey. I heard a kid got attacked at your school. Were you there?"

"I didn't see who attacked her. She was already unconscious when I found her. Have you heard if she's going to be okay?"

"I haven't. I'm sorry," he says, looking the part. "You've had a rough go of it lately, haven't you? Your friend Alice, and now her boyfriend turns up dead too."

I can't swallow his empathy. For some reason, Timmerman just *bugs* me. Maybe I should talk to somebody about my inherent mistrust of attractive men. "Yes. Detective Rojas and I were just talking about how suspicious that is."

"We weren't, actually," Rojas says.

"Do you think she knew he was dead?" Timmerman asks me. "And that's why she did what she did?"

"She didn't do anything but love him," I snap. "And try to find him when *you* guys gave up. If you ever really tried in the first place."

He holds up his hands. This guy's amiability really is obnoxiously unshakeable. "Hey, I'm not the enemy here."

"That doesn't make you a friend, either. Not if you're not going to do your job and find out who killed my best friend."

Whatever he might have said is lost when Detective Yates appears over his shoulder. "I'd like my witness back, if you don't mind."

"She's all yours," Rojas says.

Timmerman gives a half-wave. "See you later, Silencia."

"I didn't realize you were friends with Alice Booker," Yates tells me as we walk back to her desk. I can feel Rojas's gaze drilling into my back. "I'm sorry for your loss. From all accounts she was a great girl."

"Thank you." I start to sit down, but then my muscles freeze, locking me in place. "What the hell?"

What has caught my eye are three cops leading a hunched-over figure in a hoodie I know all too well toward a closed door on the far side of the room.

"Why is he here?" The question comes out in a whisper as my fling with manic chutzpah comes to a grinding halt.

Yates follows my stare. "He's being questioned about your friend's assault."

"He didn't have anything to do with it!"

"Then he'll be fine," Yates says reasonably. "They're just going to ask him some questions—"

"No!" I cut her off. "Handcuffs aren't for questions. They're for when you think you already know. But you're wrong!"

He can't possibly hear me at this distance, but Will raises his head anyway. His beanie is crooked, the shadows under his eyes are bruise-dark, and he looks like a dog who has been kicked so hard and so many times that the entire world has become a boot.

I can't watch this.

"Will!" I push past Yates to run toward him.

Two of his escorts close ranks, and someone calls my name, but I don't stop until I am stopped, and then I glare at the large hand holding my arm.

"Cia," Sean Walsh says, quiet but firm. "Come with me."

"But that's Will." I hate how young and small my voice

sounds. I try again. "That's *Will*, Uncle Sean. You know he didn't do this."

Sean's eyes flick to Will and back to me. "Come with me," is all he says. I follow him back to his office, glancing over my shoulder, but Will is no longer looking my way.

"I'm sorry I wasn't available when you first got here," Sean says when we get inside, holding a chair for me. "Yates treated you well?"

"She's fine. What is Will doing here?"

He takes the chair beside mine, leaving the leather throne behind his desk empty. "He had spray paint in his locker, Cia."

That throws me, but only for a second. "It's not his."

"Then whose is it?"

I don't have an answer he'd like. "Will would never hurt Santi. Look, it's not hard to break into someone's locker," I say, fighting to keep the quiver out of my voice. This is wrong. This is all wrong. "Mine got broken into last week."

He raises his eyebrows. "Did you report it?"

"No. That's not the point, Uncle Sean. The point is that it's a high school locker, not a bank vault."

Sean is patient with me, which only makes me angrier and, honestly, more scared for Will. "Did you know Santi Malhotra was a drug dealer?"

"Santi's not a dealer." It's not a lie. Santi doesn't sell. You tell her what you want and she connects you with the people who can make it happen. Santi's immaculately manicured hands may not be totally clean, but of this I am certain.

"I have half a dozen sources telling me otherwise. And at least that many telling me that Will's been trying to find out who sold to his mom." When I don't bother to argue, he goes on. "In one night, Will lost his mother, for all intents and purposes, and a whole lot of friends. I know how kids can be. He hasn't had it easy. All of that can add up to a mighty grudge."

I am a broken record, scratching out the same lyric over and over. "Will is my best friend. He was in Little League with Remy. You *know* him. You know this isn't him."

He comes back around the desk to sit beside me. "You're right. Will was always a good kid. But good kids mess up sometimes, especially when they're hurting and confused. And you know better than most that since his mom went to prison, he isn't always in the driver's seat of his emotions and actions."

Uninvited, the image of my cell phone invades my mind, shattered on the floor of my bedroom. Will's own words haunt me.

Santi looks out for Santi. She doesn't give a shit about me, my mom, or anyone else as long as she gets hers.

I hate these things for poisoning my brain. I hate Uncle Sean for putting them there, hate Will for being an easy target, hate myself for the unfairness of that thought, hate pretty much everybody in this moment—but one more than anyone else.

Wolf_theChemist: If you really want to play, we can play. But you won't like my rules.

He'd practically signed his name on Santi's wall. But I'm not going to convince Uncle Sean of that, not without giving him everything else, and I know in my gut that it still wouldn't be enough to change his mind. Because, all said and done, nothing I can give him would equate to an airtight alibi for Will.

So I'll find the Chemist myself. It was easy enough to get his attention. He's cocky, needs to be in charge. I can use that. I don't know exactly how yet, but that need to not just win but to *crush*—that's his weak spot. I just have to figure out how to draw him out, get him to make a mistake. Will won't need an alibi if I can give them the real monster.

"You're wrong about Will." I stand up. "Can I talk to him? Just five minutes?"

He hesitates.

"Please, Uncle Sean. Everything's been so messed up with Alice gone. He's all I have left. *Please.*"

The carved granite of his cop-face softens. "Five minutes," he says. "And Silencia?"

I follow him out the door, pause when he does. "What?"

"He isn't all you have left," Sean says gently. "You know that."

I nod, because that's what he wants. But I don't mean it.

———

"I didn't do it," Will says. He looks so freaked out. "I didn't hurt Santi."

"I know. It was the Chemist. He told me last night I wouldn't like his rules, and this is his punishment for not backing off. I'm so sorry, Will." I want to wrap my arms around him and steal him away from this place, where all anyone sees is a damaged kid and an easy solve. Sean had them move the cuffs so that Will's hands are resting in his lap, not wrenched behind him anymore, but every clink of chain makes my breath catch.

This is all wrong.

"I have to tell you—" he begins, at the exact same time I slip the card out of my pocket.

"Santi was holding this, Will." I flash him the business card, its edges brown with dried blood; I'm careful, so that all anyone looking in could possibly see is the back of my hand.

He leans forward and squints. "Mercy Clinic? So what— with her dying gasp, Santi was trying to give you the insider scoop on low-cost STD testing?"

"Santi's not dying, Will, Jesus," I snap, harsher than I need to because I have no idea if I'm telling the truth or not. "*Look.*"

"What—" He looks closer. "Ohh."

"Yeah." I glance at the name in glossy print one more time before sliding the card back into my pocket: DR. A. MILLER, MD, FACS - MEDICAL DIRECTOR.

"This would be the same Arnold Miller you found on Rearden's board of directors?"

"It sure looks that way. Will, I think Santi knew Noah was dead this whole time." When I explain why, he frowns.

"It's . . . a little thin," he says.

"It gets thinner," I say grimly. "Santi's the one who helped me ID Jenna, which is how we ended up finding out where Noah was buried. I think the Chemist attacked Santi to shut her up, Will. And I think this card is her way of telling us where to look next."

He shakes his head. "That's not just thin, Cia. That's single-ply after your dad's chili."

"You're gross." I lean on the table. "I *know* there's something here. The only reason you're sitting here in handcuffs, and Santi's lying in the hospital, is because we're getting too close to the truth."

He rotates his wrists in the cuffs. They've left angry pink ridges in his skin. "Okay, let's talk through it then. Dr. Miller runs a clinic for the poor and downtrodden, bless his philanthropic heart. And Noah was collecting a paycheck for some study run by this guy's side gig, Rearden Health whatever. No big surprise there, Noah kind of embraced the poor and downtrodden thing when he took off. And this Miller guy probably has lots of research going on, especially if he wants to keep that donor money rolling in. Kids like Noah are his cash cows. So what kind of—" Will's eyes drift over my shoulder, and his whole demeanor changes. "What the fuck is *he* doing here?"

I turn around. On the other side of the window is . . . Judah? He's talking to Yates, who tilts her head toward the room Will and I currently occupy.

"I don't know," I start to say, but Will jumps to his feet.

"Cia, listen to me. Don't trust him. This is what I tried to tell you before. I saw Judah this morning."

"So? Don't you have homeroom together?"

"Yeah, he wasn't in it! Nobody expected him to be, not with Noah being found. But I saw him afterwards. Coming up from the auditorium. He looked pissed, and he practically ran past me out to the parking lot."

And then we're no longer alone. The cop at the door points at Will. "You. Sit down. Time's up." He nods at me.

The clamor of the busy police station compresses into a low hum as I try to make sense of what Will just said. His eyes plead with me to understand.

"Do you hear what I'm saying, Cia? I saw Judah coming out of the auditorium *right after Santi was attacked.*"

Chapter
28

Out in the lobby, Dad and Uncle Sean are deep in conversation. Dad's probably asking him if it's legal to put prison bars on your daughter's window. Judah is nowhere in sight.

"Dios mío, Silencia. Can you have one normal day? Just one?" He hugs me, holds me at arm's length and looks me up and down. I feel stiff and uncomfortable, for the first time in my life unable to melt into the comfort he offers. Dad isn't blind. He lets go and steps back. "You aren't hurt?"

That's a bold question for him to be asking after the way he'd snapped at me last night. "No. What was Judah Hayes doing here?"

"Just follow-up about his brother," Uncle Sean says. "He and his mother are meeting with the lead detectives on Noah's case. Are the two of you friends?"

"Through Alice." I'm getting better at these half-truths. At least, I think I am. But here's a whole one for them: "Will didn't do it, Dad."

"Then he doesn't have anything to worry about," Dad says.

The trite response annoys me. "Yeah, because nobody has ever gone to jail for a crime they didn't commit."

He just looks at me, and I'm suddenly struck by how tired he looks. When did his hair get so gray? There's more silver than black, now, and the furrow between his brows that scrunches up when he's stressed out doesn't completely settle anymore. Or maybe he's just been in a constant state of brow-furrowing lately. Which is probably, almost definitely, my fault.

"Can we just get out of here?" Other than seeing Will, this has been a huge mission fail. I'm frustrated, I'm scared, and my pants are still damp with Santi's blood. The sudden need to be anywhere else is overpowering.

"Javier," Uncle Sean says, gesturing at his office door. "A minute?"

"Wait here, Silencia." Dad moves to follow him, making it clear that I've been dismissed.

"I'll be out front. This place smells like sweat and doughnuts."

Dad turns back, his expression far from amused, but Uncle Sean responds first. "She's not wrong. I won't keep him long, Cia. I know you want to go home."

I take the long way through the bullpen but what's left of the Hayes family is nowhere to be found. Will's parting plea had flown like a stone, shattering the fragile sense of safety my alliance with Judah had brought.

Don't trust him.

But the list of people I trust who are not presently incarcerated, hospitalized, or dead is extremely short these days. I can't afford to throw away allies as easily as that.

Sorry, Will. After finding Noah, fighting for our lives, putting each other back together—I trust Judah. If he'd met with Santi this morning, he had a good reason, and I'll find out soon enough.

I exit the police station and find a perch on the far side of the wide stone steps, clear of the chaos flowing through the main entrance. Sunlight drapes over me like a soft, familiar blanket as I unlock my phone and open Snapchat. The panicked texts I sent Judah on my way here have not yet been read. I'd told him about the insomnia-fueled rage that had led me to bait the Chemist on Kik, and the consequences thereof. If he hasn't seen those messages, does he even know what's happened to Santi?

Will sure thinks he does.

cia_luc0204 10:14

i need your help. the cops arrested will. they think he attacked santi. i know he didn't, but i can't prove it.

I consider my next message carefully.

cia_luc0204 10:16

Will saw you at school this morning, before i found santi. but you told me you weren't going to be there.

cia_luc0204 10:17

make this make sense?

I lean my head against the granite pillar behind me and close my eyes against the sun. *Please, make this make sense.*

A wailing ambulance cuts its song short as it rounds the corner. I open my eyes as it pulls into the ambulance bay of Summerset Memorial across the street. I'm on my feet before the thought has even fully formed: this is the closest hospital to our school. This has to be where they brought Santi.

I have to see her. I have to see her breathing and safe, because my hands can't forget the warmth of her blood even though I've washed them four times already, and my eyes can't forget the message on the wall that makes this all my fault. I'm down the block and crossing the street without another thought. Dad will understand. I have to—

"Oh, *hell* no." A slender figure jumps in front of me with barely enough warning to avoid both of us eating sidewalk.

I take a half step back, finding my balance in case I'm about to break the no-fighting promise I'd made to Judah. "What—"

My human obstacle is wearing a tight black turtleneck, ripped skinny jeans, and major fuck-off energy. "This is a no-fly zone for you. Turn around."

I have never seen them before in my life. "Get out of my way," I hiss. "Who the hell do you think you are?"

The petite stranger's ink-dark eyes drill into me from behind purple-rimmed lenses. "I'm damage control. You're the reason Santi's in here. You need to turn around and go back where you came from."

Their words land like burrs in my skin. "What do you mean I'm the reason she's in here? What do you think you know about me?"

Their nostrils flare. "There's nothing for you here, Silencia Lucero. You need to go before you do more harm than you already have."

They clearly care deeply about Santi, and I hold on to that to force down my own desire to shove past them and their righteous indignation. "I'm not going anywhere until you tell me who you are and what you know about Santi. Obviously you care about her. So do I. If you know who I am, you should know that much at least."

"I know that Santi caring about *you* is why there's a machine breathing for her and twenty-six staples in her head." Their glasses have slipped down their nose and they slide them back up with a middle finger, a gesture I don't interpret as co-incidental. "You and your friends who ask so many questions and let others pay the cost of the answers."

That cuts *way* too deep—it's exactly how I've been think-ing about Serpico. Did I bleed my painted target onto Santi by coming to her twice for information I knew had already gotten someone else killed? Unbidden tears burn the rims of my eyes.

"Oh, don't even," the stranger growls. I'm no one's definition of tall, but they would have a hard time reaching the healthy cereal shelf at the grocery store. Somehow, that doesn't make them any less formidable.

"Listen." My voice is unsteady as it forces its way out around my heart in my throat. "If this is related to . . . to what I think it is, then you're right. This is because of me. And I need to make it right so the monsters who did this don't get away with it, because no one else is going to. The cops think what they're being told to think. My best friend is locked up. If I don't keep pushing, then all this happened for nothing. I don't think that's what Santi would want. Do you?"

"Santi doesn't get to decide anymore," they say, grim, and I finally recognize the ferocity behind their eyes for the love that it has been the whole time. I hadn't known Santi had a partner. But their expression softens by nanometers, taking in my scars, the scabs on my palms where I'd been prepared to defend Santi and myself with a shard of mirror. "You're a tenacious thing. I can see why Santi likes you. And I can see why you're nothing but goddamn trouble."

"I've been called worse. By you. In the last thirty seconds."

They don't say anything right away. I hold their gaze, will-ing my heart up from my throat into my eyes, needing them to see that we are kindred in pain and fury. Finally, they give a little huff-sigh. "You have blood in your hair."

I examine the ends of my ponytail, a more auburn shade of brown than nature gifted me with. Instead of grossing me out, it just donkey-kicks me in the stomach instead. "I was so afraid they had killed her, too."

Their lips tighten. "They won't get a second chance. Give me your phone." I hand it over and they punch in a number rapid-fire, listen for a moment, and then hang up. "I'll text you later. Wait for it. Don't do anything dumb and get anybody else killed in the meantime, okay?"

It sounds flippant, but we both know it isn't. "Do you know what they didn't want Santi to tell me?"

"I know lots of things. Including how to keep my mouth shut." They toss my phone back. "Santi's usually pretty good at that too. Helping you was a mistake, but I guess we're past that. What's done is done."

"Whoever is behind this has made their move," I agree quietly. "But this is not the endgame. Not unless we give them the board."

"Santi would be horrified if I let her wear that awful hospital gown for the closing act." They shake their head, and a few strands of black hair escape from their topknot. "She would be horrified if I let it end with her being a victim," they add softly. "No matter what I want, this is what *she* would want."

I don't know that the words are even meant for me, so I don't ask what they mean.

They nod once, curt—a decision made. "Wait for my text. And Silencia? Stay away from her. I mean it. I don't want Santi anywhere in the blast radius when the people you pissed off come at you again."

When. Not if. "Hold on."

They give me an eyebrow.

"Your name?"

"You can call me Moto."

"Cia. I'd say it's nice to meet you, but—"

"It's not. Good. You were paying attention." Moto doesn't bother with a goodbye, pivoting back to the hospital entrance without so much as a wave.

I want to see Santi so badly it hurts. But . . . she's in good hands. I can do nothing but put her in more danger, and my want is entirely selfish.

I turn back to the police station just in time to see my Dad pushing through the double doors. By the time he reaches the bottom of the stairs I am standing beside his car, the very picture of an obedient daughter.

He doesn't tell me what he and Uncle Sean talked about, and I don't tell him about my new ally, and I guess we've drawn our lines now. It's anyone's move.

————

Papa's waiting for us at home. He crushes me in a hug, inspects me up and down twice, and sends me off to change. I am happy to oblige. My phone had buzzed several times during the drive home, but I hadn't dared look at it in front of Dad.

Bad news travels fast at Summerset High, and I have messages from people I haven't talked to since middle school asking if I'm okay. Some are genuine, some are double-edged, fishing for gory details. I ignore them all.

judah_runs_good 10:30

> block the chemist and delete that app, cia. you CANNOT let him have a direct line to you. this is way too dangerous. promise me.

judah_runs_good 10:31

I'm still at the police station. i saw you leave. can't talk for a while. sorry. thinking about you.

judah_runs_good 10:40

i'm sorry about will. are you okay?

judah_runs_good 11:26

i'm here when you can talk.

I know my reprieve is short and they expect me back in a few minutes tops, but this can't wait. I dial Judah's number and fish out some comfy leggings and an oversized sweater from my closet while it rings.

"Cia." The way he says my name wraps me in warmth, and I wish that was all I'd called for. It's almost enough. "Are you okay? Where are you?"

"I'm home. I'm okay."

"No," he says. "You're not. I can hear it in your voice. This isn't on you, Cia. Don't for a second think that this is yours to carry."

But it is. We have to own our choices, even when the fallout is almost too horrible to face. "Why did Will see you coming out of the auditorium this morning?"

He doesn't tell me Will is a liar. He doesn't tell me Will was wrong. "It's not what it looks like."

"Tell me what it is, then." I sit down on the floor of my closet, leggings temporarily abandoned.

"I can't," he says softly. "Not right now."

His words land like razor blades. "You *can't*?"

"I did talk to Santi this morning. But she was fine when I left, I swear it, Cia."

"What did you talk about?"

"Cia. Please." The words are strained. "Trust me on this one thing. Trust that if I can't tell you, it's not because I don't want to. I just need some time. The last thing I want to do is hurt you."

"Then don't."

"I won't," he says vehemently.

"You are," I whisper, so quiet I'm not sure he even hears.

I want to believe him almost as much as I want trees to keep producing oxygen and gravity to keep us all from falling off the earth. But I'm just not that girl.

I'm not the girl who kisses a boy and puts on blinders to reality. I'm not the girl who stuffs down the hard questions because a him-less future is worse than not knowing. I'll never be that girl.

For a threadbare second, though, I wish I could be.

"I have to go."

Hurt ripples through his voice. "Cia, *please.*"

My head is full of bees, my gut knotted with cotton and sorrow. Santi is in the hospital. Will is going to jail. My dad is keeping terrible secrets. And now Judah . . .

alice.books113 16:18

whatever you think you know, don't trust it. trust me.

alice.books113 16:19

i wouldn't hurt you.

Why do the people I care about most keep promising not to hurt me right after doing it?

He says my name again but I end the call and leave the phone on the carpet next to my bloody jeans. Right now, I want nothing more to do with either of them.

———

I dutifully answer Papa's gentle questioning with as much honesty as I can spare. More hugs follow. The bees in my head are all buzzing Judah's name, guessing at the shape of his secret. Papa knows a good therapist if I "want someone to bounce anything off of." I do not. I force myself to swallow enough Chinese food to convince my dads that they've fulfilled their parental obligation to keep me from starving to death, and kiss Papa goodbye when he reluctantly goes back to work. Looks like Dad's on guard duty today.

I plead a headache, which is less of a lie than an incomplete truth since *everything* aches, and beg off to my room after helping Dad clean up a small forest worth of cardboard takeaway boxes. Remy calls in response to the frantic text I'd sent him from the police station, and I fill him in on what I know about Will and Santi—which amounts to infuriatingly little—before he has to rush off to class.

Three Advil later I am finally ready to release my phone from its prison.

judah_runs_good 12:55
please don't shut me out.

judah_runs_good 01:04
alice wanted us to work together, cia. we need to work together. this is too dangerous.

judah_runs_good 01:10
I lost my brother. I'm not going to lose you too.

I stare at the series of messages on my phone, type and delete six different responses before sending the simplest.

cia_luc0204 01:12

> tell me why you went to see Santi. and why you were
> mad after.

judah_runs_good 01:13

> Will has a big mouth

cia_luc0204 01:13

> at least he's not using it to lie to me.

judah_runs_good 01:15

> ouch.

cia_luc0204 01:15

> i'm done with secrets, judah. if you can't tell me what
> business you had with Santi this morning, we have
> nothing else to talk about.

judah_runs_good 01:16

> i will, i swear it. soon. just not yet, okay? and we have
> EVERYTHING else to talk about.

My eyes sting.

cia_luc0204 01:17

> not from where I'm standing.

I put the phone on silent and throw it back into the
closet.

Do I truly believe that Judah hurt Santi? No. Not that he
doesn't have the ability—I have personally seen him cause a
whole lot of hurt, when the situation called for it. I just can't

see the boy who had traced my scars so gently hunting Santi—our *friend*—down like a rabbit and using those gentle hands to beat her within an inch of her life.

But if he can't trust me with whatever this is, then I need to re-evaluate how unequivocal my own trust is. I can't stop thinking about Will, caged and cornered. Framed. Because that's on me too. Will wasn't on anybody's radar until I put him there. Well, Judah and I put him there, but he'd been targeted because it would hurt me.

If you really want to play, we can play. But you won't like my rules.

According to the Chemist's rules, there's no such thing as collateral damage. There is just damage, and who can inflict the most of it. So far it's no contest.

Which means it's my turn to do some damage.

My laptop hums back to life with a brush of my fingertips. I keep coming back to Rearden Health Alliance, its connection to the clinic and Dr. Miller, and why it sounds so damn familiar. I pull up their corporation registration again, and something small but very, very important slides into place.

BOARD OF DIRECTORS:

Chairman of the Board: Arnold S. Miller, MD

Director: Elizabeth Gehrling, PhD

Director: Daniel Perez, DO

Director: Tetsuya Sato, MD

Director: Henrik Winther, JD

A thrill shivers through my core. T. Sato had signed off on the death certificates of dozens of kids without explanation, because nobody that mattered was *asking* for explanations. It was no coincidence that the number of fatal fires dropped when Sato came to town. They no longer needed fire to hide their secrets once he set up his no-questions-asked shop.

Whatever they were hiding has to be more than just the bodies of dead kids. It's something *about* their bodies. That's the intersection of the utter destructive power of fire and a corrupt medical examiner—both are extremely good at hiding physical evidence.

My thoughts crawl with an army of centipede legs. As if it isn't bad enough that they died before they'd ever gotten to really live. These adults, these doctors that were supposed to be a safety net for kids who'd been persistently and pathologically let down by the rest of the world—they did something so unspeakable that they had to burn the evidence away.

Once again I flash back to my fire. The Fire.

Besides my dad—what's the link? Is there one?

Coincidence costs more naivete to believe in than I have left anymore.

Humans may not be the only beasts that prey on our young, but we do it with the coldest hearts.

I prop the Mercy Clinic card up between the F-keys and the screen. Google, for once, doesn't let me down.

MERCY FOR SUMMERSET'S LOST CHILDREN: LOCAL CLINIC OPENS DOORS TO ALL, NOT JUST THOSE WHO CAN PAY

The article is almost as old as I am. The few embedded photos are grainy, low quality, but I spend several minutes staring at the image captioned *Dr. Arnold Miller talks with homeless teen*, in which a middle-aged man with a thick mustache and a long white coat sits beside a girl with huge dark eyes and an even bigger baby bump. The man's expression is earnest as he leans in, his hands open, everything about the photo supporting the article's portrayal of a man driven to help others, for whom a successful career as an emergency department physician was not enough. Along with his lesser-seen partner, Dr. Daniel Perez, Dr. Miller opened Mercy Clinic to provide services to a particularly vulnerable subsection of his community.

Dad's characteristic one-thud knock startles me, and I quickly swap windows to the AP World History report I'm supposed to be writing.

"I have to run to the office," he says, and the comma between his brows is practically a semicolon. Must not be good news.

I know how that feels.

"Okay."

"I may be a while. I'll arm the alarm on my way out. Are you okay until Papa gets home?"

Working hard not to show my relief at the not-so-metaphorical leash loosening around my neck, I nod. "Ms. Fletcher talked to my teachers and emailed me all my homework for tomorrow." That part is no lie, unfortunately, though the implied intention to address said homework might be less than sincere.

Dad doesn't look any happier, but he nods, hesitates in the doorway as if he has something else to say. I wait, but nothing comes. Two minutes later the garage door grinds shut and the whole house seems to relax. Or maybe I'm projecting.

"Free at last," I say to Pancakes, lying in her usual spot between my bed and the door. She doesn't hear me, but her old-lady snoring makes me smile. The memory of the Chemist's not-so-veiled threat that she wouldn't hear him coming freezes my smile in place, and the knowledge that my address is out there in the hands of people who clearly mean me harm shatters it entirely. I double-check the alarm, then do a lap around the house making sure all the windows are locked, and deadbolt the front and back doors before going back to my laptop.

I find a few more recent articles, all tipping their collective hats to Dr. Miller's work with low-income and homeless youth, with the obligatory links where interested donors can make tax-deductible charitable contributions to the good doctor's mission. In the most recent photos, taken five years ago, Dr. Miller has traded the mustache and a lot of the rest of his hair for a sprinkling of salt-and-pepper fuzz and some serious grandpa glasses. That article mentions that Dr. Miller continues to work with Summerset Memorial Hospital, training a new generation of physicians on the complexities of care for the city's homeless and indigent youth.

I finish reading and lean back on my elbows. I don't doubt Dr. Miller had his reasons for opening a clinic that specifically caters to the most vulnerable. But I call bullshit on those reasons being compassion and beneficence.

All of those words, all of that good intention oozing out between lines of text, and all I see is a predator.

Noah's his target audience, Will had said, and I see it too.

I see a group of kids no one will miss, and the man who looked at them and saw opportunity. But opportunity for what?

I delete my browsing history, and close the laptop. After taking a quick selfie with the trash can at the curb in case Dad asks why I disabled the alarm, I leave the door open a crack while I type in my code and race back outside before my thirty seconds are up and the security system reengages.

It's time Rearden and I get to know each other.

Chapter
29

alice 13:55

they're calling off the search.

alice 13:55

a 17-year-old goes missing, and he doesn't even get 48 hours before they write him off. this town is so messed up!!

me 13:56

he left his phone and his keys, al. he doesn't want to be found.

alice 13:56

sometimes when you push people away is when you most need them to find you. when you need the people who love you to remind you who you are. maybe that's

what love means, always having a light to guide you
through the storm.

me 13:57

maybe. sometimes I think you have to believe people
when they tell you, through their words or their
actions, that they aren't good enough for you.

alice 13:57

that's not fair, cia.

me 13:58

it wasn't fair that he hurt you the way he did. it's not
fair that he's hurting you again now. i think you have to
ask yourself, is he your light or is he your storm, alice?

alice 13:58

maybe both. maybe not everything is that simple.

me 13:58

maybe not always. but i'm your lighthouse, not his, so
for me it is that simple.

me 14:03

alice?

alice 14:04

promise me we'll always find each other, cia. that you'll
always be my fierce, stubborn-ass lighthouse.

me 14:05

i do solemnly swear.

alice 14:05

good.

alice 14:06

because sometimes I think I might drown without you.

Chapter
30

The bus drops me off half a block down from the clinic. My leg still aches but I don't mind the walk—it gives me a chance to scope out the neighborhood, which, as it turns out, is only a few blocks from where Jenna Reglin lives.

From where Noah died.

Rent must be cheap for Dr. Miller's pity project, and it doesn't look like much of the grant money the articles described went into prettying the place up, either. The clinic is a standalone building between a sprawling Mexican grocer and a vacant warehouse-style place with more windows broken than intact. One side of the clinic is weatherworn gray stucco while the other is a riot of bold color, a mural depicting white-coated saviors with gentle eyes and their sick and broken flock in some kind of garden, with a Staff of Asclepius at its center.

Only someone had spray-painted over the Staff, and recently: a splattered red oval with a horizontal line through it seems to negate the message of beneficence.

Apparently I'm not the only one with doubts about Dr. Miller's altruism.

I'm forced to revise my opinion of Mercy Clinic when I step inside, though. It's no Upper West Side Botox clinic but it's clean, and a corner of the lobby is a carpeted play area for kids, with a cube-shelf stocked with enough toys to keep even the most hyperactive rugrat busy for a while.

The receptionist is a pretty young woman with a tidy bun and the kind of super-lightweight glasses you almost don't notice until light glints off the edges. There are two people ahead of me in line, so I glance around.

This part of my plan is what my science teacher would call exploratory research, which is a fancy way of saying I don't actually have a plan at all. I don't know what I'm after, but I'll know it when I see it. This place . . . this is the dragon's den. I know it. I know it because Santi knew it, and that's why she pointed me in this direction.

And that's why she's lying in a hospital bed.

Moto had told me not to do anything dumb. But dumb is subjective and sometimes looks a lot like brave, and anyway I don't know exactly where this falls on the dumb-brave spectrum but staying at home, being the obedient daughter, is not an option anymore.

I didn't make the rules. The Chemist did. But I refuse to be broken by them.

Brochures about everything from prenatal yoga to intimate partner violence overflow from a rack near the door. A whiteboard with neat, round handwriting lists places to go to eat and sleep every day of the week, as well as support groups for eating disorders, substance abuse, and everything in between. A kid about my age sits on a beanbag in one corner with a toddler and a book in his lap, sounding out the words to Margaret Wise Brown's *Runaway Bunny.*

Something old and half-forgotten twists in my chest.

The boy squints at the words as if they're written in Latin. "'If you be . . . *become* a bird and fly away from me,' said his mother, 'I will be a tree that you come home to.'"

I know the next words by heart, but not from any book.

Books weren't allowed in the Bennett household. But my mother used to murmur this story to us at bedtime, a promise to hold us as we drifted off to sleep. "'If you become a tree,' the boy says, 'I will become a little sail . . . sailboat, and I will sail away from you.'"

The child in his lap warbles something unintelligible but happy.

"'If you become a sailboat and sail away from me—'"

I will become the wind, my heart whispers.

These memories are like landmines, buried shallow and waiting. Forgotten but not gone.

The receptionist wrenches me from my ghost-mother's arms. "Can I help you?" she says, smiling at me with the kind of patience that suggests she hasn't been in the world of customer service very long. She stands up and tugs the sign-in sheet, now full of scribbled names, free from its clipboard. "Just one moment." She walks behind a half-wall, tucks the sheet into a drawer in one of three tall filing cabinets, and returns quickly. "Sorry about that. Can you sign in, please?"

The sign-in sheet wants my name and appointment time. "I don't actually have an appointment."

"That's completely fine. We take walk-ins." She hands me a pen with a fake flower taped to it. "Just sign in here and we'll get you going."

Something fragile and green pokes out of the seed of an idea. "Is Dr. Miller available?"

"He's actually not here on Wednesdays," she says apologetically. "But one of our nurse practitioners can see you. Is that okay?"

"That's fine." I write my name and hand over my ID— last year's school ID, since this year's is now in the custody of a baseball bat-wielding maniac. She runs off a copy and hands it back. "Can I use your bathroom?"

"Sure. Any chance you might be pregnant?" The receptionist waves a clear plastic cup.

"Not unless you believe in immaculate conception."

"Fair enough. If you're older than twelve and have a uterus, I have to ask." She puts away the pee cup and reaches for a button on her desk. "I'll unlock the door. Straight down the hall, third door on your right."

"Thank you." I walk around the counter. The heavy door clicks twice as I approach, and opens easily.

The hall branches off to the left, where a woman in light blue scrubs leans over another counter, talking in a low voice and glancing back and forth between a tablet and someone hidden from my view. Patient exam rooms line this hallway, most of the doors closed.

Damn.

"I got lost" will only get me so far as an excuse for being places I shouldn't, and I won't get very far at all down that hallway. I turn back to the main hall. The first door I pass is open, and it leads to the receptionist's area. From the doorway I can see a tiny rose tattoo on the back of her neck as she types a million words a minute at her computer. She pauses and shifts in her seat and I quickly retreat back out into the hall.

I pass the bathroom. The hall splits. To the right are two locked doors, both bearing engraved metal placards: one for Dr.

Miller and one for Dr. Perez. To the left are three more locked doors, and at the end, double stainless steel doors with narrow panes of glass. I push on the doors but they don't open. The room is dark, but light from the hall filters in through the glass, illuminating the sterile metallic surfaces of what is unmistakably an operating room.

Junior EMT or not, I don't recognize half of what I'm looking at. I press my phone to the glass and take a couple of panoramic photos.

There are a lot of reasons why a medical clinic would need leather restraints, I tell myself. I just can't think of any that don't make me sick to my stomach.

Before the receptionist can send a search party, I retrace my steps. I may not know yet exactly what Rearden is doing here, but there's a way I can find out who they're doing it to.

My heart skitters with anticipation of what I am about to do, but I have to move fast or I'll lose my nerve. Without hesitation, I walk into the receptionist's file room as if I belong there. Her back is still to me as she multitasks with impressive efficiency, talking into her headset while handing a clipboard of paperwork to a nervous-looking girl wearing a vintage D.A.R.E. shirt.

I find the filing cabinet she had used only minutes before and slide the drawer open as smoothly and soundlessly as possible. My eyes scan the sea of manila folders containing insurance documents, privacy notices and the like, until I see what I'm looking for: SIGN-IN SHEETS, each labeled with the month and year, with subsections going back five years.

There's no way I can fit them all into my backpack, and the savvy receptionist would notice the second she went to file the next sheet if too many are missing. The realization that I have to leave so much potential evidence behind maddens me, but the outlook is even more grim if I get caught. I know Noah came here this summer, so I grab July and August, as well as the one from today with my name on it. Looking further back, I take October for Reggie Goodwyn, last September for Serena Clay, and last January for Rohit Shah, because Alice had named them specifically and their death certificates are burned into my memory. I choose one more month at random from each year previous and gently slide the drawer shut. Back in the hall, I only remember to breathe when I've closed the bathroom door behind me. I shove the files into my backpack and zip it shut, then sit on the lid of the toilet and look through the pictures I've taken. The glare of the flash on the glass washes out some of the details on the top half of the photos, but I can see enough to wonder what a community health clinic needs with such a well-equipped surgical suite.

I flush the toilet and run the sink in case the hand washing police are listening, then step back out into the hall. Blue Scrubs Lady is just walking in from the lobby with *Runaway Bunny* Boy and his kid. She smiles at me and leads them to an exam room.

The lobby suddenly feels claustrophobic, and it only now occurs to me to wonder if the clinic has security cameras. Of course they would, right? Unless they're sacrificing security in the name of minimizing evidence, but that seems improbable.

Just because I haven't seen any cameras doesn't mean they aren't there. And if anyone is watching them, they just saw everything—with a photocopy of my ID as icing on the cake.

"Marie will be with you in just a few minutes," the receptionist says.

I move toward the exit. "I'm actually not feeling very well," I say lamely.

She looks curious. "That's usually why people come here."

"I think I'm just going to go. I'll, um, call to reschedule. Thanks." I push open the door and walk out into the sunny afternoon, forcing myself not to rush, keeping my pace even and casual.

I wait until I'm at the bus stop with my back safely to a thick metal grate before I let my guard down enough to pull out my phone. There are two new messages from Judah, which I leave unread for the moment.

It was only yesterday that we kissed, that his warm fingers lifted my jaw to brush my lips with his . . . only twenty-four hours for him to win my trust and betray it again.

Judah makes me vulnerable, and he is keeping something from me, which makes him a wildcard. I can't afford him right now. But that doesn't stop me from wanting him with an ache that makes my fingers curl into my palms, digging eyeless smiles into my skin.

God, I wish Will were here. I'd even let him believe he's Sherlock to my Watson if it meant not doing this alone.

They can't keep him locked up. He will not be okay. The darkness that has circled him since his mom went to prison is like a pack of patient, giggling hyenas closing in on carrion. He needs to be out here, with me, where he can use that rage against Alice's killer. Not in there, where it will consume him. Even if he, like me, had skipped homeroom, *someone* has to have seen him. You can't pick a wedgie in that place without someone putting it on Snapchat; we are in each other's business all day long, whether we want to be or not. I just pray it's someone with the integrity to come forward and alibi him before it's too late.

I'm halfway home when my phone vibrates again.

Wolf_theChemist
Rough day, sweetheart?

My heart skitters. Judah was one hundred percent right—I should have blocked him and deleted Kik already. I should do it now.

But I don't.

Wolf_theChemist

> Tough break about Will. Everybody
> knew it was only a matter of time
> before he snapped, though. Never
> been quite right since his mom killed
> that football player, has he?

silencia_luc

> if that was your best attempt at a
> set-up, i'm embarrassed for you.
> it won't work. he's innocent.

He's enjoying this, which is almost enough on its own to make me block him. But I just need him to make one mistake. One.

Wolf_theChemist

> Maybe he is, maybe he isn't. Good
> thing he's in the right place for them
> to sort that out, isn't it?

silencia_luc

> he won't be in there long. so did
> you do it yourself or are you too
> much of a coward to get your
> own hands dirty?

Wolf_theChemist

> How many more of your friends
> have to bleed before you learn
> your place?

My whole body trembles, fear and rage at war for dominance as my shaking fingers move over the fractured glass. These messages alone would be enough to clear Will, or at the very least, cast enough doubt to get him out on bail.

But as if he's read my mind:

> **Wolf_theChemist**
> I like our little chats, Silencia, I really do. But if you even think about showing them to the cops I'll brick your phone faster than you can fucking blink.

Ice floods my veins at the possibility. *Can he do that?* I don't know. But I can't afford to underestimate him.

> **silencia_luc**
> I don't need the cops to find you.

> **silencia_luc**
> Lots of threats today. You wouldn't be so scared if I weren't getting close, so thanks for the encouragement.

> **Wolf_theChemist**
> Don't fuck with me, Silencia. You won't like the consequences.

> **silencia_luc**
> It's a little late for that.

Wolf_theChemist
You're right. It is getting late. Better
hurry home.

My whole body tingles, all my senses roaring into overdrive.
How the hell does he know where I am? *He can't*, I try to reassure myself. *He doesn't.*

But he can. They have my address. He might not know exactly where I am, but they could be watching my house. They
could have watched me leave.

They could be there now.

Wolf_theChemist
You don't have much time.

———

I swear at every red light and when the bus finally reaches my
stop, I run the two blocks home, full-out, shooting stars burst-
ing in my sore leg but not slowing down, because something is
wrong, I *know* something is wrong. The Chemist doesn't make
idle threats, and I'm not naïve enough to believe his last message wasn't exactly that.

"Cia!"

The sound of my name bleeds into the background of my
panic, unregistered, until it's repeated, louder.

Judah.

He jogs toward me from the opposite end of my block, on
a collision course that sublimates in my driveway. "Look, I . . .
why are you running?"

"Something's wrong," I breathe, turning up the drive and
ignoring the way my heart leaps at the sight of him.

"What do you mean?" He instantly shifts focus from whatever he'd been about to say, eyes going to the door. "What's wrong?"

"I don't know yet!" I cry, jamming my new key in the new lock and fighting with it until the door swings open.

I drop my backpack to the floor. Judah's thuds down beside it. My pulse hammers the inside of my skull.

"Dad?" I call out, my voice echoing off the walls. "Papa?"

I check the alarm panel. It's flashing angrily—it had still been armed when I blew in the front door.

Judah touches the small of my back. "Wait."

"The house is empty. The alarm—"

"Isn't foolproof," he finishes quietly. "Please." His other hand briefly cups my upper arm, slides down to my elbow before slipping away, leaving mothwing flutters in its wake as he moves past me. I enter my code with shaking fingers and the alarm settles down.

"If you tell me to stay here," I say, "I will undo that patch-up job on your face faster than you can say 'misogyny.'"

"I think you mispronounced 'chivalry.'" Judah holds up both hands to fend off attack, then touches the dark red lightning-bolt split through his lower lip and smiles ruefully. "I wouldn't dream of it. Just let me go first?"

I shove away the memory of how that lip tastes. "No. But you can take the living room."

He nods, disappears through the threshold. I move into the kitchen, the ragged sound of my breathing painfully loud—until it stops completely, trapped between lungs and scream, as I see the dark, wet smears glistening on the tile, the trail of blood stamped with the unmistakable imprint of paws.

Chapter
31

I find her under the table, in a den of furniture legs. Her favorite place to wait for dropped treats, accidental or otherwise.

I shove a chair aside to crawl beside my dog. Her spotted lips are flecked with blood, the fur of her muzzle mottled with maroon flakes, and though her ribs rise with rapid, shallow gasps, the shape is wrong, the curve of her is *wrong*.

"Pancakes!" I cry, reaching for her but not knowing where to touch that won't hurt her. I stroke the top of her head and her eyes open, the color of quarry water.

Judah narrowly avoids slipping on the blood as he runs into the kitchen. "What the hell? Cia! Where—" It doesn't take him any longer than it took me to follow the blood trail from the back door to the dining room, and then he is kneeling beside me, half under the table with us. "Oh no. Is she . . . ?"

"She's breathing," I half-sob, moving my fingers hummingbird-light down her shoulder to her chest. Several of her ribs look caved in, and it seems unlikely that her left lung is working at all, which is probably why she's gasping, and even through all of that her tail lifts once and thumps on the floor, and I just about lose it but I know I can't afford to yet because it isn't *safe* yet.

Judah jumps up and disappears again. I yank my phone out, stare at it. Who do I call? Does 911 deal with injured animals? Is there an animal 911? There probably is and I don't know what it is, I'm not prepared, I wasn't expecting this, and now Pancakes is going to die because I wasn't expecting *what I was warned was going to happen—*

I slam the door hard on that line of thought.

The cops will tell me to take her to an animal hospital. But I am petrified to move her, to make things worse. My first instinct is to call Dad. He's a paramedic, he'll know *something* . . . but if his meeting was downtown, it's smack in the middle of rush hour and he wouldn't get home for an hour, and I need someone *now*.

Remy's pre-med. That's got to be worth something. His phone rings once, twice. "Cia? Is everything okay?"

"Remy, I need you." I manage to keep the horror out of my voice but probably not the fear, because he is instantly on alert. "Something happened . . . Pancakes is hurt. It's bad."

"I'm on my way," he says, and four more welcome words have never been spoken in the English language. "What happened?"

"I don't know. I came home and found her . . ." This isn't helping. I force myself to focus. "I think her ribs are broken on the left side. The high ones and some of the middle ones. She's breathing really fast and there's blood on her mouth."

"Is she awake?"

"Yes. And she's a good girl," I whisper fiercely into her ear, kissing her satiny forehead.

Judah returns with a blanket and several towels. I don't ask how he knew where to find them; I guess every house is kind of the same when it comes to bathrooms and linen closets.

"Who are you talking to?" Judah asks me.

"A friend."

"Who's there with you?" Remy wants to know.

"A friend," I repeat.

Judah's frown deepens his dimple but he doesn't say anything. He slides a folded towel beneath Pancakes's head while I gently support her neck.

I hear the engine of his car starting as Remy walks me through safely rolling out the blanket underneath Pancakes with minimal movement of her body. He promises to be here in ten minutes and I hang up so he can focus on all the red lights he'll have to run to stand a chance at making it here from the university that fast.

We get Pancakes on the blanket. Her gasping changes to include a soft high-pitched whine at the end, as if she's trying so hard not to complain but can't help it anymore. I run out to the garage to find something to use as a makeshift litter and come back with a plank that I think used to be the shelf of an old bookcase. Judah helps me carefully slide Pancakes onto the board with the blanket.

He takes my hand, sticky with blood and fur, and doesn't say anything. It's exactly what I need. We stroke her face and listen to her breathe.

The front door slams open. Judah leaps to his feet and whirls around, putting himself between me and the door.

"Cia!" Remy shouts, and the tentacles of terror squeezing my chest ease a fraction.

"He's my friend, Judah, it's okay." He nods, comes back to my side. "In here!"

Remy skids to a halt in the kitchen doorway, taking in the scene with alarm. In two seconds he is at my side as well, examining Pancakes without touching much, just as I had.

"I don't like that breathing at all," he says. "I'm guessing she's working with one lung at best, less if she's bleeding into the space around it. Let's get her into the car. Do you know where the nearest emergency vet is?"

I don't, but Google tells me that it's less than a five minute drive away. I call them as the boys carefully load Pancakes into Remy's Prius. They promise to be ready.

Judah and I ride in the back seat, Pancakes across our laps. Beneath the heaviness of her body, rocking with gasps for air, his hand finds mine again. He doesn't take it this time, but he rests his there, letting his touch say what I refuse to hear from his lips right now.

Because he's still hiding something from me. We're still not okay.

But he's here, and I'm steadier because of it, and I don't move my hand away.

"Hey, man," Judah says after the first mile. "Where do I know you from?"

Remy glances at us in the mirror. He's clean-shaven today, his golden hair combed at some point today but slightly rumpled now. "I saw you outside the Bookers' house being a jerk to Cia last weekend."

Judah doesn't blink, but I can see the skin around his ears darken, his jaw tense. "Right. Before that. I've seen you somewhere else."

"I'd be surprised if you hadn't. It's a small town." Mossy eyes flash on mine, then back to the road. "I've never heard Cia talk about you. How do you know each other?"

Judah gives me a beat before answering. Waiting for me to define us?

You know better than I do, I think, something bitter and sad twisting in me. *What I would have said two days ago is not what I would have said yesterday is not what I would say today. You made this space between us for a secret to fit. You label it.*

"We used to run track together," he says at last. "Well, she ran. The rest of us ate dust."

I snort but it tastes like tears, so I look out the window and let the boys size each other up on their own.

"And my brother used to date Alice."

"That's right. You're Noah's brother. The guy who broke her heart and skipped town." His words make me wince, particularly considering the body of the guy in question had just been dug up *yesterday.*

"It didn't go down like that," I say sharply. "I told you it didn't. And Noah didn't *skip town.* You know they found him yesterday."

"I heard. Sorry. It just . . . still hurts, I guess." He doesn't meet my eyes in the mirror, and the discussion is tabled while we guide the makeshift stretcher out of the backseat and into the clinic. The vet is ready, a wiry woman that looks like Jamie Lee Curtis's twin in gray scrubs. Two of her techs take Pancakes from us, bookshelf and blanket and bloody towels and all, and hustle her back through silver double doors before we've even been inside for ten seconds.

The vet puts cool fingers on my arm when I start forward to follow. "Give us a few minutes to assess her," she says, firm but not unkind. "I'll be back out in a few minutes to talk about what we can do for her. The desk will have some paperwork for you when you're ready."

I'm definitely not ready.

Remy beckons me to a chair in the lobby near where Judah has dropped his backpack, but I am way too keyed up to sit.

"Tell me what's going on?" Judah asks me, low. Remy doesn't even pretend not to be listening in. "You knew something was wrong before you got home. Did someone threaten you?"

I am tempted to be petty, to keep from him the same way he is holding back from me, but I think about the mountain of secrets piling up between us, between me and my parents, between Alice and all of us, and I am just *exhausted* by them. So I pick one, lob it at him before I can doubt my decision. "The Chemist messaged me again."

"He *what*?!" It's not a shout but it's near enough that the girl behind the desk startles. "I thought you shut that down!"

A flush creeps up my neck. "I was going to. But it seemed like a waste of an opportunity. Maybe I can get him to make a mistake. To give us something he shouldn't. He's *so* cocky—"

"Because it's probably a fucking *trap*, Cia, damn it!" He drags his hand across his face and back through his hair, a habit I've noticed when he's frustrated. Usually with me. Brown tufts stick up in a few places, and it occurs to me that it doesn't look like he's slept much in the last twenty-four hours.

Of course he hasn't. His twin brother is in a refrigerated metal cabinet and his mom is at the bottom of a bottle of Scotch.

"What's this about?" Remy interjects, leaving his seat to stand beside me, completing our little triangle. His hand brushes my back briefly, a little wordless *I'm here for you* that I am grateful for.

"The Chemist set Will up," I tell Judah, suddenly needing him to understand. "He basically admitted it. If he didn't do it directly, he made it happen. And he threatened Pancakes if I didn't stop digging." My vision blurs. "He said . . . he said she wouldn't even hear him coming. Because he *knows*. He knows she's a sweet deaf little old dog and he knows about Will being an easy target for the cops and he knows *us*. He knows everything and I'm sick of not knowing and I'm sick of people I care about paying for it, so I didn't stop, I *won't* stop, and now here we are and if Pancakes dies—if Santi dies—it's all my fault."

The tears push, and they push, and still I won't let them take me even though a few creep out through my defenses.

Judah looks like he wants to either shake me or embrace me and never let go. His dark eyes shine with emotions I can't name, but soften when he wipes the tears from my chin with the back of his finger.

"She's going to be okay, Cia," he says, like it's his to promise. I cling to his words anyway. "They both are."

Remy glances between the two of us. "I think I'm going to need a little more information for all of that to make sense, kid."

"Don't call me kid." I sniff.

"You said someone threatened you?"

"Yeah. This guy—this person Alice was talking to before she died. He threatened her, too."

Remy brings me a kleenex. "This will be the last time I ask," he says carefully, watching my face. "Because you told me once, and I just want to make sure *you're* sure."

"Sure of what?" I fold the tissue, drag its edge beneath my eyes.

"Sure that what happened to Alice isn't the simple, awful tragedy that it looks like. Sure that you're not weaving together this whole complex plot out of coincidence and . . . and maybe guilt. Guilt you don't deserve, but can't let go of."

There it is. That's what he's been dancing around. I step back from him abruptly, from both of them. "Is that what you believe?"

Remy shrugs helplessly. "No. I don't know. Tell me, Cia. You're working with information I don't have, and holding it against me for drawing different conclusions. Tell me what I don't know so I can see it the way you see it."

I look at him, one shirt tail untucked, blood on his sweater-vest, and I look to Judah, who I'm pretty sure is wearing the same jeans he had on the day before, a black long-sleeved thermal tee hiding the beating he'd taken—and given—yesterday.

The mountain of secrets grows smaller again by one. But it's a big one.

"What you don't know," I tell them both, "what *neither* of you know, is that Alice was pregnant."

Chapter
32

Remy visibly wilts, as if the pull of gravity has increased but only marginally, just enough to make it a little harder to stand up straight. But Judah . . . Judah couldn't look more stricken if I'd slapped him.

"How do you know?" he asks me, and the hurt in his voice adds a *why* to the question. As in, *why do you know and I didn't?*

The receptionist is looking our way, concern written all over her face. I lower my voice. "Will found the ultrasound a week before she died. It was real early. She didn't want anyone to know yet. I . . . I'm sorry, Judah. Part of me feels like it's her secret to keep, hers and her family's, if that's what they want. But it was Noah's baby. There wasn't anyone else for her, not like that. And she . . . she would *never* . . ." I can't finish the sentence, but I don't need to. They both know.

Judah is pale, too pale to blame on the relentless incandescent lights that cast all of our hollow places in shadow. I think he should probably sit before the vet has two emergency assessments to perform, but before I can suggest it he turns and runs into the bathroom, bolting the door behind him.

Remy sighs. "That's heavy. I'm sorry, Cia."

"Yeah. And there's . . . there's more I should tell you."

He nods. "I want to hear it. But you should call your dads first. Let them know what's going on."

I swear. "You're right. Crap, I'm a terrible daughter."

"You're a distracted daughter," he corrects, "who just saved the family dog's life. Cut yourself a little slack."

"Dad won't," I mutter. I dial Papa's number first, but when he doesn't answer, I hang up on his voicemail and ring Dad instead.

The receptionist points up at a PLEASE RESPECT OUR QUIET ZONE AND TAKE PHONE CALLS OUTSIDE sign above her head, mouthing the word *sorry* and seeming to mean it. I step outside, my legs made of lead but not as heavy as the knowledge in my heart that somehow, I could have—should have—stopped this from happening.

———

Dad doesn't even address the fact that I'd gone AWOL from the house—to take a walk and clear my head, as far as he knew—during our brief but intense conversation, which means I'm either off the hook or so deeply speared on it that my lizard-brain sense of impending doom is broken.

I don't tell him that I'm almost one hundred percent certain this is punishment for my sins.

I don't tell him, but a hateful part of me wonders if he already knows.

Five minutes into the conversation, the vet pokes her head outside. I can't read anything in the creases around her eyes, in the set of her mouth, but she says something with the word "stable" in it and the weight pulling my heart down into my gut lightens by half an ounce. Dad asks me to put her on the phone and I do, and Remy follows her outside and I let myself be enveloped in his hug for just this minute, because he'd told me Pancakes would be okay and the vet just proved him right, and because he's warm and I have had pure glacial runoff running through me since reading the Chemist's last message.

I can't stop shivering.

"Are you cold?" Remy steps back, eyes probing mine.

"Not anymore. I just . . . can't stop shaking."

"That's the adrenaline." He pulls me in for another quick hug, lets me go. "I'm going to tell your dad that I'll take you home, okay? There's no point in you waiting around here for him. Traffic is going to be a bitch and I don't want you stuck here for an hour."

"Okay," I say, and then immediately regret it. I don't know if I can face those bloody paw prints again. Remy is already talking to Dad, though, and he hands me back my phone after a brief exchange.

"So we'll keep her on the ventilator for the surgery and probably overnight, and see how she does in the morning," the vet tells me. "If all goes well she'll be on cage rest for a while, which thankfully at her age she probably won't mind as much as the younger ones do. If she moves wrong she could puncture the lung, so we need to give those ribs some time to heal."

My face must reflect some fraction of what I'm feeling, because Remy brushes a tear off my cheek I didn't realize had been drying there. "Hey. All of that means that she's going to be okay, Cia."

"If all goes well," the vet repeats, not without empathy. She glances back over her shoulder. "Your father gave verbal consent for the surgery, so we're going to get started. Do you have any questions before I go back?"

"No, ma'am. Thank you for helping her."

"Of course." She pauses at the door. "How did you say this happened, again?"

An acid wash of shame burns over me at the careful neutrality of her voice. "I don't know. I came home and she . . ."

The vet nods. "Your dad says it's possible she fell from the porch?"

He did?

When I have nothing to offer, she gives my arm another reassuring squeeze and disappears back inside. We follow.

My muscles are limp spaghetti, the electricity that powered me this far abruptly cut off. I drop into a chair and put my head in my hands.

A soft rush of air signals the opening and closing of the restroom door, and then Judah is kneeling in front of me, splintered into shards by the curtain of my hair. "Cia?"

"They're taking her to surgery," I tell him. "The vet thinks she'll make it."

"Good. That's good news." But there's something in his voice that cuts deeper than compassion, the alchemy of hurt and anger that yields a uniquely acrid solution. "Cia . . . You've known this whole time that Alice was pregnant?" At my nod, he lets out a frustrated breath. "I thought you were *done with secrets.*"

I sit up then. "It wasn't mine to tell! It still isn't. Not that it's anything to be ashamed of, but Alice made a choice not to tell anyone yet and we were just trying to respect that. To respect her. But at this point, Judah, we're running pretty low on allies. I need Remy to *know* that Alice didn't kill herself. Now he does."

Judah's grim expression tells me he doesn't care for Remy

knowing anything about what we've been up to, but we need all hands on deck and I don't have time for his . . . for whatever this is.

Jealousy?

He stands up, grabs his backpack in the plastic seat next to mine. "Cia—" He lifts the bag, goes to sit down, and freezes when something clatters from the half-zipped bottom pocket to the floor.

We are motionless, all of us, confronted with the unambiguous truth of what lies on the tile at my feet. Remy is the first to break free of the spell.

"Why," he asks slowly, kneeling down to pick up what Judah's backpack spat out, "do you have Alice's phone?"

Chapter

33

I have become a stone, smooth against the storms that try to break me. I do not burn with the fires that take the forest and leave only bones and ash in their wake. I do not give with the floods that carve scars through the earth. I do not blink when Judah reaches for the phone and Remy yanks it out of reach, and rage shimmers tangible between them with the promise of violence.

"That's not mine," Judah whispers. He turns his face to me and I've never seen it so white, not even when I gave him another family member to grieve for in Alice's lost baby. The color of his eyes—I'd thought them beautiful, tiger's eyes, and now I see them for the pyrite they are. Fool's gold.

I'm the fool.

Because if he has Alice's phone, it's because he took it from me. From my locker. And that wasn't all he took.

If I close my eyes I can see you in it.

Smell you in it.

For a second I think I'm going to throw up. But then I remember that I have become a stone, and it passes.

Judah reaches for me, but he cannot have me. I am beyond his grasp before I realize I'm moving, and Remy says, "Hey, man. I don't think she wants you to touch her."

"Fuck off," Judah snarls. "She can speak for herself. Cia—"

"Did you do it?" I hardly recognize the stretched-too-thin voice as my own.

"What?"

"Did you kill her?"

"*What?* Jesus, no! Cia, listen to me. I would never hurt Alice. I didn't break into your locker. I don't know how—"

"What did you talk to Santi about?"

My question stops him short. His silence should hurt me, I recognize this somewhere in the back of my mind, but stone cannot bleed.

"You need to leave," I say softly. Stone is inexorable. Stone does not rage with violation, with betrayal, with wanting to taste the copper of his swollen lip again even though the wound he has gifted me reaches deep into my mineral core.

"I'm not leaving you with *him*," Judah hisses.

I think of all of the taunts and threats, so well-aimed it was as if the Chemist knew everything about me. About Alice.

Maybe he did. Because we'd told him. Because in my fathers' garden, drunk on honeysuckle and adrenaline, I'd let him put his lips on mine and given him everything he needed to win his horrible game.

Then I remember Moto, and the vengeance in their eyes when they promised to help me. At least that's how I'm choosing to interpret what transpired between us. I remember the clinic files stuffed into my own backpack.

Maybe I haven't given him *everything*.

He's still talking. I want to believe his words, want to run them through my fingers like river-gold and find only truth there, and I know it isn't going to happen.

"Stop."

"Cia—"

He won't stop.

So I become stone in motion. I become an avalanche and let it carry me away from him. The force of my shoes pounding the pavement slams up my spine, shudders through my rib cage. I run like it's state finals again and the gun has just gone off. I run like I can make it to the quarry on time to save her. I run because they told me I couldn't and I could. I run because he told me I could trust him and I couldn't.

I run.

———

Remy pulls up beside me half a mile down the road. We don't talk right away, and I'm grateful for the quiet. I listen to the slowing of my breath, the ebbing percussion of my pulse. We don't talk when he pulls into the coffee shop parking lot. We don't talk when he opens the door for me and lets my limp go unremarked-upon. We don't talk until he sets something frothy and steaming in front of me, and I give it a sniff.

"Is this coffee or a milkshake?" I ask.

Remy smiles. "I thought all girls liked mocha-frappa-wocka-wocka-chinos, or whatever the hell that is."

"You don't know?"

He shrugs. "I let the barista pick. She's the expert."

I take a tentative sip. It's dessert in a cup and I don't hate it, though it and coffee have about as much in common as Chihuahuas do with Dobermans. Same species, dramatically different genetic execution.

"Good?"

"Mmmm," I acknowledge. Then the world returns to laser-focus, and along with it, my priorities. "The phone. Alice's phone. Let me see it."

Remy sets it on the table, shaking his head. "It's fried. I tried to plug it in in the car and it wouldn't take a charge. I don't know what he did to it, but it's a six-hundred-dollar paperweight now."

"*Damn* it!" I don't know what else I'd been hoping to get off of it, but the fact that it's destroyed now probably means that I missed something important. I no longer need to wonder about the Chemist's threat to brick my phone. I take it anyway.

Remy stirs a packet of raw sugar into his own cup. "So . . . should we be calling the cops?"

Emotions tangle and snarl like blood-matted hair around my heart, too complex to unravel right now, lest something break and bleed anew.

"No. They think too small. If they even care that he had Alice's phone, it would end with him, and I can't let that happen. This is so much bigger than . . ." My throat catches. I drink some more of the sweet mystery concoction so my voice can find its way out again. "It's so much bigger than just Alice, Remy. I can't see the whole picture yet but I'm almost there. I think they killed Alice because she *did* see it. She figured it out."

Remy frowns. "It? They?"

I lean forward on my elbows. "If I tell you, then you're in this, Remy. And people that are in this tend to get hurt." My fingers play with the beads of Call-Me-Gwen's mala.

I will get this bastard.

I will get this bastard.

I will get this bastard.

Maybe there's something to mantras after all.

"Are you sure you want to know?"

He nods. "Whatever *this* is, if you're in it, then I'm in it."

The blood on his sweater confirms his assertion. Without him I never could have gotten Pancakes the attention she needed on time; the memory of her shallow, agonized gasping is going to haunt me for the rest of my life. I swallow hard past that annoying knot in my throat and tell him everything.

———

"So you think they're running illegal experiments out of the Mercy Clinic?"

"They're running *something* out of there. Exactly what it is, I haven't figured out yet. But they're killing kids, Remy. And it's been going on for a long time. Maybe since before we were born."

"And you think your dad . . . ?"

This part will never not hurt. "I *know* my dad has something to do with it. He was at all of those fires, making sure there would be no investigation of the kids that died in them. And even if I could write that off as coincidence, I saw those messages on his phone. He's being blackmailed, or something. You can't blackmail someone who hasn't done anything wrong."

Remy rubs his face; in the last couple of hours, tiny golden hairs have begun to shadow his jaw. They look itchy. "I can't believe Uncle Javi would have anything to do with hurting kids, Cia. I hear you, but I just . . ." He shakes his head. "I don't mean to doubt you. Please go on."

"I feel the same way," I say miserably. "Maybe they were already dead, and he was just helping to hide the evidence, or whatever." I consider this. "Actually, that makes sense. There were no signs that any of the kids tried to get out of the burning houses. And the fires dropped off pretty abruptly when the new coroner came to town. Maybe my dad was just on cleanup duty until they found a less flashy way to get rid of the bodies."

He sighs heavily. "I don't know if that makes it better or worse."

I stare into the sickly-sweet dredges of my drink. "Me neither."

My phone vibrates against my leg. Once, then again, and a third time—insistent. I slip it out of my pocket, hoping for a message from Dad even as I speculate about the blood on his hands. Maybe traffic wasn't that bad and he got to the vet early, maybe the surgery wrapped up quickly and Pancakes is in recovery, maybe . . .

My maybes wither and die when I see the notifications on my screen, and even as I open the first, another *buzz* lets me know more messages follow.

> **Wolf_theChemist**
> It's too bad you forced my hand. I really did enjoy kissing you. Even if you're not very good at it yet. I thought you'd have had more practice, like sweet Alice.

> **Wolf_theChemist**
> You wouldn't believe the things that girl offered to do for me, if I would just spare her life.

> **Wolf_theChemist**
> Her baby's life.

Stone does not tremble. Stone does not spill her coffee-adjacent drink on the table with the force of her shaking.

I am no longer stone. No longer protected by the numb and the cold. Now I feel *everything*.

But what I feel most is fury.

> **Wolf_theChemist**
> Have you had enough yet?

> **Wolf_theChemist**
> Just let it go. It's that easy.
> Walk away.

> **Wolf_theChemist**
> It is entirely within your power to
> protect the ones you love, Silencia.

> **Wolf_theChemist**
> Just walk away.

"Cia?" Remy asks, snapping me out of the Chemist's spell.

I slide my phone across the table. He scrolls through the messages, his expression growing darker and darker with every line until the last. He curses under his breath, hands the phone back after a long moment. "I should have punched him when I had the chance."

My mind is still trying to make sense of Judah as the Chemist. Judah as the shadowy figure across the chess board, if not killing Alice himself, then putting the pieces into play to have it done. And Noah . . . collateral damage, or something else? I rewind, try to hear all of the awful things the Chemist had said to me in Judah's voice, and I don't know how I feel about the fact that I can't yet, but it doesn't matter. It can't matter.

"But maybe you should," Remy is saying.

"Should what?"

"Walk away," he says, gentle, like he knows I'm going to take his words as a blow. And I do.

I recoil. "*What?*"

"This is so far past what a seventeen-year-old girl should be dealing with, Cia, and you know it. This is too dangerous. The way he's talking to you, the thought of you getting hurt . . . it makes me sick. You need help, more than I can give you. Let me bring in my dad."

I think of Sean Walsh's bear hugs. Of him saying *I know you have two dads already, and don't need a third, but . . .* and then dismissing everything I had to say about Will and Santi. I think about the price we've all paid for the meager leads I have left, and I'm not willing to let them get dismissed, too.

"Not yet," I say firmly. "Soon, but not yet. You don't get away with that many bodies without having at least a few cops on your payroll. We don't know who we can trust."

"We can trust my dad, Cia."

"I know. But he's just one man. And if the cops start asking questions—if they even would—before I have any solid evidence, that gives the bad guys all the time in the world to batten down the hatches. Cover their tracks. Whatever metaphor you want to use for 'massive cover-up' that means all of this has been for nothing. That Alice died for nothing. And I won't let that happen."

"Okay," Remy says, covering my hands with his own in an attempt to rein in my vehemence. "Okay. I hear you. No cops."

"Not yet." The dandelion glow of fairy lights strung through the rafters and along the walls softens our edges, emanating coziness and safety, but the storm in me resists. I will relax when Will is free. I will relax when I've made sure that the killers who took Alice from me have *everything* taken from them. And since some of them almost certainly wear badges, I can't trust the cops until what we have is unburyable.

"Not yet," he agrees. "But soon." He rubs his stubbly jaw again. "Mercy Clinic. You know, I did one of my clinical rotations there last year."

I blink at him across the table. "No shit?"

"None whatsoever." He takes his hands back, and I find myself oddly missing their warmth, even though the coffee shop is far from chilly. If anything, it's a little stuffy with the charred aroma of roasted beans. "It's one of the few clinics in town that really gets down with the homeless and indigent populations, and my school has a contract with them to send students there every semester for community health experience. What was the guy's name again, Dr. Mitchell?"

"Miller. Arnold Miller."

"That's it. When he was on site he always acted like God's gift to the poor. He told us to call him Dr. M, and we used to joke that the M stood for megalomaniac. Never liked him, but he's a hell of a smart guy and you can't argue with the good he's done for this town." He frowns. "I mean, I thought so anyway. Unless he's involved too."

"If he isn't, he's wearing some seriously impressive blinders."

Remy looks as if he's aged a year in the last twenty minutes. "God, Cia . . . if what you suspect is true, they have committed the grossest act of predatory exploitation I've heard of in decades. We read about things like the Willowbrook hepatitis experiments, or the Stateville Penitentiary Malaria Study, but you never think that kind of thing could happen today." I must have a blank look on my face, because he explains, "Willowbrook was a state school in New York for children considered mentally disabled. From the 1950s to the '70s they deliberately infected kids with hepatitis to try to develop a vaccine. Doctors

had done pretty much the same thing with malaria in Stateville Penitentiary in Illinois ten years before that. The United
States—well, medicine in general—has a rather murky ethical
history when it comes to vulnerable populations."

"They infected *kids*?"

"They were a burden," he says. "At least that's how they were
seen. This was their chance to serve a greater purpose than their
lives would otherwise amount to."

"That's disgusting."

He tips his head. "As the lady says. But my point being
that if that's what's going on at the Mercy Clinic . . . I mean,
I'd be horrified, but not exactly shocked. Because we've been
there before."

What he's saying sickens me, but it also makes complete
sense. "So we need to find out exactly what they're up to."

"I have an idea about that."

"Tell me."

"When I did my rotation there, security was tight by ne-
cessity—given the neighborhood—but they weren't exactly
religious about changing their door codes and passwords. I can
probably get us in for some extracurricular research. We'd just
have to time it around the guard's patrol schedule."

Excitement bubbles up in my chest. "Tonight?"

"No, Selena Kyle, we're going to have to save our burgling
for another day. If I don't get you home *as* and *when* promised,
your dads will have my head on a pike in the front yard."

I fight the crush of disappointment. "Tomorrow then."

"*Maybe* tomorrow. Let me check a few things out first."

"Promise me you won't go without me." When he hesitates, I grab his hands this time. "Promise me, Remy, or I swear
to God I will throw a brick through the front window and go
there myself tonight."

"All right, all right! I won't go without you." He squeezes my hands, then stands up. "But I'm serious about getting you home on time. I've known Uncle Javi long enough to fear his wrath."

Violet claws rake deep gouges across the sky as the sun loses its battle for dominance of the sky. I hadn't realized it had gotten so late. I suddenly want nothing more than to curl up in my bed and pull my soft blankets over my aching body, even though I know the second I do, the noise in my head that is currently an irritating background hum is going to become a cacophony of sorrow and guilt and betrayal and fear. Then I think about where Pancakes is sleeping tonight, and I think about Will and Santi, and how Will and Pancakes are both sleeping in cages and Santi and Pancakes are both sleeping with machines breathing for them, and how Alice is maybe sleeping next to Noah for the last time, and I hurt so badly I can't breathe.

Remy opens the passenger door of his car for me, realizes I haven't moved to get in, and turns to face me. He sees my expression and cuffs my chin gently with one knuckle. "Hey. Chin up, kid. I know it seems overwhelming, but you are a pretty amazing girl. You can handle this." I nod, but he isn't satisfied. "Are you worried about your dad?"

"Yeah. Both of them. If Dad did something . . . it's going to destroy Papa."

"They're adults, Cia. They can handle whatever is coming. And they would want you to do what your heart says is right. They believe in that heart and so do I."

My cheeks are wet again, but he lets me pretend like the growing darkness conceals it. "I just wish I could talk to them. They've always been my rock, which I know isn't cool anymore when you're a teenager, but it's true. And now it feels like I'm floating without my anchor."

Remy reaches into the car, grabs a jacket from the back seat and wraps it around me. It smells like it just came from the dry cleaner's and I think it might be the one he wore to Alice's memorial, but I feel just a tiny bit better wrapped up in it. "If you could talk to them now and they would just listen, no questions, no judgment, what would you say?"

I hug the jacket around myself. "That I'm sorry. Not for what I'm doing, because this is exactly what they raised me to do—to be strong, to be independent, to think for myself. And this is something I have to do. Not just for Alice or Noah, but because this sickness in our town has been festering for maybe my whole life and *no one is doing anything about it*. So . . . I'm not sorry that I am. But I am sorry for how it's going to hurt them."

Unexpectedly, he smiles, his white teeth flashing in the twilight.

"What's funny?" I ask.

Remy shakes his head, but the smile still plays across his lips. "Nothing. It's just . . . You went and grew up when I wasn't paying attention, kid. I'm proud of you."

Warmth blooms around the fragile hope that has taken root in me. "Don't call me kid," I growl.

His smile twitches. "Yes, ma'am." He tucks a tangle of hair behind my ear, and everything has been so hard today—*I* have had to be so hard today—that this small softness is like a drug. I close my eyes, giving myself permission to be soft, too, just for this sliver of a moment. But his hand doesn't move away. And neither do I. Electricity sizzles around us and sparks the parking lot lights to life as I reopen my eyes to see the planes of his face in stark relief, light and shadow, just like the rest of him: his button-down shirt neatly pressed but splotched rusty, his sweater smooth across the strength of his chest and shoulders. He dressed with care this morning but didn't give a damn about getting dirty when it mattered.

I'm not the only one who grew up while the other wasn't paying attention.

The backs of his fingers move down my cheek, enticingly slow, and it's as if he can't pull his eyes from me. His lips brush mine, all coffee and cream and warmth, familiar in every way but this one, and I am so surprised I forget how to breathe.

Remy pulls back immediately. "Are you okay?" He looks concerned, alarmed and slightly vulnerable at the same time. "Was that okay?"

"Yes," I answer before I can let myself overthink it. It's not a lie, even if *no* would be equally true. Even if my lips remember someone else's with an ache that leeches away any trace of sweetness. "It was okay."

"Okay," he says, for what seems like the fifteenth time, and I have to smile because I don't think I've seen Remy even slightly flustered since I was in fourth grade and he was in seventh and I asked him why he didn't want to come over for sleepovers anymore in front of some of his friends from his baseball team.

He opens the door for me again, and this time I get in. As Remy drives me home, even though I am confused and tired and my phone feels like a time bomb in my pocket, I burrow into his jacket and take the moment of peace for what it is, because I know with absolute certainty that all of this is only going to get worse.

Chapter
34

I am both disoriented and immeasurably relieved when I get home and find the kitchen floor sparkling clean. It's as if the last few hours have been wound back on the reel and we can do them over again, and I won't have blood on the knees of my pants and Pancakes won't be in emergency surgery and Judah . . . Judah won't . . .

I swallow back bile. There is blood on my jeans, and Pancakes is under the knife, and Judah . . .

Judah's made his choices.

Papa tucks the Swiffer sheet into the garbage can quickly when I walk into the kitchen, but not before I see the red Rorschach blots saturating its middle, or the pile of its similarly-stained mates in the trash. Swiffer: crime-scene-cleanup approved.

Papa's hug is warm like Remy's but way less complicated.

"I am so glad you were around to help," Papa says to Remy.

"So am I," Remy says. "Do you need help cleaning up?"

"No, I'm just about done. But thank you for offering. And for taking care of my girls." He offers his hand to Remy.

Remy takes it, they shake. "You know I'd do anything for

them, Mr. L. But all I did this time was play chauffeur. Cia was pretty impressive on her own." He gives me a meaningful look, and I think maybe there are layers to the compliment that aren't meant for Papa at all. My cheeks tingle, flushed.

"Of course she was," Papa says. "I just feel terrible we didn't recognize the risk sooner."

A flicker of unease. "What?" He and Dad didn't know about the threats I'd ignored, couldn't know, unless . . .

"The porch. You can see in the grass where she must have fallen off and landed on my gardening spade." Guilt is etched deep in the creases of his forehead, the shadows around his eyes. "I shouldn't have left it out, and I should have realized with as poor as her vision is getting, it was only a matter of time before it wasn't safe for her to go back there on her own anymore."

I glance at Remy. His raised eyebrows tell me all I need to know—he's not going to out me to Papa. The truth I choose to give or withhold is entirely up to me.

Unfortunately, telling Papa anything is telling Dad too, and I'm not ready for that yet. Whoever was on the other end of those messages I'd deleted from Dad's phone clearly expects him to take care of the me problem. I don't know how far he'll go since he seems to think he's protecting me by doing so, but I do know that I can't risk any more collateral damage.

So I let Papa believe what he wants to. For now.

Remy leaves, and I forget about his jacket around my shoulders until the door closes behind him, and then I run to catch him halfway down the driveway. We say good night, hug in a way that Papa—watching from the front window—will find no fault with, even if it does stir confused fireflies in my belly. Then he's gone.

I hear Dad's car pull up just as I'm changing out of bloody clothes for the second time today. I hurry to turn the shower on, lest he take the quiet as an invitation to talk. I take off my prosthetic, pull off the sleeve and sock that are meant to protect my skin but which weren't exactly made for the abuse of the past few days. Bruises flower along my leg, blossoming around my stump in an angry throb.

I turn the water up as hot as I can stand it, let it strip away the layers I don't need anymore until all that is left is the core of me, raw and red and unburnt and unyielding.

When I finally step out of the shower I leave the water running, trying to buy myself a little more time alone. I wrap a towel around my body and grab the crutch I'd left propped by the shower, hop out of the bathroom and sprawl across my bed, uncaring that I am leaving a Cia-shaped wet spot on my duvet. The cool air on my damp, heat-pinked skin feels clean and soft.

The blinking eye of my phone warns me that the rest of the world will not be held at bay by something as simple as a running shower. I reach for it with a groan, and nearly drop it when I see the messages waiting for me.

judah_runs_good 18:50

> talk to me.

judah_runs_good 18:50

> don't trust him, Cia. i know you think he's your friend
> but there's something he's not telling you.

I nearly choke on the bitter laugh that tries to twist its way out of me.

judah_runs_good 18:51

> I remembered where I saw him before. it was an
> article Alice found. he's connected to the clinic. he's
> connected to all of this.

judah_runs_good 18:51

▌ [image loading . . .]

It's low resolution but clear enough: Remy smiles from just off of the center of a group of young men and women, most of whom look a few years older than him. His path to med school is a dual major in biochem and immunology, and these must be his classmates. Polished shelves house hundreds of books in the background, and smack in the middle of the group, sitting in a high-backed leather chair with his knees crossed and a smile turning his eyes into unreadable creases, is Dr. Arnold Miller, patron saint of the Mercy Clinic and possible orchestrator of more than a decade of exploitation of Summerset's voiceless kids.

Judah hasn't included the entire article in the cropped screenshot, but the title reads, *PHILANTHROPIST PHYSICIAN PREPARES NEXT GENERATION TO PRACTICE WITH COMPASSION AND GRACE.*

"What a fucking joke," I whisper to Dr. Miller's stupid smiling face.

cia_luc0204 18:52

▌ nice try. he already told me all about it.

cia_luc0204 18:52

▌ what is the point of this? why the games? I know what
▌ you've done. It's all coming down around you. there's
▌ no reason to play anymore.

judah_runs_good 18:53

▌ i know what you're thinking, but you're wrong. i'm not
▌ the chemist, cia.

cia_luc0204 18:53

> who are you then?

Not the kind of boy whose hand in mine had trembled as we stood on the soft earth where wildflowers reigned over the grave of his twin.

The kind of boy who could infiltrate first Alice's trust and then mine, turning it against us like a weapon? Maybe.

The kind of boy who could go from zero to violence in the blink of an eye? Yes. I'd seen it.

The kind of boy who could punish Santi with such brutality it took twenty-six staples to put her head back together?

I don't know what I believe. I don't know whose side he's on. We'd found Noah together, and his grief had felt so real. But he'd taken Alice's phone from me, and I know that's not the only secret he's keeping. If he is the Chemist, maybe it hadn't only been grief I'd seen at Noah's grave. Maybe it had been guilt. And maybe losing his brother has pushed him over the edge.

Occam's razor cuts deep, but maybe the wound heals cleaner that way.

My eyes stare back at me, reflected askew in the cracked glass.

judah_runs_good 18:54

> I'm exactly who you thought I was when you kissed me in the garden.

A tear streaks down my temple into my hair without permission. I punish my eyes with the heels of my hands.

cia_luc0204 18:54

> if you were ever that boy, you left him behind when you broke into my locker.

judah_runs_good 18:55

damn it, cia. you know that wasn't me.

judah_runs_good 18:55

don't you think it's all a little too convenient? think about it.

"Silencia?" Dad calls down the hall. Time's up.

My finger hesitates over the selection I'm about to make. The memory of his lips against my hair, whispering the promise: *whatever it takes.*

I steal his promise and make it my own, give it to Alice, in her grotto beneath my heart.

cia_luc0204 18:57

goodbye.

BLOCK JUDAH_RUNS_GOOD?

I confirm.

It's time to move on.

———

Dad has brought pizza, a rare treat in a household where both parents love to cook. The alchemy that is a margherita pizza cures a whole lot of woes in my world, but tonight, this one tastes like a cardboard bribe. Dad toes the party line, that Pancakes must have fallen off the porch onto the spade, fracturing her brittle upper ribs and slicing her muzzle. But he watches me over every bite and the meal is strained with the echoes of what we aren't saying to each other.

I'm watching him, too, though. And we both know that this was no accident. I can see him trying to figure out how to turn this into a way to rein me in without admitting that the bad guys had been in our very backyard.

Papa makes small talk about one of his kids from juvie who got his GED this week. I'm pretty sure it's someone he's talked about before, one of his I-don't-have-favorites favorites, but I barely register his words, and as soon as there's a break in the conversation I take the wheel.

"What's going on with Will?"

"Silencia, your papa was talking," Dad says, frowning.

Whoops. Apparently I'd picked up on the space between sentences, not the end of the paragraph. "Sorry, Papa."

He smiles at me. "It's okay, monkey. Of course you're thinking about Will. We are, too. He hasn't come over to us yet." 'Us' meaning Summerset Juvenile Corrections.

"He's still downtown," Dad says. "He'll get a psychiatric evaluation tomorrow to determine the safest placement until his hearing."

"The only *placement* he needs is home." I don't raise my voice—I know better— but the anger shines through the cracks anyway. "You both know he wouldn't hurt Santi."

Papa gives me a look. "I'd love to believe that, sweetheart. But he did break your phone. He started a fight at school. He felt sorry afterward, but he still did those things, didn't he?"

"That's not fair!"

He sighs, puts down his pizza crust. "I'm not saying I think he did it, monkey. I'm just saying—"

"That you think he *could* have." I clench my teeth, lock the sob in. "You're not even giving him a chance!"

"Silencia," Dad says, a warning. "He'll have his chance. If the evidence doesn't support his arrest, they'll let him go. But you know what they found. Imagine he was anyone other than your best friend. It would have been grossly irresponsible of them not to bring him in, no?"

I hate his logic, want to shatter his calm the way my own has been irreparably fractured. But even I recognize the foolishness of that road. When I don't answer, he says more gently, "He's a strong boy, Silencia. He'll get through this."

"You're wrong about him," I say, unable to bear any more of Dad's relentless reasonableness or Papa's empathy.

"If you're certain it wasn't Will," Dad says evenly, "then who was it?"

It's an ambush and we both know it. I push my chair back and drop my napkin on the table. "May I be excused?"

"No," Dad says at the same time Papa says, "Yes." Their eyes meet and they do that Parent Telepathy thing again, and somehow Papa wins out this time.

"Take your dishes to the kitchen, please," Papa says, but I'm already halfway there, stepping around the memory of red-stamped paw prints to carry my plate to the sink. I wash it quickly and am nearly to my room when I hear their voices pick up again, low and terse.

They're arguing, I realize. Because of me.

No, I tell myself firmly. *Papa doesn't like Dad making unilateral decisions that affect all of us any more than I do.*

They may present a united front for the sake of parental solidarity, but things have not been copacetic in the Lucero household for some time. I've just been too distracted to notice it until now.

I close my door. Dad has a lot to answer for, but the tension between them brings me no gratification, only more misery. I open my backpack and dump the Mercy Clinic files onto my bed. Hopefully they'll give me some direction for my future

B&E with Remy. Each sign-in sheet is laid out the same way, ten rows of names scrawled with varying degrees of legibility.

I decide to work my way backwards partly because that's the order the files are in already, and partly because I know what I'm looking for: Noah.

Name	Date	Arrival Time	Appointment?	New Patient?	Insurance?	Study participant?
Riyana lewis	7/6	1:25	Yes	yes	no	No
Leandro Valdez	7/6	1:30	n	n	n	Y
NOAH HAYES	7/6	1:45	Y	N	N	N
Sara Long	7/6	2:00	n	Y	Y	n

It doesn't take long.

I'd guessed well—Noah is all over July and August. I mark his rows in pink highlighter. By July he was already a N to the new patient question. I wish I'd grabbed June. It looks like he had standing appointments every Thursday throughout July.

On July 20, Noah became a Y in the study participant category.

"Noah," I whisper, tracing the scribble of his name with my fingers. *What did they offer you?*

More importantly—what did they want from you?

He had sequential appointments August 2, 3, and 4 before resuming his Thursday schedule. Jenna's word is far from gospel, but unless she'd been outright lying, Noah being sick in early August lines up with her story. Until I know more about this study, though, I'm assuming nothing about the nature of this illness, the scars it left on his body, and whether the clinic was the cause or the cure.

And if they'd always intended for him to end up in the ground.

An hour of crossmatching names and dates of the clinic visitors with Alice's files later, I've found both Reggie Goodwyn and Serena Clay again. The earliest record I find of Reggie is in April of last year, already a Y in that far right column, and I have no way of knowing when he flipped. His last appointment was in late October, and his death certificate is dated November 4, also preceded by a string of sequential appointments.

Their official line could easily be that these kids live high-risk lives, and contract high-risk illnesses. It makes sense that they would come to the clinic more often when they were sick. It makes sense that not all of them would get better.

It makes so much sense that for the briefest of moments, I question myself. Am I looking for monsters where there are none? Was Alice? She put Noah and Serena and Reggie and all of them together for a reason. Did she see patterns in tragedy like little kids see dragons in clouds, not because they were truly there but because she needed them to be?

I could almost believe it, except—they killed Alice for what she knew. That had been a mistake for *so* many reasons, but the one that damns them the most is that in doing so they had validated every theory and suspicion she'd had. To me, at least.

Serena first appears in the clinic files almost two years ago today. She would have been my age, missing for a year, spiraling toward the eventual overdose that would close her book forever. Her grandparents had probably already turned her bedroom into a sewing room by the time Serena walked into the Mercy Clinic without an appointment, but clearly having been there before— at least enough times for Rearden Health Alliance to collect what they needed from her, and for her to collect a few bucks from them. Just like Reggie last year, and Noah this summer. And none of them made it out of the arrangement alive.

The records I've liberated only go back five years, but that's enough for the picture to begin to congeal—like standing right in front of a Monet and seeing only chaotic brush strokes, but with every step back, the chaos melts into a river littered with water lilies and the promise of sharp-toothed mermaids.

I have barely scratched the surface of my stack and I know I will find more—and I don't need to, because I can already see the sharks in the water, but I kind of *do* need to, because I feel like I owe it to these victims to read their names one last time. Not just because they deserve to be seen, but because I am Dad's daughter. Even if these records only go back five years, which made these kids Dr. Sato's problem, not my dad's—knowing that his fingerprints are on any of this, even if I don't know exactly how, stains every moment of safety and love I have taken for granted in the last twelve years.

In the clinic records I also find Juan Apreza, Shauna Zhao, and eleven other kids from Alice's files, every one of them with a Y in the "Study participant?" column. Of course there are lots of other Y's that aren't in Alice's files, and I'm not sure yet what that means. What I am sure of is that this connection is possibly the most important thing I've uncovered so far. Whatever Dr. Miller is studying at his clinic has an *exceptionally* high mortality rate.

I finish my list of surviving study participants—I'm hoping the lack of death certificates means at least *some* of them are still alive—and take the flash drive out of the laptop, turning the small rectangle over in my fingers. This is the weapon Alice has left me. This tiny piece of plastic is my blade. And I will do everything I can to make sure it strikes true.

"We make a good team," I whisper to Alice.

I grab my phone to text Remy and nearly drop it when it starts ringing—well, vibrating—the moment I pick it up.

ID BLOCKED.

My thumb hovers over the screen. The last time I'd seen those words had been on Dad's phone, and I hadn't at all liked what had come after.

But it had been something I'd needed to know.

I swipe my thumb across the glass. "Who is this?"

"Straight to the point. I respect that." The voice is familiar but not, faintly-accented. Amused and aloof.

"You have three seconds before—"

"It's Moto, jumpy girl. Been receiving some unwelcome attention lately?"

I sit up. "None I didn't ask for, I suppose. And yours is definitely welcome if you've got something that will help me. How's Santi?"

They ignore the question. "I'm not *helping* you. Let me make that perfectly clear. This isn't about you. This is about hurting the bastards that put my girl in the hospital."

The amorphous guilt I've been slowly suffocating under all day sits just that much heavier. "We're after the same thing, Moto."

"We're really not. But if the end result is the same, I can accept the means." They pause. "There is a high likelihood that you will also be hurt."

"In what way?"

"Would knowing the answer to that question mean you don't want what I am offering you?"

My turn to hesitate. "No."

"A car will pick you up in twenty minutes on the corner of Oak and Rosemary."

"Wait—it's almost ten o'clock. I'm supposed to just get into the first car that offers me a ride?"

"You've made worse decisions," Moto points out, and hangs up.

They're not wrong.

Chapter
35

Autumn slides her chill fingers up the sleeves of my belted jacket, tosses burnt leaves around my feet with her breath. I pull my beanie down over my ears and swirl my hair—finally tamed into smooth waves—into a long rope that I can tuck into my collar. If I were someone else, I might even have worn gloves, the night has that kind of teeth, but I loathe the texture of most fabrics on my hands. I'd rather ache with cold.

I hope I've bought myself a free pass for the night, but if either of my dads comes to check on me, I'm busted. After the conversation with Moto, I had found my parents in the living room and kissed them both good night, endorsed feeling a little warm to justify leaving my window open. Otherwise, if I tried to open it after they'd gone to bed, it would set off the alarm. Papa made sure I didn't have a fever with the advanced-medical-science technique of placing the back of his hand to my forehead and made me a cup of sleepytime tea, which he carried to my bedroom for me. Dad's "te quiero mucho, mija," carried something extra beneath it tonight that I wasn't ready to examine, so I left it, and them, when I crawled out my bedroom window ten minutes after turning off my light. My stump is bruise-swollen, pulsing uncomfortably in time with my heartbeat in the soft sleeve that keeps it nestled snugly in the prosthetic.

My phone is a welcome distraction, providing the illusion of being other than completely, ill-advisedly alone on this mystery mission. Remy never got into Snapchat, so I dust off my basic messaging app and find his contact.

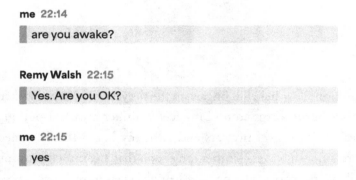

me 22:14

are you awake?

Remy Walsh 22:15

Yes. Are you OK?

me 22:15

yes

My finger hovers over the send icon. But this is Remy, and I don't have to pretend to be something I'm not. So I hit delete instead.

me 22:15

no

Delete.

me 22:15

I will be. i crosschecked the files I took from the clinic
with al's records. found a lot of familiar names on there.
alice had death certificates for at least 16 of their study

> participants, and jenna wasn't lying—noah was one of
> them. he joined the study in july.

Remy Walsh 22:16

> The one run by Rearden?

I hate that for everything I've uncovered, this study is still a big fat question mark. I'm reading this book backwards and Rearden has torn out the middle. But my next move is clear: I need to find the kids Miller has already recruited but hasn't managed to put in the ground yet. They are the parts of the story I need to know, and Remy and I will make damn sure theirs end differently than Noah's and Alice's did.

Exactly how we're going to find them, or persuade them to talk to us, I haven't figured out yet. Santi's on life support for less than I would be asking of these kids, and I'm not willing to risk any more blood on my hands. Except maybe Miller's.

Except maybe the Chemist's.

The memory of Judah's coppery kiss, of exploring his wounds with my fingertips, floods me with emotions too powerful to name. I grit my teeth and drag my thumb down the crack in the screen where the glass has begun to chip away, willing its bite to ground me.

me 22:17

> yes. with the good docs Miller and Sato on the Board.
> you'd think a study run by a guy who plays with dead
> bodies for a living would be a red flag, but who knows
> what they actually disclose? from what i can tell,
> Miller runs the clinic and recruits participants from a
> neverending supply of kids who will do anything for a
> few bucks, and Sato hides the bodies.

Remy Walsh 22:18

He's not exactly hiding them if you saw their death
certificates.

me 22:18

no, just covering up how they really died. I'm sure of it,
Remy.

me 22:19

and there are still a LOT of missing kids. way more than
a town our size should be able to lose track of. they
stopped burning down houses but that doesn't mean
they stopped hiding bodies.

Remy Walsh 22:19

And you're still anti-police?

me 22:20

I am still.

A sleek gunmetal sedan rounds the corner one block down,
nondescript in every way except that it's moving in my direction and it's been exactly twenty minutes since Moto ended
our conversation.

me 22:20

meeting a friend who might be able to help. will keep
you posted.

Remy Walsh 22:20

What, now? Who? How?

All good questions, especially the last one. I trust Santi, but Moto? Wildcard. Moto wants revenge, which puts them on my side, at least for now. And they must see me as the best way to get it, or I would never have heard from them again. They'd made that obvious this afternoon in front of the hospital. So whatever I'm walking into tonight, I am well aware that I'm being used. Moto means to make me their weapon.

Is that any different from what Alice had done?

The car rolls to a stop in front of me, and the time for speculation has run out. I jam my phone in my pocket. The sedan is eerily silent—electric, with windows so dark someone could have their face pressed against the other side and I'd never know.

I open the passenger door and get in.

The young man behind the wheel could be twenty or twice that, his features in profile fine and unlined. The back seat is empty: no Moto. Behind what I only recognize as smart glasses because of a tiny metal panel with a lens set into the top of the frame, the driver's dark eyes flick toward me and back to the road.

"Turn off your phone," is all the acknowledgment I get. He waits for me to do so, checks it, and hands it back before accelerating away from the corner, the torque silent but formidable enough to press me into my seat.

"Where are we going?" I ask, anxiety looping a queasy little knot in my stomach.

"In approximately twenty-one minutes," the driver says, "you will have your answer. Would you like to listen to music?"

Patience has never been my strength, but it's a muscle I have to flex now, and I don't enjoy it. "Dealer's choice."

He taps the screen on the dash, and ambient synth fills the empty spaces of the car. I gaze out my window as the color palette streaking past melts from the dark greens and soft neutrals

of my little corner of suburbia to the crisp whites of the freeway lights, and then to the incandescent oil spill of downtown.

We slither soundlessly through the grid. I count six traffic
lights before our car slinks up to the curb in front of . . . Summerset's oldest cathedral, St. John's. The ornate facade looms
above us with Gothic foreboding, twin towers like bones with
outstretched skeletal fingers raking the sky on either side of
three teardrop-shaped doorways.

"Beautiful, but I'm not Catholic," I tell the driver. "My parents are Unitarian Universalists."

The driver turns those rimless glasses to face me. I wonder
if anyone else is watching from behind that lens. "Moto didn't
mention how clever you are."

"What did they mention?"

"That you ask a lot of questions."

It suddenly occurs to me that nobody knows where I am,
not even Remy, and that Moto might have been on to something when they referred to the nature of my decision-making.
"This is very cloak-and-dagger."

"I'm more of a Glock guy," he says without a hint of a smile
to curve the creepy statement into joke territory, and reaches
across me to open the door. "I'll take you home when you're
done here."

"Can't wait," I mutter, but lest he think me ungrateful, add
a hasty, "Thanks." My dad might be rough around the edges but
he didn't raise a complete barbarian. I pause halfway out of the
car, eying the massive double doors in each archway. "Which
door do I use?"

Molten light limns the edges of his lenses. "The one that
opens."

The doors in the middle are scab-red with wrought iron
curling from one side to the other, and would not look out of

place in a medieval dungeon. I give one of the doors a tug and it swings open with a wooden groan.

The vestibule is empty save for a wide, shallow bowl of hammered brass on a simple column. Electric candles spill their soft light from behind opaque sconces. I pass the bowl without dipping my fingers into its still water, entering the pew-lined nave with apprehension building like a storm.

A robed man separates himself from the shadows. "Saint John Nepomucene welcomes you and all supplicants to this house of God." His face is earnest, plain; the kind you forget moments after he leaves your sight.

"Does he happen to know someone by the name of Moto?"

He ducks his head toward the confessional. "Come with me."

I follow him, the storm rumbling a low warning that I choose to set aside. For now. The man—the priest?—holds the heavy curtain aside for me.

"Kneel," he says, "and you will find what you are looking for."

"Historically, that hasn't worked out too well for us women." I peer inside the booth. "Or anyone else for that matter."

The priest looks genuinely amused. "You will come to no harm here."

I step inside the confessional and he lets the curtain fall.

I've never been in a confessional before, so naturally I bump my knees against the kneeley-part. I curse under my breath at the fresh throb.

Dropping F-bombs in church. Nice. "Sorry, Father."

"That one is free," the priest says from the other side of the dark wooden latticework. "The next one will cost you five *Hail Marys*." The smile in his voice tells me he's heard much worse. "Brace yourself, child."

"For—" I start to ask, and then the floor drops out from beneath me.

Chapter
36

I slam my palms into the walls to steady myself as I fall back onto my heels, then clamber onto the seat behind me. My half of the confessional descends smoothly into darkness with the soft whir of elegant machinery. The dim glow above narrows into a splinter and then vanishes entirely.

But I am not in the dark for long. The confessional-pod deposits me neatly, gently, at the end of a long corridor. Ultra-modern recessed strip lighting slices the walls into thirds and frames several hexagonal doors on either side of the hall. At the end of the hall is another hex door, this one striped with so many bright lights it makes my eyes ache to look at it.

So I look at the woman waiting for me instead.

Her tailored black strapless jumpsuit reveals the kind of upper body definition that you don't get from vanity lifting. I've seen it on climbers at the rock gym—not the bulky, brute force of a tank, like Dad, but the sort of sinewy power that belies agility and speed.

Like Judah.

I snap the mala beads against my wrist. *Focus.*

"Welcome, Miss Lucero," the woman says.

I unfold myself hastily from the confessional before it can betray me again. "Thank you. Who the hell are you?"

She shows me a row of white teeth. "My name is Lissa. I'll be your guide this evening." Her dark hair is knotted around two wooden sticks atop her head, and a few silken strands float loose as she turns away. "Please follow me."

The floor beneath my feet tremors faintly, as if a great beast stirs in its sleep in the earth below. At least I'm pretty sure it's not just me trembling. "My . . . Okay." I make a conscious decision to go with this for now, to trust Moto's love for Santi, because this has gone far past weird and straight into surreal-ville.

Lissa stops in front of one of the smaller hex doors on the left and places her palm on a dark panel so unobtrusive I only notice it in contrast to her pale fingers. The door retracts in petals, a mechanical flower blooming in reverse. The room inside is illuminated by the same recessed lighting but with a warmer glow, less spaceship and more Edison. A curve-backed loveseat with overstuffed pillows occupies one corner, while an antique wardrobe squats in another. The door folds closed behind us.

Lissa faces me, holds her hands out, framing my face but not touching. "May I?"

After the past few days my body's default state is hypervigilance, primed to identify any touch as a threat, and every muscle fiber hums with apprehension. I force out the breath I hadn't meant to hold and try to will my internal security system back down from *armed* to *ready*. There is no threat here. Not yet.

I have no idea what I'm giving permission for—she's close enough to kiss me, aubergine lips glossy and parted, but when I nod, Lissa only rests her palms on the sides of my face. She traces my cheekbones lightly with her thumbs, explores the curve of my ears with her pinkies, then runs her fingers through my hair from my temples to the base of my skull. The downy hairs on my arms rise with gooseflesh at her touch.

"Would you take off your hat and jacket, please?"

I remove both and tuck my beanie into a jacket pocket, nerves still at attention but none of my instincts telling me *danger* or *run*. In fact, I find my unease beginning to melt away, instead leaving me . . . intrigued.

Lissa takes the jacket from me and opens the wardrobe. Over her shoulder I can barely see what is inside, but she hangs my jacket with care and bends slightly at the waist, opens one drawer. Contemplates, slides it closed, opens the next. With a small sound of satisfaction she takes something from the drawer, closes it, and draws a dark garment from the wardrobe before turning back to me.

In her hands is a mask unlike anything I've ever seen. Carbon fiber filaments weave into a delicate lace half-mask dripping sapphire-tipped strands. Instead of holes for eyes, though, the mask unfurls around two black cups, curved eye shields like iridescent beetle wings. The unease returns with a vengeance. This place is creepy enough without losing the sense I most rely on to keep myself safe.

Seeing the question on my face, she explains, "If you seek to enter Vltava, this will protect you."

"I *seek* to talk to Moto."

"Moto is in Vltava."

"What is Vltava?"

"It is where all secrets are kept, and all prices are paid." She nods at my hesitation. "I understand your uncertainty. But the one you seek will not see you without the mask, and trust me when I tell you that you do not *want* to be seen without it. I will escort you back upstairs if you choose, and Nobu will return you to your home."

I look from her to the mask. "Will I be able to see?"

"What you are meant to. You will be no more vulnerable than anyone else."

You're a tenacious thing, Moto had said. They were right. Alice had paid a much higher price for information than this.

I uncross my arms. "Fine."

Time to be tenacious.

"It will be dark at first," Lissa tells me. "But don't be afraid."

"I am afraid of much worse things than the dark."

She only nods again, and lifts the mask to my face. The lace is cool against my skin, feather-light, as if woven from strings of spider silk instead of metal. Complete and utter darkness engulfs me as she fastens the mask behind my head, but I refuse to give in to the fear, because what I told her is true. The demons I am after don't need darkness to hide—only power.

I hear a click, and then another.

I am not afraid.

I am not afraid.

"Did you just lock this thing onto my face?" My pulse dances in my throat, the fear I refuse to acknowledge beating the drum of my ribs.

I refuse to acknowledge it because it doesn't belong here. It belongs to another time, a time I've left behind in ashes and whispered prayers, and I don't even remember the sound of the lock that closed the chain around my ankle. I don't remember the feeling of the chain that held me fast to the radiator. None of this is familiar, and yet the click of the lock has awakened something deep and dormant, the kind of horror that lives forever in the warm wet core of your bones.

Lissa touches my arm so that I can tell where she is, leaves her fingertips in contact with my tingling skin as she comes back around to stand in front of me. "Yes. It is for your protection as much as that of the others you may meet in Vltava. Your secrets are safe here, but so are theirs."

I am not afraid.

"I am only here to meet Moto."

"Even so." Lissa slips a pair of wireless earbuds into my palm, waits for me to place them. She says nothing of the clumsiness of my trembling fingers. "Very good," her voice says, now streamlined directly into my brain, or so it seems.

I sense Lissa moving, doing something with her other hand, and then the darkness evanesces. My mask must have cameras hidden somewhere in those beetle-eyes, because the room unfolds in front of me as I remember it.

Well, mostly as I remember it . . . with some additions. Such as the hex door against the far wall, traced in the white-pink of blowtorches and chemical fire, that hadn't been there a moment ago. Or the path of pale cherry blossoms that leads to the new door.

"Where did that come from?"

Lissa smiles, lifting her own simple dark silk domino mask into place. "Augmented reality. The mask you wear is both the veil and the hand that lifts it. What you need to see will be shown to you. What you must not, will not."

"That's not at all cryptic," I murmur. Now that I can see, sort of, the panic begins to ebb.

"Fitting choice of words. The space in which we stand used to be just that." Lissa trails her fingers down to my elbow. "Are you ready?"

Am I?

"Yes."

She slips her hand into the bend of my arm and leads me

down the path of petals. The door opens to a small balcony, carpeted in plush burgundy, looking out over a room so vast it must stretch beneath the entire grounds of the church. Shadows chase flickering light cast by paper lanterns, and the polished cherry floor is strewn with simple woven mats. Low rectangular tables with small flat blocks for seats are organized in a sunburst pattern, divided by sliding panels of what looks like parchment paper but probably isn't. The bar dominates half of one wall, soft golden geometric patterns glowing in the wall behind it. From the shelves I can see—and the rolling ladder tipped against them—if it gets you drunk, there is a good chance they stock it.

Most of the tables are occupied, their occupants are indistinct from my vantage point. Lissa presses a gentle suggestion into my arm and we start down a spiral staircase. Layers of music render any conversation un-eavesdroppable; a reedy flute rides the melody plucked by some sort of simple stringed instrument, with the kind of deep percussion you feel rather than hear. Figures clad in black kimonos and stark white makeup weave in between the paper screens, kneeling to deliver small crystal glasses of various liquids to the patrons seated at the tables, who are mere shadows now that I have left my perch. In my black leggings with Papa's old Nirvana shirt hanging off one of my shoulders, I am rocking the gym rat vibe while everyone else is dressed for a gala. Well, it's not like Moto had said there was a dress code. I'd dressed for quiet and easy movement, which seems like the safest bet lately. And . . . this is augmented reality, after all. Who knows what anyone is actually wearing? Or what they see when they look at me?

The staff wear their hair sculpted into flowers, bows, wings, and their simple masks mirror Lissa's. A vivid streak of red smears across the lower halves of their faces. Maybe it's meant to convey something about their vaunted secrecy, emphasizing their closed mouths, but to me the pop of bloody color makes them look disconcertingly like monochrome cannibals. Lissa escorts me between paneled rooms and when I peer into the gap between screens, I realize what she meant about the masks.

All of the patrons are wearing masks, that much I can tell. But around their masks, their features melt into a kind of blurring that is disturbing for some reason; my mind is uncomfortable trying to make sense of the visual input, and I actually feel a little queasy when I stare too long.

Augmented anonymity. It makes sense now. There is no way of knowing what is illusion and what is reality here, and that's exactly what these people are after. Curiosity tugs at me, though I don't slow to peek again. What kind of conversations are unfolding in clandestine murmurs behind those parchment walls? What kind of business is so dangerous that it cannot be spoken via telephone, or even sent through encrypted channels—and how the hell did the oldest church in Summerset become the sanctuary for the kind of people playing such games?

Threading through those thoughts with the bloodletting grace of barbed wire is the question: were any of these people involved in killing Alice? Or the hundreds who died before her?

In the middle of the room is a tiered marble fountain, presided over by a statue of a bearded man with his finger to his lips. A crown of stars rests on his brow. I glance up at him, the only unmasked face in the room, but he betrays nothing and we move past him. Lissa pauses before a section of wall indistinguishable from any other. "Up," her whisper echoes in my ear.

What you need to see will be shown to you.

Evidently I didn't need to see the spiral staircase I am now climbing, seemingly a mirror to the one I had descended on the other side of the room except with a high wall veiling us from the sight of the others. Illusion woven into illusion, keeping secrets from the secret-keepers. An invisible hex door opens to a small room, two of its walls checkered with a grid of screens that silhouette the small figure seated before them in blue-white light.

Moto spins slowly in a high-backed chair, a petite tech-monarch reigning over their faceless kingdom. Moto's mask is not a mask at all, but rather goggles, the floppy leather kind that bring to mind early aviators who were much more likely to land at the bottom of the ocean than on any tarmac. Unlike the patrons of Vltava, Moto's features are not rendered indistinct by a pixel smudge, though the giant goggles obscure more than half of their face anyway.

"Took you long enough," they say, and turn back around. Their fingers tap machine-gun rhythms on dual keyboards.

I tamp down a sizzle of anger, remembering how broken and vulnerable Santi had felt in my arms. *Moto is on my side*, I remind myself. *If only because we hate the same people.*

"Why am I here?" I insert myself into Moto's field of view by perching on the edge of their massive desk.

Moto looks up at me as if they'd forgotten I was there. "Because we needed to meet, and my time is more valuable than yours. Fiscally speaking. Do you know who John Nepomucene was?"

My reflection in their darkly mirrored lenses stares back at me, intricate carbon-fiber lace curling out from my own black eyes. "The patron saint of getting to the point?"

Moto's mouth quirks in a smile. "Close. He was a priest in fourteenth century Bohemia, in the court of King Wenceslaus the IV. As confessor to the queen, he gave her some bullshit advice about bearing her cross with grace and patience, but he also refused to break her confidence when the king demanded to know what she had said in confession. Again and again the king demanded, promised, and threatened, and still Father John maintained the sacred seal of the confessional. After some Kill Bill-style persuasion the good king eventually realized Father J was no narc, so he drowned the priest in the river Vltava." They tap their lips, mirroring the pose of the statue on the fountain. "He was eventually canonized as the patron saint of secrets kept."

"I think we met downstairs, then. Crown of stars, aging hipster vibe?"

"His halo symbolizes the stars that watched over the Vltava River as he was murdered." Moto indicates the door I'd come through with a tilt of their head. "Our Vltava honors his sacrifice by protecting the secrets shared within. To the death if necessary. Which is why I betray no secrets when I give you this." They hold out one hand, uncurl their fingers. In their palm is . . . well, a golden key shimmering with radiant glitterdust, according to my augmented vision. What I take feels a lot like a Chiclet.

"What is it?"

"The key to Pandora's Box," Moto replies. "Which you probably, definitely do not want to open. But it's yours now, and so is the choice."

There's cryptic, and then there's useless. "Enough talking in circles! How does this help Santi?"

"It doesn't. If you'd been listening you would know that I told you that already. What you hold in your hand is vengeance, pure and simple." Moto closes my fingers over the smooth square. "It's a virus I wrote that will get you into the computers at the Mercy Clinic."

I blink at them. Not that they can see it. Do they realize that they just acknowledged that Rearden was behind the attack on Santi, and likely the murder of my best friend? That the clinic's secrets are the stinking, infected black heart of this whole mess? *That's not exactly neutral*, I think, but have the presence of mind not to point out. "How did you even know—"

"I'd say it's my job to know, but it isn't. It's my job to keep my mouth shut, and I actually really fucking like my job, Silencia. I respect what we stand for. I believe in Vltava, and I will protect it to the best of my ability." They shake their head. "But I will protect Santi with everything I have, and that if that means putting a grenade in your hand, so be it. Try not to blow yourself up."

"What is Vltava?" I ask. "What are you really doing down here?"

"Vltava is the silk road of the East and the West. It is the dark web made manifest, because everything online leaves a trace, and the only people you can truly trust are those who have as much to lose as you do. Our patrons pay obscenely well for the freedom that comes with complete anonymity."

"So you play host to a bunch of scumbags who hide behind masks so they can continue to pretend to be good people by day?" Tension makes my voice rise, even though I am keenly aware of the vulnerability of my position in this nest of veiled vipers. "The only people that need to wear masks are people you'd recognize, right? So who's out there? Anyone running for office? Any movie stars I'd know?"

"Not tonight." Moto shrugs. "We don't judge the secrets, we only keep them. And make no mistake, I don't run this machine. I'm just the tech support."

"That's a bullshit position to take, Moto."

Their lips press into a thin line. "You presume too much for a girl who walked in here begging for a favor."

"I never begged. You offered. And I don't know anymore if I want to touch anything you're offering."

They lean back in their chair, but I can tell the casual posture is forced by the way their knee jumps up and down. "A lot of people believe that your fathers should not have been allowed to adopt you, to raise you as their own. That your fathers should be punished for loving each other. Right and wrong are contextual and subjective, and dependent entirely on the whim of those in power. We remove that variable, Silencia. Vltava is freedom. What people do with it is their burden to carry."

"You sound like an arms dealer."

"Maybe. Maybe someone down there is one, and maybe he or she is helping to put guns in the hands of an ethnic minority group because western civilization cares more about who gets a goddamn rose on *The Bachelor* than the genocide happening in a place that doesn't have enough oil for us to care. Maybe someone down there is arranging the shipment of lifesaving HIV medications stolen from a huge pharmaceutical company who purchased the patent and marked up the drugs five thousand percent so that those who need them most will never get them, thus maintaining systemic socioeconomic imbalance that keeps the powerful secure on their thrones. And maybe those big pharma reps are down there too, doing whatever the fuck they want to do. It is not on us to decide the balance of right and wrong in the world, Silencia. We will get the world we deserve, one way or the other."

"You're saying that the people behind those masks are just as likely to be Robin Hood or ISIS?"

"I'm saying I don't care as long as they pay their dues and follow the house rules," Moto says. "And neither should you."

I feel like I'm trying to put together a puzzle with none of the edge pieces. "I need to know exactly why Santi was attacked."

If blowing air out through pursed lips can be an act of aggression, that's what Moto does. "Because she fucking *cared*, that's why."

I stare at them. "Moto. Is Santi Serpico?"

They stare back without answering.

"Did Santi leak information to Alice about what's going on at the clinic? Is that how all of this started?"

Moto stands abruptly, sending the chair banging into the desk. "It's time for you to go. Lissa will show you out. The drive is plug and play, you can't possibly fuck it up."

Lissa separates herself from the shadows near the door, opens it for me.

"Silencia."

I turn back.

Moto smiles tightly. "Don't fuck it up."

Chapter
37

The cathedral cuts a jagged silhouette against the sky, dusted with some of the same stars that bore witness to the drowning of the sainted keeper of secrets. Not a hint of light or sound escapes the fortress of St. John's once its doors have closed behind me; true to his name, it betrays nothing of what goes on within.

And I won't either. Moto's right: some secrets do protect. Some secrets save lives, fuel revolutions. I understand that Vltava can only exist with people like Moto to defend it with rabid neutrality. But that does not mean we are not on the same side. Because when it comes to Alice—when it comes to what was done to her by people Vltava is protecting—I will never be neutral.

The fire in my marrow hadn't truly cooled until Lissa opened the locks and my eyes were my own again. The trepidation of being so deep in this place where I didn't belong, even though I'd been invited, is only now giving way to a kind of awe at everything I'd just witnessed.

Just when I think I've seen every face of this town, it shows me how wrong I can be. Vltava's whole Eyes Wide Shut vibe feels very LA, or even New York. But St. John's is over a hundred years old. Does that mean Vltava has existed here, in some form or another, for at least that long? It's clear they have other locations, but how many? Dozens, hundreds? Most of the guests in St. John's had been sitting alone, their companions visible to their eyes only, though there had been enough shimmering holograms to make me feel like I was aboard some Star Trek ship that Will would absolutely know the name of.

Will.

They have so much to pay for.

I roll the tiny flash drive in my palm: such a small thing to do the kind of damage I'm hoping for.

You might want to look away, I think to the stars. *Tonight, all of the secrets are coming out.*

St. John gave his life to protect the sanctity of secrets. Am I willing to give mine to destroy them?

Alice—the shard of her I keep alive and warm, where the moonlight can never claim her—stirs in me, whispers in her mermaid tongue words I can't understand.

Yes, she says. *Yes, we are.*

Of course, that isn't my first choice. I tell Nobu our new destination and he glides the car back onto the freeway without comment. Either he had been expecting it, or he doesn't care.

The delicate imprint of the mask is fading from my skin but not yet gone. I trace it with my fingertips and glance sidelong at Nobu. "I'm going to turn my phone on now."

He nods. Now that we're away from their precious Vltava, I'm guessing he doesn't give a damn if I'm followed or not. I'm pretty certain my dad has had some sort of uninstallable GPS tracker on my phones since I was old enough to own one, but I can't worry about that now.

Remy answers on the third ring. "Cia? Are you okay?" The question is sleep-thick, concerned.

"I'm all right," I tell him. "Can you get me into the clinic?"

A beat. I imagine him running his hand over his eyes in the darkness of his bedroom, his strawberry-blond stubble rasping against his palm. And I suddenly flush with the memory of that almost-kiss, all warmth and sweet coffee, and heat blooms in my belly. "What time is it?"

I realize I have no idea, and pull the phone away from my ear to check. "Almost midnight."

"Cia, we talked about this—"

"I know. But I have something I didn't have then."

"What is it?"

I hesitate with a sudden fear that he may not agree to help me once he knows that our minor B&E is going to tip the scales into felonious hacking territory. His willingness to help with the less savory parts of my investigation stems entirely from his desire to protect me, nothing more. He doesn't share my certainty that the path I'm asking him to join me on is the only one, because Remy is Good People. When everything shakes out, the world has done right by him, so he has no real reason to distrust it the way I do. When Remy has reached out, the world has always been there to grab onto. It has never let him fall. It has never let him burn.

And yet he is willing to risk his world to step into mine.

I roll Moto's flash drive over and over in my palm. "I'll tell you when you get there."

"When I get—Cia, where are you?"

"On my way to the clinic. Hoping that you have a better plan than mine for getting inside."

"What's yours?"

"I told you. A brick—"

"Through the front window. Right. Yes, I think I can do better than that." His voice is clearing, weighted more with apprehension than sleep now that he's imagining me with a brick in my hand. "Give me thirty minutes."

I glance at the next exit sign. "I'll be there in fifteen. Can you make it any faster?"

"I'm on the opposite side of town, Cia. Thirty minutes and I'm still screwed if I pass any traffic cameras."

"Okay."

I hear rustling; he must be trying to get dressed without putting down his phone. "Cia. That's not a great neighborhood. It's not safe for you to wait for me outside. Can you kill time somewhere safe until I'm close?"

I dredge up what I recall of the area around the clinic. My stomach chimes in with a faint rumble, reminding me I barely touched my dinner and that lunch had been a bag of almonds at the cop shop. "I know a place," I say.

———

The best thing about Taco Bell is their complete disregard for accuracy in marketing. There is no actual bell. Whether there are actual tacos is under heavy debate. And their Mexican pizza is actual pizza in the same way that putting canned tuna on a plate of iceberg lettuce is sushi. They stomp gleefully over cultural and gastronomical borders in the name of yum, and it works.

Also, most of them are open until four or five in the morning, which also happens to work for me. The only other occupants on my side of the counter are an employee on break, who sits hunched over his phone swiping right as if it's his second job, and an older man in enough layers of clothing that he can rotate which one is on the outside and have a different outfit every day of the week, who is meticulously cleaning up his area after carefully eating a burrito without getting a single crumb in his beard.

Remy arrives halfway into my second taco supreme, and wrinkles his nose as I cram the rest of it into my mouth. "You know processed meat is linked to colon cancer, right?"

I roll my eyes and offer him a nacho fry. He clearly spent at least one of those thirty minutes combing his hair, and he looks fresh and clean in a long-sleeved V-neck and jeans that I am certain were tailored, but the skin under his eyes is slightly darker than usual and he definitely hasn't shaved since at least yesterday.

Remy frowns. "Why are we here, Cia? I thought we agreed to wait until tomorrow, to give me time to figure out how we can find what we're looking for."

I pop the rejected fry into my mouth. His loss. "We did. But now I have this, and we don't need any more time." I hold the flash drive up between two fingers.

"And what is this?"

I drop it back in my pocket before he can reach for it. Not my jacket pocket, which is way too roomy for something so small, but the slim sleeve on the hip of my leggings. Whoever invented pockets on leggings should win a Nobel prize. "A virus," I tell him, keeping my voice conversational but soft. "It will get us onto their network. Going through their paper records is one thing, but Rearden is a multi-million-dollar corporation, not someone's basement startup. They're not going to keep incriminating records in filing cabinets. This will get us to the real story." I hope. I'm putting a hell of a lot of faith in the purity of Moto's vengefulness, in their coding skills, in their loyalty to Santi. I'm very aware that any one of those pillars could crumble and take me down with it.

Take us *both* down. A frisson of guilt crawls through me. "Listen, Remy. You don't need to be in this any more than you already are. It means the world to me that you showed up here in the middle of the night to help me. I shouldn't have asked. Why don't you just give me the door code and I'll do this on my own?"

He looks at me as if I just suggested he roll his shoe up into a burrito and put green sauce on it. "One," he says, ticking off a finger, "they don't change them very often, but they do rotate door codes, so it could be one of several, and you only get three chances before it locks you out and activates the alarm. Two, I know where the cameras are, and you don't. Three—" He fixes me with those green eyes, made almost fluorescent by the tube lights overhead, and reaches out to wipe nacho dust off the corner of my mouth —hello, embarrassing. He licks it off his thumb, his finger a messenger between our lips reminding us both of the time they had met without a middle man, and warmth pinks my neck. "Three, there is no chance in hell I'd let you do this alone, even if you had a key and a handwritten invitation."

I can feel the blush rising to my cheeks. "Okay then." I gather my wrappers and stand up, turning away before he can see the evidence that his words have left on my skin. "Let's go jeopardize our permanent records."

Chapter
38

The security guard looks like the kind of guy who joined the Army at eighteen and took his retirement after twenty years but still wants to occasionally be justified in smashing faces. He circles the property on foot twice, checking every lock and tapping every window, then takes out a small tablet and plays around with it for a few minutes.

"Checking the alarms and camera feeds," Remy whispers.

I smile, though it is mostly nerves. "Why are you whispering? I doubt Captain America over there is going to hear you, unless his military training also included super serum." We are parked down the block and around the corner, lights out, windows up.

"Doesn't hurt to be careful."

*The guard looks up and down the street before getting back into his truck, evidently satisfied with the nothing he saw there. When he pulls away, Remy whispers, "We should have an hour, but just to be safe, we'll call it forty-five minutes."

Though we've both dressed to blend into the shadows, Remy

has suggested that we act normal, walk up to the clinic as if we belong there, rather than slinking around like ninja burglars. His logic seems sound, and when he takes my hand, that seems right too. I tell myself it's to give credence to the illusion that we are just out for a walk.

We step off the sidewalk behind the building, gravel crunching quietly beneath our shoes. "The clinic has a strict no-smoking policy for employees," Remy says by way of explanation, nodding at the glass eye watching the back door. He lets go of my hand, climbs up onto the Dumpster that squats against the back wall but behind the camera in exaggerated slow motion so as not to make any more noise than necessary. From there, he reaches over to the camera and gives it the slightest turn, so that it is angled more toward the rear parking lot, before dropping silently back to the ground. "One of the secretaries used to sneak back here for smoke breaks. This is how she got away with it. You really have to look closely at the feed to see that the angle has shifted. It usually took a few days before someone would notice and put it back. They figured it was stray cats or pigeons since nothing ever came of it."

"Why, Remy Walsh, you have all the makings of a professional criminal," I tease him, though my pulse is already quickened. Eyeing the camera's new angle, I press myself against the wall and creep over to join Remy at the heavy metal door.

"Don't speak too soon," he mutters.

I wait while he eyes the keypad, a standard three-by-three grid of unmarked buttons. And wait a little longer. Then: "Performance anxiety?"

He hisses out a laugh. "Funny girl. I actually enjoy a challenge. But we only have three attempts before the alarm goes off, and I don't plan to waste them. They cycle through five different codes. My rotation here ended late last December, and the code that day was 6741. I just have to do the math to figure out which code they'd be on now, if nothing has changed."

"Big if." I squeeze his shoulder. "Take all the time you need, criminal mastermind."

That turns out to be only about thirty more seconds. He punches the buttons with certainty, and I'm pretty sure my heart and lungs made a pact together to go on strike until the little bulb at the top of the keypad turns green. My loud exhale makes us both jump.

"Did you doubt me?" Remy looks wounded.

"Not for a minute."

"You've never been a very good liar," he says.

I think of a file labeled FIRE, and a fire labeled accidental, and a girl labeled orphan, and the man that replaced that label with his own name. "It is nothing so special to be a good liar," I whisper.

He must hear something in my voice, because he turns around in the open doorway. "Your dad is a good man, Cia. I know you have questions, but that should *never* be one of them."

I'm not sure whether I'm supposed to feel reassured or reprimanded, and I kind of feel both, but he presses a quick, dry kiss to my forehead before pulling me inside behind him. The door bleeps in mild annoyance until we pull it closed.

The darkness in this hallway is a viscous, sticky thing. I try to calm the rabid bird beating against my ribs from the inside; I am totally disoriented, and in this undiluted blackness, it terrifies me. I close my useless eyes, draw a deep breath through my nose, and try to remember.

When I'd been here last, I'd followed a hallway back past multiple examination rooms and storage areas, to something resembling an operating room that I'd only been able to see through slivered windows. The building is L-shaped, so a left and a quick right should take me back to that long hallway.

"You know the codes to get into the filing cabinets?" My voice is steadier than it has any right to be.

"Yes," comes Remy's disembodied reply.

"Okay. You're on paper records, I'll take hacker duty. Let's regroup in fifteen minutes." I start down the hall toward where I'm about sixty percent certain the reception area is, accepting as inevitable the forty percent chance I'm about to faceplant into a wall.

Remy grabs my arm. "Wait. Let me get you into an exam room before you go all Girl with the Dragon Tattoo. That way no one passing by will see the light from the screen."

"That's probably a better idea than turning on a computer in a room full of windows," I allow.

Remy chuckles under his breath. "For such a smart girl, you sure have some big blind spots." He slips his fingers into mine. "Good thing I'm here to be the brains of this operation. Let's go."

"Pride goeth before the fall," I tell him. But his words, a near perfect echo of Will's just days earlier, hit me like a gut punch. As grateful as I am that Remy is by my side, this was our mission first, Will's and mine. He should be here. He cannot stay in a jail cell; it will break him. Maybe not physically, but *my* Will, the sweet, nerdy, not-as-funny-as-he-thinks-he-is Will, who kept Alice's secret even after she was gone because his loyalty is that fierce, who plays guitar backwards because that's how his left-handed grandfather taught him—that Will has no chance in jail. Whatever comes out, it won't be him, and the knowledge that yet another one of the people I love could be sacrificed on the altar of Rearden's secrets is enough to make me want to burn this place down.

"I think the Bible verse you want is the one about the blind leading the blind," Remy whispers. Our pace is slow, each step careful. The last thing we need is to knock into a cart full of beakers or something.

"Here," Remy says, opening a door I hadn't realized was there. Finally, the darkness is something less than absolute, the LED lights of hibernating electronics casting soft haloes around the room.

"Perfect." I move toward the computer while he flicks something at the top of the door to keep it open.

"Cia?"

I look up from the computer.

"You're the one who should be proud. What you've done for Alice—you're an incredibly strong girl."

"Dad said kind of the same thing, only the words he used weren't as nice as yours." The reflected blue-white light makes his smile garish. "But you know what they say about well-behaved women. Now get out of here while I misbehave."

"Fifteen minutes?"

"Fifteen minutes." The darkness swallows him back into itself.

I slide the two halves of Moto's drive apart, and push it into the waiting port.

A small gray box pops up, obscuring the login screen.

ⱻΦ⌐± ü π Σ   Ⱶα√δ⌐§   §Σẞ¤ ᴸÐ, it proclaims. I squint at it, then let my eyes drop to the next line.

run.exe?

My options: **yes** and **no, I'm a stank-ass coward.**

If this program can do what Moto claims, I'm lucky as hell we're on the same side. For now, at least.

I click **yes.**

The images on the screen melt like ice cream in the sun, swirling technicolor eddies that yield to a single crisp window with eight icons. In the bottom right, a goggles-wearing Bitmoji holds out one hand, the number in its palm ticking up from 1 percent to 2 percent the moment I notice it.

Moto must have coded the virus to transmit any files I'm able to access directly to them. Clever, and also slightly unsettling, the implication that Moto has a backup plan that does not require me getting out of this alive. Hopefully they're not leading Rearden straight to their doorstep, but Moto can worry about Moto. They're clearly not worrying about me.

Distantly, I hear the sound of metal sliding on metal. Remy is much more exposed than I am, by his own design. *Please, please be careful*, I pray, willing my thoughts to find him.

I start with the first icon, OMNI_FI SUITE. A login screen pops up and vanishes almost instantly, leaving me with equal parts impressed with Moto's skill and apprehensive of what I'm about to look at. But the time for hesitation, if there ever was one, is long past.

At first pass, OMNI_FI is every OCD accountant's dream. A banner in the upper right corner reads REARDEN HEALTH ALLIANCE. Countless elements form a grid of information, from revenue projection to customer growth to accounts receivable and beyond. I hope Moto knows what to make of all of this, because it is Greek to me and I don't have time to make it make sense. **RECEIVABLES** seems self-explanatory, so I click that. I don't have to be an accountant to see that contributions by Galt Global, Inc. blow every other income source out of the water. Without Galt, Rearden would barely have the resources to patch a skinned knee. I take a picture with my phone, send a few pages to the printer, and move on.

Something is tickling the back of my mind with downy mothwings, demanding to be seen. Something that's been whispering at me in the quietest parts of the day ever since Judah and I visited Jenna Reglin and saw Rearden's name on Noah's pay stubs. The whisper grows into a shriek, refusing to be ignored, and I give in.

Maybe I already know.

I click **EXPENSES**. Change the date to the year of my fire, go back six months. And rock back in my seat, my entire body slapped backward.

[EXPENSE REPORT] BENNETT, JOHN—EMP ID #01658—
DEPT: OPERATIONS—APPROVED: Y

I hadn't been able to remember where I'd seen those words before because I couldn't *read* when I'd seen them. My brain had held onto the images all this time, vestiges of a childhood that has begun clawing its way back into my memory after years of haunting my nightmares.

From what Dad told me, and everything he'd sworn to in writing, there was only one service my bio dad had been qualified to provide. And if Rearden was paying him to make bonedust . . . then their link to the plague of addiction spreading through Summerset isn't just one of exploitation, a cheap source of guinea pigs for their research, but something even more malicious.

Remy's name forms and dies on my lips. I can't call him back yet. Though everything in me wants him near, I need him right where he's at.

Alice was right all along. There is more to the story of my fire, but Rearden buried it, covering their tracks with the ash of my childhood home.

With the bones of sisters I only remember in nightmares.

Mind racing, I go back to the main expenses page. I search for my dad's name—my *real* dad's name—and come up with nothing for Javier Lucero. The relief that spreads through me is like ice on a burn, soothing but temporary. Just because he isn't on the official payroll doesn't mean he isn't a player on the board.

CLINICAL TRIAL MANAGEMENT SYSTEM shows me three active projects. I check the begoggled face at the bottom of the screen: 43%. I am as aware of our time ticking down as I am of my own heartbeat, both of which are currently racing away far too quickly.

PROJECT: OAK TREE
Pharmacopoeia . . .
Total subjects enrolled . . .
Currently in treatment . . .
Completed trial . . .
Serious adverse events . . .

PROJECT: HARMONIZER

PROJECT: ATLANTIS

Pharmacopoeia opens a recipe book of various iterations of something called Compound 1905—1905.1, 1905.2, and so on, all the way up to 1905.44. I shouldn't know what I'm looking at. But thanks to Alice decoding the autopsy reports, I do.

"Bonedust," I whisper.

Rearden isn't just profiting from the sale of dust. They *created* it. Engineered it at the molecular level to their definition of perfection.

Have I finally met the Chemist? This has to be his work. With their perfect drug, Rearden has ensured themselves a completely dependent pool of test subjects who will not complain or, if they do, will not be heard.

ELECTRONIC HEALTH RECORD [OAKTREE] fills a blue box that quickly fades to a gray search box. **Surname?** it suggests helpfully. **First? Middle? SSN? DOB? MRN? OPTN? Facility?**

I spell his name gently, as if he can feel my keystrokes. **Hayes. Noah.**

He's here.

They're all here. I can feel their presence coalescing in the shadows around me. Noah. Reggie. Amy. Serena. Shauna. Toby. Juan. Rohit. Adeline. All of them begging me to see what they've been waiting so long to show me.

A link on Noah's profile labeled **RPT** launches a new application, which again demands a password and again is backhanded into submission by Moto's virus. The loading screen reads **RESOURCE PROCUREMENT AND TRADE** above open hands cupped around the shape of a heart, as if in offering.

Offering.

But you cannot have an offering without a taking. Something dark awakens within me.

No.

The hands and heart disappear.

DONOR REGISTRY

[LAST, FIRST] Hayes, Noah

[DONOR BLOOD TYPE] AB pos

[ACTIVE] Kidney, DOS 0y 1m 6d—note: no lesions, size normal

[STATUS] deceased—note: COD unrelated to donation

[RECIPIENT] Georgios Nicolaides—note: paid in full, maintenance payments only

It was just, like, his gallbladder or something, Jenna said. *Just a couple little cuts.*

The darkness creeps around the edge of my vision.

Everything is going to be alright, murmurs my smoke-mother.

But it isn't. It will never be again. Because now I know what they have on my dad. The only possible reason a good man would ever take part in this madness.

My hands are shaking so hard I miss the first few keys entirely, but it doesn't take long.

I find Papa's name under RPT's list of active clients. His double lung transplant the year after my adoption was finalized, when it became clear the cancer would never, ever let him go, let him breathe.

Love.

Love is what they have on my dad. And his unwillingness to let the man he loves die. No matter the cost.

There is a high likelihood that you will also be hurt, Moto had said, after a rare moment of hesitation.

They knew.

Had Alice known? She'd figured out my dad's involvement in hiding the bodies before Rearden got itself a pet coroner, but had she figured out why? Something tells me I'm in deeper now than she ever got the chance to be.

Dad isn't on the payroll because they didn't pay him with dollars. His debt to them is written in Papa's blood, and renewed with every breath Papa was never supposed to live to take.

Breath stolen from someone like Noah, used and discarded once all of the potential profit had been wrung from his body.

"Oh, Dad." The words wrench out of me, quietly and

painfully as razor blades, bringing with them the warmth of tears. My head sinks down onto my forearms, none of the bones in my body strong enough to hold the weight of what I know. A sob racks my body, stifled by my fist pressed so hard against my mouth I taste copper.

I almost don't hear the noise from down the hall, muffled as it is, and when it comes again, it takes longer than it should for my senses to register it for what it is: the dull thud of something heavy hitting something heavier. A grunt, and then another thump.

We're not alone.

Every hair on my body jumps to attention as the primordial part of my brain flips into survival mode, snapping off the blood supply to my grief as something no longer to be afforded.

Had Rearden planted an extra guard inside, tipped off by the Chemist that we'd be nosing around? Or had we been followed?

I look around for a weapon even as the tears dry on my face. Nothing. There is *nothing* here! Except . . .

I grab a tongue depressor from a jar, snap it at an angle. Another meets the same fate before I wrap the rounded ends in a strip of gauze. It's no Excalibur, but my little shiv could do some damage if it needs to.

I resist the urge to call out Remy's name as I enter the hall, keeping my back to the wall so I don't get disoriented. Four doors down, faint light spills from the storage room where Remy had told me the older records were kept.

My breath reverberates cacophonously in my ears, so I hold it, trying my damnedest to live up to my name as I close the distance between myself and the open door. The light is constant, unwavering—wherever its source, there is nothing moving between it and the doorway.

I lower myself into a crouch. If there is someone waiting for me on the other side of that door, the least I can do is not be where he expects me to be. Spine pressed so tight into the wall I can feel every vertebra digging into the plaster, I close my eyes, permit myself one deep breath, and spin on one heel to see . . .

. . . complete and utter shambles. One filing cabinet is tilted precariously against another, and boxes that most likely were not crushed and disemboweled of their contents all over the floor prior to our arrival now, well, are. The narrow sliver of light is coming from the cell phone facedown on a pile of papers—Remy must have had the flashlight on—and it's just enough to illuminate the crumpled form on the floor.

An animal moan escapes my throat as I jam the makeshift blade into my pocket and run to Remy's side. He's breathing, but the knot above his temple is rapidly purpling and trickling a not-insubstantial amount of blood.

"Remy!" I hiss.

He doesn't move.

"Shit. *Shit!*" I pick up his phone. The screen is shattered and dark. Useless now, except for the fact that the flashlight stayed on. So in balance, slightly less useless than my own phone, forgotten on the desk in the exam room four doors down.

I have to get help. We have enough proof now. We have it by illegal means, and maybe completely inadmissible, but enough to get the right people asking questions. Or I will ask them, as loudly and in front of as many cameras as possible, until Rearden is buried and the earth salted above it.

It has to be enough. Because Remy's life is in danger, and I don't know that I can protect him on my own. Not now. Not here.

So it has to be enough.

I move to the doorway. The edges of my makeshift blade dig into my palm.

No signs of movement. The hall is empty. Trashed room aside, there is no sign that anyone else has been here. Except —

A sound reaches my ears. A drawer opening? Something soft but purposeful, coming from the direction of the reception area.

The opposite direction of my exam room, and my phone.

I don't hesitate to think about whether I can make it or not. I enter the hall just as Remy's phone gives up the ghost and plunges us both into black.

The sound stops and so do I. A lethal game of freeze tag. Then:

Footsteps pound the floor behind me. I break into an all-out run.

I am fast. I win races. Trophies with my name on them live behind glass at school, proving it.

I am not fast enough.

The entire airborne weight of another body slams into mine. I feel the heat of him the instant before contact, and I twist and lash out with my fists, with my knees, with everything I have and am that could hurt him, and I hear a grunt of pain but then something cool and wet and incredibly fucking stinky is covering my nose and mouth, and I've read enough books to know not to inhale but when you're fighting with everything you have against someone bigger than you, your body needs fuel, and that fuel is oxygen, and I only have enough time to wish I'd taken up swim instead of track because then I'd be better at holding my breath and the darkness wouldn't be closing over me like the sea,

like the quarry,

like

giving

up.

PART THREE

The wind of silence has become a wind of violence
The present, the future or the past. What would you choose?
Or shall I say: What have we to lose?
If we want our children to be happy and proud,
Then we have to shout and shout out loud:
Mouth to mouth, throw the dice
But hurry and don't think twice
It's only your voice you have to sacrifice

Elisabeth Karlberg

Chapter
39

I don't wake up as much as I'm exhumed, into a world of sharp edges and confusion and everywhere, everywhere pain. And a faraway voice that is growing unpleasantly louder and louder, refusing to give me back to the darkness, back to the not-knowing. For a beat, I fight it. I pull back. I reject the pain and the knowing and reach for the dark nothing, try to wrap it back around myself.

Then I hear my name again, and realize I'm fighting the wrong enemy. I reach for the pain, grab onto it like a drowning girl offered a rope of razor wire. The back of my skull throbs riotously, my left side splinters into agony when I inhale, and my left leg . . .

My prosthetic is gone. I can tell even before I open my eyes, through the veil of pulsing red pain coursing down from hip to knee, that part of me is missing.

"Cia, please, you *have* to wake up!" The voice, no longer distant, is now an urgent plea in my ear.

"Only because . . . you said . . . please," I manage, hoarse, wondering why my throat feels like I inhaled a swarm of angry bees until I remember the cloth mashed over my face, wet with whatever I had inhaled that had scorched a path into my lungs.

"Thank God." Remy, or the vague shape and size of him at least, takes shape before me. "Here." I am lying on my left side on what feels like a mound of clenched fists but probably isn't, and Remy's arm slides under my shoulder, tipping me into a sitting position.

My vision smears, and I almost throw up. *Concussion then. Definitely a concussion. What else?* Pain. Pain with breathing. *Maybe a broken rib. Maybe more than one.*

The two Remys beside me finally coalesce into one. The bruising on his temple has spread like a wine stain down his brow and cheek, and blood is caked into his hairline. His eye is already raccooning, which can't be good.

"Where . . . ?" But I don't need Remy to tell me. I know before the question has even left my lips.

The moon is a mirror, shattered into a million pieces on the rippling surface of the quarry. I am almost close enough to gather them into my palms, if I just reach out my hands, lean a little further over the edge . . .

I am sitting less than two feet from the edge. From an eighty-foot drop into the part of the quarry that is equally likely to catch me in rocky arms as frigid water. I jolt involuntarily with the realization.

"I woke up in the trunk of my own car," Remy explains, helping me scoot further from the edge. "He must have thought I was still out. He had his back to me, dragging you over here, so I was able to catch him by surprise, but I don't know how long we have before—"

"He?" My world lurches again, but this time it has nothing

to do with my bruised brain and everything to do with my bruised heart.

Judah.

He is sprawled out in the rocky dirt with the boneless abandon of someone who's had way too much to drink or was, indeed, caught completely by surprise. "Is he . . . ?"

"No," Remy says grimly. "But he should be, for what he did to you."

The sight of him, even unconscious, even like this, makes my pulse gutter, and I hate myself a little for it. "Why would he bring us here?"

"I don't know. Maybe he wanted to make it look like suicide, because just killing us would raise too many questions. It worked before, didn't it?"

He means Alice. He means that Judah killed Alice.

The bile in my throat has nothing to do with my concussion. I have so many more *why*s, but they can wait. They have to wait. Even if they carve at my chest like razor blades with every breath I don't give them voice. "Okay, Remy. I think I'm ready to call the cops now."

"Good. But I want you safe first. I'm going to get my car— it's about fifty yards back in the woods." He doesn't look down, but he doesn't need to. I know what he's thinking. "Cia—"

"He took my leg so I couldn't run," I say so he doesn't have to, and the vulnerability of it sickens me, but it's nothing I'm not used to. Nothing I haven't lived the last twelve years with, and despite. "Get the car. You'll be faster without me, and we can put *his* ass in the trunk this time."

Why did you kill Alice?

"Here." He presses something icy cold into my hands.

I blink at the gun, momentarily mystified. "Where did this come from?"

"My glove compartment. I knocked him out with it, but if he wakes up, you'll want to point the other end at him."

I've shot guns before, even took a basic firearm safety course so Papa could sleep at night even though Dad keeps all of his weapons locked up in a safe. But I've never shot to kill, and I've *never* aimed one at another human being.

Up until the past few days, I'd never been kissed by a killer or hacked into the files of an evil megacorporation, either.

Why did you make me trust you?

I take the gun. It surprises me with its heft.

"Careful," Remy says. "There's one in the chamber." His lips press against my hair. "I'll be right back. Promise me you won't hesitate to protect yourself."

It's too late for that, I almost tell him. *The damage is already done.*

But I know he means my body, not my soul, so I just nod until he's gone.

Why did you kiss me?

"Wake up." Rage and anguish drive the words out of me in a broken whisper. The breeze drags its claws across my skin, riffles Judah's hair across his forehead, across the split brow that I'd so carefully repaired, now bleeding fresh red into the earth. "Wake up, you bastard."

The ache in my marrow roars out of me, weaves itself into a spell that makes Judah's dark lashes flutter, his lips pull into a grimace of pain even before his eyes open. Twin rivulets of blood trace meandering lines across his cheek toward his mouth—Remy must have really nailed him with the butt of this gun.

Judah plants his palms on the ground, stabby with shards of quartz and other things Will would know the names of but can't tell me because he's in fucking jail. He pushes himself up with a groan, reaching instinctively toward the back of his head and freezing almost comically when he sees me less than ten feet away. My left knee stabilizes me as I rise into a half-kneel.

"Cia? What the hell—"

"No." I keep the gun trained on his center mass. "You don't get to talk."

Something passes behind his eyes as he fights for calm. It looks like fear, but as a master of masks, one is probably just as easy to don as another. He gets his feet underneath him and starts to rise. "Cia, I don't know what's going on—"

We both startle at the abrupt *thud* of something heavy hitting the dirt. It glints silver, and my lizard brain recognizes the threat before I can name it, before I can do anything more than shout, "Don't!"

Judah picks up the gun anyway. It must have fallen from his waistband when he changed positions.

Oh no. No no no. "Drop the gun, Judah!" I have the advantage. He's not even holding it right, not even pointing it at me, and yet I do the opposite of what Remy begged me to do.

I hesitate.

Judah looks at the gun, then slowly lifts his gaze to mine. "This isn't mine."

"Then put it on the ground."

His eyes, shadowed by those stupidly long lashes, are black, absent the sunlight to make them glimmer green-gold. "I can't."

"You can."

"I can't protect you without it," he says.

I want to cover my ears. Cover my heart. "You never protected me," I tell him. "It was you I needed protecting from."

The roar of tires churning up rocky projectiles drowns out his reply, and headlights wash over us, drawing our edges in stark relief. Judah whirls and points the gun at the windshield.

"Stay in the car!" I yell, but Remy listens about as well as

I do. He's out of the car before I've even finished the sentence, the still-running Prius left to mutter to itself.

Judah's gun is trained on Remy, who skids to a halt, palms out.

Remy turns wide eyes on me. "Do it, Cia!"

"Don't listen to him!" Judah keeps the gun on Remy but angles his body toward me. "Cia, he's been lying to you the whole time. I followed him—"

"We know!" Remy interrupts, inching toward me almost imperceptibly. I don't know what he thinks he's doing—putting himself between me and Judah's gun? "We know you followed us to the clinic. We know what you did."

"What did I do?" Judah demands.

"You attacked us," Remy said. "You killed Alice!"

"You're the Chemist," I whisper.

The sound Judah makes is half laugh, half desperation. "I fucking failed chemistry, Cia!"

I can't help it, I laugh too. But there's no humor in mine either. "You had Alice's phone. You kept secrets from me. Someone attacked Remy and me at the clinic, and you just admitted you followed him!"

"I told you I don't know how that phone got in my bag! But I have good fucking guess," he growls, staring at Remy. "Listen, Cia! Only one of us is telling you to do something you can't turn back from. Only one of us is pretending to know what the hell is going on here, and it damn well isn't me."

"You can't trust a word he says," Remy tells me, barely farther than an arm's length away now. "Think about Alice. Think about what he did to Pancakes! He only wants to hurt you. Shoot him!"

The thunder in my ears breaks his words into shrapnel, burrowing bloody trails into me. He's right. I have the gun, he doesn't. If I don't take the shot, if Judah hurts him again—kills him—it will be one hundred percent my fault, because I hesitated. Because I can't stop seeing the boy in the garden in the boy with the gun.

—*Alice*—

—*Pancakes*—

—*hurt you*—

Judah looks at me, really drills me with those onyx eyes, and I force myself not to flinch.

—*shoot him*—

Sadness writes its name in every line and shadow of his face. "You know me. You may not trust me right now, but you know me. And I know you."

—*shoot him*—

Slowly, deliberately, Judah lowers the gun. "I trust you, Cia."

"Oh, for fuck's sake," Remy says, and slams me to the ground.

"Stay away from her!" Judah roars, but it's too late. He raises his weapon.

Nothing happens.

Remy rips the gun from my hands and fires straight at Judah.

Chapter
40

Judah spins with the impact and crumples. Beyond the glare of the Prius's headlights, all I can see is the white edges of his Converses, and they're not moving.

A scream tears out of me as I lunge for Remy. I catch him at the knees and we go down in a writhing knot, a grunt of shock escaping him as he hits the ground. I seize the opportunity to grab the gun. It tangles in his fingers, but I don't give a damn if every single one of them breaks—I yank it away as hard as I can. It skitters a few yards away.

Remy drives an elbow into my face. The pain is exquisite, blinding, and I curl up against it instinctively. Hot blood slithers onto my lips. He takes the moment I've unwittingly given him, rolls away and comes up to a crouch.

"I'm disappointed." He is still breathing hard, but the mask of calm has already slipped back into place. "I really thought you had it in you."

"To kill an innocent person?" I seethe at him, still reeling from what just happened. "You gave me a loaded gun but his was empty? That's a cowardly move if I ever saw one."

"I wasn't willing to risk you, Cia."

I've been so fucking wrong. I am sick with the wrongness of this, and with the fact that Remy used Judah's trust in me, his desire to protect me, to set this whole thing up. Alice, Santi, Will, and now Judah—one by one, trust in me has spelled catastrophe for the people I care about.

"We need to call an ambulance." I staunch the bleeding with my palm, crane my neck to see past Remy, but the night has Judah fully wrapped in its shadowy arms.

"That's definitely *not* what I need." Remy smiles, and I'm both sickened and satisfied by the blood between his teeth. I eye the gun, just far enough from both of us to carve out this stalemate—and just close enough to the edge of the quarry to make a hail-Mary lunge an extremely bad idea. "It's not too late for you to make the right choice, Cia. Your dad did."

The world tilts. *Do not throw up. Do not throw up.*

"What do you know about what my dad did?"

"Everything, Cia. I know everything." His voice gentles at the look on my face. "He was desperate, Cia. The man he loved was dying, and when the solution presented itself, he loved Liam enough to say yes. And he was strong enough to pay the price."

"The price being whoever died to give Papa his lungs. And covering up dozens more murders since."

"You say murder, I say euthanasia," Remy says blandly. "Look. These people aren't like us, Cia. They are nothing. Their *lives* are nothing. The world will be exactly the same after they die as it was the day they were born, because they won't leave so much as a smear on its surface. They *don't matter.* We can change that. We make their lives count for something."

For such a smart girl, you sure have some big blind spots.

I should have heard it then. I can't unhear it now. Remy had gone and grown up, all right . . . into a monster I couldn't recognize even standing right in front of me. "God complex much?"

"Maybe some men *are* gods, or as good as. Maybe it's time we stop catering to the sniveling lowest common denominator, and take the greatness we make for ourselves." He pauses, softens. "Oh, man. Did I break your nose?"

The blood on my fingers speaks for itself. I feel like I'm choking on molten pennies.

"Try to see things from your dad's perspective, Cia. He did what he did for love. Have you ever been in love?" A curious, cautious smile. The memory of those lips haunts mine, warm and coffee-sweet. "Were you falling in love with me?"

I can't think about his lips. I can't feel this pain. "You're going to make me vomit."

"Don't be petty. I wasn't lying about being Alice's first kiss. Was I yours?"

"Don't flatter yourself."

"Just the best then."

"Not by a long shot. You disgust me." I swallow hard. Judah's Converses remain statue-still. *Please be okay. Please don't be dead. Please don't bleed out in the dirt while I can't do a single goddamn thing to help you.*

"Ah, you wound me." He puts a hand to his chest in injury. "I mean, you actually did wound me. I think you broke my finger."

"Come closer and I'll break something else for you."

Remy gives me a come-on look. "You couldn't even shoot the guy you thought was a killer. What are you going to do, Cia?"

"Want to find out?"

He shakes his head. "You and I go back too far. I'm in your heart, and you're in mine. I love you, Cia. Why do you think you're still alive? You've been nothing but a pain in Rearden's ass, and you better believe they wanted you in the ground the second you started asking questions. I fought for you. I didn't want this for you, or for Alice. I tried to protect you. I tried to scare you both away, so many times. Why couldn't you just fucking listen?"

"In the coffee shop. You . . . I got messages from the Chemist, but you were sitting right in front of me."

His look is pitying. "*That's* what you can't wrap your head around? I scheduled the messages in advance. They did exactly what they were supposed to do. You really do trust too easily, Cia."

I've gotten my knees under me but the world splits into two again, taking even longer to congeal back into one image this time. "What did you do to me?"

"I might have accidentally bonked your head on the wheel well when I was stuffing you into my trunk," he says apologetically. "But it's no worse than what I did to myself, to get you to drop your guard back at the clinic."

My skull throbs. "Why the games, Remy? Why didn't you just kill me when I came to you with what I knew the first time?"

Remy's face is disorientingly sincere. "I never wanted you dead, kid. Why can't you see how much I care about you? I told you, I put my neck on the line with Rearden for you. They wanted you *and* Uncle Javi put down. They don't like loose ends. They haven't stayed in business this long because they're sloppy, love. I honestly didn't think you'd get anywhere. If Santi had shut the fuck up, none of this would have happened."

"Don't you dare blame Santi for what you've done," I growl. "But why all this?" I gesture at the quarry, at Judah, lost to shadows beyond my seeing. "Why the show?"

"He's a loose end, Cia. I know you care about him. You've always been a good person. Too good for someone like him. He's going to disappear either way, but you have a choice."

"What *choice*?"

"Liam is alive because of Rearden," he says gently. "All of the lives he touches, all of the good he does, is fruit of their tree. I know you don't like their means, but the ends are *good*, Cia, I promise you. You and I, we could change things from the inside. It doesn't have to be the way it is. Do you know how many people would *volunteer*, if we promised to take care of their families? Their children? A one-time payout to change so many lives, and end their suffering. We could make that happen, Cia. Rearden has been around for a long time, but they haven't exactly evolved with the times. Their leaders are old and so are their ideas. It's time for new ideas, new voices—and I want those voices to be ours. Yours and mine."

The word *ours* makes me want to gag. "What *happened* to you?" What I'm really asking is, *What happened to the boy I knew?*

He answers the question I didn't ask. "I was always going to change the world, Cia. It's what I was born for. When they killed my mom, they showed me exactly how I would do it."

The bleeding is slowing. I drop my stained hands. "Your mom died of liver cancer."

"My mom died waiting for a new liver," he corrects me. "My mom bled out from every orifice in her body waiting for a donation that never came, while her junkie clients poisoned themselves day after day because our system values their lives more than hers. She changed lives, Cia. She was a good person, but she sacrificed everything, and what did it do for her? What did it do for her family?

"These people are *parasites*. And they get to live—off our dollars, our hard work—while good people like her die every day." There is pain in his voice, coarse and real. "What happened to me? I opened my fucking eyes, and got on the right side of the war. And it *is* a war, Cia, make no mistake. We are outnumbered, the greatest of us chained to the entitlement of the weakest. *That's* why the show. That's why you got the loaded gun. I wanted to see if you could make the right choice. If you could be one of us, if you could break those chains and take your place, or if it's too late."

He speaks with the terrifying self-righteousness of a true believer. "My place. Beside you."

"Yes."

"What did you do, Remy?"

"Everything I could," he says fervently.

"What is Project Oak Tree?"

"Oak Tree is just the beginning." He tilts his head. "Who gave you that virus, by the way?"

I ignore the question. "What did you do for Rearden, Remy? Besides kill my best friend."

"Technically speaking, Alice killed herself," he says. "I gave her a choice, too. I'm not a monster, Cia. I loved her just like you did."

"Tell me what you did to her," I whisper. "If you really loved her, tell me how she died."

"She was so wrapped up in that Hayes kid. What is it about them that gets under the skin of good girls like you? They're *nothing*." His lip curls as he glances at Judah's unmoving form. I don't dare take my eyes off of him. "So I brought her here and gave her a taste of what he'd chosen over her. She *loved* it, Cia. You should have seen her."

I have never wanted to punch a face so badly in my life. "You're lying."

"I'm not. But even high, she was still being a sanctimonious bitch. She wouldn't back down. So I gave her another choice: the needle or the water."

"The . . ." The pieces come together too sluggishly. "You were going to OD her."

"It's not a bad way to go, Cia. Better than drowning. But I guess she thought that in the water, she might still have a chance." He looks thoughtful, shrugs. "Or maybe she slipped. She was pretty fucked up."

I can't tell anymore if the wet on my face is blood or tears. "She was *pregnant*, Remy!"

"I know that *now*!" he says defensively. "But even if I'd known it then—she gave me no other option! She thought too small, refused to see the big picture. She should have thought of what kind of world she wanted that baby to grow up in before making that decision for both of them."

"She did." I say it more for myself, for *her*, than for him. Alice had known exactly what kind of world she was fighting for, and it looked nothing like the class war Remy and Rearden dream of.

"She didn't suffer. Much. You can thank me for that. The current formulation of bonedust is mine, and it blows everything that came before out of the water. Nothing else on the market comes close to its potency with no end organ damage. Oak Tree wasn't my idea, but with my product, it's become something greater than even Arnold and Perez ever envisioned.

"People like Noah Hayes only know how to tear down, never to build. They are begging to be given a purpose, because they are lost without one. You've seen how they hurt, and how they inflict that hurt on everyone around them. Addiction is the collar they willingly cinch around their own necks, and society just lets them suffer. All we did was pick up the leash and guide them to their purpose, and that purpose is Oak Tree. Under the umbrella of the study we can make sure they stay healthy until their gifts can be matched with the right buyers."

"Buyers." I spit the word. "Do they know where their *gifts* come from?"

"They know how much they spend to secure said gifts."

Remy raises his eyebrows. "People tend not to ask many questions when they know they won't like the answers. It's too bad that never stopped you. Or Alice."

"That's because I'm not a coward. And neither was she."

"Is that going to give you comfort when you send your dad to prison?" Remy asks softly. "When you break your papa's heart?"

I don't let his words land, because I know if they do, they might break me.

"Rearden is an idea, Cia. A powerful one, shared by powerful people. We can be part of it. We can shape it, make it ours. Make it better."

The blood on my fingers has turned tacky, which means my nose isn't bleeding anymore. My head is starting to clear and the gun is starting to look like a much more viable option.

"Answer me!" he demands. "Tell me you don't think Liam's life was worth the cost. Tell me you'd choose differently."

I can't imagine a world without Papa's goofy notes and Elvis toast. A world with a hollowed-out version of the dad I know, his heart a garden full of dead peonies. I don't have to, because Rearden gave Papa back to us.

I owe Rearden.

Remy isn't wrong about that. I think about Noah's spray-paint-spotted hands, Reggie Goodwyn's kind smile, Toby Aguilera's taped-together glasses, the word MOM tattooed in a heart on Serena Clay's wrist. Can I look Remy in the eye and say that I wouldn't have traded any of their lives for Papa's? For Dad's?

I am a hypocrite. If Rearden falls, other Cias will lose their Papas. Other Javiers will lose their Liams, and it is the kind of losing that makes skeletons of those left behind, all bone and ache and the memory of warmth.

"I know you, Cia. I know your heart, and I know how fiercely you love. You take after your dad in all the right ways, and I think you would make the exact same decision he did. For love. For family."

Rearden gave me Papa. Rearden took away Alice.

People are going to die. That is not up to me. The choice Remy poses to me is not if, but who.

Remy is right—I am my dad's daughter.

But I am also Papa's.

And once, a very long time ago, I was my mother's.

Remy sees the decision in my eyes before I know I've made it. "That's your choice?" he asks, quiet and sad, as if I'm the one betraying him, as if it's his heart breaking and not mine. Maybe it's both. Maybe we'll just stab each other to death with all of our broken edges and the stars can watch, as silently as they did the night St. John died keeping the faith of his queen. "You choose them over me?"

"There is no world in which I would choose you," I tell him, and I don't know if it's a hundred percent true but none of those worlds are this one, where tears shimmer-wash my vision but I can still see what he can't, that behind him the darkness is moving, it has grown arms and legs and fists and anger and it comes for him *fast*.

Remy starts as one of those arms snakes around his throat, but he has no room to turn, no space to breathe before Judah takes them both down to the ground. Somehow Remy lands on top, clawing at Judah's arm.

There's so much blood. Too much, and I know Judah's advantage right now is surprise, not strength, because you can't lose that much blood and stay conscious for very long.

"Cia, *get out of here!*" Judah shouts, ragged, and for the first time I can see his face behind Remy's, and he's paler than moonlight, and sweat gleams on his skin, and I know he is not okay.

So I take the gift he's given me and go for the gun.

Remy chooses the exact same moment to tuck his chin and dig his feet into the ground, bucking and twisting, and Judah's blood is his own enemy, refusing to stay in his veins where it belongs and making his arms slippery enough for a worm like Remy to writhe free.

The gun is heavier than I remember from five minutes ago, maybe because now it has history as well as promise. I turn just as Remy jumps to his feet.

Our eyes meet down the length of the barrel.

I will the threat to be enough, but it isn't. Remy steps toward me, palms up but not out—inviting, not surrendering.

"Give me the gun and this will be over. Let me show you the world we're building, Cia." Remy's gaze on mine is painful in its sincerity, belied by the streak of red smeared across his jaw. "I know you'll come to believe in what we're doing as much as I do. Just give us a chance. Give *me* a chance."

"You killed Alice." My voice is shaky but strong. "You killed her *child*. What chance did you give her?"

"I gave her every chance," he snaps, and the mask slips. "She made her choice."

"And I'm making mine," I say, and pull the trigger.

Several moments collide in time:

Judah grabs for Remy's ankle, misses.

Remy staggers as the bullet shreds into his hip. Doesn't go down.

His hands, wet with all of our blood mingled together, close around my upper arms. An almost-hug, an echo of an embrace we'll never share again, the gun mashed between us and useless and its barrel *burning . . . burning my chest . . . searing my skin*

his lips on my forehead

a simple push, the release of his fingers

and there is no more ground to catch me, only sky and stars.

Chapter
41

For the second time in my life I am flying, the scent of smoke on my hands, the roar of the air rushing past me and the terror running through me drowning out any other sound.

Am I screaming?

Probably.

The gun is gone, belongs to the quarry now.

I gouge my palms to ribbons on the side of the cliff searching for something, anything to deny gravity its prize. When something thick and ropy slaps my hand I clamp my fingers around it, but inertia takes its pound of flesh off my palm before I jerk to a halt, my shoulder wrenching up at an awful angle. I can't even cry out, the agony has stolen my breath, but I gasp and use the momentum to swing my other arm up to grab the protruding root. The rest of me smacks into the rock wall, and a hundred points of pain light up my body but I can't give them the attention they demand, I can only think of my hands, and they hurt too, but there are things worse than hurting and I can not, *will* not let go, because even if

Judah survived that first shot (*there was so much blood*) he will not survive a second.

My lungs decide we can be on the same team again, drawing in heaving gasps of cool air that clear the spots from the edges of my vision.

Focus. You can do this.

I can't. I'm going to fall.

Again.

The fear says, *You are going to fall.*

The fear says, *You are going to break.*

I squeeze my eyes shut.

If you don't believe you can do what should be impossible, you never will. My climbing coach's voice breaks through the clanging panic.

You freeze, you're dead in the water.

I take a shuddering breath, and with it, draw up my right leg. Exploring the rock wall for any hint of a protrusion, any cranny I can use as a foothold, and luck is on my side. I wedge my foot into the space I've found and stabilize myself, taking some of the weight off of my screaming shoulders.

I dare to look up, half expecting to see the barrel of a gun pointed at me. But Remy is not there. I spy my next hold, a small rock jutting out at a slightly upward angle.

I have never climbed without my prosthetic. If I had trouble trusting my body before . . .

Stop. Focus. Go.

I launch off of my foot and reach for the rock. My raw palm closes around it and sweet relief floods through me. But I jam it down deep, into the same place I shoved the fear and the doubt. They're traps, all of those feelings, and I can't afford any of them right now.

I find a flat rock and wedge my left knee onto it. It hurts. A lot.

I keep going.

My blood-slick hands slip from their holds, more than once.

I swear. Way more than once.

But I keep going.

I trust my body.

And I don't fall.

———

My right leg trembles with whatever comes after fatigue as I raise my head above the lip of the quarry, pull myself out of the demon's mouth.

Remy has his back to me, starlight electrified by halogen painting his silhouette as he crouches above Judah, leaning heavily on one side. It looks like he's barely holding on to his balance—I've hurt him badly.

He's hurt me worse.

Judah isn't moving but I hear a low groan, and I've never been so happy to hear the sound of someone I care about in pain. *In pain* means *still alive*.

Remy's holding his cell phone to the non-purpled side of his face. "—taking care of it, but I'm gonna need some help with clean-up. She fucking shot me and my blood is all over the place."

Another groan, this one sounding like it might be wrapped around an expletive but I'm too far away to hear him clearly, which hopefully means Remy is also too far away to hear the clattering of small stones as I drag my bruised body back onto solid ground.

"I know," Remy snaps, "but it's kind of hard to sell a suicide with two other people's blood at the scene."

I commando crawl outside the halo of light from the Prius's

headlights, unwilling to subject my savaged hands to any more abuse.

"We can still salvage this. Bring a tarp for the boy. He won't last long enough for Miller to use but Sato can get rid of him."

His words crawl over my skin. *I'm the suicide. And Judah—Judah's just going to disappear.*

No.

Rocks dig into my forearms. The earth smells like rain we haven't had in weeks. I make it to the car, slide my curling and useless fingers beneath the handle of the passenger door.

Gentle . . .

It's not silent, but it's close.

"Just get here." Remy jams the phone into his pocket. A moment of quiet, and then I hear him whisper my name. I freeze, but it's not recognition I hear in his voice.

It's grief.

I climb into the car, my knees screaming, my everything screaming, as Remy bends over Judah.

His hands close around Judah's throat just as my fist slams into the horn. Remy jerks like a puppet with tangled strings, tries to get to his feet about as effectively. I stomp on the gas (*don't think about it don't think about it just do it just do it NOW*) and the tires spin for a moment in which my heart completely stops beating.

Then the Prius lurches forward

and Remy's eyes are those of a cornered wolf that thought himself above the hunt, too predator to ever be prey,

and the sound his body makes when the front end of the car folds him in half will echo in my nightmares for the rest of my life,

and now I'm slamming on the brake because I don't want to crush Judah, and I don't want to fly again.

I am out the driver's side door in a barely-controlled tumble. Remy is draped over the cliff's edge like discarded laundry, fighting for purchase on the loose earth. His eyes widen when he sees me.

"Help me," he begs, holding out one hand that he immediately takes back to dig into the ground when he starts to slide further. "Cia! If you don't help me I'm going to die here!"

I have stopped just within arm's reach. My heart is at war with itself. "I thought you wanted me to be a killer," I say softly. "To be strong."

His face is contorted in pain and fear, but something like respect's twisted cousin enters his expression. "Is that it then? Will you become the monster to destroy the monster?"

"Maybe I'll just let the monster destroy himself."

"That's not how it works. Inaction is still a choice. Letting me die is a choice." He grunts, tries to pull his knee up over the edge. Fails. "You—"

I'll never know what he was about to say, because the backward momentum of his attempt to swing his leg up causes the earth beneath his arms to finally give, and he cries my name,

and I am not like him,

I will not become the monster to destroy the monster,

I have to believe that there is another way.

My hands blaze with agony as I clamp them around Remy's forearms, and his fingers close around mine. His feet kick the cliff wall, flailing for anything to put between his shoes and thin air, and all of his wriggling nearly sends me over the edge with him.

"Stop it!" I hiss.

Together, one inch at a time, we work our way back from the edge. I take my hands off of him the second I can afford to, unwilling to touch him any longer than I have to. He lays on his back, gasping for air, and I think the Prius caved in at least a few of his ribs, and I hope he knows every ounce of pain that Pancakes felt when she couldn't breathe for the blood in her chest.

From the way he is gasping, I think he just might.

"Knew . . . you couldn't let me go," he rasps.

"You know nothing about me." I yank his phone from his pocket, dial 911 and tell the voice at the other end where we are and how badly we need her help, then leave the call still active and drop the phone to the ground. Out of his reach.

The race is on. Who will find us first?

I should get back to the car. Get myself far enough away to see whether the next vehicles to turn onto the quarry road have ambulance logos or blacked out windows. But in this town either one could mean safety or danger, and besides, I've never been good at *shoulds*.

I am at Judah's side without any recollection of crawling there, my torn hands on him registering no pain, only desperation. I need to feel his warmth, feel his chest rise and fall and tell me he's still here with me.

I need him to still be here with me.

For the first time this whole godforsaken night, I get what I want.

Judah's eyelashes twitch, one gorgeous eye opening before the other. "How are you here? I saw him push you . . . Are you a zombie?" His breath barely forms the words before the wind carries them away.

"Yes. And I am going to bite you and turn you into my zombie lover so we can eat brains together forever." I kiss his mouth. Will we ever have a kiss that doesn't taste like blood?

"You're a . . . strange girl," his lips say against mine, and I smile.

"Yes," I tell him, and give in to his gravity, my head finding the curve of his shoulder—the one without a bullet in it. Judah is in no shape to move, and I can't get us both to the car. Remy isn't moving so neither am I. From the irregular rattle of his breathing, I'm pretty sure he's more broken than I am.

I will not become the monster. But I curl my fingers around my little wooden shiv—which has somehow survived intact—just in case.

Sirens trace a path through the night.

I pray they get here before whoever Remy called does.

Chapter
42

The nurse calls it "debridement." In medieval times, when I'm pretty sure this process was invented, it would have been called "flaying."

They toss around rationalizations like *substantial risk of infection* and *even wound edges will decrease scarring*. I tell them I'm not afraid of scars. My nurse says I could have to wear compression gloves again.

I will never wear those gloves again.

My hands, which always tell me too much about the world already, which feel every fiber of fabric and every strand of Pancakes's fur like the light tracing of an X-Acto blade, will not stay open. I don't blame them. My nurse has to call for a tech to help him hold me still.

At first, just my hands.

Then he calls for another to hold *me*.

If there is a silver lining to what happens over the next quarter hour, it is that my screams might be loud enough to wake Santi, three floors up, from her coma.

———

Detective Timmerman looks like he just fell out of bed. His tie is crooked, his hair like a cat's fur pet backward, dark circles under his eyes. Detective Rojas, on the other hand, looks like he never went to bed. Maybe he doesn't need sleep, just subsists on processed foods and weary skepticism.

I've been given one of two rooms in the hospital's observation unit that actually has four walls and a door, rather than curtained partitions. I suspect it's usually used for patients in police custody, but I am glad for the privacy and also not entirely sure I don't fit that description.

"I told you I don't need to wait for my dads. We can talk now." My bandaged hands rest atop the blankets. I've only taken half the dose of the pain medications the nurse offered—I want to remain sharp, but I can't think clearly if I'm shaking uncontrollably and trying not to throw up from the pain, either.

"Deputy Chief's orders," Timmerman says with an out-of-my-control shrug. "No questions until your dad and the lawyer get here."

"Am I under arrest?" I ask curiously.

"Should you be?" Rojas says, never disappointing. Timmerman frowns at him.

I consider. Definitely for the B&E. Probably for the data theft. Maybe for making Remy kiss the bumper of his own Prius, but I think that one was pretty clearly self-defense. Also defense of Judah, bleeding out in the dirt with Remy's hands around his throat.

I punt. "That seems like a question for smarter people than me."

"Oh, I think you're smarter than you let on," Rojas says.

"If we have to wait, can you please go get me some grape juice?" I ask Timmerman, looking as pitiable as I can manage.

Which is probably pretty pitiable. "My papa always used to give me grape juice when I was sick, and I think . . . I think it'd help me feel better."

"You got it, kid," Timmerman says. He closes the door behind him, such good manners.

My pathetic act goes with him. By the time I turn back to Rojas, every ounce of anger and grief and exhaustion I feel is plain on my face. "You can't ask me questions, fine. But you can listen, right?"

Rojas's gaze sharpens. "Why did you send Detective Timmerman away?"

"I don't trust him. He's too pretty." He's too something else, too, but I can't quite pin it down yet.

"You trust me?"

"I think so."

"Why?"

"Because you're the only one asking questions that make people as uncomfortable as the ones I'm asking." I shrug and instantly regret it as pain shoots down my shoulder. "It's thin, but it's all I've got. Should I not?"

He just looks at me for a long moment, long enough to make me shift my weight in the bed, which is about as comfortable as a lumpy wrestling mat. "Timmerman will be back any minute."

"No, he won't. They don't stock grape juice on this floor." At the rise of his tufted eyebrows, I explain, "I volunteered here a few times for my junior EMT class. He'll have to go to the pediatric floor to find grape juice. We have at least four minutes."

The ruddy detective shakes his head. "You kids are all too clever for your own good. Or think you are, which is even worse." His side-swipes oddly make me trust him more, but he holds up one hand when I open my mouth again. "Silencia, I

literally, legally, cannot take your statement at this time. Your
father will have my badge and the Deputy Chief will serve it
up to him on a platter."

Despair presses me back into my pillows. Dad has secrets
to protect. Whoever this attorney is that he's hired, they will
not have solely my interests at heart.

They might even be in Rearden's pocket, too.

"Don't let them bury this," I whisper, eyes squeezed shut
against the sudden burning. "Don't let them bury Alice twice."

I startle at the heavy weight that lands on my leg, so unexpected is Rojas's touch through the blankets.

"I can't take your statement," he says again, "but I *can* show
you this." He reaches down into the black duffel at his side, takes
something out of a plastic bag and hands it to me.

I unfold the paper, memory time-warping me back to that
first interview in my dining room, Rojas sliding another piece
of paper across the table.

```
Think of her still the same way, I say;
She is not dead,
She is just away
```

I bite the inside of my cheek until the pain snaps me back
to the present, and stare at the lines of text on the note Rojas
has just given me.

```
All is well.
Nothing is hurt; nothing is lost.
One brief moment and all will be as it
was before.
```

I look up at Rojas, give my head a tiny shake. *I don't understand.*

He takes something else out of the bag—Remy's cell phone. Fat-fingers it for a few moments until a crackly recording begins to play.

I recognize my voice, but not the words. Not out of context and chopped-up as they are.

And then I do.

"It feels like I'm floating without my anchor . . . I'm sorry. Not for what I'm doing—this is something I have to do. But I am sorry for how it's going to hurt them."

"That *asshole!*" My white-mittened hands rise off the bed in useless rage. That night, outside the coffee shop . . . Remy had practically spoon-fed me my suicide message. And I'd given him exactly what he needed.

"What's funny?" I ask.

Remy shakes his head, but the smile still plays across his lips. "Nothing . . ."

The sick thing is, I believe he'd meant it when he'd said he loved me. Because he was right: he could have killed me countless times before he actually tried to. He had set up the whole tableau with Judah for my benefit, to give me a chance to show him who I could be. Even as he put the pieces of his backup plan in place, he'd hoped he wouldn't have to use it. He'd hoped I would choose him. He *had* given me a choice, and he'd paid dearly for it.

"You told the officers on scene that Remy Walsh was trying to kill you and make it look like suicide."

I nod. "Just like he did to Alice. Because she was looking into the missing kids of Summerset. Because I found out who's killing them and why." I stare at Rojas, not flinching away from those flinty, bloodshot eyes. "Do you believe me now, Detective?"

He's only just gotten the cell phone and note back into the duffel when Timmerman barges back in.

"Would you believe," he says, opening the carton of grape juice and—the definition of chivalry—dropping a straw in it, "that there's only one floor in the whole hospital that carries this stuff, and I got wrong directions twice before I finally found the damn place?"

"Really." I take an obligatory sip, hold Rojas's gaze meaningfully. "You can't trust anyone these days." Remy had been insistent about calling the police from day one. Strange behavior for a bad guy, and part of why I'd trusted him so readily. People with a body count generally don't advocate police involvement—unless Rearden has their poisonous tentacles wrapped around enough cops to bury me *and* my amateur investigation.

Rojas reads me loud and clear. I hope.

———

I coerce one of the nurse's aides into helping me into a wheelchair—the cops found my prosthetic in Remy's car but my leg is too swollen for it to fit properly—and taking me to the bathroom. It's a busy floor and there is only one aide, so it's only a few moments before someone else demands her attention—which is exactly what I'd been counting on.

"I have to go check on someone else, sweetheart," she says through the closed door. "Just pull the string when you're done and I'll come back as soon as I can, okay? Don't try to get up on your own."

"Okay, thanks!" I reply sweetly, as if I haven't been getting by with 1.5 legs since before I could spell my own name. I count to thirty before cracking the door and making my escape.

The trick to being where you don't belong is confidence. The bandages and wheelchair help, even if pushing a wheelchair with hands cocooned in gauze is awkward at best. An elderly man sticks his cane out to hold the elevator door for me, balancing a cup of cafeteria coffee in his other hand.

"Thank you." I smile up at him. I hope I don't look too ghoulish.

The brim of his ARMY VETERAN hat bobs. "It must have been a rough night if whoever you're going to visit is in worse shape than you."

I don't take it personally. "I've had better."

"Me too, honey. My wife is in the ICU. They say people don't come back from the kind of stroke she had. She never slept well when I was overseas, said she had nightmares. So I promised her she'd never have to sleep alone again." His seaglass eyes are steady and wet. "I've kept that promise for forty-one years. I'm not about to break it now."

"She must be very special."

He holds the elevator door again for me as it opens. "She is my light," he says simply. He goes right and I wheel my chair left, blinking my own suddenly damp eyes furiously.

I wonder how Judah's body would feel against mine in my bed. If his warmth would chase my nightmares away, or if I am as irreparably haunted as an old hotel, too full of restless and vengeful ghosts to know peace in waking or in sleep.

I wonder if I can ever sleep again in the house of my fathers, knowing what I know now about what it cost to build.

The trauma unit is bustling with the minutiae of tragedy's aftermath, and tragedy, it seems, has had a busy night. Sensing its kind, my pain flares out of dull hibernation, and I instantly regret my choice of clear head over pharmacologic comfort.

My throbbing hands draw me to Judah as if reeling in a thread between us, a spider-silk strand of tentative hope, so fragile a breath might snap it—the breath it would take to breathe one more lie, to hold in one more secret.

The darkness of the room is softly spoiled by the glow from a screen behind the bed, relaying his stable vitals to calm my own. I find his palm and press my face to it.

"Zombie girl?" he whispers, and it almost breaks me.

I bite his finger, sort of gently. "How did you know?"

"These hands will never forget the shape of you. Especially when . . ." He takes a deep breath. "I didn't know if I would ever get to touch you again."

I close my eyes. "Are you okay?"

"The bullet passed all the way through. Apparently that's a good thing. I think my doctor was disappointed he didn't get to cut me open, though." His thumb traces my cheekbone. "Are you crying?"

"Your palm is just sweaty. Must be your excitement to see me." I wipe my tears away on his blanket.

"But I can't see you. Come closer."

The room is small, dominated by his bed, a tiny nightstand, an IV pole hung with a bag too dark to be IV fluid and just the right color to be blood, and a recliner full of sleeping mom. My chair is too wide to fit anywhere other than where it is.

So I give Judah his hand back, balance carefully on one leg, and slide the other over his knees. Quiet, so quiet, I climb up beside him in the shoebox bed, warming with his breathy laugh when I bump my elbow on the side rail and swear.

I briefly wonder how the hell he can laugh when a few hours ago he couldn't even stay conscious, but quickly realize that unlike me, he probably hadn't seen any need to go halfsies on pain medication.

I find the spaces where his body yields to mine and let myself melt there.

"Here," he whispers, lifting his head and sliding the pillow over to share. He tries to hide the grimace but I see it, I see him, and that's how we lay—just seeing each other, our breath mingling in the centimeters between us until the air I draw in tastes like him, because somehow my mouth remembers his, because even though it was really just that once I have lived that kiss a hundred times since, first with exhilaration and then with betrayal and now . . .

"I'm sorry I didn't trust you." I curl his hair around my gauze-wrapped finger, let its silken length slip away. "He set you up with Alice's phone, just like he set up Will, and I made it so damn easy for him." *He.* I am unwilling to speak Remy's name, not here, unwilling to invite him into this stolen space we've carved out that is doomed to end before either of us is ready.

He catches my bandaged hand. It sparks, settles. "Don't do that to yourself. When it mattered, you made the right decision."

"You still got shot."

He smiles. Somehow, this crazy boy *smiles.* "Your aim probably would have been better."

"Definitely," I agree, but I am shaking despite his efforts at levity, and he kisses my fingertips.

"It's going to be okay," he says softly.

I lift my eyes to find his in the dark. "Back at the quarry . . . You said you trusted me."

"I do. With good reason, it turns out."

"Then *trust me.*" It takes a moment, but I see when my meaning becomes clear, and his smile fades. "No more secrets."

He hesitates only briefly. "No more secrets."

And he tells me.

Chapter

43

"Code white." The voice crackles through the hall speakers with urgency carefully calculated to alert but not alarm. "Teenage female, white, likely in a wheelchair. Code white . . ."

Judah's smile tickles my hair. "Hey, trouble, they're singing your song."

I groan as I push myself up on my elbows from my cozy burrow. "Alas, all good things . . ."

"Not an end." Even injured, he is still fast, still strong, and his good arm wraps around me—a request, not a restraint, but I let it be somewhere in between and get my knees underneath me to protect his bruised body from the full weight of mine even as he pulls me down to him. "A *to be continued.*"

His mouth finds me, my collarbone igniting with the fire his lips leave behind. He kisses the hollow of my throat, up my neck, across my jaw, until finally—*finally*—he is exactly where I want him to be, and we kiss like starving things, memorizing the shape and dance of each other's mouths.

A shiver from down deep tremors up my body, which

demands to feel every inch of his despite the blanket between us, and the force of that want makes it hard to breathe, and I wish I never had to come up for air, that we could just pass this breath between us forever, live inside this moment forever.

We break apart.

He rests two fingers on my chin. "If we do that again," he murmurs, "I can't promise I won't pull you under the covers with me."

"Then we'd better not," I whisper back.

He means it.

I don't.

———

Security catches up with me at the elevator. It turns out Judah's judgment is much better than mine under certain extenuating circumstances, so it's only been a few minutes since the Code White told every soul in the hospital that I wasn't where I was supposed to be.

The guy is surprisingly cool about it. "Walkabout over, I'm afraid," he says, taking the handles of my wheelchair in his tattooed hands.

"Rollabout," I correct him. He smiles, reports my location to the powers that be via walkie-talkie, and rolls me into the elevator.

———

I don't recognize the woman standing between Dad and Detective Rojas outside my room, but her slick, easy smile says politician or lawyer.

Her Valentino spike heels say *try me*.

I am so not in the mood.

Papa comes at me first, bear hugs and the familiar crook of his neck where my face has fit perfectly for twelve years. An unfair first volley that almost cracks the shell of my resolve.

"Oh, monkey," he says, hoarse. He lets me go before I'm ready, and his warm hands immediately start to fuss at me. He gently takes my wrists, examines the bandages, combs my hair away from my face and when he sees my bruises it's as if the damage is instantly transmitted to his own flesh, the way he flinches. "Are you okay? What hurts?"

Everything hurts, Papa. Your fingers on my scars. Your secrets on my heart.

I don't say any of that, yet. "I'm okay. So is Judah."

Papa glances back at Dad, who hasn't given me even an ounce of shit yet, which only deepens my sense of dread. "The Hayes boy? Why was he with you?"

"He followed me. To protect me."

"You wouldn't have needed protecting if you'd been home where you belong," Dad says. At last.

"Really?" I stare him dead in the eye. The hollows around his eyes have gotten darker—he looks like a man making his last stand. "At home, where you've got everything *under control?*"

He doesn't blink, but Valentino Spikes swoops in, shooting a nasty look at Rojas's obvious interest in the conversation. "We're not doing this here. You're being discharged."

"They said they were keeping me overnight to monitor my concussion." I don't *want* to stay exactly, but whatever it is she wants, I find myself wanting to do the exact opposite. She's got that kind of charm.

"Your care will be taken over by a private physician. It's all been arranged. You'll go home with your parents and tomorrow, at a reasonable hour, the four of us will meet with Chief

Atwood, in light of Deputy Chief Walsh's clear conflict of interest regarding his son."

Uncle Sean. In the wake of my shock at Remy's betrayal, the realization that the boy I'd known was as much a stranger as the father I'd trusted, there hadn't been room or emotional headspace to really examine the implications of his involvement. My first thought: *Uncle Sean will be devastated.* Like my dad, he's devoted his entire life to the people of Summerset—for as long as I can remember he's been my Captain America, still a great bear of a man even though I'm not five years old riding on his shoulders anymore.

My next thought turns that one upside down. *Like my dad?* Uncle Sean can't be involved. He *can't* be.

He can, the mermaid whispers from her cove. *Trust no one.*

Except Judah. He's earned it, with blood and with sheer tenacity. The mermaid hums assent.

I assess the pieces in front of me. Which ones are immovable, and which have some play.

"Fine," I say. "But I'll take my grape juice to go."

———

My bed sinks with Papa's weight, tipping me against him. Maybe it should feel wrong to take comfort in his solid strength, given everything, but it doesn't, and I do.

I've kicked everyone else out of my room. For the time being, they've let me, Dad and the slithery lawyer we probably can't afford and the kindly doctor we *definitely* can't afford. Beside me on the nightstand, Papa's Elvis toast and the sleepy-time tea he's brewed for me sit untouched.

Before, I wasn't sure how much Papa knew. If he knew anything at all. Judah solved that problem for me. "I know everything, Papa."

His sigh is ragged, resigned, pulled from his very bones.

"Or should I call you Serpico?"

Papa stills, for so long I'm afraid he's never going to inhale again and that will be that, stolen lungs giving up the ghost for sheer heartbreak.

Not Santi, like I'd suspected. The phone call, as it goes, had come from inside the house. That was the secret Judah had gotten out of Santi, who had used Moto's resources to track Serpico's digital footprint for Alice but hadn't gotten results until after she was gone. The secret Judah hadn't wanted to tell me until he could confirm it, because betrayal by all three of the men I'd ever called father seemed too cruel even for the malicious fates tasked with weaving my tapestry.

Never protect me from the truth again, I'd made him swear. *Trust me to be strong enough.* Because I will be. Somehow, I have to be.

"I thought I was doing the right thing," Papa says after a hundred years. "I had no idea the 'investigative journalist' I was talking to was a high school kid—our Alice—until it was too late. She was gone and all I could do was pray that it would end there, but it didn't. Not with my daughter on the case." His pride is double-edged and tired. "I only started putting the pieces together this past year. I never suspected anything was wrong with how I got my transplant. You have to understand—you probably don't remember how sick I was in those days, but I was dying, and I felt it in every cell of my body. I had no strength to even pick you up anymore. Every breath cost more than it gave. I was so tired all the time. Your dad was working so much overtime to afford my medications he often didn't make it home to sleep—he was buying more days for my life, but they were days without him, and I felt like a ghost haunting my own home. Like I should just let go. Let him go, so he could have his life. I felt like a sinking ship taking everyone I loved down with me."

I do remember. I was little, but I remember the ever-present plastic mask, tipped up to deliver breathless kisses when I demanded them. I remember not understanding why I had to go to the Masons', or the Bookers', when Papa was home but too weak to take care of me. I remember Dad's thunderous fury when a home health nurse said the word "hospice." I remember never seeing that nurse again.

"But Javi never let me give up. He planted the garden, cooked whatever I could stomach, paid the bills, took me to every appointment. Reminded me every day what we were fighting for—and you were such a big, big part of that, monkey. I could almost see a future for Javi without me, but I couldn't imagine anyone else being your Papa."

I tip my head back, let the tears flow in instead of out.

"When the call came, everything changed. Your dad handled everything. There's so much I don't remember about that time, but I remember the first time I was strong enough to hold you in my arms again, and that moment was worth everything that had come before."

Papa sighs. "At least that's what I thought, until I started putting the pieces together six months ago and found out my transplant hadn't gone through UNOS. Found Rearden all over our old bank records. When one of the kids at my work told me that he was happy to be in lockup because three of his friends had gone missing in the past year and at least he knew he was safe there, I started making connections. The same ones you made." His voice goes quieter. "Connections that explained why it seemed like your dad was on call so much more than the other guys, why so many fires needed his personal attention. And how a blue collar family like us could afford a black market transplant."

He looks at his hands, flexes his fingers in empty air. "I've spent my whole career trying to help kids that no one else thinks is worth the effort. If the choice had been given to me, I would never, ever have chosen this. Your dad knew that, which is why he fought so hard to keep this secret. Five years ago, he paid off his debt. All he owes Rearden now is his discretion."

"I owe Rearden too," I say softly. "For Alice."

"Cia—"

"Tell me you didn't know that it was Remy who killed her. Tell me Uncle Sean isn't involved too."

"Oh, monkey. I had no idea Remy was with Rearden. Neither did your Dad, I'm sure of that much. Sean . . ." He shakes his head. "I just don't know. At this point, the only two people I know for certain we can trust are in this room."

"What about Dad?" When Papa doesn't say anything right away, I clarify. "Does he know that you know?"

"As of this afternoon, yes. When I realized you were in it as deep as Alice had ever gotten, I went to Javi with everything." That explains the tension between them at dinner, the raised voices. A thread of fear warps Papa's voice into something I almost don't recognize. "I want them to pay, Silencia. I do. There is a sickness in this town that has been allowed to fester—that has been *fed*—for far too long. But . . . call me a coward, I'm not willing to risk you."

"That's not your decision to make, Papa."

He pulls me close. "I know."

"The lawyer. The doctor. They're Rearden, aren't they?"

"Yes."

I can almost feel the fingers of Rearden's corporate fist closing around us. Is there anything, anyone, they can't buy?

"I'm asking you to wait. We can't beat them head-on. We'll find another way."

I wish I could tell him what he wants to hear. "What other way?"

"We'll make one."

It's a non-answer, and so I give the same. I breathe in his Papa smell, the clean cotton of his T-shirt, the warmth beneath. "Papa?"

"Yes, monkey?"

"Why did you start looking into your records six months ago?"

His chest rises under my cheek with stolen breath, falls again.

Nevermind, I want to cry out, because suddenly I know what he's going to say and it's too much to ask me to bear this, too, and his shirt is already damp beneath my lashes when he says, quiet as if this blade could ever be dulled, as if it will make me bleed less from this truth —

He says, "The cancer is back," and I shatter.

Chapter
44

Papa is going to fight, of course, but not in the way Dad wants him to. Not in the way that leaves collateral damage.

By the time Dad comes in, my eyes are dry, if swollen. My heart battened up for the storm I know is coming.

But the one that lands isn't the one I prepared for. It isn't even a storm at all, not the kind made of thunder and fury. It is the titanic shifting of tectonic plates, a quiet earthquake. It is the silent shaking of my Dad's shoulders when he takes me in his arms without a word.

"Quizás no te guste, pero siempre protegeré esta familia cueste lo que cueste," he whispers finally, over my head.

The worst of the storm has passed. Or we're in the eye of it. "Like you did whatever it took to save Papa?"

"Exactly like that."

I pull away, but not roughly. Not so as to hurt him. I'm doing enough of that already. "I won't let you protect me that way, Dad."

He nods. "I know." And, as if he and Papa rehearsed it: "I'm just asking you to wait."

"Wait for what, Dad? Wait for them to come at me again because of what I know? Or Judah? Wait for another kid to be parceled out to the highest bidders?"

"Wait," he says softly, "because I don't want to spend the time Liam has left in jail."

His words land a sucker punch I had not in any capacity been ready for. "Dad . . ."

"I know I'm going to lose him. And, probably, you. I know I don't deserve the gift I am asking of you. But still, I am asking: do not make me watch the man I love die alone."

When Papa asked me to wait, it was to protect me from Rearden's wrath. Maybe it says something about my sense of self-preservation, but it was almost easy to deny him. But what Dad is asking . . .

"Damn it," I whisper, to no one and everyone.

"Delphine will tell you exactly what to say. Let her do the work; she's being paid obscenely well for it."

My brain doesn't want to give Valentino Spikes a name. She is Rearden. She is Enemy. "I'm not saying I'll do this, Dad," I say harshly, hating the note of hope in his voice, hating what he's asking me to do, hating that I don't know if I'll hate myself more if I do it or if I don't.

His hands fall to his sides. "Then what are you saying?"

I hate seeing him like this. His fragility does not make me feel powerful. I feel like the last solid ground I had to stand on is crumbling beneath me, and there is nothing left to hold on to. Just like in my nightmares—all that's left is sky and smoke.

"I'm saying," I start, and stop, because I don't know what I'm saying.

Dad takes my bandaged hands, and I tense, but he handles them—handles me—like spun glass. "I love you so, so much, mija. There is nothing I will not do to keep you safe."

He kisses my forehead, gets up, and pauses with his hand on the light switch. "But I loved him first."

The light goes out.

———

The buzz of my phone shocks me out of the hinterland between sleep and waking I've only just fallen into. Pale light stripes the carpet near my window—dawn, slivered by the blinds, threatens full sunrise if I don't get back to sleep soon.

"I'm out," Will says excitedly, not waiting for a greeting. "But they wouldn't tell me anything. What did you do?"

An olive branch from Rearden? I rub my ground-glass eyes. "It was Remy, Will. This whole time it was him. He's with Rearden. He framed you and tried to kill me like he killed Alice. He had my suicide note all ready and everything. He's in the hospital now—I kind of shot him—in police custody."

"Holy crap," he breathes. Then: "So, not Judah Hayes."

"Not Judah Hayes. Who took a bullet for me, mind you, so you can start being nicer to him any time now."

"Eh," Will says. "Did I say holy crap? You have got to tell me everything."

"I will. After I've gotten more than an hour of sleep."

"Well, damn. Okay. Why are you still up?"

I knuckle my eyes. "Because you called me."

"Oh. Shoot. Okay. Call me in the morning. Or, like, whenever you wake up. Because it's technically morning now but maybe it's like how breakfast is the first meal of the day, no matter when you eat it? Morning is what happens after you're done sleeping?"

I give up trying to follow that halfway through. "Okay. Will?"

"Yeah?"

"Love you."

The smile in his voice eases the burden on my heart—not enough, but it's a start. "Love you, too."

———

The next call comes at an hour that most people would find reasonable, but as I've only gotten approximately two consecutive hours of sleep, nine o'clock feels highly offensive.

"Silencia?" My name is an emphysema rattle.

"Who is this?"

"Moto's gone. They never made it home from St. John's last night."

I sit up, finally placing the speaker. "Santi?"

Her post-breathing-tube voice is a ragged cocktail of gravel and grief. "They took Moto! Cia, what did you *do*?"

I was wrong. Will isn't an olive branch. He's a threat, the kind that doesn't bother wearing a veil. He's a reminder that there's always something to lose.

Rearden wants me to keep silent to protect its control over this town. Dad wants me to keep silent to protect his heart. Papa wants me to keep silent to protect *me*. But silence can destroy as well as it can protect, and so can I.

alice.books113 19:06

i can't do this alone. i need you.

I kick the blankets off my legs and sit up. "I'm on my way."